LEAVE NO WITNESSES

E. Howard Jones

E. HOWARD JONES

ELLIOT FICTION
ST. MARKS, FL 32355 USA

ELLIOT FICTION

Leave No Witnesses
Copyright © 2007 E. Howard Jones

Sequel to Elder Affairs – Silenced

Cover photo courtesy of NASA.

Illustration of Bahamas by Brittany L. Jones

Requests for information should be addressed to:
Elliot Fiction, P. O. Box 277, St. Marks, Florida 32355
sales@elliotfiction.com

http://elliotfiction.com

Library of Congress Control Number: 2006935309

ISBN-13: 978-0-9774407-1-9
ISBN-10: 0-9774407-1-0

This book is printed on acid-free paper.

PRAISES FROM READERS

- "This gripping, stand-alone sequel sweeps the reader from Florida to storm-tossed islands in the Caribbean, keeping the reader breathlessly turning pages to reach the satisfying end."

  A.H. Holt
  Arthur of Riding Fence, Blanco Sol and other action-packed western novels.

- "Captivating — Once you start reading you have to keep going — You get caught up and can't put it down — Good Sequel — Answers questions from the first book, but also works as a stand-alone."

  Melanie Jernigan
  Homemaker

- "*Leave No Witnesses* was equally as riveting as *Elder Affairs – Silenced* — I couldn't put it down."

  Joan Cassels
  Assistant Director of International Programs
  Florida State University

ACKNOWLEDGEMENTS

Thanks to all of the readers who requested this sequel. Without your persistence, it never would have been written.

Again, I would like to thank my editor, Liz Jameson, who continues to encourage and expand my mind.

Also, to all of the advance readers who helped to shape this book and read it in its unfinished form.

To Lieutenant Kevin Howard with the U.S. Coast Guard for his information.

And to my family:

Mom and Dad, for their enthusiasm during the book's creation process.

My daughters who enjoy seeing their dad spin another story.

My wife who spends countless hours getting the book ready for printing.

And as always, to God, who continues to provide me with countless stories.

THE
BAHAMAS

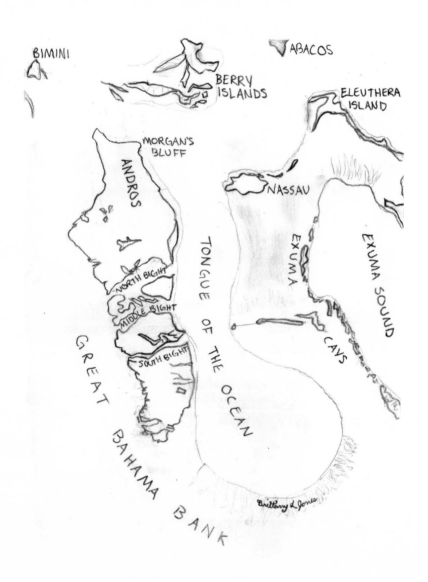

PROLOGUE

Blood oozed from the single bullet hole in the back of the man's head. The shooter dragged the lifeless body from the side of the pavement and rolled it under low shrubs, then gathered leaves and scattered them across the pale corpse.

A jet roared overhead, tucking its wheels into the broad belly as it began to ascend.

Tires screeched as a vehicle sped away into wispy fog.

Silence returned to the cool morning air. Rays of dawn stretched into the eastern sky. Approach lights flashed in a systematic pattern, leading to the end of the runway. A mockingbird's call echoed and a brown hare hopped out from under the low shrub, which now held a secret. The bunny stopped and nibbled a blade of grass.

CHAPTER ONE

Shelly Roble jolted upright in the unfamiliar bed, searching for the noise. The headboard creaked as she tussled with the sheet tangled around her neck and head. The thousand-count sheets, once warm, were now chilly and damp. Sweat beaded on her forehead. Her lungs heaved. *Where am I?* The bedroom returned to silence, except for the blood that surged through her eardrums.

She tossed off the top sheet. The dim morning light cast a shadow of a swaying tree on the far wall. She looked at the clock beside the bed. *Five-thirty.* She sighed, realizing it was Thursday morning, and she was a guest at Bessy's house.

After a couple of deep breaths, she lay back down. *What was that noise? Did it come from outside? Or, did I dream it?*

Thoughts of Mr. Otman, a man whose size intimidated most people, raced through Shelly's mind. At forty-one, she had experienced the man's threatening presence while her father, Arthur McCullen, was a trapped resident at Southern Retirement Community. A shiver raced across her body, thinking of how close she came to losing Arthur from the near-lethal injections administered by that terrible man.

Otman was being held at the Palm Beach County jail, awaiting trial. She assumed a long rap sheet contained numerous charges against him. Arthur told her stories of patients leaving in early morning hours, covered by a thin white sheet, on the back of a golf cart driven by Otman. She knew it was only a matter of time before First Degree Murder would be added to the notorious list. Sensing the noise was only part of a dream, Shelly closed her eyes.

Just days before, Arthur, a sixty-seven-year-old widower, married Bessy, another victim of Otman's abuse. Their marriage ceremony took place the same morning that Arthur, Bessy and Walter—Arthur's best man—were exonerated from all criminal charges stemming from the incidents involved in their escape from the nursing home.

Suddenly a loud thud echoed around Shelly.

"No." The muffled shout penetrated the bedroom floor.

Shelly swung her feet onto the floor, and sprang from the bed, mumbling. "What's wrong with Walter?" He was staying at Bessy's too, until the courts could clear up his assets, both the property and the money stolen from him.

Her nightgown fluttered behind her as she rushed to the closet and grabbed a pink robe. She pushed an arm through the terrycloth sleeve, flung open the door, and thundered down the stairs. The vast family room was empty. Light etched around the closed kitchen door. She snugged the belt on her robe, ran straight for the door, and thrust it open. Walter, his full head of salt-and-pepper hair now disheveled, swatted the table with the newspaper again.

"What is it?" she gasped and grabbed his shoulders, looking at him eye-to-eye from her slender five-foot-six frame.

The newspaper fell open. Walter jabbed his finger at the headline—JUDGE POSTS BAIL. "How could he?"

Shelly dropped in a chair. Her hands trembled; she propped her elbows on the table and covered her face. "They granted Judge Blair bail! He built Southern Retirement Community to lock away his ex-wife, Bessy, while he took control of her money and the bank her dad had built."

Shelly shuddered. "Then he hired Otman to make sure she was kept in a drugged stupor. Are they crazy? He kept everyone there doped up. We're in danger. And what about Dad and Bessy? Do you think? . . ."

Walter squeezed her shoulders. "We're not in danger." His

finger pointed to the last paragraph in the article. "I bet Blair will be on his best behavior until after trial. He'll be wearing his pinstriped suits and walking down that straight and narrow road. A model citizen. He'll never get his just reward."

Shelly read the paragraph that incensed him:

"I did not attempt to kill my wife Bessy, or her new husband, Arthur. I'm innocent and want to clear my name. I'll show up at trial, Your Honor," Judge Harrison T. Blair said. Circuit Judge Jonathan K. Sanchez rejected the prosecutor's suggested bail of $3 million and set it at $150,000, after concluding Blair was not a flight risk. Blair agreed not to leave the country, forfeited his passport, and is out on bail.

Shelly looked up from the paper, "Can you believe that?"

"Sure can," Walter answered. He picked up his coffee cup and took a swig. "I'm glad I'm leaving for Oregon today. I'll be away from him forever. I'm only sixty-six years old and having a lot of living to do."

"But, what about your testimony? You've got to testify against Blair and Otman."

"Absolutely. I'll come back and testify. But after that, I never want to see this town again."

A knock rattled the side door. They froze and held their breath, staring at the door.

CHAPTER TWO

Walter set the coffee cup down, eased his chair back from the kitchen table, and crept over to the door. He pulled the curtain slightly to the side, peeked out the window, and breathed a sigh of relief. "Hello," he said as the door swung open.

"Hi. I'm Jane Winchester. I'm a friend of Bessy's. Is she here?" The woman who almost came up to his nose beamed. The vibrant flowered dress hung loose on her shoulders and a wicker basket dangled from one of her freshly manicured hands. She stepped inside and looked Walter over from head to toe. "Hmm."

"No, she's not." Walter slid a step backward, away from her scrutinizing eyes. He didn't like the way she was studying him. It felt like she undressed him and he was standing there in his boxer shorts. Unwilling to shake her hand, he dug his hands into his pockets.

She stepped around Walter and headed for the table. "And who might you be?"

"I'm Shelly Ro-," she faltered, then stood, "Roble, for now that is. I just got a divorce."

"Oh, I'm sorry to hear that. My husband died a few years back. He worked himself to death. I tried to tell him to take a little vacation every now and then, but he never listened to me." Her words flowed faster. "Toward the end of his life, I saw him less and less. Eventually I started going on vacations without him. At first, I didn't think I would have much fun, but it didn't take long before I realized it beat sitting home alone. There were always plenty of older divorced or widowed women to socialize with."

Walter rolled his eyes at Shelly and motioned for her to get rid of the woman. *I know why he worked all the time. To get away from you.*

Shelly mouthed, "Shush," and grinned. "This is Walter Clemmons. We're having a cup of coffee. Would you like to join us?"

"No! No!" he mouthed; his face reddened.

Jane placed the basket on the table. "Shelly, I'd like that." She took a step toward the cabinets. "Keep your seat. I know where the cups are." She hurried over to the cabinet and reached inside. "I've shared many cups of coffee with Bessy over the years. Sometimes we'd drink the whole pot while sitting and talking. It's terrible what Judge Blair did to her. I never did like him." She took a cup from the shelf.

Shelly and Walter watched her pull out the drawer under the counter and remove a butter knife.

"He was so arrogant," she said as she opened the refrigerator, pushed aside a jar of jelly, and a carton of eggs. "I always knew he was no good." She grabbed the tub of butter and carried it to the table. "You could tell by the look in his eyes." She stopped and looked down at the table. "Walter, where are you sitting? I'd like to sit beside you while you tell me about yourself."

Walter cringed.

"He's sitting right there." Shelly pointed, suppressed the smile, and held up the pot. "Coffee?"

The tub of butter wobbled as Jane placed it on the table, then sat in the chair beside Walter's. Shelly poured the coffee.

Walter edged into his seat. He tried to hobble-horse the chair away, but Jane grasped it and held tight.

Shelly gave Walter a behave-yourself stare, causing him to sulk.

Steam and a delightful cinnamon aroma escaped when Jane flipped back the blue napkin that covered the basket. "Hot cinnamon rolls," she said, lifted a roll out, and then sliced into it with the knife. She dug into the butter, lifted up a glob, then slathered it between the two halves.

Walter frowned at the butter hanging off the sides.

"Here you go, Walter," she said and placed it on a napkin. She reached in, grabbed another, and buttered it. "Now tell me about yourself," she said before she bit into her roll.

"There's not much to tell. I'm retired."

I don't believe him. Everyone has a story to tell. He's bashful or too polite to brag about himself. That's a quality I like.

As Shelly reached for a roll, Jane pushed the butter toward her.

"Aren't these good?" Jane asked Walter. She moved her chair closer to him and nudged him teasingly, and then winked at him.

Yes, but I'd never admit it to you.

Shelly kicked Walter under the table.

"Yes ma'am," he answered with a mouthful.

"Would you like me to butter you another one?" Before he could answer, Jane grabbed another roll and sliced into it. She reached for the butter and again applied ample amounts to both sides, then laid it down on Walter's napkin and batted her eyes at him. "I like a hungry man."

The cinnamon and butter baited his taste buds as he took another bite. The flavor burst alive. He glanced at Jane as his lip curled. *She's too forward.*

Jane looked at her watch. "Oh my. Where has the time gone? I've got to get home." She giggled. "The house is a mess, and I'm expecting company." She turned and patted Walter's thigh. "Wow!" her eyebrows rose. "Firm."

Shelly gave Walter a sheepish grin.

His first instinct was to grab Jane and throw her out of Bessy's house. His hands trembled.

"Well," Shelly said, as she stood to stop Walter before he

could do anything rash. "Thanks for stopping by." She reached for the basket, folded the napkin across the other rolls, and handed it to Jane.

Jane smiled. "We'll have to do this again."

Walter snarled at Shelly, then stepped around her. He couldn't wait to shut the door on Mrs. Winchester. "Good bye," Walter said, and pushed the door closed, almost before she could step outside. Anxiety rushed through his body as he inched open the curtain, peered through the glass window, and watched her disappear around the house. He turned to Shelly. "What a woman!" His head and shoulders shuddered. "Her dead husband didn't work himself to death; he stayed at work to keep away from her. I bet he enjoyed himself while she was off on those trips. Probably made the arrangements himself, just to be rid of her."

"Now, Walter," Shelly said. "She's very nice. I'm glad she came over."

"Not me!" Walter bit his lip to keep from saying anything else.

"She's adorable. Isn't she? I was just trying to help you. You need to get out and meet women."

"No, thank you." He rolled his eyes. "That's the last thing I need. What I *need* is to get home to Oregon."

"I think she likes you."

"She doesn't know me," Walter huffed and sipped his coffee.

"I'm just teasing you," Shelly said as they finished their last sip.

On the way to the spiral staircase, Walter froze. Out of the corner of his eye, he noticed someone coming down the driveway. He stepped over to the window and peered out.

"That brassy woman is coming back."

The wicker basket with the blue cloth swayed at the woman's side. Her little red tennis shoes windmilled down the driveway.

"Is it Mrs. Winchester?" Shelly asked from behind the front door.

He gritted his teeth. "Yes and she's headed for the kitchen door. Don't answer it."

At the sound of the knock, Walter stopped breathing. He prayed she'd go away. The knock sounded again, but louder. Then they heard the side door squeak open.

"Yoohoo! Walter!"

As the kitchen door shut, Walter moved to open the front door, but Shelly blocked his path. "Get out of my way. Did you see the way she looked at me? I'm getting out of here before she catches me."

"You can't leave. She'll see you running down the driveway."

"I don't care."

"She'll probably catch you before you pass the gates."

"Then I'll hide in the bushes and you can get rid of her. Tell her I went for a jog."

"I . . ." Shelly mumbled.

"There you are," Jane interrupted.

Walter gave Shelly a dirty look. "Thanks," he mouthed, daggers shooting from his eyes.

Shelly smiled and looked at Jane. "We were just going up-stairs; we thought we heard someone."

Jane walked up to Walter and held out the basket. "I can't eat these cinnamon rolls. I want you to have them. Oh, I ran into the mailman; here's your mail."

Shelly nudged Walter. He glanced at her and then looked at Jane. "Thank you," he said through clenched jaws. He reluctantly reached out and took the basket and the mail. The fresh baked rolls did smell wonderful.

CHAPTER THREE

Judge Blair pulled open the side door at the Palm Beach County Jail and walked up to the security window. "I'm Judge Blair; I'm here to speak with my client, Mr. Otman."

The deputy pulled opened the thick metal door. "This way, Judge." He led Blair to a small private room with two chairs and a table. After a short wait, the door swung open and Otman ducked and entered the room, a smirk plastered on his face.

Blair waited until the guard closed the door.

Otman's meaty hand clasped Blair's. "I thought you'd never come. I can't believe they let you in here."

"They had to," Blair chuckled. "I've stepped down as a judge and now I can legally represent clients. Remember, this is America, and everyone is innocent until proven guilty."

Blair continued as he approached the small table. "You just don't know the system like I do. Stop worrying. I'll have you out of here soon."

Otman snickered. "So, it's true, the system can be manipulated."

"You don't manipulate the system, you orchestrate it." Blair sat. "Listen, when we get to court, I'll do all the talking. I'll request bail. I don't anticipate any problems. Don't say anything to the judge unless he specifically asks you a question."

"Sure," Otman answered, leaning back in the chair, arms crossed.

"Be polite and smile a lot."

In less than one hour, they were downtown in the courtroom. The prosecutor, Mr. Ashdown, and Blair stood before Judge Garret.

"Your Honor," Ashdown said, "bail should be denied for Mr. Otman. He's a cold-blooded killer."

"Your Honor," Blair said, looking at the judge. "I didn't know that my client had been charged with murder." He turned toward Ashdown and grinned, baiting the prosecutor. *Go ahead; charge him with murder. I'll demand a speedy trial. The lab testing won't be completed in time and a jury will find my client not guilty. With double jeopardy, you can't retry him.*

Ashdown grimaced and lowered his head. *The State hasn't identified anyone that Otman killed. Without an autopsy and lab work, we won't have a case, yet. If he demands a speedy trial, it could start within five days. I need to be patient.*

"I'm sorry, Your Honor. My mistake. At this time, the State of Florida has not charged Mr. Otman with murder. He's being charged with aggravated assault." He bit his lower lip.

Blair looked back at the bench. "Judge, my client pleads not guilty and requests that he be released on his own recognizance."

"The State requests that bail be denied," the prosecutor snapped.

"But, Your Honor," Blair continued, "at this time, the State doesn't have sufficient evidence."

"The State has three residents all claiming Otman abused them."

"Those claims were manufactured by three residents who banded together and falsely accused my client. The State hasn't found any other residents claiming that they were abused. None of the nurses collaborate their stories. And until the State comes up with sufficient evidence, an innocent man shouldn't be held."

"He's not innocent. He routinely overdosed them."

"He followed the doctor's orders." Blair stared at Ashdown. "The State has copies of the medical records. Each entry is substantiated by Dr. Sinclair's signature."

"That's not true and you know it," Ashdown thundered, glaring back at Blair.

"All right you two," Judge Garret said. "I need additional information and then I'll decide. First, does Mr. Otman have a prior arrest record?"

"No, sir," Blair said. "This is his first offense. Up until now he has been a model citizen."

"I wouldn't consider him a model citizen," Ashdown answered.

"But, he does have a clean record, right?" Garret asked. "And the State has little evidence at this time?"

The prosecutor looked down.

"The next matter before the court is to set bail," Garret said.

Blair leaned into the bench. "I'd like to ask the court to release him on his own recognizance. He's not going anywhere. He's determined to clear his name. He wants his job back."

"I object, Your Honor. These charges against Otman are heinous. You can't grant him that."

"Judge Blair," Garret said. "You of all people should know that the court can't just let Mr. Otman off on his own recognizance. And Mr. Ashdown, with the lack of evidence presented, I can't set a high bail. If at a later time evidence is sufficient for me to raise bail or revoke it, then I will." He turned to Otman. "Bail is set at ten thousand dollars. Will you post bail?"

Otman didn't know how or where he'd find that kind of money. He looked at Blair, who nodded his head. "Yes sir," Otman answered.

"The court will allow bond to be posted. Mr. Otman, you are not allowed to leave this country. Is that clear?"

"Yes, sir."

"Do you have a passport?" Garret asked.

"No, sir."

It was not long before Blair and Otman emerged from the

courthouse into the bright sunlight. "We've got work to do. I want my money back."

"I've never had a patient walk away from Southern Retirement Community before," Otman said, clenching his fist. "Those three aren't going to ruin my perfect record, and they are *not* going to testify against me."

Blair walked over to his black Lincoln and they climbed in. The Towncar moved away from the curb and merged with traffic. "We're going to get Arthur, Bessy, and Walter."

Otman let out a long devilish laugh. "I'm going to love this. I can't wait. When do we start?"

"Right now. I know where they're staying."

"Great," Otman said, and cracked his knuckles. "Let's go."

CHAPTER FOUR

Warm rays shown from the baby blue sky as the sun climbed over Freeport, Bahamas, penetrating the top floor windows of the honeymoon suite. Arthur and Bessy lay snuggled under the king size sheet as cool air blew from the vents. The living area in their suite overlooked the Blue Water Resort and was separate from the spacious bedroom. Anchors Away, their sixty-foot Hatteras they abandoned for room service, was docked at the marina. Waves lapped at the shore as a gentle sea breeze blew. Seagulls swooped past their window.

"Doesn't life have unexpected twists?" Bessy giggled.

Arthur nodded. "Too many, sometimes."

"Yeah, but haven't our lives turned out wonderfully?"

He leaned over her and kissed her lips. "And we have the rest of our lives to spend together. It's a perfect dream."

"Ahhhh," Bessy sighed. "A fairy tale and I got the prince."

Arthur laughed. "I'm glad I didn't have to be a frog."

A knock rattled the door.

"Who could that be?" he asked.

Bessy smiled. "The Fairy Godmother to grant us a wish."

Arthur slipped from the sheets, into his terrycloth robe, and hurried to the door. "Who is it?"

"Room service."

Arthur looked through the peephole and could see a man dressed in a tropical print shirt. He cradled a tray in both hands.

Arthur pulled open the door. "We didn't order anything."

The man winked as he leaned into Arthur, his eyebrows raised. "It's your honeymoon breakfast. Remember?"

"Oh, thank you," Arthur said softly and took it. *Why didn't I think of this?* He closed the door and hurried back to the bedroom. He slipped out of the robe and carried the tray to the bed. "Something for you."

Bessy sat up and propped against the headboard, smoothing out her silky lingerie. She scanned the tray of sliced fruit and saw a folded note. She reached for it, opened it, and read aloud: "Fruits are the foods of kings and queens. For strength and endurance."

They laughed.

Bessy's laugh faded as she looked past Arthur, out the sliding glass door, to the balcony. "Why don't we take our breakfast outside and enjoy the fresh air?"

"That sounds romantic."

They slipped into their robes. The sea breeze greeted them as Arthur placed the tray of goodies on the table, then pulled two chairs together, holding one out for her.

She kissed him and sat.

"Ladies first."

Bessy leaned over his lap, moved the fruit around, lifted an orange slice, and pulled off the peel.

"I'd rather feed you. Open up." She pushed it into Arthur's mouth. "Is it sweeter than me?"

"Not even close." he mumbled.

"Look," Bessy squealed, as a parasailor floated past their balcony. She stood and pulled her robe tight.

Arthur joined her, wrapping his arm around her waist. "He's kind of high, isn't he?"

"Wow," she said. "Let's go do that."

Arthur grimaced and hesitated. "Really?"

Bessy pulled him tight into her body and smothered him with a lingering kiss. Then she looked into his eyes. "Right now."

He couldn't believe she was serious. With a deep breath, he suppressed the pressure cooker within. "Let's go."

They changed into their bathing suits. Bessy laughed as she saw Arthur pulling up his suit. "I haven't seen a plaid bathing suit like that in years. We'll have to buy you a new one later. Come on."

Arthur wished he'd put on the suit he'd worn yesterday. They rode the elevator down to the lobby.

Bessy stopped at the front desk. "We'd like to go parasailing. Can you tell us where to go?"

He looked the two grandparents over and snickered. "Sure. Stand at the water's edge, and I'll phone one of my buddies. He has the best boat around. I'll have him pick you two up." He reached for the phone and punched the numbers.

Bessy grabbed Arthur's hand and pulled him to the front door. "I can't wait." As they made their way to the beach, exuberance swelled inside her and jitters caused him to sweat.

Soon she saw a sleek yellow boat bouncing across the water. It seemed to head straight for them, and she began to flag it down.

The boat's bow slid up the sand. "Are you the ones that want to go parasailing?" a young, dark-tanned man asked.

"Oh, yes," Bessy said and began climbing in, with assistance from Arthur.

Once aboard, he wondered what kind of person this friend of the desk clerk was to have an empty boat available on such short notice. "I'm Arthur, and this is my bride, Bessy."

"Bride, huh?"

"Yes, we're on our honeymoon," Bessy answered.

"I'm Steve. Hang on." The engine revved and the bow slid off the beach. The boat sliced through the small breaking waves and stopped about five hundred feet from shore. It idled as he picked up two harnesses. "Put these on."

Bessy noticed how anxious Arthur was and helped him into the harness. "It's going to be fun," she said, then tightened hers.

"All right now, has either of you done this before?"

Arthur shook his head.

"No," Bessy answered.

"There's nothing to it. All you do is stand on this platform. I'll clip you in and then you'll be off."

Arthur's mouth hung open. *I'm going to die.*

"Sounds easy enough," Bessy said, and stepped up on the platform.

"Up you go, Arthur." Steve helped him climb up beside Bessy. "You'll be going tandem this morning." Then he clipped them into the parasail line. "Get ready. I'm going to give us a little speed; then I'll begin to release the line from the boat. Soon you'll be airborne."

Arthur clung to the post. *I'm going to have bruises on my knees, the way they're knocking together.*

The boat bounced across a wake as it moved further offshore. Arthur didn't budge.

The parasail pulled and the wench whined as it began to unwind. They floated off the platform, their feet dangling.

"Oooo," Arthur gasped. The air around him grew quiet as their altitude increased. *That's high enough.*

Steve noticed Bessy was enjoying herself and decided to let all the line out. He increased the boat's speed as the parasail flew higher and appeared smaller and smaller.

Bessy turned and kissed Arthur. "Isn't this great?"

As his confidence grew, Arthur began to breathe more easily. His grimaced face transformed into a gigantic smile. "This isn't bad. I can't believe I've never tried it before. Life with you will always be an adventure." He looked down into the water. "It looks like a swimming pool. I can see the bottom."

Bessy glanced at the miles of beautiful white beaches. People scurried around like ants. Down in the water a fish darted across the boat's turbulent wake.

"Look," Arthur gasped, pointing to a dark silhouette slinking through the water.

"That's one big shark," Bessy said.

"I'm glad we're up here, and not down there swimming."

Steve watched the reel stop. He looked up at his two customers as they dangled three hundred and fifty feet behind. Fifteen minutes passed. He steered the boat into the wind and slowed their speed. The winch growled as it began to retrieve them.

Slowly Bessy and Arthur dropped toward the water. "Oh boy," Bessy squealed, "he's going to dip us into the water."

Arthur's eyes swept below, "I hope we aren't going to be shark bait." Satisfied the creature wasn't waiting for them, he relaxed. Before long, their feet and legs dipped into the water.

"Isn't this great?" She knew their sightseeing was about over as they were lifted out of the water. Soon they were standing on the platform and Steve released them from the line. "Well, what do you think?"

"I've never experienced anything like that. It was a blast," Arthur said.

Bessy wrapped her arms around Arthur and kissed him. "Thanks for taking me."

After Steve folded the parasail and put it away, he headed the boat back to their resort. As the boat bumped the beach, Arthur pulled out a hundred-dollar bill. "Thanks for the ride. We'll tell our friends about Steve and his amazing parasailing boat."

Steve helped them off. "I'm glad you enjoyed yourselves. Have a good day, and be careful."

"Thank you," Bessy said as they hurried off.

Steve backed the boat away from shore. *Parasailing at their age—hope they survive their honeymoon.*

CHAPTER FIVE

Walter stood in the foyer at Bessy's, staring at the basket of rolls. "Gee, what a woman! Is she for real?"

"I'll take those." Shelly pulled the basket from his hand, headed to the kitchen, and began to put the muffins in a paper bag.

"Why are you doing that?"

"I don't know; that's what Mom always did."

He thumbed through the mail and began to laugh. "Jane reminds me of the first time Bessy saw your dad at Southern Retirement Community. She would always appear when he least expected her. Chased him all over the place, thinking that he was her husband, Harry. But, Bessy had a reason to act the way she did. Otman kept her doped up." He shivered. "Jane's peculiar and she's not on drugs. Who cares if she bakes good cinnamon rolls? Not me."

Shelly stood at the table and continued to place the still-warm rolls in the bag. "Now Walter, she's a sweet person. She didn't have to bring us anything to eat. She went out of her way. You could have at least been polite to her."

"Polite! That woman was checking me out, prodding and poking me like a doctor."

"Maybe she *is* a doctor."

"Doctor my foot; she wants to play doctor, and I refuse to be her patient." Glad for the diversion, he held out a colorful postcard of underwater sea life. "Hey, Shelly, you've got a card from your dad and I've got one too."

"Really," Shelly squealed, as she rolled up the bag and

placed it in the refrigerator. She dashed over to Walter, took the card, flipped it over, and read:

> Honeymoon great. Weather perfect.
> Miss you. We're at Blue Water
> Resort in Freeport and are planning
> to leave for Nassau on Thursday.

She glanced up at Walter, "They're leaving Freeport today." She continued reading.

> We might anchor at an island in the
> Berries before heading across to
> Nassau. We'll send another postcard
> later. We have reservations at
> Providence Resort in Nassau for
> Friday.

Walter finished reading his card and stuck it in his shirt pocket. He pulled out a pen and jotted his cell phone number down. "Here's my number. If you get another letter from Arthur for me, call me. I'll tell you where to forward it. I'd like to stay in contact with both your dad and Bessy. We've become real close."

"I'd be glad to."

"Thanks," he said, moving out of the kitchen. "I'm going up to my room and finish packing my few things. Court will be in a couple of hours. After that, I'll go straight to the airport."

Shelly sat fingering the postcard, smiling. *Dad and Bessy. I bet they're having the time of their lives, swimming, eating, and, being in love. I hope one day I'll find someone good to spend my life with. I'd like to spend a romantic week in the Bahamas.* The card slipped from her fingers and landed on the table.

Upstairs in her bathroom, Shelly began applying makeup.

She promised Walter that she'd accompany him to court. Sitting in front of the dresser mirror, she brushed her hair and sang, "Love will meet me in the Bahamas someday and I'll melt in his arms."

Outside, a black Towncar car drove past the eight-foot wrought-iron fence that skirted Bessy's estate, an expansive two story Mediterranean beauty. Two men craned their necks and scanned the yard and house as it slowed. Satisfied no one was around, they eased down the street and around the neighborhood, checking to see if anyone was out for a morning walk, or if yardmen were at work.

"Everyone's at work or the country club," Blair said to Otman and steered back to Bessy's house. "Let's go get Bessy."

The quiet car rolled through the double gates, past the circle driveway and alongside the house, and stopped. Otman fidgeted. "Judge, I've got to hand it to you; I can't believe you're this brazen. It's the middle of the day, and you're not worried about pulling this off."

"The neighbors don't know that I no longer live here and won't suspect a thing if they see this car drive up. If a cop shows up, I'll explain I drove here out of habit." The car stopped at the side entrance. They eased the car doors open and glanced around. "Everything appears normal," Blair said. He gave a soft push and closed the door.

Otman pulled his black medical bag, concealing his drug-inducing syringes, off the front seat, and barely pushed the door shut. He caught up with Blair, who was headed to the front of the house.

Blair stepped up on the front porch, glanced across the front lawn and without anyone in sight, stepped over to a flowerpot, reached behind it, and pulled out a key. "Did they really think they could keep me out of my own house?" He snickered. "Never."

They darted back around the house, up the concrete walk,

and to the side door. Blair pushed the key into the lock. The door creaked open an inch. "No one's in the kitchen," he whispered. "Come on."

Otman stepped around and entered first.

Blair's veins bulged as he grabbed Otman's shirt. "Wipe your feet before you enter my house. I don't want to have to clean it later."

"Grouch," Otman mumbled, scuffing his shoes on the welcome mat.

Blair slipped the key into his pocket, then muttered under his breath, "Bessy, I'm home."

Otman rubbed his hands together. "Let's do it."

Blair stepped past the kitchen table and froze. The bright Caribbean postcard lying on the table caught his peripheral view. He picked it up and flipped it over. "Hmm," he groaned, "now that doesn't surprise me. Arthur and Bessy are married and honeymooning in the Bahamas." He glared at Otman, who was standing beside the sink devouring a banana.

"What?" he garbled with a mouthful.

Blair shot him an infuriated look and motioned for him.

"I'm hungry. I didn't get enough to eat in jail." Otman's shoes squeaked as he moved across the tile floor.

"Shh!" Blair snarled.

Otman tiptoed the rest of the way. At the table, he grabbed the postcard and read it. Then he looked up at Blair. "Now what? Are we waiting here until they come back?"

Blair combed his fingers through his thick graying hair. "No way. We can't wait for Bessy and Arthur to return. They might appear the day of my trial. Bessy's testimony is the one I'm worried about. Walter and Arthur have nothing on me."

"In Walter's case, I'll explain to the jury that I was duped by a slick, fast-talking lawyer when I ruled he should be institutionalized. And in Arthur's case, I followed the Florida Statutes and the recommendation from the court-appointed guardianship committee. Any jury will believe me, but for

Bessy, there's only one thing I can do. We're going to the Bahamas." Bahamas echoed off the walls. Blair grabbed the postcard and stuffed it in his shirt pocket.

"You may not be worried about Arthur and Walter's testimony," Otman sighed, "but I am. If they testify, I'll go to prison."

"Stay here," Blair whispered, "I'll be right back. I've got to grab some documents." He tiptoed down the hall and into the dark library. He crept over to the huge desk and twisted the knob on the antique desk lamp. A soft green hue cast shadows over the room. Inching the bottom drawer open, he rummaged through the files, pulling documents from each.

"I'm almost ready," a man's voice drifted into the library.

Blair froze, then rushed back into the kitchen, forgetting the open drawer. "Let's get out of here."

Otman swung open the door. They stumbled over each other, as they rushed outside. Blair glanced back into the kitchen. With no one in sight, he carefully pulled the door shut.

The car pitched as Otman dropped into the front seat. Blair ran around the front of the car and jumped in. The engine purred as the car began to move backward.

"Get down," Blair snapped, looking through the back window as the car raced to the gates.

Upstairs, Shelly heard the rumble of an engine. She stepped over to the window and pulled back the curtain, just as a black car backed out of the driveway into the street. *Hmm, someone's turning around.*

CHAPTER SIX

Walter dropped the last pair of slacks into his suitcase. The phone rang as he closed the lid. After the third ring, he glanced at the phone. *Why doesn't Shelly answer it? I'm busy.* He lifted the brown suitcase off the bed and lugged it to the door. The next ring seemed louder. Walter rushed to the phone.

Shelly lifted the receiver.

"Hello," Walter sighed.

"Oh, hi Walter. This is Jane. The house is clean and I'm cooking lunch for you and Shelly. Be here at twelve o'clock."

"I . . ."

"And come casual. You can get dressed up for dinner tonight."

Walter gulped. *Lunch? Dinner? She's crazy. I'm not eating with her.*

Shelly pressed the phone to her ear. *That's five minutes from now.* With the receiver covered, she laughed. *I'd like to be a fly in Walter's room.*

"I'm sorry Jane, but we can't . . ."

"Hi, Jane," Shelly butted in. Her cheeks puffed as she tried to suppress the laughter. "We'd be glad to come. We've got time before we have to be at the courthouse." After covering the mouthpiece again, she grabbed her sides laughing, and sat on the floor. *I bet Walter's face changed from red to a sickly green.* Deep down, she sensed that Jane was really a nice woman. She appeared a little brazen, but she meant well.

"Great," Jane said. "Come to the front door."

Shelly heard Walter's phone slam into its cradle. She

stopped laughing as she listened to footsteps racing toward her and pushed herself up off the floor.

"What were you thinking?" he asked, storming into her bedroom with clenched teeth.

"We've got to eat somewhere, and besides, it's free. If you judge lunch by her cinnamon rolls, it's bound to be good."

"So what! I'll never get out of there alive."

"Now, Walter, she isn't that bad. You just haven't gotten to know her."

"And I'm not going to either." Walter started to chuckle as a smile formed across his face. He laughed louder and louder. "You didn't get her address. We can't go." He grabbed his stomach as he laughed.

Suddenly the phone rang.

Walter's jaw dropped. "Don't answer it."

"Hello."

CHAPTER SEVEN

Arthur and Bessy stood under the twin showerheads in the honeymoon suite. Hot water cascaded down their bodies. Steam filled the room and frosted the mirror.

"If we're planning to anchor in the Berry Islands this afternoon, we'd better think about packing and checking out of here," Bessy said.

Water sprayed into Arthur's face, "Right now?"

"Not right now," Bessy laughed, shut off the water, and grabbed two towels. "First, I want to shop at the straw market."

Arthur ran the towel through his hair. "Can't you wait until Nassau?"

"No, I can't."

A faint knock sounded from the other room.

"Who can that be?" Arthur asked.

Bessy wrapped up in the towel and hurried into the bedroom. The cool air sent a shiver up her back.

Arthur snugged the terrycloth robe and headed for the door while Bessy went back into the bathroom to dress.

"Who is it?" He looked through the peephole at a bouquet of pink roses. Water dripped from his hair.

"Florist."

Bessy pulled on capri pants and a shirt and stepped out just as Arthur opened the door.

A huge vase with two dozen pink roses was pushed through the doorway. "To the sweetest lady," the man said, reading the attached note.

Bessy rushed to the door and took the vase. "Oh, Arthur.

They're beautiful." She looked at the card in the center of the stems and read aloud: "From your husband." Bessy's face radiated.

Arthur turned to look at the man, but he was gone. *I didn't order flowers. Who sent them?*

Bessy placed the flowers on the coffee table. Then she jumped into Arthur's arms. She pulled him tight into herself and smothered him with kisses. "Thank you. They're beautiful."

Arthur caught his breath as Bessy went back and inspected the roses. He closed the door wondering if this was included in the price of the honeymoon suite. Was it management's way of helping the new husband who hadn't learned the "do's" for a romantic honeymoon? The more he thought about what happened, the more he liked this hotel. They were making huge points for him.

While Arthur dressed, Bessy smelled the roses and then carried the vase over to the table by the window. Sunlight shimmered off the pink petals. She rushed to Arthur's side and grabbed his hand. "Come on. I want to buy you something." She pulled him out the room to the elevator.

Soon they made their way across two blocks and into the crowded straw market. Bessy nudged Arthur into a small booth of men's shirts. "You need an island shirt or two. How about this one?" She lifted a colorful shirt. It was a large banana-leaf-and-parrots print. She held it up to him. "Wow!"

Arthur swaggered behind the shirt. "So, I'm an islander now?"

"Oh yeah," Bessy said. She turned to the woman who was sitting at the booth. "How much?"

After a short exchange of price bartering, Bessy and Arthur were on their way with their purchase, inching along with the crowd.

Arthur stopped and fingered a cotton wrap. The island print was splashed with brilliant colored sea-life. He draped it across

Bessy's shoulder. "Now we both look like islanders."

"Won't we be the talk of any room when we appear?" Bessy tossed her head back, shook her hair, then raised an eyebrow. "Or this could be a lounging-around-the-pool or beach outfit."

"We'll take it." Arthur pulled out his wallet. "How much?"

Bessy rolled her eyes. *He's going to get taken.*

"Forty-five dollars," the woman said, holding out her hand.

Bessy put her hand on the wallet. "I think we'll look around some more."

"What, you don't want it? How much you wanna pay?"

"We're going to look around at the other shops," Bessy whispered, leaning closer to Arthur. "We can get it cheaper at one of the other booths."

"Today, I give it to you for forty dollars."

Arthur's eyes glimmered.

"We're just looking." Bessy pushed Arthur's wallet into his pocket, and tugged. "Come on."

"How much you wanna pay?" The woman followed them through the crowd.

Bessy sighed and stopped. "Twenty-five."

"Too low. Give me thirty-five."

Arthur started for his wallet, but Bessy pressed her thigh against his pocket and stopped him.

"Let's look elsewhere," Bessy said, through clenched teeth.

The woman grabbed Arthur's other hand and pulled. "Just for you, thirty dollars."

Arthur froze as he looked into Bessy's eyes.

She smiled.

"Really? Thirty dollars?" Arthur asked.

The woman looked at Bessy and then to him. "Just for you, but don't tell anyone."

Arthur pulled out the money and paid the woman. "Thank you," he said, as she folded the outfit and dropped it into a generic plastic bag.

They stepped into the never-ending swarm of shoppers. As they wove their way along and looked into other booths, Bessy leaned into Arthur. "These people expect you to barter. It's part of their culture. It's part of the game. That's why this place is so crowded."

"Yeah, I know, but they look so poor. I just don't have the heart to do it."

Bessy patted him on the back. "I agree, but when you stop and think about the price you paid for that outfit, you could get it cheaper in one of the discount stores back home."

Arthur thought about it for a moment. Then he smiled. "We paid too much didn't we?"

"Probably, but didn't we have fun?"

CHAPTER EIGHT

The two-story, Spanish stucco estate dwarfed Walter and Shelly. They stood on the spacious front porch. "Can you believe the size of this place?" he asked. "It's as big as Bessy's. How can people live in a place like this?"

She pressed the doorbell. "Very comfortably, I guess."

The wait was short; the eight-foot door swung open. "Come in," Jane said as she reached out and grabbed Walter's hand and pulled him inside. He stumbled, but caught his balance as she closed the door. He shot an evil look at Shelly.

"We're eating out back under the cabana." Jane smiled and ignored Walter's standoffish behavior, then led the way into the family room.

"You have a very nice house," Shelly said as she glanced at the enormous furniture and fireplace that appeared to have had little use.

"Thank you," Jane said, releasing Walter's hand to tidy up a pillow on the leather couch. Walter scooted behind Shelly.

"This way," Jane said. They snaked through the family room, around an ottoman to the back door. Outside was a pool with a cascading waterfall at the far end. At the other end was an oversized octagonal cabana. The glass table was set with crystal and china. The polished silverware glittered in the sunlight. A candelabra held flickering candles as its centerpiece. She led them up the two steps. "Shelly, you sit here, and Walter, you'll sit here, beside me."

Walter flinched as he observed the two chairs positioned close to each other. He shot a defiant glance at Shelly and mouthed, "I want to leave, now!"

Shelly ignored his demands. "You shouldn't have gone to such trouble. This is incredible. Walter and I appreciate the invitation." She avoided his glare.

"Have a seat and we'll get started with lunch," Jane said, then hurried off into the house.

"Sit," Shelly demanded of Walter, as she pulled out her chair.

"Sit," Walter mimicked, and sat. "What do you think she has planned for me after she fattens me up?"

Shelly leaned over the table. "Shh! She might hear you."

The door opened and Jane stepped out, balancing a tray.

"Walter, go help her," Shelly whispered, without moving her lips.

Walter forced a smile and stood. Jane scurried up to the bottom step. "Keep your seat, Walter, I've got it. You're my guest."

She's being very cordial. The least I can do is be amiable during lunch. Then I'll never see her again. With a forced smile, he reached out and took the tray.

"Thank you." At the table, she removed the three, long-stemmed glasses and placed them in the center of their plates. Large shrimp tails hung over the edge of the goblets.

After Jane was seated, Walter picked up a shrimp. As it approached his lips, Shelly exclaimed with a raised eyebrow. "Walter, shouldn't you say grace?" She knew he was in a hurry to eat and leave, but she meant to slow him down. She had no intention of sitting at the courthouse for hours. "You might get a stomachache," she said and closed her eyes.

"Sorry." Thwarted, he placed the shrimp back on top of the bed of lettuce. Walter bowed his head and gave a short blessing. He raised an eyebrow and looked at Shelly to see if she approved.

"Thank you," Shelly said, then picked up a shrimp.

"Walter, I hope you like shrimp." Jane watched him nod.

"Good. Would you like cocktail sauce or tartar sauce to go with it?"

He swallowed. "No thank you, this is perfect."

"I hope you don't mind eating out here without air-conditioning; I enjoy eating outside. It relaxes me." She batted her eyes. "You get to hear birds and bees busily at work. Sometimes you can smell the Atlantic," she drew in a deep breath, "but not today. The winds must not be blowing from the southeast."

Walter lifted the last shrimp from his goblet, then looked at Jane's. "Aren't you going to eat yours?" he asked.

"I had a few earlier. You know, I tasted them as I cooked. You may have mine."

Walter started to reach for her shrimp, but held back, fearing he'd send the wrong message. "I think I'd better pass, but thanks for offering."

"Oh my. It's time for the second course." She rose and hurried off to the kitchen. The turn-around time was short as she came out carrying salad. "I hope you'll forgive me for not putting the salad dressing in cute little crystal bowls. I forgot to ask what you'd like." She placed four different bottles of dressing on the table.

"Don't you worry about that," Shelly said. "You've outdone yourself."

"I use these fancy bottles all the time," Walter added, and a small, genuine smile eased across his face. He realized it and forced it away. He picked up the blue-cheese dressing and drowned the lettuce and tomatoes.

"So, Walter, what are your plans?" Jane asked.

Walter finished chewing and swallowed. "I have an appointment with a judge in a little while. He's going to make a ruling on some legal matters and then I'm flying home."

"Where's home and when will you be back?"

"Oregon and I don't plan on returning anytime soon."

Jane sighed. "You can't leave now. We're just getting to

know each other. There are a lot of things we can do around here. Why don't you stay a few more days? That way I could introduce you to things that you might not have seen. I know we'd have a great time."

"I agree," Shelly added. "He doesn't have family there, except maybe distant relatives. He's an only child, and both of his deceased parents were only children."

Jane smiled and leaned into Walter.

He inched away, but Shelly's foot pressed down on his foot causing him to stop. "Shelly, we've been over this many times." His eyes bore into hers. "There's . . ."

Jane sat with big eyes looking at him. "Do you like to swim? We can swim here anytime of the day or night. The sun's the hottest around one o'clock. And if you'd like to swim at night and the water's too cool, the pool's got a heater."

Shelly smiled as she watched Walter's ghastly expression. Again, Shelly pressed down on his foot.

His eyes darted her way. "Ow," he mouthed.

"Please stay," Shelly pleaded.

Walter abandoned any further explanation of his plans. He lifted another bite of salad and chewed. *I'm not staying.*

"The main course is coming up," Jane said. She hoped the wining and dining would sway his decision. She knew it affected most men.

Walter glanced at her salad plate, which hadn't been touched. He turned and watched as she disappeared inside. Then he averted his attention to Shelly. "Did the two of you plan this? Beat up on old Walter and get him to stay. You know my dislike for this place. It only brings back horrible memories." He leaned across the table. "Jane's a hungry piranha waiting to devour me." He straightened back up. "I can't stay."

"I hope you like baked grouper. It's cooked in a puff pastry," Jane said, stepping from the house.

"You told her what I like?" Walter moaned. "I can't believe you."

Shelly leaned over the table and smiled. "Bessy put me up to it. Blame her, not me."

Walter leaned back in his chair, pulled the postcard from his shirt pocket, and read:

> Hi, Walter. Bessy hopes you're enjoying yourself so much that you've changed your mind and will stay. If I don't see you when I get back, I understand. Thanks again for helping us escape Blair and Otman's imprisonment. I'll never forget what you did for Bessy and me.
>
> Forever grateful, Arthur.

CHAPTER NINE

A hush hung over the courtroom as Walter, Shelly, José Snead, and his attorney, Robert Hernandez, watched Judge Waldenberger flip from one document to another.

Walter leaned into Shelly. "That man in the dark suit is Mr. Snead. He's the one who was in cahoots with Blair and brought those false claims that I was a danger to myself and society and committed me to Southern Retirement Community. It was all a plot to take my money. I wonder what he'll say to this judge to weasel out."

"All judges aren't like Blair," Shelly said. "I bet Snead won't have much to say, especially with his lawyer present."

Snead, who appeared to be in his fifties and slightly overweight, fidgeted, and avoided eye contact.

"Mr. Clemmons, have you read over this new sales contract for your property?" the judge asked.

"Yes, Your Honor, I have."

"And you agree that this is a fair price for your property?"

"Yes, sir. It's more than fair."

Shelly stretched her legs out and took a deep breath. *I wish Walter wasn't leaving. It's too bad he didn't like Jane. I hope he'll be happy in Oregon.*

"Mr. Snead, with this signed agreement, you'll be allowed to keep the property and there will be no further litigation in either criminal or civil courts."

"Thank you, sir." His legs shook under the table.

The judge signed the documents and then handed Walter the check for a little more than one million dollars. "Mr.

Clemmons, I hope that you will never have to experience anything as grievous as this again." He turned to Snead, "And Mr. Snead, I expect never to see or hear that you have taken advantage of anyone again. If I do, I will make sure you spend time behind bars."

"I've learned my lesson," Snead said, then turned to Walter. "I am truly sorry for taking advantage of you."

Walter nodded, accepting his apology. "Thank you, Judge." He pocketed the check. "I'm just glad everything turned out as well as it did." After a quick handshake, Walter and Shelly exited the room.

Walter pushed open the front door of the courthouse, and Shelly stepped through. "Shelly, I want to thank you for cooking for me. I've enjoyed your company. But most of all, I'm glad I met your father and you. If I hadn't, I'd still be locked up at Southern Retirement Community or dead."

Shelly hugged him. "I'm glad I could help. Are you sure you won't stay?"

Walter shook his head.

"Well, I hope you'll have a good time back in Oregon getting to know your relatives and meeting new friends. We're going to miss you." She felt the emotions rising deep from inside. Not wanting to spoil a wonderful moment of success in the courthouse, she pulled away from Walter. "Come on. We've got to buy you an airline ticket."

"First, I'd like to stop by a local bank and have this money transferred to my account in Oregon."

"How about Bessy's bank?"

"Sure, it'll be safe there."

CHAPTER TEN

The sun glared off the windows on the top floor of Blue Water Resort. Arthur lugged the last suitcase to the front door and placed it with the others. Bessy sat on the couch and looked out the window. People lay sprawled on towels. The white sand sparkled. A man and woman raced into an oncoming wave. "I sure have enjoyed our stay here."

"It has been fun," Arthur said. He opened the door and looked up and down the empty hallway. "The bellhop should be here shortly." He left the door open and embraced Bessy. "How long will it take us to get to the Berry Islands?"

"Two hours at the most."

"Mr. McCullen," a man called from the doorway.

Arthur turned and saw a young man dressed in the same tropical print shirt that all the hotel staff wore. "Thanks for coming. That's our luggage beside the door."

The man leaned inside the doorway and grabbed one suitcase in each hand. Soon, the other bags were loaded. "I'm ready when you are."

Bessy rose off the couch, grabbed the vase of roses, and handed it to Arthur. "I'll make one last sweep of the rooms. I'd hate to leave something." She surveyed each room and found nothing. "Are you ready?"

Arthur held the flowers away from his nose, stepped out into the hallway, and reached back for the door. The phone rang just as the door began to close. "Should we get that?" he asked Bessy.

"Maybe we should," Bessy said, and squeezed past Arthur.

"Hello."

Arthur smiled at the bellhop. "It shouldn't take long."

"I'm used to it," he answered. "It happens all the time."

"Hello, my name is Basil Adderly," the raspy voice began.

"I can barely hear you," Bessy said, and pressed the phone tight into her ear. "Can you speak up please?"

"Is this better?"

"Yes," Bessy said, listening closely.

"I'm with management and I'm doing a survey of all our guests that stay with us on their honeymoon. I'd like to ask you a few questions. That way we can better serve future honeymooners. Do you have a minute?"

"I'd be glad to help," she answered, turned to Arthur, and mouthed, "One minute."

"Was your room cleaned to your satisfaction every day?"

"It was spotless." She thought the voice sounded familiar, but was unable to place it. She shrugged it off.

"And the accommodations in the room?"

"Perfect."

"Great, and how about room service?"

She thought about breakfast and how it led to their morning excursion. "Oh, it's been wonderful."

"I'm glad to hear that. And how would you rate our hotel?"

"Five star. Your staff has been wonderful, from the room service to the front desk."

"I'm glad you're enjoying yourself. Thanks for taking a few moments to improve our service. And to show our appreciation, I'd like to come by with a gift. Could I meet you in three to four hours?"

"Oh, I'm sorry, but we won't be here. You caught us as we were walking out the door. We're leaving."

"Oh . . ." the voice faltered.

"Are you still there?" Bessy asked.

"Yes . . . I'm here. I was uh . . . hoping to give it to you personally."

"Well, could you meet us down at the front desk?" Bessy asked.

There was another short pause. "I'd like that, but the gifts aren't here yet. We're expecting the freight company to deliver them in the next couple of hours."

"Why don't you give it to the next honeymoon couple? I'm sure they'd like it," Bessy said, smiling.

"I'm sorry to hear that your honeymoon is ending," the caller said, but his tone didn't match his words.

"Oh, it's not. We're going to another island."

"You wouldn't be going to Nassau would you?"

"Yes, that's the plan."

"That's wonderful. We have an office over there. We'll send it to your hotel."

Bessy smiled. "We have reservations at Providence Resort for Friday night."

"Wonderful. We'll send it over to you. Again, thank you for helping us ensure that our staff and hotel accommodations are superior. Have a good day."

She hung up and hurried out of the room.

Arthur pulled the door closed. "Who was that?"

"Someone from management checking to see if we enjoyed our stay. But his voice sure sounded familiar." She stepped into the elevator. The elevator door closed and she wrapped her arms around Arthur's waist.

Arthur bent down and kissed her. "It's probably just one of the employees you've spoken with here at the hotel."

"Yeah, you're probably right," Bessy said, wondering at the nagging thought.

CHAPTER ELEVEN

Jets thundered down the runway and rose into the air. Traffic flowed in and out of Palm Beach International Airport in a systematic pattern. Shelly drove into the parking garage. Vehicles packed the bottom floor. She turned right and drove up the ramp. "Look at this place. It's full." The Suburban bounced across an expansion joint.

"You should have dropped me off at the departure terminal," Walter said. "You don't need to come inside with me."

"I know, but I want to say good-bye." Shelly looked to the back of the second parking deck, saw a vacant space, and sped into it. She glanced at the clock radio and turned off the car. "We'd better hurry if you don't want to miss your flight." She dashed around the back of the Suburban and opened the rear door. "Walter," she yelled through the vehicle to the front seat. "Are you sure you don't want to change your mind and stay?"

"I'm sure," he said. "I really want to get home." He drew in a deep breath and opened the door. He slid out of the seat, stepped around to the back, pulled out the largest suitcase first, and then picked up the small carry-on.

Shelly opened the driver's door, grabbed her pocketbook, and locked the doors.

"I'm ready." He pulled both suitcases along into the terminal building, located Delta's ticket counter, and headed to it.

"I need a one way ticket to Portland, Oregon, please," Walter said as he stepped up to the ticket counter.

"One way," she mumbled and typed out the information into the computer.

Walter pulled out a wad of cash, paid the fare, and pushed the large suitcase onto the scale.

Shelly stood to his side and wiped her eyes. *I can't believe it's so hard to say good-bye. It's not as if we've known each other for years.*

Walter stepped away from the counter and pushed the ticket into his shirt pocket. He pulled the small suitcase as they walked up to the security screening area. "I guess this is it. I want to thank you again for your help. Without you and your dad, I'd be locked away for life, or have met an early death."

Shelly threw her arms around him and struggled to speak. Her eyes blurred. "You saved my dad. I'll never forget you."

"We saved each other." He pulled her tighter. "Why don't you, Arthur, and Bessy come see me in Oregon. You'll love it out there."

"I'd like that. I've never been west of the Mississippi River."

They ambled with the line of travelers waiting to pass through the metal detectors. "This is as far as I can go," Shelly said. He dropped his bag on the floor and they hugged. "Don't forget us once you get settled in out there."

"I won't. I'll call often." He straightened, grabbed the suitcase, and stepped up to the detector. "Good-bye."

"Bye," Shelly softly said as he stepped through.

He waved and disappeared into the crowd.

Shelly wiped a tear from her cheek. *I guess it's better like this.* She turned and headed to the parking garage.

When she reached the second deck, Shelly stepped out of the staircase and hurried to where she left her car. *I've got a lot of work to catch up on. I'll be up late tonight.* At the Suburban, she dug into the pocketbook for the keys.

"What are you going to do when we find them?" a deep voice echoed across the parked vehicles.

Shelly froze. *I know that voice.* She turned and searched. *It can't be Otman. He's in jail.*

"You mean, after I get my money back? I'm going to make them wish they never interfered."

Shelly cowered between two parked vehicles. *That sounded like Blair.* The hairs on her neck stood up as she tried to focus on the tall man and then the shorter, heavyset man. Dim lights cast shadows across their faces. Her hands trembled. She crouched lower beside the sedan and peered around the trunk. She looked across the lane at a minivan. *I've got to get over there without being seen.*

The two men ducked back inside the dark colored car.

Shelly held her breath, and in a crouched position hurried across. She slipped in behind the minivan. Her heart raced as the men's heads popped up above the car's roof. She squinted. *I still can't tell. I've got to get closer.* She crept out from behind the van, up to a sports car.

"Do you have everything?" a voice asked.

"Of course," the deep voice boomed.

She took a deep breath, then scooted around the sports car and up to a large sedan.

Why am I doing this? Just call the police. If it's not them, I'd look foolish calling the police. She raised her head and tried to peer through the tinted side windows. Ducking down, she crept to the bumper, and eased her head out around it.

"Oh my gosh," she wheezed, pulling her head back. "It's them." Her heart pounded as she sidestepped back behind the car.

What do I do? Where are they going? Calm down. They haven't broken any laws yet, have they? I've got to find out what they're up to before I call the police. Maybe they're here to pick someone up.

The car doors slammed. "Do you have your black bag?"

"Got it," Otman said, and held the bag tight under his arm. "I might forget other things, but not this."

Shelly cringed. *The black* bag? She visualized the court-room: Otman withdrawing a syringe and rushing to Bessy's side. She squinted, chasing away the memory. *Why didn't the cops confiscate his black bag?*

"Come on," Blair said.

Follow them. Shelly crouched and moved around each car. The profile of the two men enlarged as she closed the distance.

"Wait. My ID must have fallen out of my pocket," Otman shouted. "I'll be right back."

Shelly winced and stopped breathing. Her eardrums pulsated. *Hide!*

She looked at the full-size silver Chevy pickup on the other side of her, and then scurried between both vehicles up to the front bumpers. Her heart sank. The bumpers of both vehicles were inches from the wall. Otman's footsteps grew louder. She dropped down on her hands and knees and watched as his size fifteen shoes approached. Her ears reverberated with each thunderous step. *I'm trapped.*

CHAPTER TWELVE

The concrete parking deck dug into Shelly's knees and hands. Her heart throbbed as she pushed her pocketbook under the truck and then wiggled beneath it. Otman rounded the bumper the split second she drew her legs underneath.

Otman slipped between the two vehicles.

Did he see me? Shelly lay motionless, afraid her pounding heart would give her away. She held her breath. Time seemed to have stopped.

What's he doing? Is he grabbing a syringe? She listened, but heard nothing. Her heart drummed louder, waiting for a hand to reach under and grab her.

If he injects me, I could lie here dead for days. No one would know I was missing. She drew into a tight ball and inhaled, ready to scream. Her muscles constricted, ready for the fight.

"I found it," Otman shouted as he slammed the door.

"Now, do you have everything?"

"Everything. I'm ready."

Shelly felt the blood surge through her body. She tried unsuccessfully to slow her breathing. *Where are they going? They're up to something. But what?*

Otman caught up with Blair.

Shelly scooted out from under the truck and froze. *The black Towncar.*

She shuddered as a chill ran up her back. *They were at Bessy's this morning. Follow them.*

The voices faded into the stairwell. She took a step after

them, but stopped as she caught a glimpse of her soiled slacks. She brushed at the areas. *Who cares?* She followed, as the door to the stairwell closed.

Shelly slipped into the airport terminal behind a small group of foreign travelers. Inside, she glanced at the different airline counters. On tiptoes, she searched and found Blair and Otman standing at the Continental counter.

Her temples throbbed. Her eyes darted across the sea of people to a security guard. *What am I going to tell him? My speculations? But, what if Blair and Otman see me talking to him? They could be gone in a flash and come back when I'm not here.*

First, I've got to find out where they're going. Breathless, she stepped into the short line of Continental travelers, and crouched behind the couple at the front of the line.

"Next," a ticket agent called.

The couple stepped up to the vacant counter.

Shelly trembled as she stood at the front of the line. She turned her body away from Blair and Otman. *Why am I doing this? Why don't I just yell for the police? Because . . ."*

"Next!"

Shelly hesitated.

"Ma'am, you're next."

Shelly slowly turned around and saw Blair and Otman make their way down the corridor. Her legs wobbled as she stepped up to the same counter that they just vacated.

"Ticket, please," The man said.

Shelly looked at the man with a weak grin. "Where are those men going?"

The agent looked her over. "I'm not allowed to give out personal information. You understand. Security procedures."

Security. She winced at the irony. Shelly glanced down the corridor, but they had disappeared.

How did they get permission from the courts to leave? Oh right, he's a judge, she gasped softly. *He knows the right people.*

"Ma'am."

Silence buzzed in Shelly's ears.

Say something. "S-s-orry, I-I'm nervous; I d-don't like flying. That tall man is my dad's brother. I'm with them. We're flying in to surprise Dad for his birthday."

"So, you're Ms. Sinclair. I'll need to see some identification please."

Sinclair? Identification? Shelly looked left and right. *Run.* Her temples pounded. "I . . . I . . ."

"Ma'am, your ID please."

Tell him another lie. Tell him that your wallet was stolen. Her mouth went dry. Her fingers fumbled as she opened her pocketbook. She looked up at the agent with a weak smile. "It's here somewhere." She dug deep into the purse. Her hands trembled as she pushed aside the checkbook and keys. As her hand touched her wallet, a smile etched into her cheeks. She pulled out her driver's license. "It's not Sinclair anymore. I'm married and my last name is Roble. I need to buy a ticket."

"Yes, Mrs. Roble," the ticket agent said. With the ID in his hand, he quickly typed in Shelly's name into the computer. "Will this be a one way ticket, or round trip?"

"Round trip." Shelly placed her credit card on the counter.

It wasn't long before the agent pushed a ticket across the counter. Shelly picked it up, turned, and headed to the security check. *Where am I going?* She ripped into the envelope and pulled out the ticket. "Nassau!" She cringed, realizing the volume in which she spoke. A quick glance around, assured her that no one cared what she had said.

Oh no. Dad and Bessy are going to Nassau. But then she breathed more easily. *Blair can't possibly know they're in the Bahamas.* She took a couple of steps and slowed. *Or does he? He was at the house today.*

She stopped and glanced around for Blair and Otman, but didn't see them in the crowd of travelers.

I bet they've found out where Dad and Bessy are. I've got

to warn them.

She scanned the ticket for the flight number and departure time, then made her way to the security area. Along the side wall, she saw a bank of pay phones. *I've got to call Walter.*

As she reached into her purse for her cell phone, a woman clad in a colorful Caribbean shirt and a large straw hat passed by. The woman's shirt hung loose and fluttered behind her.

Perfect. I need a disguise. She turned and glanced at the different boutiques.

CHAPTER THIRTEEN

The line of travelers waiting to pass through the security checkpoint swelled. Blair and Otman shuffled along with the other anxious passengers and now stood next in line for the metal detectors. The light flashed red as the elderly woman in front of them walked under the archway. Security personnel asked the woman to remove her orthopedic shoes, then swept the wand down her portly frame. Finally, she collected her belongings and headed for the gate.

"I'm Doctor Sinclair," Otman said, presenting his ID. "I'm doing a clinic in Nassau."

"Step through," the young woman said, watching as the light stayed green. "I hope your clinic goes well."

"Thank you," Otman said and picked up the black bag. He spotted Blair up ahead and rushed to catch up.

Blair looked at his ticket, found the sign directing him to Continental. Otman followed at a safe distance.

Shelly stood outside a woman's boutique.

How did Otman get out of jail? She shuddered and shook her head.

I'm sure Blair had something to do with it. I bet they've been cleared to fly wherever they like. How can our government be so naive? She stepped into the boutique.

Nothing surprises me anymore. You've just got to know the right people. She made her way around a display with coffee mugs.

Now, what do I need for a disguise? She fanned through

several racks of clothes.

These clothes aren't my style. She chuckled to herself. *Like now's the time to be picky. Just grab something and get on that flight.* She moved to another rack. Her eyes landed on a wide-brim hat and an extra-wide silk scarf. She made her way to the cash register and paid for the merchandise.

Shelly stepped in front of a mirror, carefully wrapped the colorful scarf around her neck, and settled the hat down on her head. She reached into the pocketbook, pulled out an oversized pair of sunglasses, and perched them on her nose. The mirror reflected a floppy hat that hid her face completely. *Wow! They'll never recognize me.*

Shelly made her way to join the line of travelers waiting to pass through the scanners.

Should I ask one of the security guards how Blair and Otman could be flying out of the country? Shouldn't their names be on a list with mug shots of people not allowed to travel? But what if they have permission to leave? I'll blow my cover. I can't take a chance. I've got to get to Nassau and find Dad and Bessy first.

Sirens wailed, growing louder as they approached the airport. Tires screeched as police cars slid to a stop at the glass entrance doors.

Travelers stopped and stared at the front doors. Officers rushed inside.

Blair and Otman have been recognized. They should be escorted out any minute now. Shelly smiled and inched along in the line of passengers approaching the security scanners.

Officers' voices blared from portable radios. Footsteps pounded the floor as officers raced around.

Shelly moved to the side, allowing two to pass. She watched one officer run down the corridor to the left and disappear into the crowds. The other darted to the right.

Travelers in the line, moved along and soon Shelly stood in front of the metal detector. The female security guard watched as she entered. The light stayed green when she passed through.

All of the police commotion faded and the airport corridors were relatively quiet, except for a child's laughter. Shelly shuffled toward Nassau's departure gate. *I guess Blair and Otman were kept away from the general public and were hauled off through one of the side doors. I'm glad that's all over with. Maybe I don't need to go to Nassau after all.*

"Get out of my way," an undercover officer yelled and bolted through the scattering travelers.

Shelly watched as officers ran in front of her. *Did Blair and Otman slip away?* Soon the corridor of travelers returned to the normal hurried pace. *I've got to warn Dad! It's not safe for them in Nassau.*

She smiled as she felt the breeze of an officer run past. *At least they won't be on my flight.*

Up ahead was Continental's departure gate for Nassau. Shelly hurried into the crowded waiting area and found the last empty seat. She snickered when she realized the woman in the Caribbean garb sat behind her and wondered if the woman was also hiding from someone or if that was how she usually dressed. Shelly set her purse at her feet, sighed, and slumped in the seat. "What a day."

Shelly leaned her head back; her hat brushed the floppy hat directly behind her. She scanned the corridors. *I wonder what's happened to Blair and Otman.*

An overhead TV broadcasted the extended forecast. "And down here," the weatherman pointed to the tropics, "we have our first low of the season . . ."

"We're now boarding flight twenty-three, to Nassau. We'll be seating those traveling with small children first," a woman's voice resonated.

Shelly watched as a mother traveling with two-year-old twin boys made their way to the ticket agent, presented their boarding passes, and disappeared down the Jetway.

"We're now boarding those passengers traveling to Nassau

holding tickets for rows twenty-five through thirty-eight."

Travelers rushed to form a line and present their tickets. The line quickly dwindled.

"If your seat is between row fifteen and twenty-five, please begin boarding at this time."

Shelly shifted in her seat. Her eyes widened.

Blair and Otman! How did the cops miss them? She fidgeted. They were seated by the far wall, in front of the windows. *Where's a cop when you need one?* As she scanned the area for an officer, she sank further in her seat and twisted the hat lower on her head.

Otman stood and Blair followed.

She turned and looked the other way, but watched them out of the corner of her eye. She tugged the scarf tighter around her neck, bunching it under her chin. A shiver ran up her back. She pulled out her ticket and looked at the seating assignment. *What if I end up sitting next to one of them?*

A police officer stepped into the departure area and glanced around. Blair and Otman remained calm.

Shelly flinched. *Tell that cop.* She tried to rise, but her legs and arms were uncooperative.

The officer disappeared into the crowd.

Otman stepped up to the ticket agent and showed his boarding pass. She thanked him for flying Continental and he hurried down the Jetway.

"What?" Shelly gasped as she watched. *Maybe the police have set a trap at the end of the Jetway and are arresting them one at a time.* She watched Blair thank the ticket agent and turn to board the plane.

"We're boarding all other passengers at this time."

With a nervous twitch, Shelly picked up her pocketbook and entered the line, her boarding pass in hand. *I wish I was already in Nassau. I'd feel a lot better if Dad knew they were headed to Nassau.* She gritted her teeth and stood next in line.

"Boarding pass, please," the ticket agent said.

Shelly smiled and presented her boarding pass.

"Glad to have you traveling Continental, Mrs. Roble," the ticket agent said, louder than necessary.

"Thank you," Shelly replied. She took a step into the Jetway.

Suddenly, a hand grasped her arm. Shelly's arm throbbed as she was yanked off her feet and pushed to the floor. "You can't hide behind that disguise," the large man's voice boomed.

CHAPTER FOURTEEN

The Jetway was empty, except for Shelly lying on the floor, staring up at the man that pinned her to the floor. Shelly winced in pain as someone else stepped up and a second set of heavy hands helped to pin her down. The ceiling above swirled as she focused on the large man.

"Mrs. Roble, you're not going anywhere," Detective Newberry said as he stepped up to the other officers and peered into her face. "You're under arrest."

"W-What? Y-You've got the wrong person. Judge Blair and Mr. Otman are on that plane. They're getting away. They're flying out of the country. You've got to stop them."

"Mrs. Roble, you're under arrest for murder."

"WHAT?" she cried. Her heart felt like it was going to leap out of her chest. "MURDER!" Her mouth gaped and her eyes widened.

"Cut the acting. We found your husband's body a few hours ago. I suspected foul play days ago when we found blood inside Justin's BMW. All we needed was the body."

A female officer stepped beside the other two officers. She pulled out a set of handcuffs.

"Isn't it ironic," Newberry continued, "that we found Justin's body on the airport perimeter and now here you are, trying to fly out of the country? You can't hide under that disguise. You're under arrest. Read her her rights and get her out of here."

Shelly remained rigid. Her head swirled with confusion. Tears streaked down both cheeks, smudging mascara.

Passengers congregated outside the departure area, watching. Other people turned to investigate.

The female officer grabbed Shelly's hand and pulled it behind her back. Shelly cringed as the cold steel snapped around her wrist and clicked. With another fluid motion, her other arm was pulled behind her back and secured.

"I didn't do it," Shelly pleaded. "And Blair and Otman are on that plane."

"I don't know anything about Blair and Otman. You thought whoever stole his BMW would be accused of the murder," Newberry stated. "We didn't fall for it. We never believed it from the moment the car thief was stopped. He had no motive to kill Justin. You did."

Shelly's eyes were bloodshot. Her cheeks were wet; her head throbbed.

"Ms. Roble, I must read you your rights," the female officer said. "You have the right to remain silent. You have the right to have legal counsel represent you. Anything you say can be used in a court of law. Do you understand your rights?"

"But, I didn't do it. He left me. I . . ."

"Ms. Roble, do you understand your rights? Do you want your lawyer present while you are questioned?"

"You've got it wrong." Shelly sobbed. "He tried to kill me."

"Get her out of here," Newberry said.

The officers pulled Shelly up off the floor. Her legs buckled as she stood; strong arms supported her.

Passengers backed against the wall, opening up a passageway.

"She doesn't look like a killer," one older woman said to her husband.

"These days you just can't tell who's got it in for you," he replied, staring at Shelly as she passed by.

Shelly's eyes focused on her feet.

Passengers kept glancing backward over their shoulders, as

they hurried down the corridor to their designated departure gate.

"This is the final call for flight 23. All passengers holding tickets for this flight need to board now."

The female officer pulled Shelly from the Jetway. A few late boarding passengers eased around them. The woman wearing the Caribbean shirt and floppy straw hat hurried past. Shelly looked up; her head snapped around.

Connie? Justin's secretary? Shelly's feet tangled and she stumbled to the floor. The officers surrounded her. Shelly strained to see the woman from her position on the floor, but all she saw were blue trouser legs. As Shelly was lifted off the floor, she careened her head, but it was too late. The woman was gone.

"Move it," the female officer demanded.

Detective Newberry walked beside Shelly. "You almost got away in that outfit," he said, while he looked from her head to her toes. "You're good, but not good enough. We knew you purchased a ticket using your credit card and were planning to fly out of the country. We knew if we couldn't find you anywhere else, we would find you at the gate. All we had to do was wait until you presented your boarding pass. You did everything we predicted."

Shelly heard only a mumble as Newberry spoke.

That Caribbean woman looked like Connie. But, it couldn't have been. Connie and Justin are far away from here. The woman's face blurred as Shelly reflected on the vision.

But is all of this a diversion set up by Blair? If the woman was Connie, why was she disguised? Is Justin really dead? Did Connie kill him? Is all of this a plot by Justin and Connie? Whose body did the police find? Where's Justin? I bet he's on that plane with Connie.

The police led Shelly down the corridor, around the corner, and toward the entrance. People stopped and stared. Shelly drooped her head forward and stared at the ground.

How will I contact Dad? Who will warn him about Blair and Otman? I've got one call, but who?

The entrance doors opened as a police car screeched to a stop beside the curb, lights flashing. Another officer rushed to the back door and swung it open. "Watch your head," the female officer said as she pushed Shelly into the back seat and slammed the door.

Stop staring at me. I'm innocent. Shelly cowered on the back seat.

The sirens wailed and the engine roared, as the police car swept Shelly away.

CHAPTER FIFTEEN

The woman in the Caribbean shirt stepped from the Jetway to the plane and presented her ticket just as the flight attendant began to close the door.

"Welcome aboard," she greeted and looked at the ticket. "Your seat is in the last row." As Connie slipped down the aisle, the flight attendant pulled the door closed.

Passengers crowded the aisle as they pushed and shoved their carry-on items into the overhead compartments. Chatter filled the cabin. Connie waited and kept her head down. She eased past one passenger and then another. Dark sunglasses shielded her eyes, which momentarily locked on a large-framed man whose body hung over the outside seat. His stare—cold and devilish—caused her to look away. She hurried past with the back row in sight.

"Excuse me," Connie exclaimed, becoming lodged between the seat and the man's knees. A daily newspaper blocked his face. "Excuse me!"

He shifted his knees to the side.

Connie slipped past and dropped into her seat, pushing her pocketbook under it. Eeriness engulfed her. She couldn't shake the feeling that someone was staring at her. Two magazines hung from the seat back at her knees. She grabbed one, slid low in the seat, and hid behind the open spread. Her hands trembled as goose bumps spread. Again, she felt the unwelcome eyes.

The jet's engines hissed and whined as the plane jolted and moved backward. Connie breathed more easily as she watched the plane roll down the taxiway, pull onto the runway, and stop.

The man holding the newspaper lowered the right side. "Connie," he said, "I'm surprised to see you on this flight."

Connie turned and gasped, "Judge Blair!" Her voice was drowned out by the roar of the jet. The acceleration forced her back into her seat.

Blair grinned and laid his head back against the headrest.

The plane rotated and began its ascent. The ground grew smaller and smaller; soon they were over the dark blue waters of the Atlantic.

As the plane leveled out, Blair leaned into Connie. "Relax, you made it safely out of the country. You know," he chuckled, "I could use your help."

Connie trembled and shook her head.

"Your choice. I wonder why you're disguised and acting like a nervous mouse. I bet the Bahamian Government would be interested in knowing, too."

She put her head into her hands, trying to control her quivers. "What is it that you want me to do?"

"All you have to do is meet someone."

Connie didn't say anything. Her hands continued to hide her pale face.

Blair smiled and pulled the newspaper back up to read. "I'll give you some time to think about my proposal, but don't take too long."

Connie felt sick. She wished she could jump out of the plane. Neither she nor Blair said anything for the next fifteen minutes.

After a short hop over to Nassau, the plane began its descent. "Well, Connie," Blair said and nudged her with his elbow.

Connie's eyes held a blank expression.

Blair looked at his watch. "We'll be landing shortly and I need your answer."

Connie drew in a deep breath. "What choice do I have?"

"None, but until you complete our deal, I'll expect you to stay with me. If you leave, I'll phone the authorities." Blair grabbed her upper arm, tightened his fingers, and pulled her to him. "I mean it." His eyes burrowed into hers.

Connie couldn't breathe; she was afraid she was going to wet her pants. "You're hurting me."

Blair released her. "You think that hurt? Just try and double-cross me, then you'll know what pain is."

Connie hunched over, trying to conceal the tears.

Blair chuckled under his breath. *She'll do it.*

CHAPTER SIXTEEN

Shelly swayed to the left as the police car moved through traffic. She peered through the bottom portion of the window. *Who's going to help me? I'm just kidding myself if I believe someone's willing to get involved with an accused killer.* She leaned forward as the car slowed and turned into the police parking lot.

Walter! I've got his cell phone number.

The police car rocked to a halt at the rear entrance of the West Palm Beach Police Station. The back door swung open. Shelly scooted across the seat and climbed out, squinting under the bright sunlight. "I didn't kill Justin."

"Save it," the officer said. "Tell it to the judge. I'm just doing my job. Now get moving." He clasped her arm and pulled.

Shelly winced, but followed. *Why don't they believe me?* The back door of the jail opened and she stepped inside, shuddering as the stale air hit her.

"Over here," the officer said, as he pulled her, not too gently, to a counter. He grabbed her hands and removed the handcuffs. "I've got to fingerprint you."

Shelly's fingers were rolled across the inkpad and each finger pressed on the fingerprint card. She stared at the black prints. *Those should be the killer's prints, not mine.*

Before she cleared her mind, a board of numbers was thrust into her hand. She held it across her chest and stared into a camera. *This is so humiliating.* She gasped as the camera flashed.

"Follow me," the officer said.

Shelly dropped the numbered sign on the table and moved down the hallway. She took a deep breath, stepped into a cell, then froze when the door clanged shut. She shivered as she glanced at the walls, floor, and bed. *It's cold and nasty in here.* Minutes passed. Shelly remained rigid.

What's going to happen to me? She exhaled, stepped beside the bed, touched it, and cringed. After pacing back and forth, she reluctantly sat and waited.

Finally, the door screeched open. A female guard stood in the doorway. "Mrs. Roble, you can make your one phone call now."

Shelly's bloodshot eyes pleaded with the woman. "The phone number I need to call is in my pocketbook. Can you get it for me?"

"I'll see," the officer answered. The cell door clanged shut.

"It's on a white sheet of paper. Walter Clemmons," Shelly shouted through the bars.

The guard returned. As she stepped up to the cell door, she held the pocketbook open. "Mrs. Roble, there's nothing in your pocketbook."

Shelly gasped, "That's not mine."

"What?" the guard asked.

"It's similar to mine, but it's a little different."

"This is the pocketbook that you were carrying when you were arrested."

"Well, it's not mine." Shelly stared at the bag. Her jaw quivered.

Whose pocketbook is that? How am I going to call Walter? What am I going to do? The cell felt colder. Loneliness pressed heavier as she tried to think of who she could call.

I've got to call someone. But who? Dad's in big trouble. Her head throbbed.

She paced from one wall to the other, two steps in each direction and then turned to do it again. Shelly froze. *Jane*

Winchester. Why didn't I think of her before?

After getting the guard's attention, Shelly was led over to a bank of phones on a concrete block wall. "Five minutes."

Shelly thumbed through the tattered phonebook. She slid her finger down the page. "Wh-Wi-n . . . there's her number." She lifted the receiver and dialed. Her heart raced as she waited. *Please be home.*

"Hello," Jane said.

"Jane, I'm so glad you're home. This is Shelly." Her voice quivered. "I need your help. The police have arrested me; they've charged me with murdering Justin, my ex-husband."

"What?" she exclaimed.

"I didn't do it. Honest. Justin can't be dead. He's with his girlfriend, Connie, and they're supposed to be out of the country. It doesn't make sense. I don't know what's going on, but I think I saw Connie at the airport. If it was her, you can bet Justin's somewhere around. I've been set up," her voice was barely audible between sniffles.

"Shelly, take a couple of deep breaths. It'll all work out."

"I . . . I can't! Blair and Otman are on their way to Nassau. They're after Dad and Bessy. Otman has *that* black bag."

"Don't you worry. I'll warn them. Where are they staying?"

"It's a marina. I don't remember the name. You've got to call Delta Airlines in Atlanta and have them page Walter. He'll know where they're staying. Hurry. He's changing flights and you've got to catch him before he boards that plane. Tell him what's happening. Tell him he's got to come back immediately. I need him. Dad and Bessy need him. Please hurry."

"Shelly, I'll find him. I'll call you back and let you know what Walter said."

"They won't let you call me," she remembered from trying to contact Arthur when he was held in the county jail on erroneous charges, after his escape from Southern Retirement

Community. "I'll have to call you collect from now on. This was my only free call."

The phone went dead as they said goodbye. Shelly sighed and slumped over. *Please Walter, put aside your feelings for Jane; don't let her annoy you. I need you. You've got to come back.*

She grasped her knees and began to cry softly. *Please Jane, find Walter.*

CHAPTER SEVENTEEN

Walter stepped off the plane at Hartsfield in Atlanta and followed the line of passengers through the Jetway. Once in the concourse, he looked overhead at the flight board and searched for the connecting flight. With the gate and directions, he turned left. His walk slowed. *I hate it when a part of life has to end and a new part begins.* He sighed and walked up to the departure gate. "I'm Walter Clemmons." He slid the ticket across the counter.

"Mr. Clemmons," the young woman said as she read his name. "I have a message for you." As he began to pull the paper from her hand, her grip tightened, and she leaned over the counter. "The caller seemed anxious for you to call. It seems to be an emergency." She released the note.

"Really," Walter said, staring at the note. He read:

> Shelly has been arrested. Arthur and
> Bessy are in trouble. Call me!
> Jane Winchester at 555-647-5263

"What?" he gasped. He hurried away from the counter and pulled out his cell phone. He stood beside a bank of windows that stretched from floor to ceiling, and looked down at the tarmac. Delta employees scurried below. His palms were sweaty as he flipped open the phone and punched in the number.

"Hello," Jane answered.

"Jane, this is Walter. I got your message."

"Walter, thank goodness it's you. Shelly's been arrested for murder."

"Murder? I don't believe it."

"It's true. The police have charged her with killing Justin, her ex-husband."

"Justin's dead?"

"Yes. No. She doesn't believe Justin's dead."

Walter took a deep breath. "She couldn't have. It's not in her to kill anyone." Again, he took a deep breath. "Tell Arthur I'll be on the next flight back."

"I haven't been able to contact Arthur. I don't know where he's staying. Arthur and Bessy are in trouble. Shelly saw that no-good Judge Blair and Mr. Otman board a plane to Nassau; he was carrying his black bag. What's going to happen when Blair finds them?"

"We can warn them; I know where they're staying," Walter said and pulled out the postcard from his pocket. He scanned it. "Oh, no. Shelly's card is the one that told where they were staying, not mine."

"Think."

Walter rubbed his forehead and squinted as he tried to pull the name of the resort from the blank void that he was seeing. "It's . . . Blue Water Resort or something." He continued massaging his head. "No, no, that's not it. That's where they were staying in Freeport, I think. I can't remember. It's some resort with a marina. There can't be many."

"Don't worry, Walter." Jane fidgeted. "You'll remember it. Just get back here. Are Bessy and Arthur going to be all right?"

"If we get to them first," Walter said as he scanned up and down the concourse. *Where can I purchase a return ticket?*

"I've got to go," he said and flipped the phone closed. He raced back to the ticket agent. "I need your help!"

CHAPTER EIGHTEEN

The jet rolled to a stop on the tarmac at Nassau International Airport. A flight attendant stepped up to the door, unlatched it, and pushed it open. Warm tropical air rushed inside. Two Bahamian men pushed a rolling staircase to the side of the jet and locked its wheels. The attendant waved at the men.

The air inside the cabin grew warmer. Passengers jammed the aisle as they retrieved their belongings from overhead compartments and then waited to exit. The single file line of eager travelers passed the attendant, who smiled and said over and over again, "Thanks for flying Continental." They stepped out into the hot air, each with a smile on their face, ready to begin their vacation.

Connie stared at Blair. "That's all I have to do? Just give Bessy a present and then I can go?"

"Yes," Blair said, nodding, "and then you can do whatever you'd like. You'll never have to see me again."

"If you're giving her a present, why don't you do it yourself?"

"We've got to go," he said. He stood and blocked the aisle. "Are you going to give Bessy the present or not?"

"I said I would, and then I'm out of here."

"Good."

Otman bumped and nudged passengers as he entered the aisle. His black bag jabbed a well-built man in the back.

The man's squared jaw tightened as he swirled around, then looked up at Otman. "Oh, excuse me." He turned and hurried down the aisle.

Otman followed the man to the door. The man rushed down the stairs as Otman ducked and stepped onto the metal stairs. He stood on the top step, closed his eyes, and took a deep breath. The hot, salty air filled his lungs. *I've always wanted to come here.*

"Please move along," the attendant said.

The stairs shook as Otman hurried down them. Connie and Blair were the last to deplane. Inside the rustic terminal building, they searched for their suitcases, as the carousel circled. Otman and Blair picked up their small suitcases and stood impatiently, while Connie retrieved three huge bags.

Otman stepped into one line to pass through immigration and customs.

Blair put his arm around Connie. She cringed. Blair instructed a porter to load their suitcases. They proceeded to a different line from Otman and waited their turn. "We're traveling as a couple," Blair breathed into Connie's ear. "Smile and act like you're enjoying yourself." He smiled and pulled her closer.

Connie forced a smile, but was unable to control the tremor.

"Relax," Blair said, as they were next in line. "Everything will work out fine." He fingered a one-hundred-dollar bill.

"Next," the customs officer announced and waved them up to the counter.

Blair smiled as they stepped up.

"ID, please."

Connie pulled out her passport. Blair handed the man a fake passport.

The officer looked at Blair and then at his ID and then back at him. "And what's the nature of your stay?"

"Vacation," Connie said with labored breath and a forced smile.

Blair smiled and nodded. "Honeymoon."

The officer grinned. "Ever been to the Bahamas before?"

Connie shook her head.

"Yes sir," Blair answered, "before I met my new bride." Blair watched Otman clear customs and walk outside the terminal. Otman leaned against a post and waited.

Blair slid the one-hundred-dollar bill across the counter. The man looked at the bill and smiled. He palmed it and pulled it across the counter. "Enjoy yourselves," he said, pocketing the bill. The rubber stamp smacked the paperwork for both immigration and customs.

Blair grabbed Connie's hand, and they walked out of the terminal building. The porter followed, pulling the mountain of luggage on a cart. As they approached, Otman stepped up to the curb, and flagged down a cab.

The taxi pulled over to the curb, and the cabby hopped out. He opened the trunk and struggled with Connie's three large cases, then tossed the small ones in after them. The cabby reached for Otman's black bag.

"I'll keep this with me," Otman said and snatched it away. He stepped up to the front door and climbed in. The car squatted to the right. His hair brushed the headliner.

Blair and Connie climbed into the back seat. He tried to sit close to her, but she moved away and rested against the far door.

The cab lurched away from the curb. "Where to?" the cabby asked.

Blair pulled out the post card. "Providence Resort."

"Man," Otman gasped and grabbed the dash, "you're driving on the wrong side of the street."

The cabby laughed. "This is the side we drive on. You Americans drive on the wrong side."

Otman gave the man a dirty look and released his grip. He leaned back in the seat, unable to relax as they wove in and out of traffic, inches from other vehicles. Faster cars and trucks muscled past.

Otman grasped the seat, as tail lights from the car in front of him glowed red. He pressed hard on the floorboard with his feet and gritted his teeth as the cab's front end rocked to a stop. His mouth hung open, staring at a fraction-of-an-inch separating both vehicles. *These people drive crazy.*

As the miles zipped past, Otman relaxed. Before he knew it, they were downtown beside the harbour and in the parking lot of Providence Resort.

Blair dug into his pocket, pulled out a wad of bills, then counted out the fare. They lugged their bags inside to the registration office. Otman and Connie stood over to the side and watched Blair approach the counter. "We'll take two rooms overlooking the marina, please."

The dark-tanned woman behind the counter looked the three over. "How long will you be staying?"

"One night, maybe two."

Connie stared at Blair; he could sense she was about to become demanding. "We'd like those two rooms to be adjoining, please," he added. "Two beds in one room and, . . ." he looked at the clerk, ". . . and a queen-size or bigger in the other." He shook his head at how he was having to pacify Connie.

"Do you have a swimming pool?" Connie asked, stepping up to the counter.

"Down that hallway, first door on your right. It'll take you out to the pool," the woman said as she pointed. She reached behind her and pulled three keys from the pigeon-holed cupboard. She handed both men keys to 414 and gave Connie the key to 412.

Blair gave the woman a newly-acquired credit card and then they were off. They rode the elevator up to the fourth floor. As they made their way down the corridor, Otman scratched his head. "You said Bessy canceled all of your credit cards."

"She did, but it's amazing how many people are willing to accommodate you, with the right incentive."

They came to Connie's room first. She slipped her key into

the door and opened it. Otman continued to the next room and did likewise. Blair followed Connie into her room, waited for the bellboy to leave, and shut the door. "Now, get one thing straight. We're not here for a vacation. We have work to do and you aren't going to the pool. I can't afford for you to be at the pool when they arrive. Is that clear?"

Connie pulled one of the large suitcases over to the king size bed. Grunting, she wrestled it on top. "You might not be here for a vacation, but I am. I'm going to the pool, and you can't stop me."

"You want to bet. I'll call the cops and tell them you're wanted back in the states."

"And while you're telling them that, tell them where they can find me. I'll be at the pool. If I see them, I'll assume our deal is off." She pulled out one of her bikinis. "Anyway, you made the deal. I agreed to meet someone, not to be held prisoner in a room in the Bahamas. I'm going to enjoy myself. When Arthur and Bessy arrive, come and get me. I don't believe you'll make your move the second they pull up to the dock."

"Enjoy yourself," Blair snapped.

"I will." She turned, stepped over to the adjoining door, and opened it. Otman stood in the doorway sideways. "Now, if you don't mind, I'd like to put on my bathing suit."

Blair stepped through the door and closed it.

"Wow, she's going to be a real pill, isn't she?" Otman asked.

"No, she's not." He lowered his voice. "She's not getting away with talking to me like that."

Connie slipped on her glimmering black two-piece. She grabbed a tube of sunscreen and a towel, then headed down to the pool. She found a lounge chair and stretched out. Within minutes, the warmth of the sun erased all of her problems.

Blair and Otman made themselves comfortable on the balcony, staring down at the marina and waterway. Otman glanced at Connie, lying on her stomach. "What're you going to do with Connie, once we've got Bessy?"

"I don't know, but we're not leaving any witnesses."

CHAPTER NINETEEN

Walter stepped outside of Palm Beach International Airport in the dim evening light and flagged down a taxi. "Palm Beach County Jail, please." He tossed the small carry-on suitcase into the back seat and climbed in.

The cab driver gave him and his suitcase a quick glance. "County jail, huh. You planning on checking in?" He chuckled and pulled away from the curb.

Outside the jail, the cab pulled into the back parking area and stopped next to the visitor entrance sign. Walter paid the fare and retrieved his suitcase. He looked up at the thirteen-floor facility and shivered, remembering that awful night weeks ago, when he was incarcerated after Arthur, Bessy, and he escaped from Southern Retirement Community and forcibly withdrew Arthur's money from West Palm Beach Bank. *I hoped I'd never see the inside of this place again.*

He drew a deep breath, followed the visitor sign up the ramp to the second floor, and stepped inside. After checking the suitcase at security and signing in, he hung the visitor's badge around his neck. He was led to a row of windows with individual compartments, each having a phone, and waited for Shelly. He didn't have to wait long.

"Walter!" Shelly cried into the phone. "I'm glad Jane found you."

"Are you okay?"

"No." She reached up to the glass, touched it, and shook her head. "It's awful in here."

"I know." He put his hand up on the glass, against Shelly's.

"I'll get you a lawyer. Just hang in there; I'll get you out."

Shelly nodded.

"Tell me what happened at the airport."

"After we said goodbye, I returned to my car. That's where I overheard voices that sounded familiar. I turned and saw Blair and Otman. So, I followed them back into the airport to see where they were going. At the ticket counter for Continental, I found out they'd bought tickets to Nassau. I bought one too. I didn't want to be noticed, so I bought a disguise, a hat and a scarf." Shelly stared at Walter. "The next thing I know I'm being arrested, and Blair and Otman are flying off to the Bahamas." Her hands trembled. "The police discovered a body they claim is Justin's." She sniffled. "But I swear, I didn't do it."

Walter swallowed the lump in his throat. "Of course you didn't do it. You couldn't have." He began to smile. "It's obvious the cops have made a big mistake. That dead man isn't Justin. By tomorrow morning they'll have it all figured out and you'll be free."

"Really?" Shelly said with a forced smile that quickly faded. "Have you been able to contact Dad and Bessy?"

"No, but they're okay. They're not supposed to be in Nassau until tomorrow. Remember? They were stopping at another island first."

Shelly squirmed. "I'm afraid something terrible is going to happen to them."

"Stop worrying. I'll call and leave a message for them tonight. They'll get it as soon as they check in. And . . ." he rubbed his eyes and yawned. "By morning I bet the police will have everything sorted out and realize they've made a mistake."

"I hope so. I want to go home."

"I know; those nights spent in here were the worst of my life. Trust me, everything will work out."

Shelly nodded. "Yeah, you're right." Her tight facial skin

softened. "Oh, I almost forgot! I remember seeing a woman pass by me when I was being arrested. I think it was Connie. Justin must have been around there somewhere. I just didn't see him."

"Sure, maybe he's waiting for her in Nassau. He could have been catching the next flight across, or maybe he was already on the plane. It wouldn't surprise me if he had something to do with plotting all of this. In fact, Justin and Blair could have planned this whole thing together."

"They had to." Shelly's face reddened. "I bet Blair offered him a piece of Bessy's estate if he'd help. Justin would never refuse easy money."

"And that would explain how Blair and Otman got enough cash to post bail."

"Justin!" Shelly spat.

Walter laughed. "Their plan is going to fail; I'll warn Bessy and Arthur before they can find them. I'd like to see Judge Blair's face when he discovers Bessy and Arthur aren't in Nassau."

"I'd like to see all of their faces when they finally realize what has happened."

Walter looked at his watch. "It's getting late. I've got to find a hotel and check in."

"Oh, you don't need to do that. You can stay at Bessy's house. There's plenty of room."

"No way. Jane lives a few houses down." Walter hesitated. "Thanks for the offer, but . . ."

". . . but nothing. You'll have the whole house to yourself. Bessy would want you to stay there."

"Okay, but if Jane bothers me, I'm going to a hotel."

Shelly smiled as she pictured Jane patting Walter's thigh. "I don't think Jane will bother you. I think she got the message you aren't interested."

"I hope so."

"Make yourself at home. Bessy won't mind. The key is

hidden behind the flower pot at the front door."

"I'll see you tomorrow," Walter said. "And don't worry about your dad. Everything will be fine. You'll be out of here tomorrow morning and I'll be here to pick you up."

Walter stepped from the room, returned the badge, and claimed his suitcase. After asking the officer at the counter for the phone number, he pulled out his cell phone and requested a taxi.

He paid the fare when he reached Bessy's house and watched the taxi drive away.

Shelly said to look behind the flowerpot. A search turned up nothing. *She said it was right here.* He scrutinized the rest of the porch for the key, but didn't find it.

I'll just go to a hotel. He pulled out his cell phone and pressed the redial button.

"Hello," Walter said. ". . . Hello . . . Are you there? Hello?" He looked at the cell phone screen. It was blank. *I can't believe the battery would pick now to die.* He looked down the long driveway.

I'll walk back to town. Or, maybe . . . Jane will drive me into town. No way, I'd rather walk. He grabbed the suitcase and headed up the driveway.

Boy, it's humid. He felt like a salesperson going from house to house and laughed. When he reached the street, he looked left toward Jane's house and shook his head. "Absolutely not." He turned right and headed for town. With each step taken, exhaustion began to take its toll.

I'll never make it. I could use Jane's phone. Shoulders drooped, he turned and headed for her house, sighing.

Once he reached the front door, he paused, building up courage, then knocked. He drew in a cleansing breath. *The Atlantic. You can smell it just like Jane said.* The overhead light illuminated the enormous porch.

"Walter," Jane said, opening in the door, her gaze taking in the suitcase. "Come in." A large smile spread across her face.

Once the door was closed, she flipped the dead bolt in place.

Walter felt a chill run down his spine.

"This way," she said, as she stepped up on the first step on the long sweeping staircase.

"Um," he stuttered. He didn't move. "I need a ride to the hotel."

"Nonsense. You're not staying at a hotel, when I've got five empty bedrooms."

Walter felt the hairs on his neck prickle. He thought of Southern Retirement and how he'd been locked up and couldn't leave. "I . . . I can't stay."

"Sure you can."

"N–n–o–o, it's not right." He turned his head and looked at the front door. "I don't want to put you out."

Jane grabbed the suitcase. "I'm not taking no for an answer."

Walter's eyes grew large. He tugged on the suitcase, but she pulled back. He thought about letting her keep the bag and running.

"Now, Walter. You'll have your own bedroom and if you'd feel safer, you can lock your door and put a chair up against it for extra security."

I bet she has a back way into the room.

"That is, if you're scared." She smiled. "I know these big houses can seem ghostly for someone not used to staying in one. But I assure you," she said as she turned to the key pad and punched in the code, "with the security alarm installed here, you won't have to worry about someone breaking in."

It's not someone breaking in I'm worried about. He gritted his teeth to keep his thoughts private and decided that locking the bedroom door was a wise suggestion. With Jane almost pulling him up the stairs, he agreed to stay and let go of the suitcase.

It whizzed past Jane. "Walter, you travel light. This suitcase is practically empty."

Walter grinned. "That's because I changed planes and they didn't have time to pull my other suitcase. Most of my clothes are in Oregon, at the Portland Airport."

Jane gave him a brief glance. *I guess he'll be wearing the same outfit for days, unless . . .*" She wasn't going to suggest it. She turned and led him to his room. "You'll like this room. Mine is on the other end of the house. You'll have complete privacy." She flipped the light switch and stepped inside. "What do you think?"

"Wow!" He looked from the ornate king size bed to the matching armoire, then on to the six-foot long dresser complete with a full-length mirror. On one side was a wall of windows, which he assumed overlooked the back yard and the swimming pool. In the corner were two matching chairs and end table, which formed a reading nook. "I need to make an international call," he said. "My cell phone's dead. I've got to warn Arthur and Bessy."

"Use the phone on the nightstand. I don't mind."

Walter fidgeted.

Jane moved over to the bed and turned down the sheets. "If you need anything, just ask. Make yourself at home." Their eyes locked for a moment, but he glanced away. "Use anything that I have. There's no need to ask. I'll leave you alone."

He glanced at her again. "Thank you for the hospitality." *I think.*

"It'll be nice to have a house guest." Her eyes softened.

Walter noticed. "I bet you have guests all the time."

"No, not really. I haven't been out much since Bessy went away. I have a hard time trusting men. Most seem to want what I have, more than who I am."

Walter nodded. "Yeah, I know. A man wanted what was mine, stole my money and property, and put me in Southern Retirement Community." He stepped over to the bed and laid the suitcase on it.

"You can stay as long as you need. Bessy spoke highly of

you. I trust you. Sorry for my earlier behavior. She . . ." Jane blushed. "She said I should get to know you. I tried too hard."

Walter's face turned red. "She did?"

"It was just girl talk, you know. She told me what a great guy you were." She blushed again and hurried to the door. "I'll leave you alone."

Walter watched her red shoes disappear into the hallway. *Did I misjudge her?*

"Sleep tight." She grabbed the doorknob and pulled the door shut.

He hurried over to the phone and pressed zero. He closed his eyes and tried to recall the resort Arthur mentioned on Shelly's postcard while he waited for the operator.

"International operator," the soft voice spoke. "How may I help you?"

"I need the number for a marina and resort in Nassau, but I can't remember the name. Could you read them to me?"

"Let's see, there's Nassau Yacht Club, White Sands Resort, Providence Resort, Bayside, . . ."

"Wait, the one before that."

"Providence Resort?"

"Yes, that's it." He wrote down the number and hung up. Walter looked at the number for a moment and then dialed it.

"Hello. Thank you for calling Providence Resort. How may I help you?"

"My name is Walter Clemmons. Have Arthur and Bessy McCullen checked in?"

"Uhh . . . no sir, they haven't," the receptionist said, glancing over the register.

"I know they have reservations for tomorrow. I need to leave an urgent message for Mr. McCullen."

"One moment, please." She searched the desk for a pen.

Walter paced in front of the window.

"I'm ready. What's the message?"

"Tell him that Blair and Otman, yes Otman, O-T-M-A-N,

are in Nassau. Have him call Walter Clemmons the minute he gets in." He took another step. "Please, don't forget. This is urgent." He scrambled to the nightstand and read the number from Jane's phone to the resort operator.

"Is that all?" she asked.

"Yes ma'am," Walter said and hung up. He looked out the window, over the swimming pool. *Arthur, please be careful.* His eyes drifted to the shallow end and stopped at the gazebo. *Careful!* He chuckled and looked at the locked door. *Look who's telling whom to be careful.*

CHAPTER TWENTY

The afternoon breeze had long since died down and the night sky darkened. Out on the balcony, Otman shifted from one hip to the other as he tried to get comfortable. He straightened in his chair and then slouched again. "How much longer do we have to stay out here looking for Arthur and Bessy? I'm hungry."

Blair looked at his watch. "I guess they're not coming today. We'll go get something to eat."

Otman led the way inside and flung open the adjoining door.

Connie lay sprawled on top of the sheets, clad in her two-piece bikini. Crimson radiated from her skin. Blair stood beside the bed shaking his head. "I told you not to go down to the pool. Now look at you. You look like a broiled lobster."

"I feel like one, too." She glanced over at the nightstand. "Please rub that aloe on my back."

"No way." Blair said with a grin. "You had to go to the pool. You'll have to put that on yourself or suffer."

Connie moaned.

Otman lifted the bottle and twisted off the cap. "I'd be glad to rub it on you, Connie."

Connie glared at him with contempt. "Don't you dare touch me."

"If you want that stuff rubbed on your back, you'd better let him do it. Otherwise you'll have to do it yourself," Blair snickered. He swore he could feel the heat rising from her body.

"Well?" Otman smirked, exposing his yellowish teeth. "Do

you want me to, or not?"

Connie's skin hurt all over. "Okay! But you'd best watch those hands. I'll scream if you try anything."

He turned the bottle upside down and squeezed. Green gel pooled in his hand. He slapped his hands together sending little green blobs across the bed and onto the carpet.

Connie flinched as the cold gel came in contact with her burning skin. His hands ran up her thigh. "That's far enough! I said my back."

Otman frowned and slopped the goo across her back. As he finished, he wiped his hands on the sheets.

"Otman and I are going down to the restaurant for dinner. Do you want us to bring you something?"

"I'm not hungry," she moaned, "I just want to sleep. On your way out, please turn the air-conditioner down."

Otman stepped over to the thermostat and thought for a split second of turning the heat on, but instead he pushed the lever to the left. Cool air blew from the vents. "Don't wait up for us." He laughed as they stepped from the room. "We'll have an enjoyable dinner without her."

Blair nodded. "And tomorrow we'll have Bessy."

"And Arthur."

Blair laughed. "No, he'll be in Nassau on his honeymoon without his bride."

CHAPTER TWENTY-ONE

The sky appeared as a jeweler's black velvet, scattered with thousands of diamonds. Bessy and Arthur cuddled on the flybridge. Bessy's hair fluttered as the light breeze kept the bugs away. She gazed into the heavens. "It's a beautiful night."

"Very relaxing," Arthur said, looking from the sky to the water. A bottle of red wine sat on the table, and the wine in their glasses swayed ever so slightly from one side to the other.

Anchors Away drifted at anchor in eight feet of water.

"Oh look," Bessy said, "a shooting star."

Arthur watched as it streaked across the sky. "That lasted longer than any I've ever seen."

Bessy took a deep breath and closed her eyes. "I wonder what Walter decided to do."

"He left. He wanted to put the past behind him and start over."

"Do you think he'll like Oregon?"

"I hope so." Arthur stretched for the wine glass, picked it up, and sipped. "I'm so glad we all met."

"Me too," Bessy said. "Isn't it ironic how Harry and Otman changed places with us? They're locked up and now we're free."

"Justice might be slow, but it always seems to win in the end." Arthur scanned the horizon. The lagoon blended into the darkness.

The boat shifted as a small swell ran under it. Seconds later, the wave was heard lapping at the shore.

Arthur turned and looked into Bessy's eyes. They twinkled.

"What?" Bessy asked.

"You have beautiful eyes."

Bessy batted her eyes. "And you'll follow them anywhere," she said as she sat up, clasping his hand.

"Anywhere?"

She stood and he followed her down the stairs and back to the master stateroom. "Sweep me off my feet."

Arthur lifted her in his arms and gently placed her on the bed.

Bessy threw up her arms and pulled him down beside her. Their lips met.

CHAPTER TWENTY-TWO

The night air in Palm Beach was muggy. In Jane's back yard crickets chirped and bugs smacked into the window outside Walter's bedroom. A light breeze swayed the palm branches beside the pool. Inside the house, everything was dark and quiet.

"Help!" pierced the air.

Walter's eyelids fluttered as he fought to focus. *What was that?* He held his breath as his heart raced. Splash–splash–splosh echoed dimly outside the window. He sprang upright in bed.

"Help! Please help me!"

Walter threw off the sheets, leaped out of bed, and raced to the window. Down in the swimming pool he saw someone's arms flailing. "Oh no!" He pressed his nose into the window and stared. "JANE!" Pushing away, he raced from the room, down the stairs, through the large family room, dodging and leaping over the furniture, to the back door. He swung it open and ran out on the patio toward the deep end of the pool. The breeze bristled against his bare chest causing him to stop and look at himself. *I'm in my boxer shorts.*

"Walter, help me!" Jane sputtered and then went under.

Walter's knees bent to spring, but locked stiff as he stared through the clear water. *Good grief! She's swimming in the buff. Is this a trick or is she really in trouble?* He stood and glanced from one end of the pool to the waterfall at the other end, hoping to find something to reach her with or something to throw to her. *I'm not getting in.*

Jane's head popped above the water as her arms slapped the water. Her eyes were wide with fright.

Walter's throat tightened; his heart pounded. With nothing in sight, he dropped to the concrete on his knees and reached far over the water. "Jane! Grab my hand." His fingers wavered above the pool's surface.

Jane slapped the water, sending droplets in his direction. She groped for his hand.

Walter felt the breeze from Jane's flailing hands. *Just a little farther.* He grunted as he stretched, teetering on the edge of the pool.

Jane grabbed his hand and pulled.

"I've got you," he yelled. His knee slipped off the concrete. His eyes closed as he sucked in a deep breath and flipped into the pool.

Jane's hand disappeared.

Walter surged to the surface and shuddered, "Jane!" He twisted right, then left looking down into the water, but could not see her. He pulled himself up on the edge of the pool and stood. He rubbed his eyes and raced around the deep end as he searched the pool's bottom. *Where is she?*

"Jane!" He ran back to the other side, gasping.

"Walter," Jane called, as she dashed from the house wrapped in a robe, holding a towel, "what's wrong?"

Walter looked from Jane, to the pool, and back to Jane. He looked down at his wet boxer shorts that clung to his legs. He clasped his hands below his waist. "Uhh."

Jane held out an open towel. "Here, take this."

Walter slid one hand up and grabbed the towel. "Thanks," he grinned and pulled the towel around himself. "I'm sorry I woke you. I, uhh, I must have been walking in my sleep. I could have sworn I saw you out here in the pool. I thought you were drowning. I came down to rescue you."

"Oh Walter, thank you." Jane smiled. "I saw you in the

pool from my bedroom window and thought you were calling me to come swim." Jane let the robe slip from her shoulders, revealing a bright multi-color, one-piece.

Walter stood speechless.

"Since you are already wet, why don't we go for a swim?"

Walter pulled the towel tighter. "I . . . I don't think so. I don't have a suit."

"Your boxer's are fine. Come on." She leaped into the pool. "Aren't you going to join me?"

"I don't know."

"Do I have to start drowning for you to get in?"

Walter tossed the towel on a chair and jumped in.

CHAPTER TWENTY-THREE

Anchored off a secluded spot between Frozen and Alder Cay in the Berry Islands, morning dew beaded on Anchor Away's deck. Shafts of light darted through the porthole and shown on Arthur's face. The white sand of the beach glimmered as if it was freshly manicured during the night. Small waves chased the birds at the shoreline.

"Coffee?" Bessy asked as she carried a tray with two steaming cups into the master cabin. "It's so nice to leisurely wake up."

Arthur yawned and stretched. "And it's so peaceful." He sat up in bed, reached out, and took the tray from Bessy.

She climbed across the bed, up against Arthur. "We just might have to stay longer on our honeymoon before we head back to West Palm Beach."

"I'll clear my calendar. I don't have any pressing appointments back home."

Pillows propped them up in bed. They sipped their coffee, glancing at each other with contented grins.

"I've ordered bread from Flo's at the next island up, Little Harbour Cay," Bessy said. "I bet you've never eaten fresh Bahamian bread. If we hurry, it'll still be hot. It's only a ten-minute dinghy ride away. Once we get to the dinghy dock, it's another ten-minute walk."

"I've never heard of taking a dinghy ride to buy bread. Do they serve breakfast as well?"

"Yes, I'll raise her on the radio again and let her know

we'll be having breakfast. It'll be fun."

"Shelly would love Flo's. As a teenager, hot, fresh bread with lots of butter was always her favorite. I wish we'd talked to her before we left Freeport. I can't believe she wasn't home when we called."

"We'll try her again when we get to Nassau."

CHAPTER TWENTY-FOUR

Jane stood over the stove and dropped another slice of bacon into the black iron frying pan. Grease sizzled and popped. She turned to the pan beside it and stirred the eggs. Over on the counter, toast sprang up. Beside it, coffee dripped into the glass pot. Through the picture window, puffy clouds drifted past in the blue sky. Soft fifty's music resonated from the overhead concealed speakers.

Walter strolled into the kitchen. The aroma filled his senses; he stopped and took another deep breath. Eyes closed, he envisioned his grandmother's warm kitchen.

"Walter," Jane's soft voice interrupted his thoughts, "I hope you eat breakfast." She caught herself staring. She pivoted. It was all she could do not to picture him in his boxers. They had such a great time last night, swimming.

"You bet; everything smells wonderful."

"Grab a cup of coffee, and if you'd like to read the morning paper, it's at the end of the driveway. I haven't had time to get it."

"No problem. I'll find it." Walter stepped over to the coffee pot. He picked up a china cup and marveled at its light weight. Then he filled the cup and sipped. "Wow, that's good coffee."

"Thank you." Jane grabbed the third frying pan's handle and flipped a pancake. "By the time you get the newspaper, I'll have the table set for breakfast."

Walter took another sip and then hurried outside.

Jane pulled the china from the cabinet and set the table. She placed the last dish on the table, as Walter entered, newspaper in hand.

Hmm. Eggs, bacon, sausage, toast, and pancakes. Three different jams in leaded crystal bowls sat clustered together. Light refracted off the large glass bowl of fruit that sat in the center of the table. "Who else is coming for breakfast?" He wondered if Shelly had been released and Jane had invited other guests to join them.

"Sit," Jane chuckled. "It's just us. Why?"

"I can't eat all of this!" Walter said as he laid the rolled up newspaper in the empty seat beside him.

"I'd hope not," she chuckled louder and sat, bumping the table, causing the fruit to jostle.

"Then why did you cook so much?"

"It was in the refrigerator. I figured we'd be heading to the Bahamas and I was afraid the food might go bad."

Walter's eyebrows rose. The hairs on his arm bristled. "Oh no. I'm not going to the Bahamas. It's not safe. I've left word for Arthur to call me. They've got to get out of there."

"I know," she said with a mischievous grin. "I thought it might be nice to surprise them. It won't take us long to get there. We'll just zoom across and be there in no time at all. We'll rescue them."

"We don't need to be anywhere close to Blair and Otman. Otman's capable of administering horrible drug-induced stupors, and he doesn't hesitate to inject anyone that gets in his way." Walter breathed deeply and shook his head, trying to block out the memories. "I'm not going to the Bahamas while either of those men are there. And besides, Shelly's expecting me to pick her up this morning from the county jail. They're bound to discover that the body found at the airport yesterday isn't Justin's." He wondered whose body it was and felt sorry for the victim and the family.

"Shelly can come with us. It'll be safer in numbers."

"There's no reason for any of us to go to Nassau." He

glanced at the food.

"Let's eat," Jane said, not wanting to put a damper on breakfast.

Walter found himself glancing at Jane while they ate, realizing how much effort she expended in preparing breakfast. As he swallowed the last bite of bacon, it reminded him of the times as a boy going to his grandmother's to eat. She was always up earlier than anyone else. He looked at Jane and marveled at how some things never changed from that generation until today. The cook is always up first. He couldn't believe that Jane took so much time to prepare breakfast for him, especially after the way he treated her in the past.

Maybe Bessy knew something after all. . . . Get rid of that thought. I'm not staying. He thought of Shelly. *Only bad things happen in this city. I'm leaving once Arthur and Bessy are safe. And that shouldn't be long.*

Walter rubbed his full stomach as he scooted away from the table and stood. "Would you like some help cleaning up?"

"I've got it. Sit back down and read the newspaper." She grabbed their plates and hurried to the sink.

Walter picked the newspaper up off the chair and set it on the table. It rolled open, exposing the front page. "What?" he gasped as his heart stopped.

CHAPTER TWENTY-FIVE

The kitchen went silent; time seemed to stop. Jane stood motionless at the sink holding the soapy dishrag against a plate, glancing over her shoulder at Walter. His shoulders tensed as he stared at the bold black letters:

EX-HUSBAND KILLED EXECUTION STYLE

"Oh no," Walter gasped. "Shelly needs a good attorney." He pointed to the headline as Jane rushed to his side.

Jane's spirit sagged; her eyes dropped to the large unflattering picture of Shelly taken at the airport being pushed into the squad car. "I'll call my attorney. He's really good."

"Is he qualified as a criminal lawyer?"

"I don't know, but if he isn't, he can recommend the best." Jane pulled out a chair and collapsed into it.

"Oh," he moaned and looked back at the article. "She shot him in the back of the head with a single shot." He dropped the paper to the table. "I . . . I mean someone shot him in the head."

Jane stared at him.

"I didn't mean to say Shelly did it. She didn't."

Jane leaned over and took the newspaper from his hands. "I know she didn't. She's too sweet a girl to kill anyone. Maybe you shouldn't read any more."

"They identified Justin's body with his dental records," Walter said, as he lowered his head. "I can't believe it. I just knew the police would find out it was one of the homeless men around here, not Justin."

Jane rubbed Walter's back and shoulders. "It'll all work out."

Walter's throat tightened as he thought of the days he was locked away, wrongfully accused. He knew how Shelly felt, but didn't know how to help her.

Jane scrambled around the kitchen, putting bacon and sausage into zip-lock bags and then into the refrigerator. The leftover eggs were scrapped into the garbage. As she picked up the last of the dirty plates, she noticed Walter, deep in thought. A small smile emerged as she carried the dishes to the sink. *Bessy's right. He's a gentleman. . . . But, he's not interested in me. Although he sure was adorable in those boxers.* She looked back into the sink and washed off the breadcrumbs with the soapy rag. After she washed the china platter and dried it, she carried it over to the cabinet.

She stretched on her tiptoes for the second shelf and pushed the platter with the tips of her fingers. Her ankle buckled and she fell to the floor. The platter flipped through the air over her head and crashed on the tile floor. Fragments scattered everywhere.

Walter sprang up and saw Jane, in a heap, staring at the broken pieces. "Are you okay?" He took a step toward her, but stopped as he heard a crunch under his foot.

"Yes, I'm fine," she said, then laughed. "The older I get, the clumsier I become. I need to be more careful." She eased to her feet and began picking up the ceramic shards.

"Let me help," he said as he bent down and began picking up the larger pieces.

"Thank you." A twinkle sparked in Jane's eyes as she piled pieces into her hand.

Walter scooted over to grab the last large piece of china. As he reached for it, his head collided with Jane's head.

"Ouch!" they said simultaneously. "I'm sorry," they again said in unison. Their eyes met.

I've really misjudged her. Don't fall for her. Remember, nothing good ever came from this place. Walter forced his eyes away.

"I'll finish cleaning it up," Jane said. "Why don't you go shower and get dressed." She blushed as she remembered he didn't have any clothes to wear, other than the ones he wore when he arrived.

Walter smiled, realizing the irony in her instructions.

She looked over at the wall clock. "I'll call my attorney after I sweep the floor. He'll know what to do." She hurried to the closet and pulled out the broom and dustpan. Soon the kitchen was clean and Jane held the phone to her ear. "Hello, William, this is Jane Winchester. I need legal advice. I have a friend that has been charged with murder. Can you help me?"

CHAPTER TWENTY-SIX

Manuel Marconnet, a robust and dark-tanned man, who was recommended by Jane's attorney, sat across the table from Shelly. He tapped his pen tip on the legal pad, which was full of notes. Arrows and lines inserted additional points to the scribbled mess.

"Now, let me see if I understand these facts: First, Justin was murdered." He looked up at his client as she nodded her head and then back at the page. "Second, you were arrested at the airport wearing a disguise, trying to board a flight out of the country. And third, you have a motive for killing him, revenge; he tried to kill you."

Again, he glanced at her and drew a long breath. "He emptied your bank account and your dad's. Hmm, he locked your dad away in a nursing home, divorced you, and ran off with a younger woman, his secretary." He sighed. "It'll be evident to any jury of your hatred for your ex-husband. And we can bet that the State Attorney will introduce it that way."

"But I didn't kill Justin," Shelly sniffled and rubbed her eyes. "I'm not guilty. I'm innocent."

He stared at her. *Can I believe her?*

"Why don't you believe me? I didn't kill him."

"Okay, okay," Manuel said. "I just want you to understand what we're up against." He stood and patted Shelly on the back. *Oh, this isn't going to be easy. I'm going to lose a lot of sleep before this case is solved, but I'll get her off.*

"We're going to need more than your testimony. We need physical evidence to show the jury. Seeing is believing. Do you know of anyone who hated him?" He waited for an answer. "Other than you?" He smiled.

Shelly shook her head. "I don't know. He never shared his work with me."

He sat back down and thought. His pen tapped the legal pad. "What was Justin doing at the airport?"

Shelly gazed at the floor. "Maybe he was to meet Connie there and . . ." her head snapped up as she looked at Manuel, "that could explain why she waited and was the last one to board the plane. She obviously was waiting for him and he never showed up."

"You saw Connie at the airport."

"Well, I thought it was her, but . . ."

"Did you or didn't you?"

"They were arresting me. I didn't get a good look at her, but I thought it was Connie."

Manuel jotted a note to himself. Call Continental and see if Connie was on that flight.

"Did Justin carry large sums of cash with him?"

"If he did, I never saw any."

He flipped the page over and wrote at the top: Shelly Roble vs. The State of Florida. He wrote as he spoke. "First, I'll have to ask for all of the evidence the State has. Then, I'll interview any witnesses." He stopped and looked at Shelly. "There probably won't be many." She nodded. He looked back at his notes and again continued the annoying habit of tapping his pen. "There is always the possibility that someone will come forward. Someone might have seen something."

"When can I post bail and get out of here?"

Manuel ran his hand through his hair. "I'm working on your release. Hopefully it won't be long."

"Really?" Her eyes brightened. "Today?"

Manuel looked at his notes. "That's one of the things we'll discuss with the judge later today." With the evidence he'd seen, he assumed bail would be set. "Tell you what, I'll check on that first thing when I get back to my office."

Shelly squared her shoulders and sat straight in the chair. "Thank you. I can't wait."

"At today's appearance before the judge, you'll have to tell him if you're guilty or not."

"Not guilty!" Shelly shouted.

Manuel looked at her. "You have to answer calmly in court."

"Sorry. Not guilty," she said, more subdued this time.

"That's good." He looked back at the page.

"At some point, you might be presented with a plea bargain." He raised his eyelids and peered at Shelly.

"No plea bargain. I'm innocent." She shook her head.

He looked back down and wrote: second or third degree murder. *She'll serve some years, but with good behavior, she'll still have most of her life ahead.* He held the pen still.

The State Attorney will never agree to accidental homicide with such domestic hatred. And that bullet hole in the back of Justin's head. His eyes closed at the thought.

That hole is condemning. We'll never get any plea bargain, except . . . he shook his head. *Except first-degree murder, without any chance of parole. She'll spend the rest of her life behind bars.* He took a deep long breath and scratched out second or third degree murder.

He looked at his watch. *Where has the time gone?* He scribbled: insanity plea.

CHAPTER TWENTY-SEVEN

Blair sat on the balcony with his feet propped up. A fat, stubby, Cuban cigar protruded from his lips. A cloud of smoke rose above his head. Red embers glowed as he took another drag. He watched the docks and waterways through half-open eyes.

Otman fanned at the thick smoke, but it didn't disperse. "Do you have to smoke that thing out here?"

Blair shrugged his shoulders and turned his head. Smoke drifted across the railing. "No. I guess I could go inside and smoke it."

"No! No! Just stay out here," Otman pleaded. "I'll never be able to go back inside with all of that smoke." He scooted to the edge of the chair and peered over the handrail at an approaching yacht. "Nope, not them." He remained with his head hung over the railing. "What if they don't show?"

"They'll be here." Blair drew another puff and slowly blew the smoke through the slats in the railing. The smoke dispersed upward. He watched as another yacht motored into view and nodded toward it. "She's a beauty, isn't she?"

Otman stood and looked at the mega yacht. "Now that's a boat. It's got to be over one-hundred feet long." He watched the vessel motor pass, but kept an eye on the young ladies lounging on cushions. "Ummm. Look at those girls," he added with hungry eyes.

Blair glanced at his watch again and knew it shouldn't be much longer. "Keep an eye out for them. I'm going in to check on Connie." He snubbed out the cigar.

Connie, dressed in a lightweight cotton jumpsuit, lay in

bed, surrounded and propped up by pillows. The TV blared. The room was chilly and the air-conditioner, set on high, continued to blow. Yesterday's sunburn faded during the night and she now sported an almond tan. She just returned from renting a car from downtown and was exhausted from the stifling heat. She wanted to go swimming, but Blair packed her suitcases while she was gone. He carried them down and locked them in the trunk along with his and Otman's, the minute she returned. The only thing left on the dresser was Otman's black bag and a green glittery package.

"Can I get you something?" Blair mocked as he stepped in front of the contestants of the game show. "You'd better be ready when they arrive."

Connie shifted herself in the bed and peered around him. "I'm ready. Now step to the side if you still have something to say. You're blocking my view."

"I mean it. You'd better be ready."

"What? You don't like what I'm wearing?"

Blair snarled.

"I bet Otman approves of it," she said, and gave a quick smirk.

"I'll get him. I'm sure he will."

Otman rushed inside. "Judge, you'd better get out here. There's a boat coming toward the marina. Check it out."

Blair ran to the door and peered out. "It's them! Come on!"

Connie sprang out of bed. Otman stood goggle-eyed at her outfit. She gave Blair an I-told-you-so look.

"Connie, you know what to do?"

"I'm to give Bessy your present. I still don't see why you can't do it yourself."

Blair looked beyond her at Otman.

Otman slipped a syringe from the black bag, slid it into a pocket, and nodded.

Connie craned her neck and looked at Otman. "What?"

Otman's yellowish teeth shown behind a smug grin.

"Perfect, and I'll be in the car waiting. Let's go." Blair stepped to the door.

Otman nudged Connie forward.

With the shimmery-green box in hand, Connie was ready to get this over with. Otman handed the black bag to Blair and they hurried out of the room down to the elevator. When they reached the first floor, Connie, the only one they wouldn't recognize, exited first and scanned the lobby. Arthur and Bessy weren't anywhere to be seen.

They walked calmly past the empty registration counter, and down the hallway, which lead to the swimming pool and the yachts. Blair and Otman stepped into the stairwell opposite the door to the pool. Blair descended the steps to the ground-level parking lot. Remaining hidden, Otman stood on the first floor landing, peering through the ever-so-slightly open door.

Connie leaned against the floor-to-ceiling pane of glass and watched Anchors Away bump the dock. A dockhand lashed the lines to the cleats.

Blair sat in the car with the doors unlocked, his pulse quickening. He scanned the garage and saw no one. His hand rested on the ignition key, ready to crank.

Connie shifted from one foot to the other as Arthur finished checking the lines on the dock and Bessy stepped down to join him.

"She's coming," Connie whispered and held the present close to her mid-section.

Otman tightened his grip on the doorknob and took a deep breath. He pulled his other hand up, ready to reach out and grab her. *This is going to be easy.*

"She's turning around," Connie gasped.

"What?" Otman strained to see through the crack. *Did they see us?*

Bessy stood on the dock looking up at Arthur who was now on the boat's deck. He tossed her a black object and she caught it. She turned and headed back toward the building, bouncing the object from one hand to the other.

He gave her his wallet. Otman tensed, his hand ready to spring into action.

"Here she comes," Connie muttered. "She's almost at the door." *Why does Blair want me to do this?*

Otman drew in a deep breath and held it, leering.

The glass entrance door swung open and Bessy hurried inside.

"Excuse me," Connie said, stepping up to her.

Bessy stopped and glanced at Connie.

"Are you Bessy?" Connie asked, as she stepped between the glass door and Bessy.

"Yes, I am," Bessy replied, as she turned her back to the stairs.

"I'm from Bahamian Resorts, and yesterday you spoke with Basil Adderly. I've been asked to give you this gift as a thank-you for taking part in our customer survey." Connie held out the present.

"You didn't have to do this," Bessy said as she lifted it from Connie's hands. "What is it?"

"Open it and see." Connie forced a smile.

Bessy pulled at the sparkling paper. It crackled as it tore.

The stairwell door eased open and Otman's long arms reached out as he crept up behind Bessy.

Connie glanced past Bessy. *What's he doing?*

Bessy popped the taped edges.

Otman's right hand reached for Bessy's head. His other reached for her back.

Connie glared.

Bessy's eyes brightened as she lifted the lid.

"What a nice Caribbean wrap," she cooed. She picked up the card.

> To: Bessy
> From: Nassau International, Ltd.
> Harrison T. Blair, President

"Harry!" she gasped at the same moment a large meaty hand slapped across her mouth and another grabbed her waist. Her body was jerked into solid muscles. The box and wallet fell to the floor. Bessy's eyes bulged. Her chest constricted; only a muffled squeak emerged from under the enormous hand.

Otman lifted her. She kicked out, but the blows only made him squeeze harder. Unable to breathe, she stopped kicking.

Connie trembled, looked right then left, and scooped up the wrap. "Otman, what are you doing?"

Otman. Bessy's heart raced. She gasped for air through the slit between the meaty fingers.

Otman thrust Bessy into Connie. "Downstairs," he said as he corralled Connie toward the door.

"What are you doing?" Connie demanded.

Otman carried Bessy down the stairs and out into the parking garage.

"Come on, Connie. We're leaving."

Bessy trembled as she saw Blair emerge from a parked car. Her arms and legs flailed. "Ahh!" Her muffled scream faded.

"Hi, Bessy," Blair said. "Did you miss me?"

Bessy squirmed. The vehicles around her blurred and then dimmed. Her lungs ached for air. *Arthur!* Her body fell limp.

CHAPTER TWENTY-EIGHT

Arthur locked up the boat and hurried inside the resort, glancing around for Bessy. He approached the woman behind the registration desk. "Hello. I'm Arthur McCullen. My wife just checked in. Could you tell me my room number, please?"

The woman looked up from the pile of papers. "Mr. McCullen, I haven't seen your wife, but I've been expecting you." She scooted her chair back, stood, reached up into the pigeonhole, and pulled out a message and a room key. "Your room is on the third floor. Room 316. Will you be charging or paying cash?"

"My wife didn't check in?"

"No sir, I haven't seen her, but I do have this urgent message for you," she held out the note. "You need to call Walter. Will you be needing a separate key for your wife?"

Arthur flipped open the note, tuned out her last question, and read:

> Arthur, be careful. Otman and Blair are in
> Nassau. Call me immediately. 555-647-5263
> Walter Clemmons

A chill ran up his back. "Blair and Otman are here?" He turned and looked back at the receptionist. "Are you sure you haven't seen my wife, Bessy?"

The woman shook her head.

Arthur's heart raced. He glanced around the lobby and hallway. "Bessy," he called. His throat tightened. The long halls only echoed her name.

Again, he looked right, then left, but no one was in sight.

"Where's the ladies' room?" Arthur demanded.

"Right across the hall." The woman stepped around the counter and pointed.

Arthur lunged for the door and knocked. "Bessy, are you in there?" Silence hung in the air. "Bessy!"

The receptionist stepped up to the door. "I'll check," she said, then pushed the door open. "Bessy," her soft voice called. The door closed and Arthur waited.

The door swung open. "There's no one in there."

"Thank you." He scanned the halls again. "Didn't you see or hear anyone? My wife just came in a minute ago."

The woman shook her head. "No, I didn't see her, but I did hear two women talking. Their voices seemed to come from that direction." She pointed into the hallway that led to the pool.

"What's that lying in the floor by the door?" Arthur asked, and sprinted for it. The receptionist was on his heels. Arthur reached the shiny green paper and scooped it up. His wallet lay beneath it.

"What is it?" the clerk asked.

Arthur flipped the paper over and read the card. "To Bessy from Harrison T. Blair." His heart hammered. "Call the police. Her ex-husband has kidnapped her!"

The woman scanned the hall. "Are you sure?" I didn't hear any harsh words or anyone scream."

"What's behind this door?"

"Stairs. They go up to the guest floors and into the parking garage."

Blair's got Bessy. He shoved the door open and rushed through it.

An engine revved and tires squealed, echoing in the stairway.

Arthur and the woman's eyes met for a second. He dashed

past her and down the hallway to the front door. He flung it open and froze.

A white, four-door sedan sped out of the driveway and disappeared around the corner.

CHAPTER TWENTY-NINE

Buildings flashed by as the white sedan sped through downtown Nassau. In the back, pinned to the floorboard, Bessy began to stir. Otman lay in the back seat, crunched on his side. He pressed his large hand on her back, immobilizing her.

Blair spun the steering wheel; the car slid around another corner.

"You kidnapped her," Connie yelled, staring at Blair. "You told me you just wanted me to give her a present."

"You're too gullible. Bessy ran off with my money. I want it back. I'm no guiltier than you and Justin, taking Arthur and Shelly's money." He grinned at her. "Am I?"

Bessy cringed. "You're hurting me!"

Otman continued to press her to the floor. "Judge, do you want me to give her that injection now?"

Bessy stiffened.

Connie gulped. *Injection?*

"Not yet. Let's wait until we arrive at the airport."

The airport? Numbness swept across Bessy's body. The roar of the tires drummed in her ears. *If they get me on a plane, I'll never be found.*

"You're driving on the wrong side," Connie hollered. Her eyes bulged as she stared out the front windshield. She grabbed the steering wheel and snatched it to the right.

Up ahead, a car rounded the corner and headed straight for them.

"Let go," Blair yelled as he gripped the steering wheel and pulled left. "We're in the Bahamas. They drive on the left!"

The horn blared and at the last moment, the car up ahead swerved off the road. The old man shook his fist out the window as they sped past.

Connie released the wheel and grabbed the dash with both hands as the tires screeched into the left-hand lane.

Otman's free hand groped for Connie. "You just about killed us." He snatched her shirt and pulled her back into the seat. "If you touch that steering wheel one more time, I'm going to give you one of these injections and you'll never grab anything again."

Connie inched toward the door. "Get away from me you, you . . ." She freed herself from his grip.

"Both of you, shut up," Blair yelled. "Otman, don't waste any of those injections. Now both of you sit back and try to relax. We've got what we came for, and we're almost out of here."

Otman sat up and placed his feet on top of Bessy, keeping her pinned to the floor.

Out of the corner of her eye, Connie watched Otman settle into his seat. *Am I next? He's going to kill me. They'll find me dead, locked inside the trunk, at the airport.*

As the floorboards warmed, Bessy's nose twitched, smelling Otman's shoes. She tried to ignore the odor as she thought about Connie. *Otman's not going to leave any witnesses.*

Blair pulled out a city map. The cold air from the vent caught it and unfolded it. His eyes moved across the page, trying to pinpoint their location. "Here we are," he said as the car slowed. He put the map between Connie and himself and pointed to their location. "If we turn here," his finger pressed at the intersection, "this will take us to the highway and then to the airport. We should be there in ten to fifteen minutes, the way these people drive."

Blair turned the white sedan and merged into heavier traffic, then picked up speed. He braked with the traffic and followed the cars as they turned onto the four-lane divided highway. "I hope all of these people aren't going to the airport," he said, and turned up the air-conditioner.

Connie hesitated, then said, "Wh-when we get to the airport, I-I'm through with you two. That's the deal, right?"

"Now Connie," Blair snapped. "Don't go making such rash conclusions." He reached across the console and patted her leg.

She tried to scoot away, but was already pinned against the door.

Bessy's bones ached. The odor from Otman's feet continued to build. She tried to move, but he only pressed harder. Carpet loops pressed into her face. "Please stop pushing so hard," she mumbled, "you're hurting me."

Otman chuckled, then turned and stared out the window.

"Connie, I bet you haven't given any thought to what you're going to do next," Blair continued.

Connie tensed. *He's right.* Her head throbbed as she thought of what options were available.

"Why don't you come with us? We're flying to . . ." He glanced back at the road, then back to Connie, and smiled.

Otman leaned forward to listen.

"On second thought, I think I'll keep that a secret." Blair breathed. *I'm certainly not telling her where we're going; she'd turn us in.* "If you want to come along, you're more than welcome. The U.S. can't touch us where we're going." He glanced at her. "You can't stay here. You'll need a safe place to live."

Connie didn't breathe. *The U.S. government.*

"If they find you, they'll extradite you back and you'll spend the rest of your life in prison. Is that what you want?"

"N–no," she answered, her jaw quivering.

He swore he could see perspiration beading up on her upper lip.

Connie glanced at him. "What are you saying, that I can come with you?" *What if he's setting a trap?*

"Sure, why not?"

Bessy squirmed. Carpet fibers dug at her lips. "I'll never get on any flight with you."

"Oh, but you will," Blair snapped. "Mr. Otman, I think it's time for you to take care of Ms. Bessy for us."

Connie's throat constricted and her muscles tightened into knots as she heard the zipper opening. *If I don't agree to go, I'm next.*

Bessy squirmed; her joints throbbed from the pressure.

Otman grabbed Bessy's arm with one hand and reached into the black bag with the other, and grabbed a syringe.

Connie glanced behind, to see Otman popping off the safety cap from the needle. Her hands trembled.

I'm doomed if he grabs me. She glanced at the door handle and clasped it, watching the scenery fly by.

Open the door and jump out. The landscape flashed past. *I'd end up killing myself. They'd like that.*

Blair noticed Connie's fidgeting with the door handle. "What are you doing?"

"Nothing," she stammered and released the handle. She peered over the seat at Otman. *What choice do I have?*

Bessy's ears burned as she listed to Otman chuckle. She remained tense, waiting for the prick of the needle.

"Look what I have for you," Otman said, sneering. "It's just like old times, when you were a patient of mine. You remember, don't you?"

Bessy took a deep breath. "I don't care if you kill me; you'll never get my money again. Go ahead." She trembled uncontrollably.

"Hmm," Blair murmured and held up his hand. "Otman, wait a minute. Let's think about this." He smiled. "She might have a point."

"Judge, leave her to me," Otman smirked, as he held the syringe less than an inch from her arm and waited for permission to proceed.

Connie read the fast approaching roadside sign. "Slow

down. You're going to miss the turn," she shouted. "There's the airport."

Blair focused on the sign and pressed the brake. The car decelerated and swerved left. He pulled the car over to the shoulder, squirmed around, and peered over the seat into the back floorboard. "You know, Bessy, you'll never understand, but I'm smarter than you and you'll do as I tell you."

Bessy didn't bother to look up. *I'll never do what he says again. Never.*

Blair turned back in his seat and put the car in gear. "We're going back to the marina and get Arthur." He looked into the rearview mirror. "You'd like that wouldn't you, Mr. Otman?"

Otman's eyes gleamed.

"If Bessy wants Arthur to live, she'll do whatever I tell her," Blair chuckled.

Otman laughed too, "I'd like that."

Connie's hands trembled as she grabbed the door handle and pulled. The door popped open. "I'm through; I'm not helping you any more."

"Run," Bessy yelled.

Otman reached over the seat and grabbed Connie's hair. "You're not leaving us until the judge says so."

Tires squealed as the car slid around. Connie squinted in pain, the roots of her hair holding her prisoner.

"All right, I'm not leaving," Connie yelled, and slammed the door.

Bessy swallowed the lump in her throat. *Arthur, get out of there.*

CHAPTER THIRTY

Manuel sat in the small room with a coffee pot, table, and chairs, downtown in the State Attorney's office. The table held an open file folder and a photo taken from an airport surveillance camera of Shelly lurking under a large brimmed hat. Her eyes were undetectable as she passed the boarding gate.

She's going on vacation to the Bahamas. Tourists wear this clothing all the time or the shops wouldn't sell it. Manuel pulled out the yellow legal tablet and jotted: evidence, photo one, outfit, same as others that are going to the Caribbean.

Mr. Douglas sat across from him, sipping coffee.

Manuel flipped the photo over and another photo showed Shelly entering the airport terminal wearing dress slacks, a crisp pleated shirt, and no hat. He turned it over and looked at the following photo of Shelly entering a boutique.

The fourth photo placed Shelly exiting the shop, sporting the Caribbean apparel. A police officer scrutinized the crowd. The next photo showed her walking away from the officer, an anxious look on his face. Manuel scribbled a description of the five photos on his tablet. A tourist doing what all tourists do, spending money.

"Do you need to see more photos?" Mr. Douglas asked.

Manuel stared at him. "This doesn't prove she killed anyone."

"No, but it sure shows she didn't want to be recognized." He smirked. "I wonder whom the jury would say she's hiding from."

"She told you. She disguised herself so Blair and Otman

wouldn't recognize her."

"That's what she said, but I don't believe her. She would have found security and notified them. We've checked the flight manifest and neither Blair nor Otman's names appear. And besides, if they were on that flight, the Bahamian government wouldn't have allowed them into their country without proper identification."

"It still doesn't prove anything," Manuel said, then looked at the next photo. It was the steering wheel of Justin's BMW, with blood drops. And another photo of the front, driver-side floorboard carpet with splotches of blood."

"We just sent those samples to the lab to be tested. They will be back in a day or two."

Manuel set aside the pictures and looked at Douglas. "Have you found the gun?"

"Not yet."

Manuel made another entry on the pad: not much blood for someone shot in the back of the head.

"But, that nine-millimeter will show up sooner or later," Douglas said, with a smug face as he poured another cup of coffee.

"She doesn't own a gun."

He set the coffee pot down.

"Good grief, Manuel. She had the motive. Hate and revenge. She plotted and waited for him. She shot him in the back of the head, execution style, and tried to flee the country. That's cold-blooded murder, and you know it. Who cares if she owns a gun? It could have been her dad's. She could have bought it that morning on the street corner before she found him." He took a sip and pointed his finger at Manuel. "And you can bet we're looking into whether Arthur had any guns. She had access to his house."

"It doesn't make sense. He's stronger than she is. She would have never gotten close enough to him to kill him."

"Come on. It's very reasonable. She pointed the gun at him

and made him get on his knees and beg for his life. It happens all the time. She hated him. Hate grows and festers. She put the gun to his head and pulled the trigger. POW!"

Manuel flinched.

"It's that simple. She had the motive and the opportunity. The State is charging her with first degree murder."

Manuel's head throbbed. The evidence was weak, but circumstantial evidence leaned heavily in the State's favor. He knew all logic said that Shelly killed Justin. She had access to him and hated him for divorcing her. He stole her dad's money and left her broke. All for a younger woman.

Douglas put his hand on Manuel's back. "Listen, the people of this state aren't fond of sending women to the electric chair. So the state is offering a plea bargain. If she confesses, she'll be given life without parole."

Manuel gritted his teeth and lowered his head.

"If she doesn't accept," Douglas continued, "the State's going to seek the death penalty. Think it over." He patted Manuel on the back, then departed.

Manuel's mouth was dry. *If she's found guilty, I'll have ten to fifteen years to find the truth before she's . . .* A lump lodged in his throat. He refused to think it.

CHAPTER THIRTY-ONE

Arthur shifted from one foot to the other as he stood under the covered archway in front of Providence Resort. *Where are the police?* The sun beat down on the black pavement. Heat waves radiated across the parking lot.

Minutes passed, and sweat ran down his face, as he heard a siren wail in the distance. Anxiety swelled as the siren became louder and louder, and a small car with a single blue light swerved into the parking lot. The siren whined to a stop.

As a dark-skinned officer exited the car, Arthur rushed to his side. The officer barely reached Arthur's chin. "My wife's been kidnapped. You've got to put out a bulletin on a white, four-door sedan."

The officer held up his hands. "Slow down, sir." He pulled out a pad and pen from his shirt pocket. "I'm Officer Garraway. Now, why do you believe your wife, . . . what's her name?"

"Bessy McCullen. She's missing and I saw a four-door sedan speeding away. She had to be inside it. Judge Blair and Mr. Otman kidnapped her."

People in their rooms peered down from their windows. A man and a woman stepped from the street into the parking lot, stood under a shade tree, and watched.

Arthur rubbed his sleeve across his face.

"Mr. Otman? What's his first name?"

"I don't know. People just call him Otman."

"Did you see her?"

"No."

"Did you see the judge or Otman?"

"No."

"Who was driving?"

"I don't know. From the back, the man looked like Judge Blair."

"So you're not sure these two men are really here or not?"

Arthur shook his head, "No, sir. I didn't get a good look at the driver. But," he pulled out the wrapping paper, "this tag says 'To: Bessy, From: Harrison T. Blair.' That's the judge. I found this on the floor, near the stairs to the garage."

"All right. You stay here and I'll be right back. I'll run these fellows through our computer."

The officer sat on the seat and looked back at Arthur. "You really think a judge kidnapped your wife?"

"Yes, he was married to her and tried to kill her and steal her money."

The officer scratched his head. "Wow, a judge, huh?" He pulled his feet into the floorboard and picked up the radio. "This is Officer Garraway. I need two names run through the computer. Check and see if Immigration lists them as entering the Bahamas." He gave their names, laid the radio down on the seat, and waited.

Arthur paced from one side of the bumper to the other. He bit at a fingernail. *Bessy, where are you?* He looked at the officer sitting, relaxed in the seat. He gritted his teeth. *Please hurry.* He continued pacing. After what seemed like an eternity, the radio squawked and the officer lifted the radio. Arthur strained to listen, but couldn't hear the conversation.

Garraway slid off the seat and made his way around the front of the vehicle. "Immigration doesn't show that anyone named Blair or Otman entered the Bahamas in the last forty-eight hours."

"They've got to be here." Arthur pulled the message from his shirt pocket. "I know it. I received this message just a few minutes ago when I arrived." He handed it to Garraway. "Here, read Walter's note for yourself."

The officer held the note and read. Then he looked up. "I don't know who Walter is, but it doesn't prove they've made it into this country."

"But, what about the note on the wrapping paper. If they get to the airport and on a plane out of here, I'll never see my wife again."

"Okay, Arthur, I'll call the airport and have them be on the lookout for two men. Can you give me a description?"

"Sure. One man will be tall and husky. He's muscular and looks mean. He's dangerous. And the other, the judge, is an older man, say, in his late sixties. He's shorter and a little round. Gray hair."

"And your wife?"

Arthur smiled. "She's about this tall," he held his hand up to his lips. "About five-two. She has brown hair with streaks of gray and she's slim. She's wearing blue shorts and a white sleeveless shirt. Please hurry."

"I'll be right back." Garraway eased back into the driver's side and slid squarely under the steering wheel. He grabbed the radio and broadcasted the descriptions.

Up at the street, Connie, now driving at Blair's insistence, peered into the parking lot as she drove past Providence Resort. Blair slid as low as he could in the front seat.

Otman was stretched out on the back seat, pressing Bessy to the floor with one hand. "Shhh," he hissed in her ear. In his other hand he held the syringe—its needle an inch from her arm.

"What did you see?" Blair asked as he craned his neck toward Connie.

"Arthur was speaking to a police officer." Her jaw quivered. "I'm getting out of here."

"No!" Blair snapped and grabbed her arm. "We can't panic. Everything is going to work out perfectly. You'll see."

"Maybe we should dump Bessy's body somewhere and get

out of here," Otman said, with beads of perspiration growing on his forehead. "Turn up the air conditioning. I'm roasting. We don't need Bessy's money; we have Connie, and Connie has Arthur's money."

Connie twitched.

"Why don't you be quiet," Blair said, "and let me do the thinking? We're not getting rid of Bessy. She has *my* money and I want it back. Besides, Bessy has more money than Connie and Justin took from Arthur. We wouldn't be able to live like I want to on Arthur's money."

Connie swallowed hard.

Bessy listened, but didn't move.

Connie's foot eased off the brake and she steered the car off the road.

Otman's head popped above the backseat as he looked behind them. "I'm getting tired of pinning Bessy to the floor."

"Stop complaining," Blair snapped as he sat up. "Connie, have you ever met Arthur?"

"No, why?"

"I need you to walk back there and see what's going on. Ask some questions if you need too, but don't use your real name."

"I'm not walking back there."

"The sooner you find out, the sooner we'll get out of here. Do you want a cop showing up asking questions? How would we explain why we're holding Bessy hostage in the back seat?"

Connie opened the door. Her knees shook. With a soft touch, she pushed the door closed, and settled the sunglasses on her face. Up ahead she saw the officer climb out of the vehicle and make his way up to Arthur. She pulled the floppy hat low, covering her face, and eased up as close as she dared, an ear toward their conversation.

"I've notified the airport and there are guards asking each individual as they check in if they are under duress. We've also notified the U.S. embassy and requested photos of Judge Blair and Otman. The photos should be here shortly. If Blair and Otman are here, we'll find them. Don't you worry. They can't get off this island."

Arthur breathed more easily. "I'm staying in room 316."

"Let's hope she shows up. I'll let you know if we find her or those other two men. In the meantime, keep your door locked."

Connie intermingled with the crowd of gawkers. She heard enough and waited for her chance to get back to the car, unnoticed.

The officer climbed back into his car, disengaged the blue flashing light, and eased the car backward. The throngs of people began to disperse.

Arthur dragged his feet as he walked into the resort. He headed up to the suite.

Connie turned and shuffled along with the crowd of strangers to the street. As they turned to go right, she made her way to the left and scampered to the parked car.

Otman watched as she approached and slipped into the front seat.

"You'd better change your plans," Connie said, her voice shaky. "We'll never get on a plane and fly out of here. There are police all over the airport looking for both of you." She looked at Blair and then at Otman. "Soon they'll have your photos plastered everywhere."

"Quiet," Blair fumed as he rubbed his temples. He rested his head on his hands, propped on the dash. "I'll figure something out."

CHAPTER THIRTY-TWO

Walter sat on the leather couch looking up at the tall ceiling wondering when Arthur and Bessy would arrive in Nassau and when they would call. Every couple of minutes he'd look at the large ornate grandfather clock against the far wall; its hands crawled around the dial. Sometimes he stared at the pendulum and watched it sway from side to side.

Jane sat in her favorite wingback chair and read. She, too, was anxious to hear from the honeymooners. Each time she'd turn another page, she'd glance at Walter over the top of her book. He hadn't moved in more than an hour. Finally, she couldn't take it anymore. "Walter, why don't we go sit out by the pool. It's more relaxing out there and I'll take the phone with us. It'll help get our minds off those newlyweds. Time always passes quicker when you're doing something."

"I know." Walter turned and looked at Jane. "But I'm concerned and feel so helpless. It reminds me of being back in that nursing home, under Otman's scrutiny."

"If you don't want to relax by the pool, how about lunch? You must be hungry. It's almost one."

Walter glanced at the grandfather clock. He couldn't believe the time. He hadn't been keeping up with the hours, only the minutes. Now that she mentioned eating, he did feel hungry. "All right," he said and rose off the couch, "but I don't need as much as you fixed for breakfast."

"Okay, I'll just make sandwiches," she said and headed for the kitchen.

"I only want one."

At the refrigerator, Jane pulled out the cooked bacon and placed it on the counter. "How about a grilled BLT? I make a great one."

"Sure, that sounds good?"

"Two BLTs coming up." She pulled out a large iron skillet and placed it on the burner. She turned the knob and the gas ignited. "It won't take long. I'll just warm up the bacon." She dropped in the bacon, then pulled out the mayonnaise and grabbed the loaf of bread from the counter top just as the phone rang. "Walter, would you please answer that?" she said over her shoulder, then placed the items on the table.

Walter leaped for the phone. "Hello. . . . Hey, Arthur. Did you get? . . ."

Silence filled the room as Walter listened. His smile faded, "What?" He looked at Jane. "Bessy's missing!"

Jane dropped the knife with mayonnaise and spun around. "Missing?"

Walter covered the mouthpiece. "He can't find her."

Jane rushed up beside him and pressed her cheek against his. Her ear rested beside the receiver.

"I found my wallet and wrapping paper on the ground with a tag on it. It was to Bessy, from Blair. Then I saw a white car speeding away from the hotel. I think he's got her. The cops are out looking for her. I'm scared. I don't want to lose her."

"I'm coming to help you find her," Walter said, his heart racing.

"We'll be there in a couple of hours," Jane blurted. She dashed over to the counter and grabbed her pocketbook. She pulled out her cell phone and dialed. "Hello, Ben. Fill her up. I'll be there in a few minutes." She hung up and stuffed it back into her purse. She passed by the stove and switched off the burner. The bacon began to sizzle in the skillet. She moved it off the burner, then darted out of the kitchen.

"Don't worry," Walter said, turning to look for Jane. "I'll be there soon." He slammed the phone down and sprinted for the stairs. "Jane?"

She rushed to the head of the stairs and looked down. "Grab some clothes. We'll change on our way there." Jane's little red tennis shoes disappeared around the corner as she scurried off.

I guess I'll have to let her come if I'm going to fly over in her plane. Walter raced upstairs and into his room. He pulled out the small suitcase and opened the dresser drawer. It didn't contain much more than toiletries and underclothes. He tossed them in, zipped it up, and grabbed its handle.

Within seconds, they met downstairs and made their way to the garage. Jane cranked her bright blue Jaguar and backed out. The Jag zoomed down the driveway and squealed as it turned onto the street. Walter quickly buckled his seatbelt. The tires squealed again as the car pulled onto the highway and sped away.

A few miles down the road, Jane pressed the brakes. Walter looked up and read the billboard: Palm Yacht Club, Next Right. "I've been here before."

Jane spun the steering wheel to the right. The sports car raced forward.

"Oh, no!" Walter stared at the same marina that Bessy turned into weeks ago, when they were fleeing from the police. He looked at Jane. "I thought we were flying. I thought you had an airplane. You said we'd be there in a couple of hours."

"And we will. She smiled. Wait until you see my boat. My husband bought it. He wanted something to get him there fast." Her small foot pressed the brake and the car slid into a parking place in front of a large yacht.

"I . . . uh . . . get seasick."

"No, you won't; I promise."

Walter grabbed his stomach. His face flushed. "Oh yes, I will."

"Come on." Jane flung the door open and grabbed her purse and a small suitcase. "We've got to find Bessy."

Having doubts about any boat, he inched off the seat. Jane ran around the front of the car and grabbed his hand. "Trust me, you won't get sick. Come on. You'll be okay."

He took another deep breath, looked down at their clasped hands, and wondered what he was doing. Her warm touch began to calm his nerves. Before he knew it, he found himself being pulled down the dock.

Jane ran up to a long cigar-shaped yacht.

His jaw dropped. "That's a torpedo. Is it safe?"

Jane laughed and tossed her purse into the open cockpit. "Untie the ropes." She climbed aboard. Ben had left the keys in the ignition. He always kept the yacht in top condition, ready to leave at a moment's notice. She stepped up to the helm and turned the keys. Puffs of smoke rose from each exhaust port as the engines roared to life.

"All of the ropes are untied," Walter yelled, as he carefully and methodically climbed aboard.

Jane worked the yacht off the dock and turned the wheel. As the boat eased out of the marina, she pushed the throttles forward until the boat leapt up and settled out on a plane. The boat clipped along at twenty-five knots, the maximum allowed in the Intracoastal Waterway. Water rolled off the bow on each side, fanning spray outward.

Walter's knuckles whitened; his grip tightened by the minute. The Atlantic Ocean emerged as they zipped past buoys. The yacht rose across a small swell and into the next, slightly larger wave. They raced out of the inlet. Perspiration dotted his forehead as he watched the last buoy approach. They zoomed past it and out into the open waters.

Jane put a hand on his shoulder. "Don't worry. Relax. It's only three-to-four footers out here."

"Ohhh!" Walter moaned, bracing himself as the bow rose in the air. "These waves are larger than the last time I was out here on Bessy's boat." Walter's chest heaved with each breath. He closed his eyes, hoping to maintain some semblance of calm.

Jane slid out of the captain's seat and tugged on his shirt. "Walter, why don't you drive?"

Walter stared with wide eyes. "You want me to drive. I–I've never driven a boat. I–I don't know how."

"It's easy, just like driving a car. See this electronic map and this arrow?" She pointed to the twelve-inch LCD panel. "The GPS indicates a southeast heading. If the arrow points left, then turn left. It's that simple."

Walter grabbed the dash and steadied himself as the boat bounced across the next wave. *What have I gotten myself into?* With his hands on the steering wheel, he slid into the seat, and stared straight ahead.

"Now, what do you think?"

Walter's sweaty hands clung to the wheel. He heard nothing, except possibly his teeth chattering. His hands trembled.

Jane smiled and put her arm around him and gave him a tight embrace. "Relax, Walter. It's just like driving a car, but easier. There aren't streets out here that you have to stay on. No lines to stay between."

The wave height remained the same as they moved offshore, but the waves were spaced further apart and the boat skimmed across the inky blue water.

He exhaled and slowly drew in another breath. His grip relaxed as he leaned back in the seat. A small smile emerged. "This isn't bad."

"Now if we're going to get to Nassau in a couple of hours, you're going to have to push those throttles forward."

Walter glanced down at the two red-knobbed controls. "Aren't we going fast enough?"

"Not at all. This boat will do fifty-five, easy. Now push the throttles forward."

He held his breath and slowly did as she said. The engines whined louder. The boat smoothed out as it skipped effortlessly across the tops of each wave. Within five minutes, Walter was sitting back in the seat with a big smile and the wind in his face. "This is great. I can't believe it." He looked at Jane. *What's more amazing is that I'm on a boat with Jane, and I'm having a good time.*

Jane smiled as she realized her arm was still draped across his shoulders. "I thought you'd like it." She knew most men would give anything to experience this thrill at least once in a lifetime.

Some sport fishing yachts dotted the horizon, but other than those, they had the ocean to themselves.

After an hour passed, an island appeared on their left. "See that island?" Jane asked.

Walter turned, his hand resting on the wheel. "Yes, what island is it?"

"Grand Bahama Island. Freeport is over there."

He could see tiny buildings along the shoreline. He turned back and focused in front of the boat.

"Next, we'll pass the Berry Islands on our right, then we'll be out in open water again. It won't be long and we'll be in Nassau. I hope Arthur will be waiting for us."

"Let's hope so. We don't have any time to waste." His brow furrowed. "We've got to find Bessy and tell Arthur about Shelly."

CHAPTER THIRTY-THREE

A dull hum reverberated in courtroom five. The court reporter arranged the small desk with her laptop computer and exhibit stickers. She placed a pillow in her seat. The bailiff sat straight in his seat, arms-crossed, and scanned the room.

Manuel sat at the defense table jotting down notes while he waited for Shelly to be brought in. As he checked his watch for the third time, the side door swung open and Shelly entered, escorted by a deputy. Her hands were cuffed in front. Her orange jumpsuit hung limp on her thin frame. The officer led her over to the defense table.

Manuel stood. "Have a seat," he said and pulled it out for her. "We need to talk before the judge gets here."

Shelly stared at his illegible notes.

"I've got the coroner's report which estimates the time of death between 5:00 a.m. and 8:00 a.m. I spoke with Walter; he remembers you coming into the kitchen at 5:30 while he was reading the morning paper. You were with him all morning up to the time you dropped him off at the airport that afternoon. We can account for all but the first thirty minutes. So, I drove from Bessy's house to the airport. The time it takes to drive that distance was well within thirty minutes. The prosecutor will claim that at five in the morning the driving time would be even shorter, since there would be less traffic. So, we can't claim you didn't have enough time to make that drive."

The back door squeaked as Douglas entered wearing a huge smile. He swaggered past the benches and dropped his briefcase on the plaintiff's table. Then he made his way over to

Manuel and hovered. He stooped down and propped his hands on the table. "Well, are you accepting the offer?"

"What?" Shelly snapped, as she looked from Douglas to Manuel.

"I haven't had a chance to discuss it with my client." Manuel said. "My calendar was already full today before I unexpectedly woke to a phone call of this magnitude."

"We're all busy." Douglas glanced at Shelly and then back at Manuel. "I'll wait and hear her answer when she tells the judge." He pivoted on his heel and stepped toward the rear and out the door.

Shelly squirmed in her seat.

"I hate that guy," Manuel breathed.

"What offer? I'm innocent," Shelly said. "I'm not accepting anything other than an apology from that man for falsely accusing me of murder."

"Don't let him get to you. The evidence the State has is all circumstantial." He repositioned the notes and continued. "I'm sorry. I forgot to ask how you're holding up."

"So-so," she said, her face sullen. "I just want to get out of here and go home." She pulled at her jumpsuit. "This doesn't fit very well."

He glanced at her and nodded in agreement. "Yeah, those clothes never fit anyone. They're one-size-fits-all." He turned and looked back at his notes. "Where were we?" He ran his finger across the page.

The guard stood against the wall behind Shelly and watched.

"Here's what the State's going to show," Manuel said. "Your ex-husband, Justin Roble, was murdered. They'll claim you had a motive and that you were arrested at the airport, disguised and fleeing the country. The evidence is weak. I *can* convince the judge to let you out on bail."

The back door opened and Douglas rushed inside. His arrogance sent a chill through Manuel. Douglas stepped up to

Manuel, and with delight, dropped papers in front of him. "Here's some new evidence you might want to see." He spun and made his way to the plaintiff's table.

Manuel grabbed the papers.

Shelly twitched.

He scanned the important sections on each page as he flipped through them. He stopped and stared at the last page and read carefully: Lab Results for the State of Florida, item number thirty-seven: Pocketbook. Manuel slumped over the table.

"What?" Shelly asked. "What is it?"

"All rise," the bailiff said as he entered the room. "The Honorable Anthony Zapata, presiding."

Manuel pushed up off the table and stood. He extended a hand, helping Shelly to her feet.

The judge entered and made his way up to the bench. "Be seated."

All eyes focused on the judge.

After taking a moment to glance over the documents, he arched his eyebrows. "Ms. Shelly Roble, the State of Florida charges you with first degree murder. How do you plead?"

Shelly sat mortified. She knew what the charge would be, but the words seemed so cold.

Manuel looked at her and then stood. "She pleads not guilty."

"Is that correct, Ms. Roble?" the judge asked. "You're pleading not guilty?"

Manuel helped Shelly return to her feet.

"Yes, sir. I didn't kill anyone." Her lips quivered as she tried to keep the hysteria out of her voice.

The judge looked down at the folder. "Now, we need to discuss bail."

"Your Honor," Douglas said as he stood. "I request a side-bar. May we approach the bench? There's new evidence that you need to consider before we discuss bail."

Manuel glanced down at Shelly, who was staring up at him. "You may approach," the judge said, and motioned them to the bench. Both attorneys made their way to the front. The judge leaned forward. "What do you have Mr. Douglas?"

"Your Honor," he said and handed the judge the papers. "I apologize, but I just received this."

"What is it?" the judge asked.

Manuel exhaled heavily as he listened. The timing couldn't be worse.

Shelly leaned forward and listened.

"The lab results, taken from the pocketbook Ms. Roble was carrying when she was arrested. This photo," Douglas said as he handed the judge a picture, "shows blood splatter on that purse. Shelly previously notified us that Justin's BMW was missing. The police found the car several hours later; there was blood inside. Samples have been sent to the lab for DNA analysis."

"What?" Shelly gasped.

Douglas glanced at Shelly and then back to the judge. "Your Honor, the pocketbook proves she was at the scene. She was there when that bullet went into Justin's head. She killed her ex-husband, execution style. The State of Florida requests that bail be denied."

"But, Your Honor," Manuel said. "She didn't kill Justin. She's innocent and doesn't pose any danger to the community."

"If she is granted bail, she will flee and we'll never see her again."

"That's not true," Manuel countered. "She has no other place to go. She wants her name cleared. She is young and has a full life ahead of her. She does *not* want to live on the run and in hiding. She's innocent."

"Your Honor, she will flee. Her dad has plenty of money to enable her to live comfortably on the run. We cannot forget where Ms. Roble was arrested. At the airport. She was wearing a disguise as she tried to slip out of Florida to the Bahamas. She *is* a flight risk. She tried it once and she *will* do it again."

"I wasn't fleeing the county," Shelly yelled. "I was . . ."

"Quiet in the courtroom," the judge snapped, and pounded the gavel. Then he turned his attention back to the lawyers. "Counselors, please give me a moment to review the findings and then we will continue."

Manuel dragged his feet as he went over to Shelly and sat.

"That's not my pocketbook," Shelly said.

"Shhhh. It's not the time or place to discuss our case."

"But, he's lying. I wasn't trying to flee."

He put his hand on top of hers. "Don't say anything." Manuel looked over his shoulder at Douglas. "We don't want to say anything that he might overhear and misinterpret."

The judge looked up and cleared his throat. "After reviewing the facts, I am going to deny bail at this time."

"What?" Shelly gasped, her head dropping in her hands.

"You will remain in custody at the Palm Beach County Jail."

"I want to go home," Shelly sobbed.

Manuel put his arm around her and hugged her. "It'll just be for a little while. I'm going to work hard and get you out. There has to be someone who saw something that can clear your name. Maybe a neighbor was awake that morning and will testify that your vehicle never left the driveway."

"Is it too early to try to set a trial date?" the judge asked.

"Your Honor," Douglas said and stood, "it appears to me that Ms. Roble might want to demand a speedy trial. It is obvious that she wants to go home as soon as possible," he smirked. He knew the State would be ready to proceed within days. It was a tactic he'd plotted in college, and this would be the perfect chance to try it. "If a jury finds her innocent, then she can go home." He looked over at Shelly.

"Is that true, Ms. Roble?" the judge asked.

Shelly sniffled and stood, wiping her checks. "Is that possible? Can I have a speedy trial?"

Manuel grabbed Shelly and pulled her back into her seat. "We don't want a quick trial date." He pulled her closer and whispered, "The evidence is mounting in their favor. We don't have anything yet. We'll lose if we go to trial early."

Shelly grabbed his hand. "You don't understand. If I can't get out on bail, I want a speedy trial. I can't stay in that place much longer. I . . ."

"Excuse me, Counsel," the judge said, then turned to Shelly. "Ms. Roble, I must caution you that an early trial could be devastating to your legal representation. Most murder trials are tried at least a year to eighteen months away. Your counsel needs time to gather all of the evidence so a thorough case can be presented before this court."

"A year to eighteen months," Shelly said, jumping to her feet. "I'll never survive that long. We'll be ready sir."

Manuel gritted his teeth.

"I'll make the call date within five days. Counselors, be prepared to start at the earliest possible date," the judge said, while looking from one table to the next.

Manuel buried his head into his hands. *She doesn't understand.*

"The State of Florida will be ready," Douglas said. He glanced at Manuel and grinned.

Manuel felt sick. He closed the briefcase; its latches clicked. *I hope this doesn't backfire. Something's got to surface. But will it be in time?*

Shelly stared straight ahead. *I need Dad and Bessy. I hope Walter can get in touch with them.*

CHAPTER THIRTY- FOUR

The white sedan made a quick u-turn. The brim of the hat flopped in Connie's face. She tilted her head back, enabling her to see the road, and turned into Providence Resort. Blair and Otman crouched below the windows. Otman continued to press Bessy down with one hand. His other hand was cupped across her mouth and nose, making it nearly impossible for her to breathe.

Connie tipped the hat with her hand as she scanned the front parking lot for Arthur. A young couple climbed out of their car and headed to the front door. No one else was in view. The car's engine revved as it sped toward the underground parking garage.

She felt the veins in her temples throb. She wished she'd never agreed to Blair's demands. She should have called his bluff. Inside the parking garage, she made her way to the far side, found an empty place, and parked. Her heart raced as she scanned the garage. "It's clear," she wheezed.

Blair raised his head and glanced around. His movement stopped as his eyes focused through the latticework. Anchors Away bobbed against the dock. Blair chuckled. "I just found our way off this island. You two stay here with Bessy. I'm going to find Arthur. He's going to invite all of us aboard my yacht."

Bessy twitched. Her eyes widened. *Run Arthur.*

Bessy moaned as Otman planted his knee in her back and peered through the lattice fence. "You hear that Bessy? We're all going for a boat ride."

"When it's safe for you to come aboard, I'll motion for you," Blair said as he opened the door. "Remember, stay here until you see my signal. If anything goes wrong, get her out of here."

Connie's hands trembled as they continued to clasp the steering wheel.

Blair slipped out of the car, then stopped. He stooped and leaned into the back seat. "Give Bessy that shot. That way she won't be any trouble when I signal you. Just pick her up and carry her. If anyone asks about her, just say she got drunk and passed out."

Bessy tried to move, but Otman pressed heavier.

"Don't give her the whole thing. I want her alive."

Otman popped off the protective cap with his thumb and pushed the plunger. Air squeezed out, followed by a thin stream of liquid. He chuckled. "That should be enough to sedate her and not kill her."

Connie's eyes grew large in the rearview mirror. She gulped, but her tongue stuck to the roof of her mouth. She froze as she saw Otman's hand drop.

The needle jabbed into Bessy's arm. A peep sounded as she tried to scream through his heavy hand. The floorboard began to darken. Bessy clawed at the back of the seat and at the carpet. Her fingers weakened as her vision blurred. *Arthur, help me . . .* A dull hum droned in her ears. Her eyelids fluttered, as her body fell limp.

"She's out," Otman chuckled, and released her.

Connie watched as Blair stepped into the stairway. "I-Is he always th-that confident in himself?" She pressed her sweaty hands in her lap.

Otman laughed. "Always."

Blair made his way up to the first floor, stepped out into the hallway, and walked to the front desk. "Excuse me," he said to the man behind the counter. "Have my friends, the McCullens, arrived yet?"

The young man glanced up, with a who-are-you stare.

"I'm in room 414. Are they on the same floor?"

The man's finger slid down the registry page and stopped. "No, they're on the third floor, room 316."

"Thank you," Blair said, then walked over to the elevator and pressed the button. He grinned. *I can't wait to see Arthur's face. It's been too long.* The door slid open, and he stepped inside. As the door closed, the bell dinged and the elevator jolted. The sound of the motor drowned out the silence as he watched the numbers increase and stop at three.

Soon, Blair stood at room 316, grinning as he waited for an answer to his knock.

"Who is it?"

"I've got Bessy," he said in a low rumble, "and if you want to see her you'd better open the door." He stepped backward and watched the peephole darken.

The doorknob turned, and the door jolted open. "Bessy!"

Blair stepped forward and pushed Arthur back into the room. "If you cause any commotion, you'll never see her again. That's a promise." Blair's face tightened.

Arthur backed up as Blair closed the door, "Where is she?"

"Listen to me," Blair said, "if you want to see Bessy, you're going to invite me onboard Anchors Away. Then when I feel it's safe, and only then, I'll signal Otman and he'll bring Bessy aboard." He pulled out his cell phone and pressed the phone to his lips, as if he were in contact with Otman. "Do we have an understanding?"

"Yes," Arthur said, through gritted teeth. "You'd better not have hurt her."

"Don't worry. She's fine." Blair laughed. "At least she was when I left her with Otman." Then with a low voice, he spoke into the phone. "Arthur agrees. Get ready." He lowered the phone and dropped it into his pocket. "Let's go. You might want to grab your bags. You're not coming back."

Arthur shook his head. "Our suitcases are still on the boat."

140

"How convenient." Blair grabbed the doorknob. "Remember, if you want to see Bessy again, don't do anything to attract attention. If Otman sees the police, he won't be gentle with her." He pulled the door open. "After you."

Arthur's hands tightened into fists as he headed to the elevator. It was all he could do to keep his hands by his side. The ride to the first floor seemed long, as thoughts of Bessy raced about. Arthur stepped out and glanced around, hoping to catch a glimpse of Bessy. But she wasn't there and his heart sank.

Arthur moved down the hallway and out the side door leading to the pool and docks. He squinted as a blast of hot air hit him in the face.

"Keep moving," Blair said, then pushed him past the pool and down to the docks. Soon they were onboard Anchors Away. Blair sat on the couch and sighed. Arthur stood in front of the couch, his face growing redder by the moment.

"We're going to wait a few minutes and make sure you didn't alert the cops. You should sit."

Arthur remained rigid.

"Sit down!" Blair snapped, pointing to the couch. "If I say sit, you sit. If I say stand, you'd better stand. Is that clear?"

Arthur fell into the couch. The wait began.

Blair watched the door and his watch. After five minutes, he stood and motioned for the others to come aboard, then closed the door. "Downstairs," Blair demanded, "and not a word from you."

Down in the sleeping quarters, Arthur turned toward the master stateroom, but Blair grabbed him. "Your room's up front."

Arthur stepped into the forward cabin. Bunks, one above the other, were on the right side, with a private bath on the left. Sunlight entered two portholes, one on each side of the cabin.

Connie's legs pumped as she pulled one of her suitcases and Blair's. The wheels clattered on the dock as they bounced over each plank of wood. The air was hot and muggy. She stopped at the gangplank, out of breath. After a couple of deep breaths, she picked up one suitcase and lugged it up the steps and inside. She regained her breath and retrieved the other suitcase. As she stepped back inside, she looked at Blair, "Thanks for the help."

He grinned. "Someone has to guard Arthur."

"Why don't I guard him and you go grab Otman's suitcase and my other two?"

"Not a chance. You shouldn't have brought so much stuff. Hurry up. We've got to get out of here."

Connie huffed, turned, and descended the steps. Several trips later, she dragged the last suitcase behind her. Her fingers ached from each jolt the wheels made across the wooden dock. She struggled as she hauled the suitcase onboard, gasping for air. Her shirt was half-soaked.

Once Otman saw Connie disappear inside the boat, he did a quick scan of the parking area, then opened the back door, and lifted Bessy off the floor.

Bessy lay draped across Otman's arms, like a lover asleep. He climbed the stairs effortlessly, as if the load were nothing more than a few towels draped in his arms. He didn't stop to look as he stepped across the empty hallway. The few guests that lounged around the pool were in their own oblivious world; they never lifted their heads or opened their eyes as he passed. He carried her down the docks and up the gangplank.

Connie opened the door as Otman stepped in. "Carry her downstairs," she said smartly, "and put her in the front cabin with Arthur."

Otman stared at her, "Who put you in charge?"

"Those were Blair's orders," she said, and shrugged off his stare.

Downstairs, Otman slung open the front cabin door and jostled Bessy's body inside.

Arthur slid off the lower bunk as Otman dropped her on it. "You'd better not have hurt her," he snapped.

Otman snickered. "What if I did?"

Arthur didn't answer. He brushed Bessy's hair out of her face.

Blair dashed down the stairs with a roll of duck tape in his hand. "Grab him."

Otman snatched Arthur away from Bessy and held him in a bear hug while Blair bound Arthur's hands and feet, then slapped a piece of tape over his mouth.

Blair soon sat at the helm on the flybridge. Otman untied the dock lines, and the Hatteras maneuvered away from the dock. The boat motored west, through the shipping canal. "We're heading south, down the Tongue of the Ocean." Connie and Otman listened. "We'll be safe on this route. We won't encounter many boats."

"What's the weather forecast?" Connie asked.

Otman looked up at the cloudless blue sky. "Sunny and breezy." The wind blew in their faces. "Blondes," he breathed, while shaking his head.

Connie shrugged off the snide remark and disappeared down into the boat.

"Otman," Blair said, "in about thirty minutes, after we reach the Tongue of the Ocean, I'm going to draw up the legal documents for Bessy to sign. She's going to give me all of her worldly possessions once and for all. After she signs the documents, I want you to get rid of them. Throw them overboard. The water is thousands of feet deep."

"My pleasure," Otman chuckled. "I've always enjoyed silencing troublemakers."

Anchors Away rounded the harbour's entrance; waves caused the bow to rise and fall.

"It won't be long, and I'll have my money back." Blair smiled and engaged the autopilot.

"That'll leave one troublemaker," Otman said. "He'll be easy to get rid of."

"Don't worry about Walter. The government won't have a

case anymore. Besides, we're not going back to the states."

Otman smirked, "If I ever find Walter, I'll make sure he's history."

Connie climbed up the ladder to the flybridge in her two-piece, red bikini. She laid a towel out on one of the cushions and stretched out. "Ahhh! I think I could get used to this life-style."

Otman frowned and stared at her. *She's nothing but a tease and a distraction.* He cracked his knuckles. *Blair's right, we're not leaving any witnesses. I hope I get to throw her overboard, too.*

CHAPTER THIRTY-FIVE

Buildings grew taller on the horizon. The wind died down and waves decreased to two feet. Walter relaxed behind the steering wheel, sipping coke, and watching the skyline grow closer. The yacht held steady, racing toward the first buoy leading into Nassau Harbour. Soon land emerged around the enlarging buildings.

"That's New Providence," Jane said, pointing.

"I can't believe it. I drove all the way to Nassau, and I didn't get seasick."

"I told you that you wouldn't." She patted him on the back. "I've found out over the years that motion sickness in boating is just like motion sickness in a car. Drivers never get sick."

The boat continued on its straight path. Trees emerged and soon other boats were seen racing across the water to and from the island. A parasailor soared high above them as they approached the first channel marker.

"I'd better take over now." Jane slipped between Walter and the steering wheel. She pulled back on the throttles and the boat slowed to about twenty knots. After calling the harbour master for permission, she slowed the boat further, and entered Nassau Channel. The boat came off its plane and plowed through the water at approximately seven knots.

Walter looked up at three large cruise ships docked on their starboard. People leaned over the railings and waved as they passed by. He waved back.

"Providence Resort's on the other side of the bridge," she said. "There's the sign." They passed under the bridge connecting Nassau to Paradise Island. Jane radioed the resort and was instructed to pull into slip nine on the outside dock. "Walter, the ropes are in that locker," she said, motioning. "We'll need them to tie up."

Walter opened the door and pulled out a pile of ropes. "How many?"

"Four will do for now." She scanned the docks. "I don't see Bessy's Hatteras. I guess Arthur found her and they left."

"I hope so. But just to play it safe, I'll stay on board and out of sight once the boat's tied up. Why don't you go inside and ask at the registration desk if Arthur and Bessy are here. If Blair and Otman are lurking around, they shouldn't recognize you."

Jane brought the boat alongside the dock with a hard bump.

Walter grabbed the handrail to keep from being thrown overboard.

"Sorry. I'm not very good at this part."

He wrestled the bowline around the cleat and threw the other end to the dockmaster, then dashed to the stern and tossed him that line. With a few wraps, all lines were cleated and the boat was snug against the dock.

"You sure make that look easy," Walter said to the dock-master.

"Years of practice," he answered.

"I'll be right back." Jane sprinted down the dock and into the building. She stood at the registration desk, propped her arms on the counter, and leaned over. "Hello," she said to the man who was writing entries into a ledger. "I'm Jane Winchester. I just tied up at slip nine. I'm looking for my friends, Arthur and Bessy McCullen. I didn't see their boat, Anchors Away. Have they arrived?"

"Mr. McCullen is in his room," the man said, glancing up. "The last I heard, his wife was still missing. However, maybe she's been found. I don't know. They're in room 316." He reached under the counter, pulled out the registration book, laid it on the counter, and flipped it open. "So, how many more boats will be arriving today as part of your boating club?"

"Boating Club?" Jane asked.

"I assumed a boating club is meeting here. Others have been asking for them."

"They have?" Jane gasped.

"An older distinguished fellow came by a little while ago looking for them. You might catch him in Arthur's room. I haven't seen him come back down."

Jane stood motionless. Her skin crawled. "O . . . Okay. Thank you." She took a slow step backward, glanced over at the elevator, and then down the hallway. She raced back to the boat, trembling. "Blair's here."

"What?" Walter sprang up off the couch. "Did you see them? Did they see you?" He peered out the window.

"The receptionist said a distinguished looking fellow came by a little while ago looking for them. He thinks they're still in Arthur's room, number 316."

"If they are here, where's Bessy's boat?" Walter raced to the door. "Maybe they took Bessy and left Arthur tied up in the room. Come on." They raced inside.

The elevator door opened on the third floor. Walter leaped out and sprinted down the hall. He read the numbers on each door as he passed. At 316, he stopped and turned back toward Jane. "Go back downstairs and call for help."

Jane stepped back inside the elevator and pressed the button for the first floor.

Walter pounded on the door. "Arthur! Bessy! Are you in there?" He didn't hear anything and pounded louder. "It's me, Walter."

The door to room 315 opened behind him. "What's the problem?" the man asked.

Walter spun around. "Call the front desk. Something has happened to my friends."

The man disappeared behind the open door.

Jane stepped out of the elevator and rushed past the man who sat at the registration desk. He ran into the elevator. She sensed where he was headed and turned and jumped back inside the elevator before the doors closed.

When they reached the third floor, the man rushed to room 316 with a key in his outstretched hand. Walter stepped back as the man slipped the key into the lock and swung open the door. "Arthur?" Walter shouted, as he beat the man into the room.

The room was clean, the king size bed, wrinkle-free. "Their suitcases aren't here!" Jane said. "They're gone."

"Call the police," Walter demanded of the receptionist.

"Slow down. What's all this about? They might be out on the town."

"Their boat's gone," Walter snapped back.

"Maybe they're taking a romantic ride out front. People do it all the time."

Jane sighed. "Walter, he could be right."

Walter felt the hair on the back of his neck bristle. "We received a phone call hours ago that Bessy was missing and that the police were searching for her."

"Yes, I heard that, but all that happened before I arrived on duty. I don't believe it. People just aren't kidnapped here in the Bahamas."

A knock sounded on the opened door. "Mr. McCullen," the voice said. "Oh, I see you found Bessy," he said, looking at Jane. His eyes were quickly drawn to her red shoes. He smiled, then turned and saw Walter. "Oh, I'm sorry, I've got the wrong room."

Jane stepped up to the officer. "I'm Jane, Bessy's friend. We can't find her or Arthur."

"I'm Officer Garraway. Mr. McCullen said he'd wait here until I returned." Garraway scrutinized the room. "There doesn't appear to have been any struggle."

"Officer," Walter said. "Bessy's boat is gone."

"Gone. Arthur was supposed to let me know if he found his

wife."

Walter looked back at Jane. "They've got Arthur, too."

"What?" Garraway asked. "Are these the two men?" He pulled out two photos from his pocket and unfolded the pictures.

Walter glanced at the photos, then pointed to each. "That's Blair and the taller one's Otman."

"Oh," Jane gasped. "We're too late."

"Hmm," Garraway said as he scratched his head. "Don't worry. We'll catch them."

"You don't know Blair and Otman," Walter said. "I'm sure they have Arthur and Bessy and are long gone. We'll be lucky if Arthur and Bessy are ever found alive."

"Why don't we sit, and I'll make some notes," Garraway said, and pulled up one of the two chairs beside the window. He placed his tablet on the round table. "Now, do either of you have photos of Arthur and Bessy?"

Jane and Walter looked at each other and shook their heads.

"Okay, what kind of yacht are they are on?"

"A sixty-foot Hatteras," Jane said. "A motor yacht."

"That should be easy to spot. Let me make a call." Garraway pulled out a cell phone and dialed. "Barkley, this is Garraway. Seen a sixty-foot Hatteras out in the harbour?"

He covered the mouthpiece and whispered. "He's with Nassau Harbour. He's responsible for making sure the large ships and the little pleasure crafts don't get tangled up. He monitors who's doing what within the harbour. . . ."

"What's that?" Garraway asked uncovering the mouthpiece. "Uh huh." The officer nodded his head. "All right. No problem. I owe you," and he flipped the cell phone closed. "He did see a motor yacht that was about sixty feet leaving the west channel some time ago, but he doesn't know what make it was. They didn't ask for permission to leave the harbour."

Jane's eyes were wide as she moved closer to the edge of the chair.

"That's them," Walter said as he leaped from the bed. "Let's go get them."

"Mr. Clemmons, that would be like chasing the wind. Please, let us handle it. We have no information as to which way they went after leaving the channel. They could have gone any direction. I'll make a few calls and notify the proper agencies."

"But . . ."

"Please, sir," he said, raising both hands. "You've got to slow down and relax. You're in the Bahamas. You probably don't know, but we have planes and boats out there keeping our waters safe. The U.S. Coast Guard patrols these waters, too."

Walter sighed. "I'm sorry. It's just . . ."

"I understand. You're concerned. Remember, we're professionals here. This is the largest city in the Bahamas. Millions of people visit here every year. We are well equipped." He jotted another note and then stood. "How can I get in contact with you later?"

"We're staying here at the marina, slip nine," Jane said and rose. "If there's anything that we can do for you, we'd be glad to. Just ask."

Garraway stepped toward the door and again noticed Jane's red shoes. He blinked and looked back up at her. "Ma'am, don't you worry, we'll find your friends." He turned to Walter. "A boat that size can't hide. Hopefully by tomorrow morning, your friends will be back and you all can have a wonderful time here." He leaned into Walter and whispered. "Does she always wear those bright red shoes?"

"Always," Walter said, and rolled his eyes.

"You'll never lose her," he whispered. As he was leaving, he turned back to them. "I'll keep in touch. Don't play hero and try to find them yourselves. Remember, these waters can be dangerous. Anything can happen out there. Some places are so sparsely populated that you could get into trouble and no one

would ever know. Stay here and let us do the police work." He
turned and disappeared down the hall.

CHAPTER THIRTY-SIX

The Tongue of the Ocean, more than 6000 feet deep, was inky-blue and desolate except for one lonely yacht cresting across two-foot waves.

The autopilot held Anchors Away on a southern course. Nassau was twenty-eight miles behind, Andros, twenty miles to the west. The ocean sparkled under the hot sun. Blair sat inside, at the table in the salon, typing on his laptop. The vase of two dozen pink roses sat in the center of the table. A printer hummed on his left. Over against the wall, wadded up papers lay scattered around a trash can, few made it inside. *One more document and I'll be ready for Bessy to sign, giving me authorization to transfer her money to Grand Cayman National Bank. I'll have my money back soon.*

The printer stopped as the last document slid out. Blair grabbed it and proofread it. "Perfect." He arranged all the papers and clipped them together. "Otman," he yelled.

Otman's feet fell from the pilothouse dash, where he sat scanning the horizon. He leaped to the floor. "Yes sir," he said, rushing up to Blair.

"Bring Bessy up here," he chuckled. "The documents are ready for her to sign. This is too easy. I should have done this five years ago."

Otman turned, grinned, and went down the stairs. He unlocked the door—the doorknob had been turned around, locking them inside—and pushed it open.

Bessy had awakened some time ago. Arthur was freed from his bindings once land was out of sight. They sat on the lower bunk cuddled together and stared at Otman.

"Bessy," Otman said from a hunched-over stoop, as his body filled the doorway. "Blair wants you upstairs in the salon."

She kissed Arthur and scooted off the bunk. "I'll be right back." She gave Otman a wide berth.

Otman locked the door and pushed Bessy up the stairs ahead of him.

"Bessy, come over here and sit down," Blair said, as he pointed to the vacant seat beside him.

"Boy, it's hot out there," Connie said, strolling in, her body covered in oil and sweat. She plopped down into the recliner.

Bessy cringed knowing the fabric would need a good cleaning later.

Blair pulled his chair closer to Bessy. She leaned away.

"I see you're enjoying the roses I sent you."

"You?"

"I had them delivered to your room at Blue Water Resort in Freeport."

Bessy glanced at the roses. "Well take them back. I don't want them."

"Now Bessy, you're not being nice." Blair grinned and slipped papers in front of her. "You need to sign these documents." He handed her a pen. "Right above your name."

Bessy picked up the document and began to read. After a moment, she stopped and looked at him. "You're crazy; I'm not signing this. I'll never give you my money." She dropped the pen on the table.

"I'd do as he says," Connie said.

"You'd do anything anyone told you," Bessy snapped.

"Suit yourself. If you'd worked with him, you wouldn't be in the predicament you're in."

"I'm not giving Harry my money."

"You don't have a choice," Connie said.

Blair cleared his throat, "Ladies." The room fell silent.

"Thank you." He looked back at Bessy. "Sign it."

"I'm not signing anything. I'm going back to my room." She began to stand.

"Sit down and sign the documents," he demanded, as he grabbed her wrist and pulled her back into the seat. "Otman, go get Arthur and throw him overboard."

"My pleasure, sir," Otman said, leaping for the stairs. "I've waited a long time to get rid of him."

"No, wait," Bessy yelled after Otman.

Otman's feet thundered down the steps.

Bessy grabbed Blair. "Harry, I'll sign whatever you want. Don't let him throw Arthur overboard."

Blair laughed, "I knew you would." He pushed the first document back in front of Bessy. "Your signature goes right there." His finger pointed at the line at the bottom of the page.

She scooted the chair up to the table and clutched the pen.

Otman pushed Arthur up the stairs and into the salon. Then he grabbed him and lifted.

Arthur's toes dragged the carpet as he was carried to the back door.

Otman grinned and opened the door.

"No! Stop him," Bessy yelled and jumped up.

"Otman," Blair said. "She's agreed to sign."

Otman closed the door; Arthur looked puzzled. *Agreed to sign what?* He craned his neck trying to read, but Otman pulled him over to the couch.

"Sit," his deep voice rumbled, as he pushed him down. "She's giving Blair all of her money."

"Don't do it!" He tried to stand, but Otman shoved him back into the couch. Otman's fingers dug into his shoulders like claws. "Don't move."

Blair stared at Arthur. "If she doesn't sign, you're going swimming."

"And when she signs, you'll throw us both overboard anyway."

"That's the risk she's willing to take. Now sign," he said. His finger jabbed again at the blank line.

Bessy squeezed the pen and scrawled out her signature.

As she signed each form, he organized them in a file folder. "And this is the last one."

Bessy hesitated. "I'll sign it when we're at port."

Otman stood and pulled Arthur up with him. He grabbed the back door, swung it open, and jerked Arthur outside. Arthur clung to the handrail and strained to see Bessy, but Otman's large frame blocked his view.

Bessy snatched the document.

"Don't sign it!" Arthur yelled over Otman's head.

Otman's adrenalin pumped as he lifted Arthur. "How long can you swim?" Thunderous laughter erupted.

"Noooo!" Bessy screamed and scribbled her signature. "I'd rather have you than my money."

Bessy threw the document at Blair. "Now, let him go."

Otman flexed his arms and Arthur flew over the handrail.

"I love . . ." Arthur's voice faded. The rumble of the diesel engines drowned out all other words.

Bessy grabbed the vase, threw a punch at Blair, hitting him in the stomach and raced to the aft deck. She reared the vase back and threw it at Otman, who ducked. It missed him, landing in the ocean with a splash. The vase sunk.

Otman wrapped her up with a tight bear hug.

"Get rid of her," Blair snapped.

"Stop!" Connie yelled.

But Bessy's body was lifted and tossed over the handrail. She belly-flopped into the inky blue water.

"No!" Arthur gasped. He kicked and breaststroked, splashing madly as he swam toward her.

The back of the yacht grew smaller.

CHAPTER THIRTY-SEVEN

The yacht continued on a straight path. Inside the salon, Connie stared wide eyed out the back door. Her mouth gaped open as she sprang from the recliner. "Why'd you do that? You can't throw them overboard."

"I just did."

"You've got to go back and get them."

Otman laughed louder. "No we don't."

"We planned that out with perfection," Blair snickered.

"Just like you said," Otman grinned, looking at Blair, "Leave no witnesses."

Witnesses! Connie fidgeted. "But, but what if the Cayman bank doesn't believe it's her signature and demands to see her in person? What if they demand a notarized signature? You'll end up with nothing. I'm not giving you any of *my* money."

Blair dashed into the pilothouse, disengaged the autopilot, and spun the wheel to starboard. He reached for the GPS and pressed the man-overboard button. *It's probably too late for that.*

Everyone leaned hard right as the yacht turned a tight circle.

"Do you see them?" Blair asked.

"No," Otman said with a smirk. He barreled through the cabin, out the side door, and up to the bow pulpit. He stood rigid and scanned the waters.

"Where are they?" Connie asked. Her eyes darted across the waves.

"Keep looking," Blair yelled.

The sun retreated into the western sky. A two-foot wave lifted Arthur as he swam up to Bessy. "Are you okay?" Water sputtered from his mouth.

"A little sore, but other than that, I'm fine."

"Fine!" He sighed. "Look at us. We're in the middle of the ocean with no life vests and no land in sight."

Arthur gulped. "Look!" He pointed toward the yacht. "They're coming back to run us over. Blair isn't taking any chances. Take a couple of deep breaths and dive under water. They won't be able to find us. Stay down as long as you can." He sucked in a deep breath. They went under together.

Bessy swam down. She could hear the rumble of the diesel engines. Her heart hammered. She hoped the props would miss them.

Arthur opened his eyes, the salty water, stinging them. Seconds passed. A blurred Bessy was the only thing in sight. Her eyes were tightly closed and her cheeks puffed out. His lungs began to burn. He fought the urge to surface. The hum of the engine stayed constant, off in the distance.

Bessy's head popped above a wave. She gasped a breath of air and disappeared under the approaching wave. Arthur did the same. Soon their air supply was gone again, and they surfaced together. They gasped for air and searched for the boat. The drum of the engines remained unchanged.

The yacht drifted, its bow pointed toward them. Otman clung to the handrail and scanned the water. Connie stood on the flybridge with a pair of binoculars searching the troughs. Blair stood beside her, one hand cupped over his eyes.

"They can't find us," Arthur said.

"How long do you think we can tread water?"

"I don't know, but Connie's looking straight at us. Quick, dive," Arthur gasped and slipped beneath a wave.

The drum of the engines deepened. They knew the boat was bearing down on them. Arthur blinked his eyes and saw Bessy swimming upward. *No!* He reached out to grab her, but she had already surfaced. Fearing the props would be over them any second, he waited and watched Bessy, but she didn't swim back down. With a couple of kicks, he surfaced and noticed the yacht had pulled to within one hundred yards and stopped.

Bessy grabbed Arthur. "Listen, they're calling for us to get back on the boat."

"It's got to be a trick," Arthur said. "He just wants to get closer so he can run us over."

The yacht bobbed closer and closer.

"Bessy," Blair yelled. "Get back on the boat. Otman shouldn't have thrown either of you over." He dropped his hands from around his mouth.

A wave swept past them as they treaded water and stared at the yacht. "We'll drown out here if we don't get on the boat," Bessy said.

"But, he's up to something, or he wouldn't have changed his mind about dumping us."

The boat was less than one hundred feet away. Blair scrambled down from the flybridge and stood out front with Otman. "I can't leave you out here like this. Climb aboard."

"What are you going to do with us after you take all of Bessy's money? You'll never allow us to live," Arthur yelled. His arms and legs began to cramp and he rolled over on his back and floated.

"No, you have it all wrong. Once the money's in my bank account, I'll set you free. You won't be able to touch me." Blair looked at his watch and mumbled. "Dang. They're costing us precious time. The sun is going to be too low in the sky for us to navigate the shifting sandbars at the bottom of the Tongue of the Ocean, and it's the only way across. We'll have to drop an anchor at the south end of Andros for the night."

Bessy struggled. "I can't swim much longer. All of these clothes are weighing me down."

Arthur looked up at Blair. He knew the man's word

couldn't be trusted, but he knew they wouldn't last much longer floating in the middle of the ocean. "Okay," he said to Bessy. "Swim to the dive platform. At least this way we might have an opportunity to plot an escape."

"Quick," Blair said to Otman. "Get back there and wash them off, bind their hands, and get them below. Then get a tube of silicone and glue down the hatch over their cabin. We've got to find a passage into the anchorage through the coral reefs before daylight fades and we risk wrecking."

Otman hurried to the back. He pulled them up on the dive platform and rinsed them off. Exhausted, they lay on the aft deck, gasping, while Otman bound them with duck tape, then took them to their cabin.

Blair and Connie sat on the flybridge as they watched Andros appear.

Otman remained downstairs in the air-conditioned salon. An empty glass with melted ice cubes sat on the coffee table. Every once in a while, his eyelids would blink open.

Connie watched the water change from an inky blue to turquoise. Up ahead were many shades of seafoam, blue, and greens. She watched breathlessly and said to no one in particular, "I can't wait to go swimming."

Blair gritted his teeth. He'd been through this with her at the hotel and wasn't going to get into an argument. At least not right now. This time tomorrow, they would be well on their way to Grand Cayman Island. "Keep an eye out for coral heads. We've got to make our way past that reef."

A mile ahead, waves turned to white-water, as each washed across the massive barrier reef.

CHAPTER THIRTY-EIGHT

Detective Newberry's office was a windowless cubicle. A desk sat in the middle of the room, with one chair on each side. Newberry sat reclined with both hands behind his head. "Of course I'll answer your questions about Shelly Roble."

Manuel opened up his folder and pulled out the legal pad. He flipped it to the fourth page. "Tell me about the first time you met Shelly."

Newberry shifted in his seat. "That would be at her office. I told her the police found Justin's BMW and asked her if she would come to the police station to identify it." He smiled and chuckled. "Of course we knew it was Justin's, but I wanted to question her."

"About what?" Manuel asked, looking puzzled.

"Most officers have seen enough dried blood to become suspicious when they see it. We had questions that needed answering." He scrutinized Manuel. "People who commit a crime will try to shift the focus of an investigation away from themselves and that's what I think Shelly did when she called us and notified us that Justin's BMW was missing."

"But that's not always true," Manuel said.

"Right, but that's why I wanted to ask her questions, to dismiss her as a suspect. When we began questioning her, she seemed distant and cold toward Justin."

"He divorced her. You'd be cold toward your wife if she divorced you."

"Under questioning, Shelly was evasive."

"Like?"

"She couldn't remember much, except that she *claimed* Justin tried to give her an overdose, but she didn't filed a complaint against him. From what I gather, she was the last person to see him alive. He divorced her and no one's seen him since. I'd say his killing was domestically related, pure and simple."

Manuel finished writing and looked up. "Is there anything else that you can remember?"

"Yeah, I remember Shelly telling me that in the divorce, she got everything—the house and both cars. She seemed pleased that he got nothing." The phone on the desk rang. Newberry smiled. "One moment," he said to Manuel as he lifted the phone. "Okay. I'll be right there."

Manuel stood. "Detective, thank you for your time. May I call you if I have future questions?"

"Counsel, call me any time, and don't be surprised when you find out Shelly killed Justin. I've seen plenty of these cases in my time. When there are domestic problems, you'll find the spouse is always involved, somehow."

They shook hands and went their separate directions. Manuel hurried to his car.

After he reached the county jail, he watched as Shelly was brought into the small room.

"Have a seat. I've just come from a meeting with Detective Newberry. He believes you were the last person to see Justin alive. Tell me the last time you saw him."

"It was a few weeks ago, on a Friday. Justin returned from Atlanta. He made all the arrangements for Dad to leave Southern Retirement Community Home and we were going to drive out there and pick him up together. But, before Justin came home, he stopped and bought me my favorite ice cream. I thought he was trying to make up for being insensitive to me and my Dad, but instead, he laced the ice cream with sleeping pills. We never made it out of the driveway. I passed out in the front seat of Justin's BMW."

"Why did you have to wait for Justin to pick up your Dad?"

"I went to pick him up once, but was told Justin was the only one that could sign him out, or so Paul Thornton, the administrator at Southern Retirement Community said. He claimed Justin was Dad's guardian."

Manuel jotted a note to check on Paul Thornton. "But Justin never signed your dad out?"

"I never found out. I remember Justin came to get me and then I don't remember anything until Monday. That's when I woke and found an empty, broken bottle of Halcion beside me. By that time, Dad had escaped from that horrible place."

"So, Halcion is a sleeping pill?"

"Yes. When I woke up Monday, I had lost three days."

"Why didn't you file charges against Justin?"

"I couldn't prove it, and that Detective Newberry didn't believe me." Shelly slumped in her seat. "Do you believe me?"

Manuel stared at her. "Shelly, I'm trying to, but I haven't found the proof that will convince a jury. I know it's out there; I've just have to find it."

CHAPTER THIRTY-NINE

Walter watched Garraway leave Arthur and Bessy's hotel room. He peeked out the door as the man stepped into the elevator. "I don't care what he said. Come on Jane, we're going to find Arthur and Bessy." He flung open the door and exited.

Jane remained at the table. "Walter, wait a minute; come back in here."

He looked from her to the elevator and then back.

"Garraway is right that it could be dangerous out there." Jane motioned for him. "We can't leave today. But he's crazy if he thinks we're going to sit around here tomorrow and wait."

Walter stepped back into the room, but left the door open. "I know how vicious Otman and Blair are. We beat them once, and we'll beat them again."

Jane propped her feet on the bed. "That may be, but here in the Bahamas. . ."

He stepped beside the bed and crossed his arms.

". . . I'm more concerned with the unseen dangers in the ocean than with Blair and Otman." She noticed the blank look on his face. "You know, all the things that can wreck and sink a boat."

Walter shrugged and shook his head. "Like what?"

"The water here is different from back home. In the states, we have marked channels and if you stray from them and run into trouble, you can call someone on the radio or a cell phone for help. But here, you're on your own; there are few marked channels. Boaters are warned not to motor around the out islands after four o'clock. You can't read the water's depth.

The sun's too low in the sky to expose coral heads. If we hit one, we'd be the ones that needed rescuing. Besides, we don't have any provisions." She looked at the clothes he was still wearing. "You've gotta have new clothes."

"Clothes," Walter laughed. "Are you sure?"

"Yeah, those will be standing by themselves shortly."

"What does an airline do with unclaimed suitcases?"

"I'm sure they're placed in lost and found. Don't worry about your clothes. They'll keep the suitcase for a long time. Now let's think of what we need here. Besides clothes for you, we need food and fuel so we can leave first thing tomorrow. Nassau is the best place to purchase those. Once we leave here, the places that have supplies are few and far between, and even if they have anything, the choices are limited. We could be out there for a long time. There're hundreds of small islands to search."

Walter's head sagged forward. "Okay, but I'm not going to sleep good tonight, knowing they're in trouble."

Jane stood and patted him on his back. "Come on. Let's get started."

They made their way to the first grocery store, The City Market. Inside, Jane pushed the cart. Walter lifted a bag of potato chips and another of corn chips from the bin and dropped them into the cart.

Jane stopped. "Put those back. They're bad for you."

"What?" Walter snarled.

"They're bad for your cholesterol."

Walter pushed the potato chip bag back on the shelf and with a boyish grin said, "I'm buying these corn chips for my-self."

Jane smiled and motioned for him to drop the bag into the cart.

He did with a huge grin. "Thanks."

The cart slowly filled with more healthy food than junk food. Walter was pleased with himself, having talked his way into keeping a package of chocolate-chip cookies and a half-gallon of coconut and vanilla ice cream that was made locally.

It wasn't long before their provisions were stowed on the boat and they were back in the streets of Nassau. They made their way to Bay Street, looking in store windows as they passed. Streams of people flowed in both directions on the sidewalks. Some drifted into shops, and others exited the stores with bags and intermingled with the crowd.

Jane glanced through the window at Coach handbags, but didn't stop. "Oh look," Jane said, stopping at the next window to look at the display of men's bathing suits.

Walter cowered as shoppers heard her and stopped to look at the male mannequin wearing a Speedo.

"You need a bathing suit," she said, looking up at him.

"One of those things?" Walter squeaked. "They're called Speedos and for a good reason. You speed from the water to your towel in hopes that no one sees you."

Jane laughed so hard she doubled over. "No, Walter, not a Speedo."

The people around Walter were snickering.

Jane grabbed his hand and pulled him inside. "I'm glad I came with you. There's no telling what you'd buy."

"Me-e?"

"Yeah. You're obviously shortsighted. I was talking about the surfer's bathing suits hanging on the back wall behind that mannequin." She led him into the men's clothing department and stopped at the bathing suit rack. She began flipping through swimsuits.

Walter glanced at the Speedo selection. *Those things ought to have a warning label. Caution: Will cause Walter great discomfort and humiliation.* He chuckled.

"Walter," Jane called from the end rack after scrutinizing each suit. "Which one did you like the best?"

Walter coughed weakly as he searched the rack. Seeing two that would do, he reached in and grabbed them. "How about one of these?" He held up a tri-colored blue one and a loud yellow print with surfboards. "These look nice."

Jane ignored him. "What about this one?" She pulled out a Caribbean multi-colored print.

"I like it."

"Good." Jane smiled and stepped over to the women's bathing suits. She pulled out a string bikini.

Walter gulped. *She's got to be kidding.*

"What do you think?" she asked, grinning and holding up a suit that was three sizes too small.

"But it's nothing but a few strings."

She nudged him. "I'm just teasing with you. I already have mine. Come on."

He was concerned with what she might have packed.

After an hour of shopping, Walter owned a bathing suit, two pairs of shorts—khaki and navy blue—and two shirts, each different colored Hawaiian prints. The bags hung at his knees.

"It looks like you've gotten everything you'll need for a few days except a hat, and I know just the place to get one. The straw market. It's just down the street."

The walk to the straw market turned out to be farther than "just down the street." Walter's arms ached from carrying his purchases, and his legs cramped from trying to keep up with Jane's fast pace.

On the other end of Bay Street, Walter and Jane ambled through the market until they found the perfect wide-brimmed hat. The miniature thatch-roof hat moved above the sea of tourists as Jane and Walter wove in and out of the crowded market.

A heavy Bahamian woman holding an armload of colorful tee shirts and wraps stepped from her booth and blocked Jane's path. "Here, pretty lady, don't you wanna buy a wrap?"

Jane shook her head, "No, thank you."

"Sir," the shopkeeper said, turning and pressing against Walter, "don't you wanna see your pretty lady in this."

"Uh," Walter cleared his throat as his eyes darted between Jane, who was now smiling, to the woman, whose eyes begged for a sale. He shrugged. "Come on Jane, she might be right."

"If you don't like this one, maybe you like this one?" she smiled as she pulled out a red and white Androsian Batik.

"Well, maybe this one," Jane said, and blushed as she felt the nicer cotton fabric.

"It matches your shoes," the woman added.

Walter watched as the woman draped Jane in the fabric. "Jane, that looks good on you."

"Well, that settles it," Jane said as she pulled out her wallet. "I'll take it."

Walter handed the cash to the woman. "Let's get out of here before we have to buy something else."

Jane clutched her purchase and as they hurried off, her stomach growled. "It's getting late. How about dinner before we head back to the marina?"

Walter wiped the sweat from his forehead. "Anything but an outdoor café."

CHAPTER FORTY

Jane was up early the next morning, sitting at the galley table, with a chart of the Bahamas laid out in front of her. *Where would Blair be?* She looked north to the Abacos and shook her head. *Too populated.* She looked east to the Eleuthera Islands, but didn't really think they'd go there either. Then she looked south at the Exumas, hundreds of small beautiful uninhabited islands. A good place to disappear or have fun. A smile stretched across her face as she remembered the fun they had yesterday, shopping and sharing pie. *I'd like to take Walter there.*

"What are you doing?" Walter asked as he entered, stretching. He was wearing the new large-flower print shirt and khaki shorts.

"Wow!" She looked him over, and smoothed out a wrinkle. "I like that."

"Thanks," Walter blushed. "Any word on Bessy and Arthur?"

Jane's smile faded. "No, and their boat's still missing. I've been asking myself which way they might have gone." Her finger slid across the chart and stopped on a long slender chain of islands. "If I were hiding, I'd be down here," she pointed to the map, "in the Exumas."

He looked at the small islands that were east and southeast of Nassau that lined up from north to south. Then his eyes moved westward, back across Nassau, across the Tongue of the Ocean to the largest island in the Bahamas, Andros. It was approximately thirty miles due west of Nassau. The blue area west of the island—closest to Florida—was the Great Bahama Bank. The single digits indicated that it was shallow. The east side of the island was marked by a thin strip of blue and a wide swath of white. The first number in the white indicated a shear wall that dropped to six hundred feet. The next line out marked six thousand feet. "Is this island heavily populated?" he asked, pointing to it.

"No, not at all. It's mostly uninhabited. Lots of mangrove trees, pine and mahogany, too. It's buggy and mostly shallow water. These," she said as she pointed to the many small x's, "indicate coral heads. It's the world's third largest reef. The place where whisky runners and pirates used to hide out."

Walter's eyes brightened. "Sounds like a good hiding place to me."

"Not many boats go down there. It's a dead-end place at the bottom of the Tongue of the Ocean. Nothing but sandy shoals." Her finger moved across the lower Great Bahama Bank. "It's shallow. Down there, you're on your own."

Walter looked at her finger and saw the line dividing the six-hundred-feet drop-off from the numerous sandbars, five feet or less at low tide.

Walter glanced at the other islands in the Bahamas, especially the ones farther south. "You know, if I kidnapped someone, I'd be hiding at Andros or heading south, away from everyone."

Jane's finger tapped on top of Andros Island. "You might be right. We'll search there first. It won't take us long to run down the east side of the island."

"What about checking out the western side?"

"The mud flats. They'd never go there. It's too shallow. They'd run aground."

CHAPTER FORTY-ONE

Anchors Away floated at anchorage, just off a sandy beach. The sun continued its ascent into the blue sky. A school of minnows darted in unison in clear water behind the dive platform. Several sea gulls flew over the yacht as they headed out to sea in search of a meal.

Otman sat at the table drinking a glass of milk. "I'd like four eggs," he hollered to the galley where Bessy was cooking. "Lots of bacon, three slices of toast with butter, and . . ." he looked at Blair whose eyes tightened on him, ". . . what?"

"You're going to eat up all the food," Blair said.

"So, we'll be at the Cayman Islands tomorrow. We can buy more then."

"Fine, order whatever you'd like."

Connie stepped off the stairs and rounded the corner. The tight, yellow, two-piece swimsuit set off her dark tan. "I'm not having breakfast. I'm going to the beach."

"What is it with you two?" Blair snapped. "This isn't vacation. We've got unfinished work to do."

"You said we couldn't leave until high tide," Connie said. "I've got a few hours and I'm spending them on that beautiful beach. I'll eat later. After all, we're in the Bahamas."

Bessy stepped around the corner carrying a frying pan of scrabbled eggs and a plate of toast. "Sorry to disappoint you; there isn't any bacon. You didn't buy any before you left." She plopped the frying pan on the table.

Otman's large hand snatched the pan, held it over his plate, and raked out the eggs.

"Hey," Blair yelled, "leave me some."

A pile of eggs lay heaped in Otman's plate. "I am."

Connie stepped beside the table and looked down at Blair. "I want Arthur to take me to the beach in the dinghy."

"Now? Can't you see we're eating?" Blair said. "Later."

Connie turned and went downstairs and unlocked the front cabin door. "Get up," she demanded. "You're taking me to the beach."

Arthur propped himself up on his elbows and stared at her.

"Do I have to yell for Otman?" she asked, knowing that he probably wouldn't come even if she called.

Arthur's eyebrows arched. *This might be the opportunity I'm looking for. I could have a look around and plan an escape.* He leaped up off the bed. "I've got to change," and he stepped into the bathroom.

Connie smiled at herself, proud that she had gotten her way.

The bathroom door swung open, and Arthur exited wearing his bathing suit. "I'm ready."

Connie followed him up the stairs and into the salon. "I'm going to lie out on the beach before it gets too hot."

Blair dabbed his face with a paper towel as he stood. He drew in a deep breath to tell Connie no, but knowing she wouldn't listen, gritted his teeth and sat back down. "Arthur, remember, I've got Bessy."

Arthur glanced at Bessy to see her mouth the word, "Sorry." He turned and followed Connie to the aft door.

Blair grabbed Bessy and pulled her into the seat beside him. "You're staying by my side until he comes back."

Arthur helped Connie from the dive platform into the inflatable dinghy, untied it, and shoved off. He cranked the nine-point-nine outboard engine. It growled louder, as Arthur gave it more gas. The dinghy jumped up on a plane and zipped toward shore.

"Connie, you've got to help us escape."

Connie shook her head. "Just give them the money, and they'll let both of you go."

The dinghy approached the shore, and Arthur shut off the engine. He slipped overboard, stood on the sand, and pulled Connie toward shore. "You know they'll never let us go."

Connie turned and looked away.

"You saw Otman throw us overboard. They're not going to let any of us live, and that includes you."

"I've done everything they've asked of me. They'll let me go. They promised."

"Are you sure? Once Blair gets Bessy's money, he's going to get rid of all evidence. He'll never go back to jail. Never."

"But, he promised me."

"Okay Connie, just think about it for now. I bet he promised Bessy similar things when they got married, and you know where that got her."

The dinghy bumped the beach, and Connie stepped out holding her towel. She spread out the towel, crawled onto it, and closed her eyes. She peeped through a slit in one eye. *Maybe he's right. We have the dinghy. We could get away.*

"Listen." Connie sat up. "I'm afraid of them. But, how can I trust you? You might be setting me up."

"You can trust me. I've never done anything to you."

"Okay. Let's leave now."

"Right now?"

"Yes, let's get in the dinghy and speed away."

"I can't leave Bessy. Blair has her and there's no telling what he'd do to her if I left. All you've got to do is create a diversion. Bessy and I . . ."

". . . That's too risky for me. If we don't go now, I'm not interested. Leave me alone." She fell back on the towel.

"Just think about it. If we were to gang up on them, we could beat them." He glanced around. *I'll come up with a plan with or without her help.*

CHAPTER FORTY-TWO

Downtown West Palm Beach, on the eleventh floor of the Atlantic building, Manuel sat hunched over his desk. Photos of Shelly lay scattered before him. The digital clock on the credenza showed 9:30. The morning sun filtered through the tinted windows.

He flipped the sheet over. *If Shelly wasn't at the murder scene, how did Justin's blood get on that pocketbook? He picked up the photo and stared at the splattered bloodstains. Someone could have tampered with her pocketbook. . . . But who?*

"Excuse me," Jennie, his secretary, said. "The State Attorney's office just dropped off this envelope marked State of Florida vs. Shelly Roble."

Manuel reached out and took it. "Thank you." He slit open the envelope and pulled out the contents. He flipped the cover page over and read: Shelly Roble vs. State of Florida. You are hereby notified that the trial date is. . . .

He dropped the document on the desk. "Shelly's trial begins two weeks from today." He grabbed his planner. "Jennie, clear my calendar for the next four weeks."

"Yes sir. That's kind of quick, isn't it?"

"Too quick." He grabbed Shelly's folder, opened it, and snatched out the legal pad. He thumbed through the pages. "Jennie, please get Paul Thornton at Southern Retirement Community on the phone."

She disappeared into the hallway.

Minutes later, Jennie placed the call and Manuel picked up

the line.

"Hello, Mr. Thornton. Thank you for taking my call. I'm Manuel Marconnet. I represent Shelly Roble and would like to ask you a couple of questions."

"I don't know much about her. I've only met her once and she was irate. I was afraid for my life. I had to have her escorted out of my office and out of the building."

"Why?"

"She wanted to take her dad home, but for some reason she'd listed her husband, Justin, as Arthur's guardian. Without Justin's approval, I couldn't, by law, allow Arthur to leave."

"But Justin spoke with you and arranged for Shelly to pick him up."

"No sir. I never spoke with Justin. He never authorized us to discharge Arthur."

"Mr. Thornton, thank you for your time," and Manuel hung up. He put his feet on the desk, leaned back, and stared at the ceiling. *Hmm, Justin never attempted to correct his name as Arthur's guardian, but led Shelly to believe he had. He stole Arthur's money and now he's dead. What a character. Paul Thornton said Shelly was irate and he feared for his life. Detective Newberry says this case is domestic violence, and Shelly's involved in Justin's death. She was arrested at the airport wearing a disguise, trying to flee the country.* He closed his eyes. *Shelly, if we're going to win, we'll need something big to present to the jury.*

CHAPTER FORTY-THREE

Walter squeezed the lever on the fuel nozzle; diesel flowed into the yacht's tanks. The dial rolled over—one hundred gallons. The soft ding continued. He watched in disbelief as the gallon display rolled to two hundred gallons. The nozzle shut off as the diesel gurgled in the fill tube at just over two hundred gallons. He glanced at the amount and then to Jane.

"Don't worry Walter, I'm buying." She laughed. "This isn't much. If the tanks were empty, it would have cost thousands."

Walter rehung the fuel nozzle and tightened the deck-cap on the tank, while Jane signed the credit receipt and handed it back to the dockmaster.

Soon the slick boat was untied and on its way. Jane turned the boat on a westward heading and maneuvered out into the shipping channel. The sun rose behind them. The air was still and warming. Within ten minutes, the boat received permission to leave, cleared Nassau's channel, and was racing across calm water, heading west, to the northern tip of Andros. The boat zipped across in just over thirty minutes. They stared at Morgan's Bluff rising out of the ocean.

"There's an anchorage up there. We can stop and ask if they've seen a sixty-foot yacht." Jane pulled back on the throttles and entered the buoyed channel.

"I thought you said there weren't many marked channels?" Walter stared at the well-maintained channel.

"I did. This is one of the exceptions. Barges come here daily to fill up with fresh water. They haul approximately six million gallons of water out of per day and take it to Nassau."

She steered past the last buoy and rounded Morgan's Bluff. "Over there," she pointed, "is the acclaimed hideout of Sir Henry Morgan."

"The pirate?"

"The pirate."

Up ahead, anchored off the beach, were a Sea Ray, a Chris Craft, and a twin-outboard center console. They bobbed lazily across half-foot waves.

"Let's start with that Sea Ray first. Maybe they've seen Bessy's boat?"

Walter nodded. "Let's hope someone saw them."

Jane steered alongside the Sea Ray, a thirty-three-foot Sundancer. The two yachts drifted a foot apart.

A slender, middle age man appeared from below deck in his swimsuit and waved. "Good Morning."

"Morning. I'm Walter. We're looking for our friends. They're in a sixty-foot Hatteras."

"Hi Walter, I'm Heath. I've been here three days and haven't seen your friends. How long will the two of you be staying?"

"I wish we could stay for a couple of days," Jane said, moving beside Walter. "But, we can't."

"That's too bad. I always enjoy company, and there's plenty of buried pirate treasure up there for everyone to find."

"I'd like to stay and help you look," Walter said, his eyes eager. "I'll have to take a rain check."

"Sure, another day."

"Our friends are missing. They've been kidnapped. We've got to keep looking for them."

"I'll keep my eye out for them. If I see a sixty-foot Hatteras, I'll call the authorities."

"Thank you." Walter waved as Jane drove off.

"Next port of call will be Fresh Creek." Jane steered the yacht around the last buoy. They raced south across two-foot seas and stayed two to three miles offshore for the next thirty or so miles. Along the way, they saw a few small skiffs inside the reef.

"We're going in there," Jane said, pointing to a cut in the land. "That's Fresh Creek."

"Do you think they're up there hiding?"

"No. I'm just ruling it out so we don't have to second guess ourselves later."

Walter nodded and watched them turn toward the creek. He grabbed the side of the yacht seeing shallow water all around.

Jane navigated by staying in the darker water.

"Someone should mark the way with buoys."

"In the Bahamas you use a lot of local knowledge. The buoys never would survive in the winds and waves that come ashore here. I'm sure the locals gave up trying, years ago."

Inside the creek, eight yachts were tied up at three different marinas, but Bessy's wasn't one of them. After raising each marina on the radio and being told that they hadn't seen any sixty-foot yachts, Jane headed out of the unmarked channel.

"It's not going to be as easy to find them as I hoped." Walter sighed. "Maybe Garraway is having better success than we are."

"Well, we haven't seen any boats or planes searching. They must have started their search at another island. At least we're not duplicating each other's efforts." Jane turned right and headed south. The yacht skimmed across the waves at thirty-five knots. "Walter, go down into the salon and grab the binoculars from the drawer under the TV. We might need them."

Walter disappeared inside and soon returned with the binoculars around his neck. He lifted them and scanned the shoreline. Waves lapped at the deserted beaches.

"If we don't find them at Andros, we'll head on over to the Exumas." She smiled. "If we end up having to spend the night, there's a place halfway down that I think you'd like to see."

"Where's that?" Walter asked as the circle in the viewfinder swayed on two people walking along the waterline.

"Thunderball Cave. It's where one of the James Bond movies was made. It's a small island with an underwater cave. At high tide, you have to swim underwater on one side to enter. And on the other side is a crevice you swim through."

"Wow, that sounds like a neat place."

"Oh, you'd love to see it."

The horizon jiggled in the viewfinder. Walter began feeling woozy. "I think I should drive now," he said, a green hew on his face.

Jane looked at him and quickly moved aside.

He grabbed the wheel. It wasn't long before his color returned.

"Make sure we stay in the inky blue water. It's plenty deep. The reef is over there," she said, and pointed to the breaking water. "It runs the length of the coast, 140 miles." The distance to shore was less than a mile. She didn't bother using the binoculars unless she spotted a yacht. As the minutes passed, she saw none. She looked at the chart.

"Walter, we're getting close to the first Bight; keep a sharp lookout."

"Bite? That sounds like we're fishing."

"Not b-i-t-e, but b-i-g-h-t," she laughed. "There are three huge inlets that cut through to the west coast, and they call them Bights."

"Oh," he said, and joined in the laughter.

As they approached the North Bight, Jane grew restless. She figured that if Bessy and Arthur were at Andros Island, they'd be found somewhere south of here. This was an enormous and mostly unpopulated area.

She tapped on Walter's shoulders. "Slow the boat to about twenty knots." Jane scanned what appeared to be a large river, miles wide. *What a deception. It's very shallow in there.*

Soon they approached the Middle Bight. Jane focused on a couple of small fishing boats. The skiffs were approximately seventeen feet or less. She assumed they were paying customers fishing for bonefish—small game fish, but great fighters. At the mouth of this Bight was a small village with a few homes.

As the South Bight emerged in the viewfinder, it appeared that they were at the end of Andros, but the fact was that they just finished searching the first half of the island. She read once that the channel's entrance was dug out to a depth of twelve feet, allowing cruise ship tenders to ferry passengers to and from shore. Inside the Bight, another small community rose out of the sand. They had not seen a sixty-foot yacht either.

Over the years, she heard boaters bragging that they surfed through the island at high tide on this waterway, but that was smaller boats, nowhere near the size of Bessy's. From here on, she knew there wouldn't be many people, if any. Just a home or two and then nothing but sandy beaches.

Walter held his face in the breeze and grinned. "I'm enjoying this."

"I'm glad you're feeling better." She looked back toward shore. There was nothing but pristine beaches. Waves rolled onto the unspoiled sand.

As they began their third hour of the search, Jane's skin tingled. She saw a flicker of light in the circular view. She stared and waited for the flash to repeat itself. It flashed again. "Look there! South on the horizon," she said and pointed.

Walter's knuckles tightened on the steering wheel. "What is it?" He kept watch until his eyes blurred.

She turned and looked at the prop wash and the flat path where they had traveled. The last Bight was long out of sight.

CHAPTER FORTY-FOUR

Anchors Away bobbed close to shore. The yacht's twin generators hummed as cold air circulated inside the salon. Otman squirmed on the couch. Blair sat at the table checking and rechecking each document. "Perfect."

"I can't stay on this boat any longer," Otman said. "I've got to go to shore and stretch my legs before we leave."

Blair looked at his watch. "It's almost high tide. Be back in thirty minutes. Don't be late."

Otman stood on the aft deck, waving his hands. "Arthur."

Arthur turned and saw Otman motioning. "We've got to go."

Connie picked up the towel and climbed into the dinghy.

"Harry, I'd need to stretch my legs too," Bessy said. "May I go along?"

"Nice try, but you're not going anywhere."

"Please. What can happen with Otman and Connie there?"

"Nothing's going to happen, because you're not going." Blair looked out the window, scanning the horizon.

"I've signed your documents."

"Fine," he said, wanting a little peace and quiet. He opened the back door. "Otman, take Bessy, but keep a close eye on her."

Arthur brought the dinghy up to the dive platform. Bessy climbed in and snuggled up next to him. Otman sat on the side of the tube, beside Connie.

"Remember," Blair hollered, "be back in thirty minutes."

CHAPTER FORTY-FIVE

Close to the bottom of Andros, Walter and Jane shouted in unison. "It's Bessy's boat."

"You'd better hide inside while I get closer and have a look. Blair and Otman won't recognize my boat." Jane said.

Walter slid out of the seat.

Jane climbed into the captain's seat and pulled back on the throttles, slowing the boat to fifteen knots. Walter grabbed the binoculars from Jane's outstretched hand and disappeared into the cabin.

She pulled the charts close and made mental notes as to the position of the dangerous reefs. Keeping an eye out for shallow areas, she slowed further and steered toward shore.

Walter focused on four people in an inflatable raft, nearing shore. Arthur sat in the back and held the throttle. Bessy sat in front of him.

"Otman!" he wheezed. He focused on the other woman. *Who is that?*

"There are four people in a dinghy," he shouted to Jane, "but I don't see Blair."

Jane lifted the mic on the radio and depressed the button. "May-Day, May-Day, May-Day!" She released the button and waited for a response.

Walter pressed the binoculars back to the porthole and focused. The dingy bobbed at the shoreline, as Arthur stood in knee-deep water, holding it.

Connie slid off the side of the dinghy, headed for the beach, and spread out her towel.

Otman noticed the approaching yacht, leaped out of the dinghy, and sprinted from the water to the top of the sand dune for a better view. He cupped his hands over his eyes and stared.

Walter moved the binoculars over to the yacht and gulped. There on the aft deck, holding a pair of binoculars, was Blair, looking straight at them.

Jane gripped the mic. "May-Day, May-Day, May-Day!"

Bessy inched closer to Arthur and whispered. "That's Jane's boat."

"Who's Jane?" Arthur murmured and stared at the low profile yacht. He knew she would be in danger if she came ashore.

"She's here to rescue us," Bessy continued to whisper. "Let's make a break for her boat." She looked over her shoulder at Otman and then back to the approaching yacht. "Ease us out into deeper water."

Arthur's pulse quickened.

"Hurry," Bessy wheezed, as she shifted to the dinghy's other side.

Blair turned to see the dinghy moving away from shore. "Otman! Grab them!"

Otman leaped down the sand dune, kicking up sand, and splashed into the water.

Arthur lunged over the side of the dinghy, yanked on the crank cord, and the engine sputtered.

"Hurry," Bessy yelled, and dropped to the floor while Arthur yanked again. The engine roared to life.

Blair stared in unbelief.

"Go," Bessy shrieked.

Arthur's hand trembled as he pushed the gearshift lever into gear. The dinghy lurched forward.

Otman vaulted toward them.

"Hold on," Arthur shouted and twisted the throttle control handle. The engine whined.

Otman grabbed the rubber side, jolting Bessy and Arthur, but his wet hands slipped off.

The dinghy jumped up on a plane as the outboard roared.

Walter watched through the binoculars. "They're coming! They're coming!" he yelled, dropping the binoculars on the couch and dashing from the cabin to the side of the boat.

Jane steered straight for the dinghy.

Arthur and Bessy were over the reef before he slowed for the approaching yacht.

Otman stared in disbelief. His fists balled and his teeth gritted. "I'll get you, Arthur. One day I'll find you and you'll wish you'd never escaped." He stared at the yacht. "Walter!"

Jane's heart pounded as she reached for the throttles. She turned back to Bessy and Arthur, almost on top of them. Out of the corner of her eye, she saw Blair's hands coming up, pointing a gun at them.

Suddenly a red glowing ball soared toward them. She ducked, hearing a cracking sound against the hull. Her body fell on top of the throttles, thrusting them forward.

The engines screamed as the yacht's bow rose high out of the water.

Arthur swallowed hard. "Hold on!" He gunned the outboard. The dinghy veered to the right. The large yacht barreled toward them.

"Jane!" Bessy screamed.

Plumes of water peeled off the hull as the yacht sped toward the reef. Jane recovered and spun the wheel to the left. The boat dug hard into the water, fanning huge wakes outward.

Powerful waves raced toward Arthur and Bessy. The dinghy wobbled up the first wave. Arthur and Bessy clasped the sides as the wake washed under them, whiplashing them. The second wave slammed into them. The dinghy teetered on its side as the outboard's prop spun wildly in the air. The third wake crashed into the dinghy. It flipped and landed upside down.

Bessy and Arthur tumbled in the turbulence. Suddenly, the waves were gone and calmness returned. They swam to the surface, gasping for air. A horrendous crunching noise reverberated.

Jane gripped the steering wheel as coral raked the hull. The yacht shuddered and drifted off the reef. Jane lay up against the wheel, a vacant stare on her face. *What have I done?*

Otman trudged through chin-deep water laughing at the mayhem. He froze. *Sharks.*

Connie stood looking out over the water in horror.

"They aren't going anywhere but to shore, and I'll be waiting," Otman said as he backed out of the water. "That is *if* they make it at all."

"Aren't you going to swim out there and help them?" Connie asked.

"Nope. That's Walter, another one of my troublemakers. I'm not going out there."

"If you're not, I am," she said, dashing into the water.

"I wouldn't do that if I were you. With that kind of carnage, there's bound to be blood, and sharks."

Connie stopped kicking and looked back at Otman.

He stood glaring at the wreckage, smiled, and nodded his head. "Something's going to grab one of them."

CHAPTER FORTY-SIX

The yacht wobbled across each wave. Arthur and Bessy swam madly toward the wreck and climbed aboard. Bessy stepped over to the helm where Jane lay up against the dash. She pulled the dazed woman back into the chair.

"Bessy," Jane moaned, "Walter's downstairs."

Arthur rushed into the cabin and stopped in ankle-deep water. "Walter!"

Walter sat on the floor rubbing his head. Arthur grabbed him. "Get up. We've got to get out of here."

Walter looked up as a small grin appeared. "Hi, Arthur."

"Are you hurt?"

"I don't think so."

Bessy wrapped her arms around Jane. "Come on; we've got to get off this boat. It's sinking."

A weak smile emerged on Jane's face. "I was supposed to be rescuing you."

Bessy grimaced at the irony.

Jane wobbled as she stood.

Bessy steadied her. "Careful."

The water inside the cabin was now up to Arthur's knees. "You'd better grab your suitcases."

"Jane's suitcase is up there in the front cabin. I'll get my clothes." Walter sloshed through the water to his stateroom. He grabbed the suitcase that floated above the submerged bed. By the time he and Arthur met back in the salon, water was up to their waists.

Arthur trudged into the cockpit area. "Let's get out of here before the boat goes down." After glancing at the shore and the overturned dinghy just behind them, he placed the suitcase on the captain's chair and jumped overboard. He splashed through the water, climbed up on one side of the dinghy, reached across, and pulled. The dinghy flipped over.

Arthur stared at the transom. "The motor's missing." He stuck his face into the water and searched. The salty water blurred his vision. *I'll never find it.*

He swam the dinghy over to the submerging yacht. Its gunwales were a foot above the water.

Bessy and Walter helped Jane, who was still wobbly, into the dinghy. Then Bessy climbed aboard and Walter handed her both suitcases. She held Jane's, ensuring it wouldn't get wet, and put his already wet one on the floor.

"Without a motor or paddles, we've got no other choice but head to shore." Arthur grabbed the boat and, with Walter's help, they swam, pulling the dinghy behind them.

Otman stood at the shoreline watching. "Oh, another patient's coming back to me," he said, with an evil laugh. "My record's intact. I've never lost a patient."

The dinghy bumped the sandy bottom, and Walter sat on his knees, breathing heavily.

Otman stood at the water's edge. "Walter, who did you bring me?"

Walter straightened up on his knees, but Otman reached out and pushed him down into the water and sand.

Otman bent down. "Hello, Jane, it's been years since the last time I saw you visiting Bessy."

Jane shuddered. *Otman!* He was the reason that she stopped going to see Bessy years ago.

He grabbed her by the biceps and lifted her out of the dinghy. He roared with laughter. "Great driving."

Jane's eyes watered from the pain in her arms.

"Remember me?" Otman's eyes bulged.

"Yes, M-Mr. Otman." Jane's body quivered.

He dropped her back into the dinghy.

She landed hard on the fiberglass floor, and didn't move.

Otman looked at the back of the dinghy. "Where's the motor?" he yelled, stepping over to Arthur.

"It's out there," Arthur said.

Otman smiled. "I'm ready to go back, now." He stooped and looked Arthur eye to eye. "But since we don't have any paddles, I guess you'll have to swim us back and forth, pulling the dinghy." He grabbed the dinghy and rocked it.

Bessy and Jane tumbled out. Bessy held Jane's suitcase high out of the water.

Otman's open hand slapped the suitcase; it splashed into a cresting wave, and washed up on the beach.

Connie jumped up. Her feet kicked sand into the blowing wind and covered the suitcase. "I'm ready to go back, too."

"You heard the lady," Otman snapped, "take us to the boat." He looked from Arthur to Walter. "Arthur, it's obvious that you've got a lot of energy for escaping. I believe a good workout, swimming this dinghy around, will leave you tired for the rest of the day. You won't have the strength to plan another escape."

Walter grabbed Jane, her legs wobbling, as a wave washed past her.

Bessy sprinted up the wet sand, grabbed Jane's suitcase, and tossed it high into the sand, then raced after Walter's suitcase as the receding water pulled it back into the sea.

Arthur reached for the dinghy.

"Wait a minute," Otman demanded. "Bessy, you need some exercise, too. Let's go."

Bessy walked into the water. She and Arthur pushed the dinghy out as far as they could touch, and then began to kick and push it toward the Hatteras. Otman stuck a leg over the side and dragged it through the water.

Blair scowled, standing on the aft deck watching. The flare gun was tucked into his waistline. The dinghy moved slowly as it bobbed across the waves. Finally, it bumped the dive platform. Arthur's lungs burned.

Otman looked behind the dinghy at Arthur clinging to the transom. He knocked Arthur's hands off. "No resting. Keep swimming."

Otman turned and gave Connie a hand as she stepped from the dinghy. He looked up at Blair. "We'll be back." He turned back to Arthur and Bessy. "We'd better go get your friends."

Arthur and Bessy struggled and swam back toward shore with Otman dragging both legs in the water.

"I hear barracudas are attracted to toes that dangle in water," Bessy said.

Otman snatched his feet into the dinghy.

Finally, Arthur's toes stretched for the sandy bottom. He shoved the dinghy toward shore. Chest heaving, he knelt in the wet sand, knowing he only had a second to rest.

CHAPTER FORTY-SEVEN

Once again, Blair waited at the back of the boat as the dinghy approached. Otman stepped out, onto the dive platform. He grabbed the outside shower and rinsed off. Then he climbed the ladder and stood on deck.

Arthur, Bessy, and Walter treaded water, while Jane rested in the bottom of the dinghy.

"What do you want to do with these two newcomers?" Otman asked.

"I don't know," Blair said as he ran both hands through his hair. "Give me a minute."

Bessy pulled herself up on the dive platform and stood. Walter moved to follow.

"Get off. You're not welcome," Blair growled. "Because of you, we've missed the high tide. Now we'll have to stay another night." He stared at Jane. "Hello, Jane. You shouldn't have come. Mr. Otman, duck tape Jane and Walter, and leave them on the island. There's not enough room on this boat for two more."

Jane cringed in the bottom of the dinghy.

Bessy's head snapped upward staring at Blair. "There's plenty of room."

"No, there's not," Blair snapped. "All staterooms are full. This boat is already crowded."

Connie stepped out the door with a towel wrapped around her head and one wrapped around her body. She looked over the handrail and down into the water. "You're not putting them in my room."

"There's plenty of room in the forward cabin," Bessy fumed.

Otman started laughing. "Your room is crowded with two."

"We'll make do," Bessy said, turning to look at Jane. "Won't we?"

Afraid, Jane only nodded.

Blair stood stoically and shook his head. "We definitely don't have enough food for everyone."

Bessy knew he was right. The food aboard was enough for two and with seven, it would dwindle fast.

"I'll share my portion," Arthur said, holding the dinghy and the dive platform.

"Me too," Bessy chimed.

Otman leaned over and whispered into Blair's ear. "We can't get rid of them yet. We don't want to take the chance that their bodies could be discovered until we're long gone."

Blair's eyes narrowed at Otman as he muttered. "There are only four syringes. You don't have enough meds to keep them all under control."

"They don't know that," Otman whispered back with a big grin. "And besides, each syringe has enough drugs to kill whoever receives it."

"Just don't give Bessy one," Blair mumbled, "until I get my money back."

Otman grinned.

Blair nodded. "Okay. We'll keep them until we leave, but then they're history. Lock them downstairs." He turned and stared at them with a stern look. "If anyone tries to escape . . ."

". . . They'll never do it again," Otman said. An evil grin spread across his face as he leaned over the side and yelled. "All right. Bessy, you and your friend wash off and get up here. Arthur and Walter, I want to see you swimming. By the time you stop, you'll be too tired to even think about escaping. Swim!"

Already exhausted, Arthur and Walter began a slow swim.

Blair turned and walked inside the air-conditioned salon. He picked up a book, sat, and began to read.

Bessy and Jane used the fresh water wash-down and rinsed off.

"Don't waste our water," Otman shouted.

Bessy washed off easily since she was in her swimsuit. It was a little more difficult for Jane who wore shorts and a cotton top. As they climbed up the ladder, Connie handed them her wet towel to dry off with. "We don't have enough room to hang all of the towels and clothes. You'll have to share."

After Bessy and Jane were semi-dry, they followed Connie inside.

Walter and Arthur continued to swim.

CHAPTER FORTY-EIGHT

Connie, Bessy, and Jane stepped through the door, into the salon. "Get downstairs and don't give me any trouble or I'll scream for Otman."

Otman laughed, hearing Connie's voice from the open door. "Keep them straight Connie." His eyes bore into Bessy's. "You heard Blair. The first time anyone tries anything, Walter and Jane will disappear."

Jane quivered.

Bessy wrapped an arm around her. "Come on. Don't listen to him." She helped Jane from the salon into the passageway, past the galley, to the curved stairs that were on the opposite side of the galley and helm. Halfway down, Bessy turned and whispered to Connie. "You've got to help us."

"I can't. You know what they'd do to me."

Jane nudged Bessy. "Tell her what I told you on my boat."

Bessy shook her head. Her eyes warned Jane to be quiet. Bessy took another step.

"Tell me what?" Connie asked as she followed and stepped closer.

Jane took a deep breath. "I placed a Mayday call over the radio. The Bahamian Government must have heard my call."

"Are you sure?" Connie asked as they all took another step down. She glanced out of the stairwell at Blair and Otman and then back. "You're teasing me. You think just because I'm a blonde, I'll fall for it."

Jane shook her head. "It's true. They were out there, searching for Arthur and Bessy before we left Nassau. The police officer warned Walter and me to stay in Nassau, that they had airplanes and boats that would be out here searching. He even said the U.S. Coastguard would be called in to help in their search. That's why I'm sure they're looking for us. They must have heard my Mayday calls."

Connie swallowed hard. *She could be telling the truth. When we left, they were watching the airport for us, and now they're out here searching for us.* "Maybe I should tell Blair."

"I knew we shouldn't have said anything," Bessy said, and hurried down the stairs.

"Wait," Connie pleaded, hurrying after Bessy. "Maybe we can make a deal. Maybe I won't tell them anything."

"Deal?" Bessy asked.

"Yes. I don't want to go to jail. I didn't want to come along, but Blair made me. He . . ." She froze.

Jane and Bessy glanced at each other and then back at Connie. "Okay," they said together. "We'll tell everyone that you helped us."

"Tonight," Connie began, "after everyone's gone to sleep, I'll unlock your door, then we'll all overpower Blair and Otman."

"Maybe we should just slip off the boat," Bessy said, "and get to land so we can find help."

"I agree with Bessy," Jane said.

Connie nodded her head. Her hands trembled as she reached for the door and opened it. "I've got to get back up-stairs before Blair or Otman suspect anything." She began to close the door, "I'll be here as soon as I hear Otman snoring."

"We'll be waiting," Bessy said.

Connie closed the door, hurried back up, and dropped into the couch.

Jane looked out the porthole to shore. The sun glowed bright in the Western sky. "It's a long way back to the last house we saw."

CHAPTER FORTY-NINE

The temperature in the salon was seventy-five. The air-conditioner blew on high. Blair's hands were behind his head as he leaned back in the recliner and Otman, propped up with pillows, stretched out on the couch.

"I'm glad Connie's resting downstairs," Blair said. "I don't like her knowing our plans. Sometimes she concerns me. Like wanting to go out there and help Jane and Walter. They weren't going anywhere, but to shore."

"She concerns me all the time," Otman said. "I wish she had never come."

"We couldn't leave her. If the Bahamian cops caught her, she would panic and spill her guts."

"What are we going to do with her? Drown her?"

"No, she might be useful to us. We'll keep her as long as she doesn't get in the way."

"But," Otman said, "when she does, she'll disappear."

Blair sat up; his eyes brightened. "Why don't you go get Bessy and bring her to the galley so she can fix dinner. I'm going to get something."

Otman followed Blair down the stairs. Blair hurried down the hallway to his cabin. Otman stopped at the forward cabin and opened the door. "All right Bessy, you're coming with me. I'm hungry. You're fixing dinner."

Bessy scooted across Arthur, who couldn't move, and tiptoed around Walter, sleeping on the floor.

Jane peered off the top bunk. "Need any help?"

"You're not coming," Otman snapped, pulling Bessy from

the room and locking the door. He pushed Bessy up the stairs and into the galley. "After today's escapades, I'm extra hungry. So if you don't cook enough food, you four won't be eating."

Bessy opened the cupboard and stared at the few cans and a box of pancake mix.

Blair stood at the bathroom sink in the aft cabin and looked into the full medicine cabinet. His finger moved across each bottle and stopped at the label, Halcion. He pulled it out and stuffed it into his pant's pocket. *I won't have any problems from them tonight.* He closed the door and hurried upstairs.

"Otman," he said as he stepped past the galley, into the salon, and motioned Otman over to the table.

Otman stepped up and leaned on the table. "What's up?"

Blair pulled out the bottle, popped its top, and dumped out four pills. He leaned close to Otman. "We're going to put one pill in each of their meals tonight."

"What is it?"

"Sleeping pills. I discovered their value five years ago. Since then, I've always kept some with me." He smirked. "You never know when you might need them."

Otman grinned. "Just like old times. Let me do it." The grin widened, allowing his yellowed teeth to shine.

"Grind each pill and dump the powder into their food when I distract Bessy."

Otman picked up the pills and hurried over to the coffee table where he began smashing the first pill.

Four pots simmered on the stove. Eight empty cans lay piled in the trash can. Bessy stood at the cupboard. *I hope I've cooked enough food.* She looked deep into the shelves. *We'll be out of food by tomorrow.* She glanced over her shoulders, didn't see anyone, and quickly shut the cabinet door. *I can't let Blair know. He'll get rid of Jane and Walter tonight.* Not wanting dinner to scorch, she hurried over to the stove, stirred the contents, and then turned off the burners.

Otman glanced at Bessy as she stepped up to the table and

placed two pots down. He laid a magazine over four grayish-blue piles of powder.

"Dinner," Bessy announced, and hurried back to the galley to grab the other two pots.

Otman was careful in serving his plate and left enough food for the last four to eat. Blair ate slowly while he kept an eye on Bessy, who sat beside him. Connie ate her usual, a dainty serving.

Blair looked at the two carrots remaining on his plate. "Bessy, clear the plates and clean the kitchen. Otman, get four plates and serve our guests their food. Leave Bessy's up here and take the rest downstairs. She can eat hers later, after she's cleaned up the kitchen and their plates."

Bessy gathered the dirty dishes and carried them to the galley. She placed the plates into the sink and began filling it.

Connie wiped her mouth, scooted her chair back, and stood. "I'm going to retire early tonight."

Otman smirked as she hurried down the stairs.

Blair nodded at him and mouthed. "Make sure they each get their medicine." He moved to the galley where he could watch Bessy.

Otman grabbed the plates and slopped food onto each one. He rushed to the coffee table with two plates and sprinkled the drugs onto the food. Then he did the last two plates and served Arthur, Walter, and Jane. He hurried up the stairs, grinning.

After Bessy cleaned the kitchen and the last three plates, she ate and then washed hers.

Arthur looked out one porthole, while Walter looked out the other, hoping to see a rescue boat coming. Jane lay in the upper bunk, her eyelids closed. Outside, the winds and waves were subsiding. The sun hovered above the horizon, casting an orangish glow. Footsteps approached their door. Arthur sat beside Walter on the lower bunk. The door swung open and Bessy was pushed in. The door slammed closed.

Bessy looked up at Jane, who was asleep. "We'd all better

get a little rest before tonight. We're going to need it."

The room glowed in amber, as the sun dropped below the island. The sky was brushed with oranges, yellows, and pinks. At the beach, waves slid up the sand. A few birds stood in the soft breeze looking out over the water. A sandpiper chased along the crest of the wave, pecking at the sand, snatching a bite to eat. The room grew dimmer and dimmer.

Bessy and Arthur lay in the lower bunk and Walter sprawled out on the floor.

The boat became silent, except for the occasional splash against the hull.

CHAPTER FIFTY

An eerie silence lingered in the yacht's sleeping quarters. Connie lay in the center of the bed, staring into the blackness. *Is everyone asleep?* She eased out of bed and pressed her ear to the door, but heard nothing. She gently opened the bedroom door and stuck her head out. The hallway was pitch black.

Down the hallway to her right, she heard soft snoring coming from Blair's cabin.

She drew in a deep breath and slipped out into the hallway, closed her door, and turned left. She tiptoed to Otman's open door and looked in.

Why isn't he snoring? He always snores. She grabbed the doorknob.

If he catches me helping them escape, he'll kill me. She tried to ease the door closed, but it shut with a thud. Connie froze, listened, but heard nothing. Her hands trembled as she released the doorknob.

Hurry. Get them and get out of here. She slid her hand along the darkened wall and made her way up to the forward cabin. Connie wheezed as she groped for the doorknob and opened it. The night sky outlined both porthole windows, but wasn't enough light to identify any of the four inside. She slipped inside and stumbled over someone.

Who's on the floor?

She turned back to the door, checked it to make sure it was unlocked, and eased it closed. Then she flipped the light switch. Walter and Jane lay heaped on the floor. Arthur and Bessy lay snuggled in the lower bunk.

"Wake up," she said as she shook Walter and Jane. But they didn't move. "Get up. We've got to get out of here." She turned and poked Arthur and Bessy. "Come on. We've got to escape. Let's go." They didn't move either. *What's wrong with them?* She grabbed Arthur's wrist and felt a pulse. Then she felt Bessy's. *Why can't I wake them?* She glanced at each person and covered her mouth with both hands. *What did Otman do to you?*

Connie stepped around Walter and Jane. "I'm leaving without you." She turned, eased open the door, and stepped out into the hall. After making sure the door was locked, she crawled up the stairs. Once at the top, she made her way past the galley, and into the salon.

The dim night sky lit up the glass in the back door. She tiptoed outside. A chill ran across her body, as she looked into blackness. *Where's the beach?* Disoriented, she rubbed her eyes, but still couldn't see the shoreline. *Surely it's out that way, behind the boat.* Unable to see clearly, she groped for the handrail, followed it to the ladder, and felt her way down to the dive platform. She slipped into the dinghy, and began to untie it.

But what if the boat's drifting aimlessly and that way's out into the ocean? I'd be lost forever. She shook her head and released the line. *I can't believe it. I can't leave.*

CHAPTER FIFTY-ONE

A gentle breeze swayed the mango trees on the southern tip of Andros. Sandpipers ran along the water's edge. A pelican lowered his head and dove into blue water. It surfaced with a fish in his beak, tilted his head back, and swallowed. The orange sun evolved into fiery yellow, as it rose above the horizon.

The soft morning light trickled into the forward cabin. Arthur twitched and rolled over. He smiled seeing Bessy, but sprang up on his elbows. *Why are we still here and why are Walter and Jane on the floor? Connie didn't come and get us last night.* He turned to Bessy and shook her. "Wake up," he whispered into her ear.

Bessy's eyes fluttered open. A smile stretched across her face. It faded as she noticed his stern look. "What is it?"

"Connie didn't come for us last night. Do you think they caught her?"

Bessy shook her head. "Who knows? Maybe she got scared and backed out. I guess we'll find out soon."

"We've got to start planning an escape," he said as they sat up.

"What are they doing down there?" Bessy asked.

"I don't know." Arthur stretched down and shook them. "Wake up."

Walter opened his eyes. He glanced from Jane to Arthur. "When did she come down here?"

Arthur shrugged and grinned.

Walter raised his eyes at Arthur. "Nothing happened."

Jane stretched and snuggled into Walter as she opened her eyes. "Huh!" she gasped and tried to move away, but the small floor space held her close to Walter. She sprung up on her knees, but was unable to look him in the eye. "Oh, I'm sorry. Last night after going to the bathroom, I tried to climb back into my bunk, but my muscles felt heavy, and I couldn't pull myself up. I gave up and lay down here. I'm sorry."

Walter sat up and found himself putting an arm around Jane. "It's okay. I was so tired that I didn't even know you were there. You didn't bother me."

Arthur swallowed hard as he looked at Bessy. "I think we were drugged last night. Shelly told us that Justin forced her to take sleeping pills. She said she slept for days and never knew it. What day is it?"

"There's no telling," Bessy said.

"Otman," Walter gasped, "is back to his old ways."

"He must have put something in our food last night," Bessy said. "He served our plates. I should have known something was up when he was so eager to help. Helpfulness is not in his nature."

Jane rubbed her head as she looked at Walter. "You're right about those stupors Otman puts people in. I don't remember a thing after I fell asleep."

"We're going to have to be careful about what we eat," Arthur said. "Whoever cooks needs to keep an eye on our food and let us know whether it's safe or not to eat it. There's no telling what other drugs Otman has with him."

"I don't think we have to worry about food. There's not much left," Bessy said. "We've got to come up with an escape plan and fast. If they don't kill us, we'll starve to death."

Jane perked up. "There's canned food on my boat that'll still be good." She looked at Walter. "We stocked up before we left Nassau."

Their cabin door rattled; it was snatched open. Otman stepped inside. "Wake up," his voice trailed off as he looked at each one. "I'm glad to see you all awake. Bessy you're coming with me. The judge wants you to fix breakfast."

"Oh, I love to cook," Jane said, as she stepped up to Otman.

Otman held up his hand and pushed her back. "I'll be back for you later. You're cleaning cabins."

Bessy kissed Arthur, but Otman yanked her away. "Cut that out. I can't stand to see it."

He pulled Bessy out of the room and locked the door.

They listened to the footsteps climbing the steps.

"Listen up," Arthur said. "We've . . ." He heard the heavy footsteps on the stairs again. "He's coming back."

The door swung open and Otman looked at Jane. "You're going with me."

Jane turned and grabbed Walter. She smothered him with kisses.

Otman snatched Jane outside. "If I see that behavior again, I'll-I'll," he slammed the door and locked it. "I'll glue your lips together with super glue."

Arthur listened as the footsteps softened down the hallway.

Walter touched his tingling lips. *I haven't been kissed by a woman in years. . . . That was wonderful.*

"Walter . . . Walter," Arthur said, and nudged his shoulder.

Walter grinned, starry eyed. "Did you see that? Wow."

"Walter?" Arthur chuckled. "Are you all right?"

Walter continued to stare dreamily.

Otman pulled Jane through the hallway to the aft cabin. "You're going to clean the staterooms while Bessy cooks. And you'll start with Blair's cabin."

Jane stepped into the aft cabin. The right side of the queen size bed was turned down. The carpet was clean and the tops of the dressers were spotless. She dragged her fingers across it and found it lint free. Then she stepped into the bathroom. The sink and counter were clean. Towels hung neatly folded, draped across towel rods. Water puddled in the shower. She didn't see any black and gray hairs. *I should have known. I've heard he's meticulous.*

"Stop gawking and start cleaning," Otman huffed. "I don't have all day." He turned and sat on the side of the bed.

Under the bathroom sink, she found Clorox cleaner and a scrub pad. She sprayed the cleaner into the sink and swirled the pad around it. *That's clean.* Within a minute the tub and the head were clean.

When Jane put away the Clorox, she saw a bottle of mirror cleaner and a clean rag. Frost covered the mirror as she depressed the button. In the process of polishing the mirror, the cloth snatched open the medicine cabinet and revealed full shelves, with the exception of one space between two bottles. *I bet he drugged us with whatever used to be there.*

She began reading the bottles. Aspirin, Ibuprofen, Benadryl, mouthwash, toothbrush, toothpaste, deodorant, Ex-lax, alcohol, band-aids, Neosporin, eye-drops, Pepto-Bismol. *He's well prepared. I bet if one of us got sick, he'd let us suffer.*

Jane glanced over her shoulder at Otman. His eyes were buried in Blair's *Yachting World*. *Maybe we can give them some of their own medicine.*

She turned, reached up, and grabbed the bottle of Benadryl and quickly rearranged the spacing of the bottles on the shelf. *I hope no one notices this bottle is missing.* She wiped at the liquid streaks on the mirror and eased the door closed, then glanced back at Otman who was staring at her.

"Well," Otman asked, "what are you waiting on? Are you finished in there?"

Jane nodded her head, and slipped her hand into her pants' pocket.

"Good," Otman said and stood. "Now, straighten up this room."

Jane's hand trembled as she grabbed the pillows, fluffed them, then pulled the sheets up and tidied up the bedspread. Smoothing out the last wrinkle, she smiled. "I'm finished." She brushed her pocket while she followed Otman.

Bessy stood in the kitchen scratching her head as to what she could fix for breakfast. In the nearly-bare refrigerator were three eggs and butter. "Nothing." A box of pancake mix that only needed to have water added, and a few cans of vegetables were all that remained in the cabinet. *It's pancakes today.*

She whipped up a mixing bowl of batter and then placed a large frying pan on the stove. She poured three circles and waited for the bubbles to rise. *What can I do to cause food poisoning?* She looked into the trash can. A clean plastic bag hung inside it. *There's nothing here.* She looked into the fry pan and flipped the pancakes.

Otman led Jane past Connie's cabin, down to his stateroom. He grinned. "Mine's next."

Jane sighed as she stepped inside and saw the sheets lying at the foot of the bed. A black bag sat on the top of the dresser and a suitcase sat against the wall. *So that's the infamous black bag.*

Otman reached behind her, grabbed it, patted it, and smirked.

Jane tugged the sheets back across the bed and tucked them in. Then she pulled the bedspread up.

"That's good enough," Otman said. "Just clean the bathroom and get out." He snugged the black bag under his arm.

Jane stepped into the bathroom and saw hair lying on the floor, sink, and in the shower. *That's disgusting.* She took a deep breath and hurriedly cleaned. As she wiped the mirror, she wondered what was in his medicine cabinet. When she pressed hard on the rag, the mirror slid to the right. *Nothing but a toothbrush, toothpaste and deodorant.* She eased the mirror closed. "I'm finished in here."

"Good. Just one more room," Otman said. "Come on." He pulled her out into the hallway.

Jane opened the last bedroom door. "Connie's asleep, should we go in?"

"She sleeps through anything. Get in there and clean."

Otman pushed her inside. He stared at Connie. *She'll be easy to get rid of. One night while she's sleeping, I'll toss her overboard.* He stepped over to the bed and saw her wrapped up in a blanket. *This is going to be too easy.*

Jane gasped at the three-to-four layers of clothes hiding the carpet. Three suitcases, all unzipped, were full of clothes that spilled over the sides.

Otman laughed. "She's messier than I am."

Jane dropped to her knees beside the first suitcase and pressed the clothes back inside and shut the top. She did the same for the others and then folded the shirts and shorts on top of the dressers and laid them inside the drawers.

Connie moaned and rolled over onto her stomach, pulling the pillow over her head. "Go away."

Jane held her breath as she stepped into the bathroom. "What a mess!" she gasped. Oil covered the sink and counter top. It was littered with cosmetics, brushes, and hair spray. Parts of bathing suits hung from the showerhead, knobs, and towel rods. Towels lay piled under the bathing suits. "Good grief."

Otman stuck his head inside and laughed. He glanced back at Connie who was buried under the pillow. "On second thought, don't waste your time cleaning in here; let's go. Breakfast should be ready and I'm hungry."

CHAPTER FIFTY-TWO

Two stacks of pancakes rose from the platter. Bessy set three plates and forks on the table. She hurried back into the galley, grabbed three glasses of water, and returned. "Breakfast."

Otman's eyes brightened. He turned and hurried to the table. "What, no eggs?"

"You ate them yesterday."

Blair stepped over and looked at the platter. "Bessy, where's my glass of milk?"

"Otman drank it all yesterday."

Otman pulled out a seat and quickly sat and grabbed the platter of pancakes.

"Hold on," Blair said as he snatched the plate away from Otman. "What are you saying? We don't have much food?"

"We have *some* things." Bessy said. "Otman's eating like a horse."

Blair looked at the pancakes. "Well, if we don't have enough food to eat, I know who will be doing without." He glanced at Bessy. "Two uninvited guests."

Blair placed three pancakes on Otman's plate, three on his plate and three on Connie's. He looked at the four remaining pancakes. "That leaves one each for the rest of you."

Otman reached and snatched another pancake from the platter. "I'm hungry."

"I can make more," Bessy said and turned to head for the galley.

"No, Otman's had enough," Blair said, taking the pancake.

"We're going to have to ration our food."

"Maybe not," Bessy said. "There's food stowed on Jane's boat. We could dive and get it."

"Hmm." Blair rubbed his chin. "Maybe we can." He looked over at Otman, who was squeezing the bottle of syrup. "But until we see how much food is salvageable, you're not getting any extras."

Bessy hurried back into the galley and began cleaning.

Connie stepped up to the table, yawned, and stretched. She looked at the pancakes and plopped into the chair. "I can't eat all of these."

Otman reached around Blair, grabbed a pancake, and dropped it into his plate. "Well I can. Thanks."

"Here," Connie said, and dropped one pancake into Blair's. She stretched her arms across the table and picked up a fork.

Blair poured syrup on his pancakes. "Otman, after breakfast, take Walter and Jane out in the dinghy to her sunken boat. We're going to need that food."

Otman mopped a piece of pancake in the syrup. "Why do I have to sit out there in that hot sun?" He stuffed the wad into his mouth.

Blair dug his fork into another bite of pancake. "Because they won't try anything with you there."

"They won't try anything as long as we have Bessy and Arthur. Anyway, where are they going? We're miles from anywhere."

"All right. Just keep an eye on them."

"I'll be glad to. I'll sit up top under the bimini and have Bessy keep me supplied with plenty of iced tea." Otman laughed. "Great life, ain't it? Maybe we could stay longer."

Blair shook his head. "No, we can't risk it. The Bahamian Government is looking for them. As soon as the tides are right this afternoon, we're leaving. We should be in Grand Cayman Island tomorrow afternoon at the latest."

"Uhh!" Bessy wheezed as she stood around the corner in

the galley, listening. *We've only got hours to plan an escape.*

Light reflected off the blades of the knives in the utensil drawer. She eased out a long fillet knife and a butcher knife. *Where can I hide these?* She looked at her waistband. *Not there. I'll end up cutting myself.*

Footsteps approached. *Otman's coming.* She glanced around the galley. Soapsuds filled the sink. The footsteps pounded louder. Her hands trembled as she threw the knives into the dishwater. The footsteps stopped behind her.

Otman grabbed Bessy and jerked her away from the sink. "Back to your room."

Bessy stared into the soapy water. "But I'm not finished washing the dishes."

"You can finish them later." He pulled her downstairs.

CHAPTER FIFTY-THREE

Jane sat on the floor of the dinghy, up against the bow, with a fleeting look at Otman, who sat on the flybridge watching them. Walter rowed. Bessy disappeared below deck, obviously to fetch him something.

Walter pulled leisurely at the oars. "Otman's crazy if he thinks I'm going to hurry. I'm not in a rush to get back in that tiny prison."

Jane relaxed, her head held into the sun. "This is so ro . . ." *Romantic. I almost said that out loud.*

"What?" Walter asked.

"It . . . it's so . . . roomy in this dinghy." She blushed. "Isn't it?" *I don't want to scare him off. I think he's finally starting to like me. If only I'd packed a picnic basket.* She watched Walter's muscles flex with each pull of the paddles. She turned around and looked across the water for the submerged yacht.

"Do you see it?" Walter asked, pulling on the oars again and looking into the clear turquoise water.

"It should be right over there," she said, cupping her hand across her eyes. "Probably not much farther. Try to your left," she said, leading him away from the sleek looking yacht resting on the sandy bottom, twenty feet below to her right.

Walter pulled hard with his right hand, turning the boat left. "I'm from Oregon; I've never dived on a wreck before. What do I do?"

"How long can you hold your breath?"

"Not very long."

Jane's eyes twinkled as his muscles tightened. "I bet you can hold it longer than you give yourself credit for."

Walter pulled harder on the next stroke. *I'll find out.* The dinghy jolted as the oars dug into the water. He sucked in a deep breath and held it. The paddles dug into the water five more times before he breathed. *Wow! I can't believe how long I held my breath.* He tried it again and pulled six times before breathing.

"I see my boat," Jane yelled and pointed behind them.

Walter snapped back from the trance he was in. The paddles hung limp in the water as the boat swerved to the left and slowed. "How'd we miss it?" he asked, looking back at Jane.

"Okay," Jane said with a big smile. "I can't lie. I was enjoying our little freedom and took advantage of you, allowing you to paddle me around like in the movies."

"Really?"

"Sorry."

"Don't be; I saw the boat too, but I was also enjoying being out here with you." He pulled the oars and turned to face her. "I know that kiss this morning was to make Otman mad, but . . ." He stopped and took a deep breath.

"I'm sorry for that, too."

"No, don't be sorry," he stopped and inhaled deeply. "It's hard for me to say this, but," he sighed. "I haven't been kissed in years; it made my heart race."

Jane smiled. "I felt that same sensation when our lips met. A tingle raced through my body."

Walter glanced from Jane's eyes back to Otman. He sat reclined in the captain's seat with his feet on the edge of the flybridge. His hat was pulled low. Walter looked back at Jane. "I misjudged you that first day we met."

"No, it was my fault. Bessy called me earlier and told me that if I wanted to meet a real gentleman, I'd better hurry down to her house before you flew off. I was overzealous. I practi-

210

cally threw myself at you."

"It wasn't *all* your fault. I was definitely cold toward you."

"I understand. You wanted to go home. Who could blame you? Everyone likes to go home, especially after what you've been through."

"Well, Shelly was right. Shelly! With all our troubles, I've forgotten all about her! She's in jail, and we haven't even told Arthur what's going on."

"She'll be fine. Manuel's one of the best criminal lawyers in Palm Beach, so my attorney says. She's probably worrying about us. I'm not sure when the best time to tell Arthur is, but not now. He'll just worry. There's nothing he can do out here."

"You're probably right. It would only make him worry more."

"We'd better get down to the wreck before Otman notices our lack of progress."

Walter grabbed the oars and dug them into the water. Soon the yacht emerged beneath them.

Jane grabbed Bessy's old fins and mask that were forgotten onboard Anchors Away the whole time she was at Southern Retirement Community. Jane struggled to slip the tight fins onto her feet. She wiggled her cramped toes and then pulled the mask down over her face. She picked up the bowline. "I'll dive down and tie this to the boat. Then we won't have to worry about the dinghy drifting away while we're diving."

Walter nodded and pulled the oars into the dinghy, as Jane slipped below the water's surface. He watched her legs alternating kicks. *And to think I almost flew off and missed all of this.* Suddenly he stiffened. An object darted past. "Jane!"

Jane tied off the rope to the back cleat and looked up. The dinghy bobbed above, like a balloon tethered to a string. She froze as a shadow drifted overhead.

Jane held the air in her lungs as she watched the dark, barrel-chested barracuda. *It must be five feet long.* It seemed to smile at her, showing off its razor sharp teeth, as it circled behind her. Her lungs started to ache. She glanced forward to the boat's side where she kept a boat hook. She slowly kicked the fins and moved over to it. With a firm grip, she pulled it out and glanced around for the barracuda. It hovered overhead, motionless.

Walter clenched one oar in his hands and watched air bubbles zigzag to the surface.

Jane's knees bent to spring off the deck, but locked stiff. The barracuda darted to the transom. They stared eye to eye. She pulled the boat hook up in front of her and eased backward. Her lungs searing. She felt the cabin's doorway at her back and with a free hand, pulled herself backward. The fish moved closer. She jabbed the metal hook at the barracuda. It darted to the side. She vanished inside and shut the door behind her.

Walter stared into the water. *Jane's trapped.* He glanced from the cabin door to the forward hatch. But neither opened. *Come on Jane; you can do it. Get out of there.*

CHAPTER FIFTY-FOUR

Walter fidgeted with the oar in his grip as he watched the barracuda circling below. His body trembled. *How long can she hold her breath? She's been down for more than three minutes.* He held his breath, watching and waiting.

Jane looked up from the side window and waved her hands.

Walter rubbed his eyes. "Jane!"

She held up both thumbs.

"She's smiling," he said aloud to himself. "I can't believe it. She's found trapped air down there." He waved back and nodded.

A minute or two passed; he watched as the barracuda darted off after an unsuspecting fish. Walter dropped the oar, slipped his feet into Blair's loose-fitting fins, and pulled the mask over his face. He eased into the water and drew in a deep breath. His head submerged and his feet kicked rapidly, propelling him down.

Jane watched from the window.

He swooped into the cockpit and grabbed the door.

With a smile, Jane held onto the table underwater as the door swung open. She motioned for him to swim in. As he entered, she pushed the door shut and pulled him up into the air pocket. She slipped off the mask. "Can you believe this?"

Walter held his mask and looked around at the two-foot high air pocket. It ran fifteen feet to the front bulkhead. "I guess we'll never know how long I can hold my breath."

Jane smiled as she remembered the bet she made with the

neighbor boy in seventh grade. *Who could hold their breath the longest while they kissed? The first to pull away and breathe was the loser.* Her smile widened remembering that she'd won the bet.

Walter pulled himself into the galley and dived under to a cabinet. He reached in, pulled out his unopened bag of chocolate-chip cookies, and surfaced. "How about a picnic?" He held the bag out of the water and tore into it.

"Oh, I'd love a picnic . . . but, what if they find out?" Jane gasped.

Walter grinned. "Who's going to know? If we took them back, we wouldn't have gotten any. I'll never tell." He shook the water off his hand. Still a little damp, he reached inside the bag and pulled out a handful. "We have to eat something on our picnic."

"Thanks," Jane said, lifted two cookies, then dropped them back in his hand. "I'll be right back." She repositioned the mask, dove down, opened the refrigerator, and pulled out the bottle of Cabernet Sauvignon from the door. Then she pulled open the utensil drawer and grabbed the corkscrew. Water splashed as she surfaced. "A picnic without wine would be terrible."

Walter laughed.

Jane screwed the corkscrew into the bottle and pulled out the cork. "It's a great vintage, 1997," she laughed, "but we'll have to drink it from the bottle."

"Who'd have thought a day of captivity would turn into a day of pleasure?" Walter handed her two cookies.

After a sip each, Jane pushed the cork back into its neck. She released it and it bobbed around while they chewed another cookie.

Otman looked at his watch and then tilted his hat up as he looked across the water to the dinghy. *There must be a lot of food on that boat.* He rubbed his hands together. *We're going to eat good today.* He took a swig of tea and watched to see what they would bring up.

Thirty seconds passed, but no one surfaced. Otman twitched in the seat. *How long does it take to swim up with food?* His eyes burned as he stared without blinking. *Where are they?* The glass clunked on the dash as he set it down and continued scanning the water. The air warmed around him, as he turned his attention to shore. The beach was empty.

"Judge," he yelled climbing down the stairs. "Judge!"

Walter took another sip from the bottle. "Is this a dry wine or wet?"

"It's definitely wet . . . and fruity, black cherry I think." Jane smiled.

Walter looked into the bag of chocolate cookies. "We'd best start gathering the groceries." He rolled up the half-eaten bag and stuffed it on top of the dry microwave, which sat on a shelf above the submerged stove. He swallowed, pulled on the mask, and dived under.

Jane corked the bottle and set it beside the microwave. She stuck her hand behind the counter and pulled out a large plastic garbage bag.

Walter surfaced, cradling cans in his arm. "I'll swim these up."

"Wait, we'll put it in a bag and only have to make one trip."

"I like the way you think." Walter placed the cans inside it and submerged for another load.

Blair and Otman stood on the flybridge staring at the empty dinghy. "Otman, swim out there and check it out."

"Maybe we've missed them when they surfaced."

Blair's eyes narrowed. "What? We've been staring out there for more than ten minutes and no one's surfaced. Get out there."

"B-but, there are sharks and other things out there. I'm going to wait." Otman twitched, wondering what Blair would do if he allowed them to slip away.

"Jane, we better put the rest of that wine in the frig. We wouldn't want it to spoil," Walter teased.

Jane laughed, "Maybe we should put a message in it and throw it overboard. Someone might find it and rescue us." She tied a knot in the garbage bag. "I've enjoyed our little picnic, but we'd better go."

"What? A picnic without a kiss?"

Jane released the doorknob as Walter pulled her close and kissed her.

Walter smiled as he positioned the mask on his face. He swam out after Jane, pulling the bag behind him. Their heads broke the surface.

"There they are," Blair yelled and pointed.

Jane pulled herself up and into the dinghy. Then she reached out, grabbed the plastic bag, and pulled. "I can't lift it," she grunted.

Walter pulled himself over the rubber tube and slid into the boat's bottom. He yanked off the fins and laid his mask down. Then he grabbed the bag and pulled. "It's full of water. We'll never lift it." He punched small holes into the side of the bag and gradually lifted. The ocean flowed out of the bag, like a watering can.

"Uh oh, don't look now," Jane said, "but we've drawn a crowd. I guess we got carried away with our underwater picnic. We'd better get back to the boat. And remember, don't say anything about Shelly."

CHAPTER FIFTY-FIVE

Detective Newberry sat in his small cubical. Stacks of paper covered his desk. He stared at the newly delivered toxicology report on Justin Roble. The information indicated high levels of Benzodiazepine. "So, Justin had an excessive amount of a controlled substance in his system; sleeping pills, that's how Shelly overpowered Justin."

He moved over to the file cabinet, pulled out Shelly Roble's file, thumbed through the pages, and stopped at the first interview. He glanced at Shelly's answers. *Darn, there's no drug name mentioned.*

He grabbed the phonebook, flipped through the yellow pages until he found pharmacies, then started circling names of stores closest to Shelly's home address. Phone in hand, he dialed the first store.

"Hello, this is Detective Newberry. I'd like to speak with one of the pharmacists, please." Soft music filled the silence. "Hello, Cathy, this is Detective Newberry. I'm working on a murder case. Would you check your records and see if Shelly Roble had a prescription for sleeping pills filled within the last few months? . . . Yes, ma'am. I'll wait." He listened to music for almost a minute before being told Shelly wasn't a customer of theirs.

Newberry dialed nine more pharmacies and then heard, "Detective, Shelly Roble had a prescription for a sleeping pill called in from her doctor approximately three weeks ago."

"Does that medicine have Benzodiazepine in it?"

"Yes sir."

He looked at the toxicology report.

"Detective, that prescription was for Halcion."

"What strengths does it come in?"

"It comes in two different strengths, .125 mg. and .25 mg. Shelly's prescription was for the higher dosage."

Newberry smiled and thanked her. He hung up, looked at the toxicology report, and wrote: Benzodiazepine is found in sleeping pills, aka Halcion. *She claimed she was drugged, but in fact, she was the one that drugged Justin. Clever.*

CHAPTER FIFTY-SIX

Jane grabbed the dive platform. Walter pulled the oars into the dinghy and laid them on the floor. Otman and Blair stood on the aft deck glaring down at them.

"What kept you so long?" Otman asked, looking at his watch. "It's almost lunch time."

"Well," Walter said. "We um," he glanced at Jane, unable to contain the grin. "We were trapped inside the cabin by a man-eating barracuda. Thank goodness there was an air pocket, and we were able to breathe until that thing left us alone."

"I haven't seen any barracudas." Otman stood rigid, scanning the water.

"You can go out there and see for yourself," Jane said. "Walter saw it coming; he grabbed me, and pushed me into the cabin just as it darted toward us," she lied, covering their delay. "It was at least five-feet long."

"Otman, she's pulling your leg." Blair turned and looked down at them. "Barracudas don't attack people *unless* they're holding a fish or wearing something reflective. And they *aren't* wearing anything shiny."

"Yeah, well what do you call these?" Walter pulled out two cans, one in each hand, and held them up. The sun reflected off the lids and blinded Otman.

"Otman," Blair shouted, "get that food up here. Wash them off and lock them in their cabin."

Walter climbed out of the dinghy and handed the bag of food up to Otman.

"Is this all?" Otman asked, looking inside. "There's not much here. Where's the rest of the food?"

"Most of it was spoiled," Jane said as she climbed out of the dinghy. *Well, except the wine and cookies.* She smirked.

Otman gave her a doubtful look.

"If you don't believe me, go out there and see for yourself."

"Would you like to go?" Walter asked. "I'll take you. I'd rather do that than be locked in that small room."

"Get up here," Otman snapped. "You're not going anywhere."

Oil glistened off Connie as she lay on cushions on the flybridge. Under her towel lay a folded shirt and shorts. Her ears twitched, listening.

I wonder if while they're all downstairs, I could climb over the back and into the dinghy and slip away. She raised her head and peered down at the back as they went inside.

How far could I paddle before they noticed I was missing and begin to look for me? She sat up, stood, and looked down at the dinghy.

I could jump overboard. She looked at her dry clothes and shook her head. She noticed her legs shaking and her breathing grew shallow.

I need a better plan. If they catch me leaving, I'm dead. Maybe I should try to help the others again. Or, I could take sides with Blair. He'll make sure no harm comes to me. She lay back down on the towel and closed her eyes.

Otman escorted Walter and Jane downstairs and shoved them into their cabin. "Think of me as a barracuda. Let's see how long you like staying in there." Otman slammed the door.

Walter and Jane grinned as they looked at Bessy and Arthur sitting up in bed. Cards lay in front of them.

"Someone got under Otman's skin," Arthur said.

"Yeah, and we had a great time," Jane said, gazing into Walter's eyes.

"An underwater picnic," Walter murmured. He wrapped his

arms around her and pulled her in tight.

"And with all the amenities anyone could want," Jane said, her eyes twinkling.

After changing out of their wet clothes, they sat on the bed filling Bessy and Arthur in on all the details.

Bessy nudged Arthur in his ribs and grinned. "See!"

"I hate to be the one to spoil a good time," Arthur said, "but, during breakfast, Bessy overheard Blair say that we were leaving today and by tomorrow, we should be in the Cayman Islands. We're running out of chances to escape before they get rid of us."

"And I believe," Bessy said, "they'll start dumping bodies before they arrive in the Cayman Islands."

"Maybe," Walter said, "we should try getting Connie to help again."

"We might not need to," Jane said as she stood stretching for the top bunk.

They all watched as she pulled out a medicine bottle. She held it out. "I took this from Blair's medicine cabinet while I cleaned his room. Maybe we could give them some of their own medicine." She looked at Bessy. "When you cook lunch for them, you could put this Benadryl into their food. It's not as powerful as some drugs Otman uses, but with these quantities, it'll make them sleepy. All you'd have to do is keep cleaning in the galley until they fall asleep. Then you can slip downstairs and let us out."

Walter looked at the bottle. "Jane, you're conniving. I like that."

Jane grinned from ear to ear. "I'm going to love binding their bodies with duck tape. They'll look like mummies when I'm through with them."

Arthur stared at Jane. *I'm glad she's on our side.*

Bessy took the bottle, opened it, and dumped out the pills. "Three, four, six, there's only nine pills."

They all looked into Bessy's palm.

221

"How many should I give them?" Bessy asked.

"All of them," Jane said.

"Yeah," Walter added, "I hope they'll sleep until we get them back to the Bahamian authorities, but if they don't, I'd be glad to give Otman one of his injections as well. You know, jab the needle deep into his arm." He chuckled, "I might even have to jab it into him a couple of times for practice."

Bessy stood up. "I'd like to use that frying pan on Harry." She swatted her empty hand through the air. "I'd like to give him something that he'll remember me by for a long time." She laughed. "For a real long time."

The door rattled and swung open. Bessy shoved the bottle under the mattress and clutched the pills.

Otman stood in the doorway. "Bessy, its lunch time." He grinned. "And you're cooking." He reached in and grabbed her. She balled her hand around the pills as she was pulled from the cabin.

CHAPTER FIFTY-SEVEN

Bessy shoved her hand into her pocket, as Otman pushed her into the galley. Bessy's face warmed, as she stepped to the sink. Carefully, she stuck her hand into the cloudy water and felt for the knives. *Where are they?*

She pulled the stopper and the water drained. *Who put away the knives?* She crept over to the drawer and quietly slid it open.

"Looking for something?" Blair asked, leaning up against the doorway.

Bessy wheeled around. "Uh, no. I was just making sure everything was put away from breakfast."

"You mean like these knives?" he asked, and pulled his hand from behind the wall, holding a box. "I think I'd better keep these. I don't want you tempted to do something stupid. After all, we're miles from nowhere."

Bessy turned and pushed the drawer closed. *He took the butter knives as well. I hope these pills knock him out cold.*

"I'm keeping my eye on you." Blair stood, arms crossed, and leaned in the doorway.

Bessy glanced away from him and moved to the cupboard. She reached in and pulled out the first four cans. *They'll have to eat whatever I fix.* She took a deep breath. *Calm down. Fix something they'll eat a lot of.*

Blair eased from the galley doorway and into the salon where Otman sat on the couch. "Scoot over; I want to show you something."

The boat grew quiet except for the soft drone of the air-conditioner. Blair gathered his thoughts as he looked at the paper navigational charts lying on the coffee table. His laptop showed the charted plot of their route, from the bottom of Andros, around Cuba, past Jamaica, and finally Grand Cayman Island. "Listen," Blair said, "I've been studying these charts and tide tables. The tide will be high early this afternoon allowing safe passage across this area down here." Blair pointed to the blue, shallow Great Bahama Bank, below the Tongue of the Ocean. "We won't have to worry about the shifting sand shoals." He dragged his finger across the shoals to the deep water off Cuba. "Once we get here, we'll never have to worry about the water depth again until we motor into Georgetown, Grand Cayman Island."

"I'm tasting that seafood already," Otman said, while rubbing his stomach. "First thing I'm going to do is order two fat, juicy lobsters."

Blair reached into his pocket and pulled out an orange medicine bottle. "And this is where Walter and Jane are going to be leaving us." He dumped out four pills into the table. "We're going to do the same thing as last night. Put these into their food. Once they're asleep, we'll be able to separate them without a fight."

Otman grinned and picked up the pills. "I know exactly what to do." He bounced them in his palm and chuckled. "I've got that magical touch, don't I?"

"Absolutely. Once they are asleep, you're going to give Walter and Jane each an injection. We don't want them waking up and becoming survivors, do we?"

"No witnesses, no testimonies." Otman's grin widened. "And what about Connie? Is this where she gets off too?"

"Maybe we should keep her a little longer. We don't want a pile of bodies in any one place." Blair closed his eyes. *I'm not sure I want to get rid of Connie yet. She's good looking and has money.*

"Judge, are you all right?" Otman asked.

Blair's eyes opened. "Sure, I was just thinking."

CHAPTER FIFTY-EIGHT

Shelly paced from one wall to the other; it only took three steps each way. Endless hours ticked away. She turned her head and looked out the bars. She drew in another deep breath and sighed. *Why haven't I heard from Dad? Surely they are back from the Bahamas by now. Why hasn't he come to see me?* She wiped her damp, red eyes with the back of her hand.

She stepped over to the bed and collapsed. Unable to keep the tears in check, they streamed down her cheeks. *I knew it. I just knew it. Blair and Otman have found them. I can feel it.* Her once-soft whimpers swelled to sobs. She pulled the pillow over her head. *Dad's not getting away this time. I'm all alone. I'm going to be convicted of killing Justin. I didn't do it!* A moan of despair emitted from the tear-damp pillow.

CHAPTER FIFTY-NINE

The sun beat down on the Hatteras. One-to-two foot waves rolled past the yacht. Connie stood on the aft deck, looking down at the dinghy and then at the beach. *Maybe I should eat a good meal before slipping away. It might be hours before I'm rescued.*

"What are you thinking?" Blair asked as he stepped to the railing beside her. "Lying out on that beach?"

"Uh . . . yes," she lied.

"Maybe you'll let me to take you to one of the finest in Grand Cayman. Would you like that?"

"Really?" Connie asked. She took a deep breath. "You want to take me to the beach?"

"Sure. Why wouldn't I?"

"I don't know." She shrugged her shoulders. "I thought you wanted to get rid of me."

"Not me."

"Otman doesn't like me. He'd just as soon I'd disappear."

"That's just Otman. He doesn't trust people. He's always looking over his shoulder."

Arthur looked out the porthole. The sky was blue, not a cloud in the sky. Small waves lapped at the shore. "It's a perfect day for an escape. Once we tie them up, we'll take them straight to Nassau and . . ."

Walter and Jane heard nothing that Arthur said. They lay on their sides in the top bunk, gazing in each other's eyes.

"Walter," Jane asked, "once we're free, what are your

plans?"

"I was wondering if your offer to show me around Palm Beach still exists. We'd have a good time. Wouldn't we?"

Jane reached out and brushed a speck off his cheek. "We would. Before we go back, I'd still like to show you that island in the Exumas. We could fly down there."

"Flying sounds good to me. I'll pay for both rooms. Maybe we could stay for a few days. I'd like to eat more of their conch specialties."

"I'm sure that could be arranged as well as finding a local to take us out to pick up conch. He'll clean it and cook it. You'll never get it any fresher than that." Jane rolled into Walter and kissed him. "You better plan to stay for a long time." She grinned. "It might take a lifetime."

Walter leaned into her and they kissed again.

Arthur listened as he glanced from the window to them and back. *Bessy would love to hear this.*

Bessy stood in the galley in front of three plates. Otman's plate contained more than the others. Blair's was in the middle with an ample amount. Connie's plate held the least, a scoop of each: green beans, potatoes, corn, and a small serving of canned white chicken with Alfredo sauce.

Beads of perspiration stood on Bessy's forehead. She held her breath and separated the first capsule. *I hope this Benadryl doesn't have a taste.* White powder fell across Otman's plate. The powder dissolved into the food. After dumping four capsules on Otman's, she sprinkled three on Blair's plate of food and two onto Connie's. Anxiety raced through her body as she placed each plate on the table. *It won't be long now.*

Blair and Connie stepped inside as Bessy yelled, "Lunch."

While the three ate, and in between Bessy bring me this and that, she dished up four more plates.

Otman scrapped his plate clean. He leaned into Blair. "I'm ready," he whispered into his ear.

Blair, who was eating slower to keep pace with Connie, looked at Otman's empty plate. "Bessy," he called, and motioned for Otman to leave.

"Yes," Bessy answered, stepping up to the table.

Otman dabbed his lips, stood, and hurried off.

"Have a seat." Blair pointed to the chair Otman just vacated. "We haven't spoken in a while."

Bessy watched Otman disappear around the corner. *What's he up to? He never leaves before all of the food's gone.*

Otman stomped on the stairs as if he were going down, but turned and sneaked into the galley. He pulled out the four pills and smashed them into powder. Then he sprinkled the powder across their food. His grin widened as he picked up three plates and eased downstairs.

He fumbled with the door, careful not to spill the food. The door opened. Walter, Jane, and Arthur all looked at Otman from their bunks.

"Well, is anyone hungry?"

After Otman placed the plates on the lower bunk, Arthur swung his feet to the floor and distributed the plates.

"Enjoy." Otman hurried from the cabin, locked the door, and stood outside snickering. *That was too easy.* He patted his pockets. *I'm ready for the second round.*

CHAPTER SIXTY

Swells gently rocked the yacht. The salon was quiet. Bessy fidgeted in the chair and looked at Blair. "Harry, what was it that you wanted to talk about?" She looked from him to Connie, who was nibbling a bite of chicken.

"We'll talk, once I'm finished eating." He chewed and washed it all down with a gulp of water. He smiled. "I'm almost done." He pushed the last bite of green beans on his fork, then swallowed.

Bessy looked behind her. *Where'd Otman go?*

"Bessy, would you relax, you're making me nervous," Blair said.

"I'm sorry, but I'm thinking about all of those dishes that I've got to wash," she lied. *What's Otman up to?*

"Well, stop it." He lifted the last slice of potato to his mouth and chewed. "They'll be waiting for you when we're through talking. Connie, would you get Bessy's plate of food?"

Connie did a double take, but did as asked and hurried back with it.

Bessy stared at the food and remembered last night. *Otman must have put something in it.*

"Well," Blair asked, staring between her and the plate of food, "aren't you going to eat?"

Oh no. I was right. She glanced to Blair. "I'm not hungry. I sampled as I cooked." She rubbed her stomach.

Otman took the others their food. Stay calm. Don't panic. She drew in a long breath. *I hope they haven't eaten it.*

"Don't waste food," Connie said. "People go hungry every

day."

Bessy stared at her. "I know, but I've already had plenty. Why don't you eat mine." Bessy pushed the plate in front of Connie. "Really, I'm not hungry."

Blair twitched in his seat and intercepted the plate. "She's had plenty. Haven't you?" he asked, looking at Connie.

"Yes. If I eat anymore, I won't look good in my swim suit."

Bessy held her stomach and remembered Arthur's words when he was in Southern Retirement, "If you are given medicine, drink plenty of water to flush it from your body." *I have to get down there and make them drink water.* She looked at Connie and Blair. *We've all drugged each other. Which of us will fall asleep first?*

CHAPTER SIXTY-ONE

Manuel sat behind his desk. The office was quiet as he read the latest discovery handed to him by Douglas, who sat across from him. Manuel flipped the next page over. A half-eaten sandwich lay in its wrapper on the edge of his desk. A hot cup of coffee steamed next to the sandwich. The digital clock on the credenza showed 1:10.

"Look Manuel," Douglas said, "I know you're an excellent attorney, but this time your client is guilty. The DNA of those rabbit hairs found beside Justin's body, match those found at Bessy's side door and in the kitchen. With this and Shelly's blood-splattered pocketbook, it's undisputable that she was present at Justin's death. She's guilty."

Manuel said nothing. He stared at the police photos showing the exact location of the hair at the murder scene and the hair found at two locations at Bessy's house: On the welcome mat at the side door and on the floor beside the kitchen sink.

"And take a look at this discovery of Newberry's," Douglas said. "Shelly filled a prescription for Halcion. They're sleeping pills."

Manuel grabbed the document and began to read.

"She led him sleepwalking straight to his death. She's a heartless woman." He stood and looked straight into Manuel's eyes. "I'm going to make sure justice is served. She's never going to be a free woman again. Never. The State has Justin's killer." He stormed out.

Manuel leaned back in his chair and stared at the ceiling. *Shelly has to plead temporary insanity, or maybe, self defense.*

CHAPTER SIXTY-TWO

Seagulls circled the yacht in the early afternoon sun, squawking for a handout. After numerous passes, they flew back toward shore and landed at the water's edge, watching the waves and the yacht.

Bessy stood at the sink slowly swirling the dishrag across plates. *Blair and Otman should be asleep by now.* She grinned, but it faded. *Did Arthur, Walter, and Jane eat lunch? If so, how am I going to tie up everyone?*

Bessy looked at the ceiling as she heard Connie moving around on the flybridge. *She definitely didn't eat enough, but she won't be a problem. If Arthur and Walter ate their food and can't help me, I could get her to help me tie up Harry and Otman.* Bessy peered from the galley into the salon.

Otman was stretched out on the couch, his eyes closed. Blair blinked rapidly. He stood and shook off the dreariness. "Bessy, you need to hurry or you'll have to finish cleaning later."

Bessy ducked back inside the galley. "Not much longer." *I've got to get downstairs and help them. We've got to escape now, before it's too late.* She stepped back and peered around the wall. Blair dropped into the recliner.

Otman stretched and yawned. *I'm tired. I need a moment's rest before I get rid of Walter and Jane.* He pointed his toes and reached far over his head.

"Otman," Blair asked, "do you think they're asleep?"

"Give it a little longer," he said, yawning.

Bessy pulled back from the corner. *It's now or never.* She

held her breath as she tiptoed to the bottom of the stairs, and gently opened the door.

Arthur, Walter, and Jane stood waiting.

Bessy smiled, seeing their uneaten food. "Shhhh," she whispered, "they're almost asleep. Come on." They eased up the stairs with Bessy in the lead. Arthur was next, followed by Walter and Jane. Bessy knelt on the top step and looked into the salon. Blair looked at his watch. She crawled across to the pilothouse. Arthur followed at her feet.

"Bessy!" Blair hollered.

They all froze.

Blair stared toward the hallway. "Bessy, what's taking you so long? You said ten minutes ago that you were almost finished cleaning."

Bessy rose from the floor and bounced into view. "Yes sir," she answered. "I've got one pot left and then all I've got to do is wipe down the counter. Give me one more minute, then the kitchen will be clean."

Darn. Arthur held his breath. *He's not asleep.*

Blair checked his watch again. "One minute." He stared her way.

Bessy stepped back into the galley and turned on the water. It splashed into the sink. "Change of plans," she whispered to Arthur. "The drugs aren't working fast enough. You'll have to slip off the boat and go get help. If we're unable to escape, you keep going. You're our only hope. Whatever happens here, happens. Don't you dare come back. We're counting on you. I love you. Now hurry."

Walter and Jane peered from the stairs and waited.

The water continued to splash into the sink. Arthur kissed Bessy. "I love you, too." He turned and crawled to the pilothouse.

Bessy motioned and mouthed to Walter and Jane, "Go back downstairs and find something to use against them." As she watched them disappear, she stepped out of the galley into the salon. "I think Connie's calling me," she lied to Blair. "I'll be right back. I'm through cleaning."

"Tell her to get whatever she needs herself," he said, and stood. "You're going downstairs. . . . Otman," Blair said, kicking the size fifteen shoes off the couch.

"Huh?" Otman answered, stretching and rubbing at his eyes.

Bessy ignored Blair and hurried to the ladder leading up to the flybridge. She turned to see Arthur looking at her. "Hurry," she mouthed. She climbed the ladder, pushed the hatch open, making as much noise as possible, and climbed out.

It was perfect timing as Arthur slid the door shut and slipped off the deck. He hung from the side of the boat and looked down at his toes, which tipped the water's surface. *I hope I don't make a big splash.*

Bessy climbed out on the flybridge.

Walter and Jane heard footsteps above as they disappeared into Otman's room. "Find that black bag," Walter whispered.

"Bessy," Blair yelled, "get back down here."

Bessy stepped over to Connie who was stretched out on cushions. Oil glistened from her body. "Connie, what do you need?" She could hear Blair climbing the ladder.

Arthur pointed his toes, sucked in three deep breaths, closed his eyes, and let go. He dropped his arms to his sides and entered the water like an arrow.

Bessy cringed as a sploosh sounded.

Connie raised her head just off the cushion. "What was that?"

Bessy looked overboard to see Arthur swimming toward shore. "Must have been a fish jumping. I don't see anything."

Connie lay her head back down.

Blair's head popped above the hatch. "Bessy, get down here, now! Connie, if you need anything, get it yourself."

"Bessy, before you go back down, will you rub some oil on my back. I can't reach it."

"Sure," Bessy said, and grabbed the bottle.

"Bessy, put that bottle down and get over here." Blair's face reddened.

Bessy kept an eye on Blair, while she squirted oil on Connie's back and began rubbing it in.

As Blair climbed the next rung, Bessy turned the bottle toward him and squeezed. Oil sprayed across the floor and sprayed his clothes.

"You're going to wish you hadn't done that," Blair yelled. He climbed down the ladder. "Otman!"

Connie placed her sunglasses on her face. "I can't understand what all the fuss is about." A seagull swooped over the yacht and circled behind her. She turned to watch it dip its beak into the water. "What?" she gasped, looking toward shore. "Judge! Arthur's swimming away."

"Otman!" Blair yelled, "they're escaping." Blair ducked below the hatch and slammed it closed.

Bessy grabbed Connie. "You've got to help us escape. They're going to kill us." Bessy reached out and grabbed the hatch. Her oily fingers slipped off.

Connie's mouth gaped open; she stared at Arthur.

Downstairs in Otman's room, Jane ripped into the black bag and dumped its contents onto the bed. Two syringes plopped on the bed. "Walter, catch," she said as she tossed a syringe to him. "Let's go help Bessy."

They dashed out of the room and to the stairs.

Otman stood at the top grinning. "Walter, thanks for bringing me your medicine. Come on up here."

Walter held out his other hand and blocked Jane from climbing the stairs. "Jane, be careful. Jab him anywhere with the syringe and press the plunger. Whatever's in these things will probably kill him. Stay behind me."

Blair stepped around Otman and grabbed a chair from the salon's table. "Here Otman," he said, handing him the chair. "Hold it in front of you."

Walter and Jane backed down the hallway as the chair pressed toward them. "Stay back," Walter yelled.

Otman lumbered down the stairs, batting the sleepiness from his eyes.

Jane slipped into Otman's cabin and grabbed Walter. "In here."

Walter jumped inside as Jane slammed the door and locked it. He rushed over to the porthole. "I see Arthur. He's getting close to shore. They'll never catch him now."

Jane grabbed Walter and hugged him. "We're in big trouble." She kissed him. "I just wanted to let you know I haven't felt this way about another man since my husband died. I wish everything had turned out differently."

Walter pulled her tighter. "Jane," he touched her soft cheek, "I've enjoyed these last few days with you. I don't want to go back to Oregon. I want to stay in West Palm Beach and be with you." He pulled her head close to his and kissed her.

The door splintered. Otman stood squared-shoulder in the doorway. "Well, well, well. All good things must come to an end."

Walter reached for the lamp, but it didn't budge.

Jane placed her hand on Walter's. "Everything on a boat's bolted down so it doesn't move underway."

The chair came at Walter. Its legs pinned him against Jane. Otman laughed. "Now what are you going to do?"

Blair stepped around Otman with his chair drawn back, ready to swing it into them. "Drop the syringes."

The syringes fell to the floor.

Otman tossed the chair onto the bed, grabbed Walter, and pulled him away from Jane. Blair grabbed Jane and pulled her into the hallway.

Jane's face drooped.

"Just like Romeo," Otman said as he pulled out a syringe from his pocket and stuck it into Walter's arm. "Never to be together again." Walter fell limp onto the floor. Otman dashed up the stairs. Together, he and Blair manhandled Jane up onto the flybridge.

"Leave her alone," Bessy yelled, as she plowed into Blair, knocking him backward.

Otman wrapped one arm around Jane's neck and grabbed Bessy with the other hand. "Now that's no way to treat your ex."

Bessy swung wildly. Her blows bounced off Otman's muscular frame.

Blair caught his balance, charged Bessy, knocking her to the floor. Grabbing her by the hair, he twisted her head, making her watch Jane.

Otman dragged Jane to the flybridge's edge and held her up.

"See what you've caused," Blair said. He looked up at Otman. "If Arthur doesn't come back, give it to her."

Jane's eyes grew large. "W-what ar-re you doing?"

"Arthur," Otman yelled as Arthur stepped out of the water and up onto the beach. Otman yawned as his eyes half closed. He shook it off.

"H-e-l-p!" Jane squealed, as her feet swung over the side.

Arthur cringed and swung around. "Jane," he gasped. Water dripped from his body.

Otman laughed as he dug his hand into his pocket and pulled out a syringe. "Good thing Blair insists that I always carry a couple of these with me at all times," he said to Jane.

"Oh!" Connie shrieked. Her body trembled as she watched the needle stop an inch away from Jane's neck. Her eyes widened. *He's going to kill her.* She didn't move.

Arthur froze as he stared at Jane. "No!" he screamed. "Don't do it." He raced into the water, but stopped. Otman's warning rang in his ear. *Try escaping, you'll never do it again.* Arthur sputtered water out of his mouth. He turned and looked at the shore. It was now or never. *We're as good as dead, anyway.* He turned away. *I'm sorry, Jane.* He took a step up on the beach.

Otman's face reddened as he lifted Jane further away from the boat. He pressed the needle to her skin.

The prick sent shivers up her spine. "Arthur!"

CHAPTER SIXTY-THREE

Otman's adrenaline surged, chasing away the drowsiness. Muscles bulged as he clasped Jane's wrists in one hand and dangled her further over the side. Her feet kicked wildly as she tried to regain her footing. The water below was crystal clear. She glanced at a large orange starfish on the sandy bottom.

Connie jolted backward away from Otman. *I can't watch her die.* She hid her face.

Arthur ran up to shore. His lungs heaved.

"A-R-T-H-U-R . . . S-T-O-P!" Otman thundered

Arthur's head jerked around to see Otman's grin widen.

"I didn't think you wanted to watch."

"No! Don't!" Arthur hollered, as he plunged back into the water. He splashed deeper as he kept an eye on Otman and Jane.

Otman looked at Blair. "He's coming back."

Connie leaned over to Bessy. "What were you all thinking? Otman's dangerous. I thought Jane was going overboard."

Jane shook violently, gasping short raspy breaths.

"Connie, help us," Bessy whispered.

Connie shook her head and turned away.

Blair pulled Bessy to her feet. "I knew something like this was going to happen. When Arthur gets back, inject him; Jane, too. We'll tie up Bessy. Then take everyone but Bessy up that inlet and hide their bodies where no one will see them. By then, it'll be high tide and we can leave."

"Arthur!" Bessy screamed. "Run!"

Arthur splashed to a stop. *Bessy said, whatever happens*

here, happens. Don't come back. He turned and swam back to shore, then ran north on the beach. He didn't look back.

"Arthur!" Otman yelled.

Blair knocked Bessy to the floor. "Inject Jane."

Connie shook violently in the corner, her face buried in her hands.

"Ahhhhh!" Jane screamed as the needle dug into her skin. The sky and water blurred as Jane's eyes closed.

Otman pulled her back into the flybridge and dropped her on the floor.

"We're in the middle of nowhere," Blair said to Bessy. "By the time Arthur finds help, we'll be long gone. And Jane and Walter's bodies will have been picked over by the birds and wild animals."

"Let's just dump the bodies here." Otman started lifting Jane's body.

"We can't throw them overboard here; they might wash right up on the beach. Any boat or plane passing by would spot them. Remember, leave no witnesses. It's hard for any court to get a conviction without a body. No bodies, no evidence, no trial."

Otman's adrenaline slowed as he stepped into his cabin. Inside, he bent over, picked up the fallen syringes, and laid them on the dresser. With a grunt, he lifted Walter over his shoulder and lugged him up the stairs. He went straight for the aft deck and dropped Walter on it. Then he lumbered through the cabin and climbed the ladder to the flybridge where he and Blair bound Bessy. He carried her to the forward cabin.

Soon, Walter and Jane lay in the front of the dinghy as Otman climbed in. "I'll be right back."

"Make it quick," Blair said.

The sun beat down on Otman's sweaty body. He yawned as he dug the paddles into the water and pulled. His body slumped as he strained with the oars. The inlet lay just ahead. Otman, now close to shore, rolled out of the dinghy and splashed water into his face. *Wake up.* He grabbed the bow rope of the dinghy and plowed into the shin-deep inlet. He stretched. *Man, I'm tired.*

Otman wobbled and grabbed the rope tighter as wooziness flushed over him. He batted his eyes as a haze filled the sky. The dinghy whiplashed behind him in the surf.

Ahead were sandbars with water swirling around them. The air grew hotter. His skin radiated from the sun's rays. Water eddied at his feet as it swept inland. He dropped to his knees as his leg muscles began to quiver. *This is far enough. I'm exhausted.*

He glanced around. A flock of birds looked at him and then continued washing their feathers with salt water. Beaches and small sand dunes stretched as far as the eye could see. He looked again to the east, but couldn't see Anchors Away. *This place should be perfect. No one will ever find their carcasses here.*

He stood, grabbed Jane's limp body, and pulled her out. She splashed into the water. He dragged her up on the sand and dropped her. Then he returned for Walter, wrestled him out, lugged him over to Jane, and dropped him. Water lapped at Walter's feet. Otman bent over and grabbed their wrists. Each had a weak pulse.

"Hmm," Otman mumbled and then laughed. He dropped Jane's hand onto Walter's. "Together forever," and he chuckled, falling to his knees. He tried to stand, but his muscles felt like jelly. His smile faded as he tried again. *What's wrong with me?* He rubbed his blurry eyes, stretched weakly, and yawned. *Why am I so tired?* He crawled to the dinghy, rolled over its side and sprawled in the bottom. He tried to lift his head, but his eyes fluttered closed. His breathing slowed. *I-I can't wake-up.*

CHAPTER SIXTY-FOUR

The trade winds blew at fifteen miles per hour. Waves washed higher onto the beach as a few white-capped waves appeared across the ocean. Arthur pressed ahead. His swimsuit dried as it flapped in the breeze. He looked around and noticed fewer birds flying.

Why didn't those pills put Otman and Blair to sleep? He turned and looked behind. The yacht was no longer on the horizon.

He wiped his forehead and looked for shade. *What did Otman do to Walter and Jane?*

High on the beach, a large shrub cast a small shadow across the sand. He hurried up to it and crawled into the shade. As far as he could see to the north, only sand, shrubs, and a few trees dotted the horizon. *How much further before I find help?*

A cloud drifted overhead casting its shadow across the island. "What a relief." Arthur pulled himself back to his feet and jogged off. His feet kicked up sand, leaving pockmarks behind.

The cloud sailed past, revealing the sun in the western sky. *It must be close to five o'clock.*

As he rounded a bend, he saw a rooftop in the distance surrounded by trees. Another cloud drifted in overhead, giving Arthur the relief needed to continue. *There's help.* Renewed adrenalin surged; he broke out in a trot.

His calves burned; he stopped to massage them for a second, then sprinted forward.

The roof grew larger and larger until a window and the

front porch could be seen. Arthur's smile widened as he stopped at the trailhead leading up to the house. "Hello." He sprinted up the path and onto the front porch, then banged on the door. "Hello. Help me. Is anyone home?"

A hush hung over the house and yard. He took a step backward and waited. Arthur cupped his hands and peered through the large picture window. He banged on it. "Help, please help me."

Inside was dark. His heart sank. *No one's home.*

He turned and glanced around for a neighbor's house, but saw none. He leaped off the porch and raced down the side yard. *I bet this is a winter home for a snowbird.*

At the back door, he jiggled the knob, but it was latched tight. He stretched on his toes and checked the molding above the door, no key.

Where's the hidden key? He picked up the mat, but saw only sand. To his left in the sand were many sun-bleached conch shells. Arthur squatted and began lifting each shell. As he lifted the sixth shell, a key dangled from fishing line. He leaped to his feet and inserted the key into the door. Hot stale air engulfed him. "Hello, help me. Is anyone here? May I use the phone?"

Silenced greeted him.

"Hello-o-o-o," he called as he stepped inside. He flipped the light switch, but the overhead light didn't shine. Inside he found another switch beside the kitchen table. The light didn't work. *Where's the breaker box?* Within a minute, he located it and flipped on the breakers, but still the house remained dark.

I just need to use their phone. He searched the whole house without any luck. In the family room, which overlooked the beautiful beach, he found a VHF radio, but without power, it didn't work.

He spun around and ran into the backyard, following the electrical wire from the house to a locked shed. The backdoor key fit. Inside, a small generator sat covered by a drop cloth.

He uncovered it and yanked on the pull cord. The motor coughed. After yanking harder, the motor purred to life. A single light bulb glowed from the overhead fixture.

Gusts of wind peppered him with sand and swayed the trees as he raced out of the shed. Puffy clouds sailed overhead. He dashed through the back door and into the family room. He turned on the radio and picked up its mic. He pressed the button. "Hello. Can anyone hear me?" Static sounded from the speaker. "Hello. Is anyone out there? I need help."

CHAPTER SIXTY-FIVE

Thick sliver-gray clouds soared overhead, sending blustering winds across the islands as the tide rose. Cool air swept grains of sand across the submerging sandbars. Otman lay on his back in the dinghy, shivering. Sand plastered his body. He fought the grogginess, struggling to open both eyes. *A storm's coming.* He sputtered, spitting sand out of his mouth. *Where am I? What happened?*

Looking around, he roared, "What?" Water lapped at Jane and Walter's bodies. *I fell asleep. Blair's going to be furious.* He leaped out into the water and grabbed the rope.

"Good-bye and good riddance," he said, and dashed eastward, pressing into the wind.

Blair yawned, looked at his watch, and stood. The yacht rocked as the wind and waves buffeted it.

Where's Otman? Where's Connie? We're going to miss the tide. We should have already left. He glanced out the back window at the choppy water, stepped out on the deck, and leaned over the railing; the dinghy was missing.

Otman's been gone for hours. He looked across small white caps at the beach. *He's nowhere in sight. Look at this weather; we can't leave now.* Blair stumbled as the yacht pitched.

Wind thrashed at Otman's face as he sloshed through knee-deep water. The dinghy skimmed behind on its rope-leash, with two paddles as cargo. Finally, Jane and Walter were no longer visible.

Anchors Away materialized as Otman neared the mouth of the inlet. He stopped and stared at the frothy seas crashing on the beach. Wrapping the rope tight around his wrist, he pulled. *Look at those waves; they must be three-footers inside the reef.* He drew in a deep breath and lunged into the wind and the turbulent water.

The waves pounded the dinghy's bow. Otman climbed in and pulled hard on the oars. The distance from shore widened with each moan and groan. Waves bludgeoned the dinghy. He looked over his shoulder at the yacht.

Just a little farther. He gritted his teeth and pulled harder. He glanced at the yacht again.

A couple more strokes and I'm there. Finally, the dinghy bumped the dive platform. His muscles throbbed as he grabbed and fought with it. Otman lashed the rope to the dive platform and hauled himself out. His wet clothes clung to his massive frame.

The back door swung open, and Blair stepped out. "What took you so long? I thought you were going to get rid of them and come right back." He rubbed his eyes and yawned. "You knew I wanted to leave today, but now we can't. We'll have to wait for this storm to blow over. Hopefully we can leave on tomorrow's high tide. What kept you?"

Otman shrugged. "I-I don't know what happened. I was tired and fell asleep."

Blair rubbed his head and looked at the couch. "That's strange, I fell asleep, too." He whirled around and stared at Otman. "We were drugged. Where's Connie and Bessy?"

They darted inside and down the stairs. Otman pushed open Connie's door and rushed in.

Connie lay curled up on her bed.

"Connie!" Blair yelled, pushing Otman to the side.

Connie jolted straight up in bed. "What?" She stared wide-eyed.

"Are you all right?" Blair asked.

"Sure. Why wouldn't I be?"

"We saw you and thought you were dead."

"Dead?" Connie glanced from Blair to Otman. "After Otman left and I regained my nerves, I came down from the flybridge and found you asleep on the couch, so, I decided to lie down in my bed."

"Bessy," Blair gasped. "She slipped us something."

"But what?" Otman asked.

"Who knows," Blair said with wide eyes. "Where is she?"

CHAPTER SIXTY-SIX

The forward cabin door swung open and Otman rushed inside. Blair leaned around Otman and stared into the bottom bunk. Bessy's silhouette emerged from where she faced the wall. She didn't move. "You didn't have to kill them," she murmured with a quivering voice. "You could have let them go."

"They shouldn't have stuck their noses into my business," Blair said.

Otman pushed Blair backward out of the cabin. "They left us with no other option." Otman locked the door. He patted his stomach as he turned and looked at Connie. "I'm hungry. What are you cooking us for dinner?"

"What am I cooking? Cook your own dinner," Connie snapped. "I'm not your servant."

"I can't," Otman said. "The Judge and I have to secure the boat."

"You can cook after you finish." Connie stared with contempt. "I'm not fixing dinner. I don't cook. If we were at a marina, I'd be going out to eat."

"But we're not," Blair said. "Get upstairs and start fixing dinner."

Connie stomped up the stairs and into the galley. She snatched open a cabinet door and looked into the nearly-empty shelves. "Hmm," she said, deciding what would be the simplest meal.

Otman and Blair stepped to the aft deck, into rain, and climbed down the ladder. "We've got to lash this dinghy down tight," Blair said. "I don't want it blowing away. We're in for a stormy night."

Otman pulled the rope tight and looped a knot. He scanned the sky. "Hopefully all of this will be gone before nightfall. He grabbed the cleat beside him, as the boat swayed. "I wanted to be in the Cayman Islands by tomorrow evening, eating a big juicy steak."

"That sounds good to me, but we'll have to wait another day for that meal." Blair pulled the last knot tight, securing the dinghy to the dive platform and the back of the yacht. "Let's get out of this weather."

They hurried inside and found dry clothes. Otman fell on the couch and Blair into the recliner.

Connie clutched an unopened can in her arms as she swayed to the left. *These waves are getting worse.* She glanced around the corner at Otman and Blair. *I'm not cooking breakfast for them.* Then she stepped back into the galley and grabbed other cans. She corralled them together.

Otman closed his eyes and propped his hands behind his head. "I hope she knows what she's doing in there."

"Don't be so hard on her," Blair said, as he kicked back the footrest and reclined. "Give her a chance."

Otman opened his eyes and peered out into the darkening sky. A bolt of lightning arched in the distance; its fingers spider-webbed across the clouds. He imagined Connie heating the cans on top of the burner, hobo style. He chuckled. *She's a real catch.*

"Otman," Blair asked, taking a deep breath, "were Walter and Jane dead when you left them?"

A soft whistle resonated as the wind swirled around the back door.

"Almost. I took them deep into the island. They were as-good-as dead when I dropped them in the water-covered sand. If the drugs didn't kill them, they'll drown in the rising tide. Either way, they'll be a smorgasbord for the sea creatures tonight. No way they could survive." And he laughed.

"Good." Blair leaned the recliner further back and closed his eyes. "Now we have to get rid of Bessy . . . as soon as I get my money back."

Connie looked at the cans. "I'm not a cook. How do they expect me to cook anything without a cookbook?" She threw her hands into the air. *I'll improvise.* The can opener slit into the can of green beans. She cranked the handle until the lid was off, then emptied the contents into a pot. "Hmm." She read, "Lima beans," and dumped them into the same pot. *This will be the bean pot.* Grabbing another can, black-eyed peas were dumped into the mixture. She pulled out a large spoon and stirred.

Connie opened the last three cans and dumped the sliced Idaho potatoes, whole kernel corn, and cream corn into another pot. *This will be the starch pot.* She smiled at herself, placed a lid on each pot, and turned the burners on high.

The boat rocked and the pots slid; she grasped the pot handles. *I'd better not lose dinner after all of my hard work.* Steam rose from around the lids.

The boat pitched left and then right. Connie felt woozy.

Otman's stomach growled. "Connie, I'm starving. How much longer?"

"Not much," Connie answered. *I can't take much more of this motion.*

Otman turned his nose up at the smell drifting over them. "What's she fixing?"

After five minutes, Connie fought the nausea, turned off the burners, and grabbed the pots. "Dinner's ready."

"You don't look good," Blair said, as Connie dropped the pots onto the table.

The boat swayed and Otman grabbed the recliner, steadying his way to the table.

The pots slid on the table, but Blair grabbed both handles. "That was close."

Connie hurried back into the galley, grabbed three bowls

and forks, and returned.

"We're eating out of bowls?" Otman asked. "What did you fix?"

Connie ignored the question and hurried back for three bottles of water. As she sat at the table, she smiled. "We're having vegetables and potatoes."

"What, no meat?" Otman reached for a pot.

"Didn't find any?"

Otman lifted the pot's lid and light gray smoke snaked from the pot. "What did you do?"

"Doesn't it look good?" Connie asked, beaming.

"You've burned it," Otman hissed, staring at the blackened blob. "You've cooked the water out."

"I couldn't have. I put the lid on the moment the burners were turned on."

"Didn't you check it as you cooked?" His eyes rolled up.

"Was I supposed to?"

As they stared at each other, Blair pulled the lid off the next pot. The acrid odor billowed into the air. He dropped the lid back into place. "Connie, it's all ruined."

"I don't believe it," she said, leaning over the table and lifting the lid. "Pee-u." She slammed the lid down.

"That's a record," Otman said with a sinister laugh. "No one could burn every pot and not know it, but you."

"I only cooked them on high for a couple of minutes."

"High!" Otman yelled. "You were just warming everything up."

Connie grabbed the two pots. "If you don't like my cooking, fix something for yourself." She swayed as the boat lurched, then hurried to the back door. Balancing one pot on top of the other, she flung the door open and heaved dinner, pots and all, overboard; they disappeared into a cresting wave. She hurried back inside and rushed past the table. "I'm going to my room. I don't feel good."

"I think I'll skip dinner, too," Blair said.

Otman stood, tipping the chair over, "Well I'm hungry." Otman grabbed his growling stomach. He stomped into the galley, searched the shelves, and found a package of crackers.

Bessy listened to the rain pelting the fiberglass deck above. Wind whistled past the yacht; waves pounded the hull. Lightning flickered in the window. Thunder reverberated again. Chills raced across her body. *We're in for a stormy night.*

CHAPTER SIXTY-SEVEN

A light sprinkle fell on the beach house. Water droplets speck-led the picture window where Arthur stood looking over the agitated sea. *Hang in there Bessy. Blair and Otman aren't going to get away with this.*

"Come back," the VHF radio squawked. "Say again. You're breaking up."

Arthur jerked the mic to his mouth and pressed the button. "Hello. . . ." The overhead light flickered twice and then went out as did the little red LCD light on the radio. "No, not now," Arthur moaned and looked at the back door. *What's wrong with the generator?*

He dashed to the shed. Inside, it was steamy and quiet. He grabbed the crank cord and yanked. It sputtered. Then silence. "What's wrong with you? Crank!" He jerked on the cord three more times. Then twisted the gas cap off and looked inside. "Great, it's out of fuel." He spun around and searched for a gas can. In the corner of the room was a five-gallon container. Within minutes, he filled the tank, restarted the generator, and was back inside, clutching the radio's mic. "This is Arthur McCullen. Please help me!"

Rain pelted the roof as Arthur waited and waited. "Can anyone hear me?"

Exasperated at the unanswered pleas, Arthur turned on the TV, but kept the radio at his side. He chuckled, "No telephone, but they have satellite TV." He flipped from one station to the next until he found a weather station.

"This is the latest on the season's first approaching hurricane," the speakers resounded.

"Hurricane!" Arthur's eyes widened; he leaped to his feet. The weatherman's body blocked Andros Island, as he pointed to Florida Keys.

"Latest projections have the eye coming ashore late tomorrow afternoon anywhere from the lower keys up to the Miami, Biscayne Bay area." The camera shot zoomed out and brought into view all of the Bahamas. "The eye is now located off the Turks and Caicos Islands. If it continues on the projected path, it'll make landfall at Upper Matecumbe Key. Stay tuned; we'll be right back."

Arthur moved to the window and peered out. The sky was darker and white caps covered the sea. *I have to get out of here and find a working phone to call the authorities. Blair and Otman are getting away.* He took a deep breath and sighed.

Bessy, hang on a little longer. Help's coming.

His face reddened as he raced to the breaker box and flipped all breakers off. After locking the house, he dashed into the shed and turned off the generator. Lightning flashed off in the distance followed by a deepening rumble.

Arthur ran down the path and out onto the beach. Froth washed ashore as waves pounded. He looked south. *I'm glad they left hours ago or they'd be anchored in the path of that hurricane.*

He turned and looked north. *I've got to save Bessy and notify the U.S. and Bahamian governments. They've got to catch Blair and Otman before it's too late.* He sprinted north as wind and rain blew at his back.

CHAPTER SIXTY-EIGHT

The wind drove sea spray across the rising water and the submerging sandbars. Further inland, brush and grass swayed. Dark-gray clouds swirled above. The air grew cooler as rain fell. Small ripples curled up the inlet. Minnows swam around and bumped into the small red tennis shoes.

Water lapped at Walter and Jane's faces.

Jane's fingers twitched; one eye batted open and then the other. Saltwater gushed into her eyes. She flinched, sputtered, and sat straight up, rubbing her stinging eyes. *Where am I?* Her muscles ached. Another small wave splashed into her lap. Water extended to the horizon with a few islands interspersed. Something brushed her body; she turned. "Walter!"

Jane sprung onto her knees, grabbed his head, and lifted it out of the water. Walter didn't move. A wave momentarily shifted his body.

"Walter, wake up," she pleaded.

Another wave floated Walter's body, tugging at it. Jane grabbed his shoulders and dragged him into shallower water. "Walter, fight it. Don't give up." She laid his head in her lap. Lightning flashed and thunder echoed. Jane looked down into his face. "Please wake up." She leaned over him and kissed him. "Walter," she said gently. "Wake up." She kissed him again.

Walter's body twitched; his eyes opened.

Jane cradled his head into her body. "Oh Walter. I thought I'd lost you."

"Jane," Walter said, his voice smothered by the wind.

She relaxed her hold. Her eyes glistened as she stared into his. "I want to take care of you forever."

A smile spread across Walter's face. "I'd like that." A deep rumble jolted Walter straight up. "Where are we?"

"I don't know. The last thing I remember was Otman jabbing me with a syringe."

"Obviously Otman thought we would die out here. He thought he'd hidden our bodies." Walter pushed himself up. "Come on. We've got to get out of here."

Walter reached down and lifted Jane to her feet. Water flowed around their legs. "I can't believe we survived that overdose."

"We probably wouldn't have, if we were back in the states," Jane said with a smile. "I've heard medicine shouldn't be left in the heat. It desensitizes the drug's strength. That's how my doctor convinced me not to order any medicine through the mail from Canada. He said you'd never know how long it would stay in those delivery trucks on a hot day."

Walter looked up at the weather and then around at their surroundings. "Nothing looks familiar. Come on. The tide's rising. We'll be swimming soon."

"This is a big storm," Jane said. "We should look for shelter."

"Which way should we go?"

Jane covered her eyes as rain blew into her face. She looked into the sky for her usual east and west visual. "I'm not sure."

"I don't want to end up back at that boat with Blair and Otman. I'm sure they think we're dead, and I don't want them to think any differently. Next time they'll tie something around our ankles and throw us into the sea."

"Wait a minute," she said. "They were getting rid of us, then leaving."

"Good. Now all we have to do is figure out which way is north and head for shelter."

Jane nodded as she looked at the clouds blowing overhead and pointed. "I'd say that way is north."

"Are you sure?"

"Yes. In the summer, clouds generally blow from the southeast. It's called the trade winds. Come on." She led the way. They trudged through varying depths of water, from ankle-deep, into water where they had to swim, and then back through waist-deep water.

"This way," Jane said, tugging at his hand. "Let's get out on the beach and walk. It'll be easier." She heard the breaking surf through the heavy downpour and headed to it.

The rain hammered them, slowing their pace. They moved out on the beach. Her red shoes sloshed and gouged the sand.

The wind and rain let up momentarily, and their visibility cleared. Walter grabbed Jane and pulled her down onto the sand. "Look," he said, pointing to the yacht that materialized out of the rainy haze. "They're still here."

"Let's get out of here," Jane said. They crawled up the low sand dune and slid down its back side. "We'll stay hidden for a ways and then we'll get back on the beach."

Walter followed and ducked under a swaying branch. "Ouch," he groaned, as the stubby branch whacked his cheek.

Jane touched the red mark on his face. "Are you all right?"

He smiled, "I'm fine." Jane started to move, but Walter pulled her back. "Wait, maybe we should stay here. Arthur's gone to get help. When the Bahamian Government gets here, we'll step out and flag them down."

"Are you sure we shouldn't seek shelter?" Her hair whipped around her face. She shuddered, as rain continued soaking her.

"What if they're on their way now? We'd miss them and have to find a place to get out of the weather and then wait to be rescued. This way's got to be quicker."

Wet clothes sagged on Jane's petite frame. She shivered. "I-I've got to get out of this wind for a few minutes. I-I'm getting c-cold."

Lightning flashed and arched across the sky. "That was close."

Jane nodded through chattering teeth. "T-too close."

Walter felt a strange tingle in his body. "I'll keep you warm." He pulled her closer.

"Thanks." She felt the warmth returning.

CHAPTER SIXTY-NINE

At Palm Beach County Jail, Manuel sat in a small room. His legal pad and briefcase lay on the table. Shelly sat next to him looking at the jumbled up notes and arrows across the legal page. Manuel pressed his finger on the last paragraph. "I've been working on a theory." He repositioned the legal pad in front of him. "I want to make sure my information is correct before I lay out everything."

"Okay. Have you gotten new information?"

"No, but I think I've put together the scrambled pieces. Bear with me. Walter Clemmons was staying with you at Bessy's house?"

"That's right." She nodded.

"And you were awakened by him swatting the newspaper on the table?"

She continued to nod.

"And when you arrived in the kitchen, he was wide awake?"

"Sure, he was reading the paper."

"Was he acting strange?"

"What do you mean?" Shelly's focus tightened.

"Was he fidgety or nervous?"

"Not that I remember."

"Come on, think." Manuel eased closer to her.

Shelly pressed her temples. "I only remember he was mad."

"Mad's good."

"At the newspaper. He couldn't believe Blair had been released from jail."

"What kind of shoes was he wearing?"

Shelly thought, then shrugged. "Shoes?"

"Were they tennis shoes, loafers, house shoes?"

"I don't remember. Why?"

Manuel stood and paced to the far side of the table. "Here's what I think happened." He reached into his briefcase and pulled out a folder. He opened it, lifted the top paper, and looked back at Shelly. "The State's toxicology report shows Justin's body had a high level of Benzodiazepine."

Shelly looked puzzled.

"It's a depressant found in sleeping pills. The same narcotic found in Halcion. Did Justin take sleeping pills?"

"Not that I'm aware of."

"I'd say his conscience wouldn't allow him to sleep after stealing from you and your dad, so he took pills. The state believes you gave Justin sleeping pills and while he slept or dozed, you killed him. They discovered the pharmacy where you filled a prescription for Halcion."

"I never filled a prescription for sleeping pills. Those aren't mine."

"I didn't think so. Stay with me," He pulled out the next document. "The State also has evidence from the crime scene that matches evidence found at Bessy's house. Rabbit hairs."

"How did rabbit hair get in Bessy's house?"

Manuel grinned. "Only two people were staying at Bessy's. You and Walter. He was awake long before you were. And, in those early hours, the distance from the airport to Bessy's house is easily driven within fifteen minutes."

He stood, moved to the side wall, and pounded his fist into his palm. "It was Walter who had time to kill Justin and drive back to Bessy's and change clothes before you were awakened by his so-called anger. It was perfectly staged."

He turned back to Shelly. "Walter had the flawless get-away; everyone knew he was flying out of town that afternoon. He wouldn't look suspicious. Any evidence of the crime was packed in his suitcases, which were checked through the airline and disposed of either in Atlanta or his final destination." He stepped back to the table. "I can't believe it. What a perfect murder."

His breathing seemed to echo in the room as he pulled out a picture. "Hmm," he groaned, rubbing his chin. "You said earlier that this was not your pocketbook. If it's not yours, whose is it? How did you end up with it?"

Shelly shook her head.

He looked into her eyes. "Did you have that pocketbook the afternoon you drove Walter to the airport?"

"I don't believe so."

"No, you didn't!" he snapped. "You've got to start answering direct questions with conviction. No, you didn't! Say it."

"No, I didn't," Shelly said, timidly.

"That's not strong enough. The jury must believe you."

"No, I didn't!" Shelly said, squaring her shoulders.

"Great. Now that's how I want you to answer all of your questions." He pushed up out of the chair and ambled to the far wall. "The way I see it, you left Bessy's house with *your* pocketbook. It wasn't until you arrived at the airport that Walter somehow switched it."

"He did?" Shelly shifted in her seat. "But how?"

"Didn't you tell me that you got out of the Suburban at the airport and opened up the back doors to get his suitcases?"

"Yes."

"And then you went back to the front seat and grabbed your pocketbook before you locked up the vehicle."

"I did."

"Doesn't that pocketbook look similar to yours?"

She studied the photo and nodded. "Slightly."

Manuel smiled. "And you never knew."

He bent over the table, propping on his hands and looked her eye-to-eye. "He was very adamant about leaving that day. Wasn't he?"

"Yes."

"I wonder what we'd find in Walter's suitcase."

Shelly sat stupefied. Her mouth hung open. "Why would Walter kill Justin? He didn't even know him. That doesn't make any sense."

"Exactly. We don't really know anything about Walter. Who was he before he came to Florida? But, since he never met Justin, he would have been able to get close enough to him without scaring him off."

"But . . ."

"The blood found in the BMW could have come from any-where. For all we know, it could have been planted. But one thing's for sure, Justin wasn't shot in it, or there would be blood everywhere."

"How could Walter . . ."

"How convenient. Mr. Clemmons killed Justin Roble and now has disappeared. But he failed to consider the evidence would make you the number one suspect. I believe by present-ing this evidence tomorrow, I can petition the court and get you released on bail."

"Really?"

"Yes, and then we can look for Arthur, Bessy, and Walter. Think about it. We don't have to prove his motive. It just proves someone else had opportunity. All we have to do is make the accusation. It'll be enough doubt planted in any juror's mind that they won't be able to reach a verdict. There will be those on a jury that believe the police have arrested the wrong person. It'll only muddy up the water. At the least, we'll have a hung jury." Manuel smiled.

CHAPTER SEVENTY

Trees and shrubs leaned over, whipped one way then the other. Raindrops pounded the coast. Water cascaded across the saturated sand to the ocean. Arthur shivered and hunched down in the sand.

If Bessy put all of that Benadryl into Blair and Otman's food, they should have fallen asleep. Are they still sleeping? He looked south down the beach. The house was a quarter of a mile back.

If they didn't leave, they're right in the path of that hurricane. I've got to go back and find out.

Turning back, Arthur's hand shielded his eyes from the pelting rain. Surf pounded the beach.

He lowered his head and pressed on. Lightning illuminated the house as he approached for the second time that day. *I should go inside and look for a weapon.*

He dashed up the incline and around the house. The now-familiar generator cranked on the first pull. Arthur rushed into the house and into the kitchen where he rummaged through kitchen drawers. He saw a fillet knife and grabbed it.

He hurried to the door, saw a raincoat hanging in the corner, and borrowed it too.

Arthur locked the house. On the way out of the shed, he found a boat hook and took it. When he reached the beach, wind drove rain and sea spray into him.

A couple of hours passed, Arthur now trudged along in the dark. Lightning flashed frequently illuminating his way. He stopped and leaned over, resting.

How much farther? A lightning bolt lit up the southern sky. Arthur blinked.

Was that Bessy's boat? He strained through chilling obscurity, waiting for the next flash. Before he could take another breath, the sky illuminated for an instant revealing a yacht's silhouette.

They didn't leave!

He leaped to his feet and trudged into the wind. *I've got to rescue Bessy.*

Walter and Jane sat snug in a crevice he gouged out of the backside of a sand dune. Palm branches were wedged into the sand and sticks helped hold them in place. Water flowed down the thatched roof. "Maybe you should look around."

"Sure, I'll be right back." Walter scooted out and peered over the sand embankment. He stared into the darkness. Lightning flashed. He crawled back into the crevice. "I saw someone on the beach."

"Was it Blair or Otman?" Jane got on her knees. "Maybe we should get out of here."

"It wasn't big enough to be Otman. If it's Blair, I'll take him." Walter slipped a stick off the lean-to and crawled up the sand. He waited for another lightening strike.

Jane pulled a limb off and scrambled up beside him. "He's going to wish he'd never gotten off that boat."

Lightning again brightened the beach. Someone stood just on the other side of them, clad in a yellow rain coat. "Who is it?" Jane asked.

"I don't know, but I'll find out."

Another flash revealed the person peering through the rain at the yacht. Walter eased out from behind the bush, and reared back the stick.

"Bessy," Arthur moaned, "what should I do?"

"Arthur?" Walter lowered his stick.

The sky lit up and revealed all three, scrutinizing each

other. "Walter! Jane! I thought you were dead." They dropped their weapons, grabbed each other, and hugged. "I'm so glad to see you."

"Is help on the way?" Jane asked.

"No. No one's coming."

"Come on. Let's get out of this weather," Walter said. They picked up their weapons and climbed across the sand dune and down into the crevice.

Walter and Jane climbed back under their lean-to. Jane nuzzled against Walter, while Arthur sat beside them with the raincoat over his head. "I've got to swim out there and sneak aboard. There's a hurricane coming. We're in the projected path."

"A hurricane? I'm going with you," Walter said.

"Count me in," Jane added.

"No, it's too dangerous," Walter said, holding Jane's hand. "Stay here; we'll be right back."

Jane shook her head. "There's safety in numbers if anything goes wrong. Remember, Otman only has two syringes left. If he injects two of us, the other two can escape."

"I don't know," Walter replied, "I don't want anything to happen to you."

"And nothing will." She nudged him playfully. "You'll protect me."

"You know, Walter, she's onto something. If they wake up while I'm downstairs, you two could cause a distraction that I'll need to get away. Yell U.S. Coastguard. It'll be the perfect diversion. They'll be confused and won't know what's happening. You and Jane can stay on the back deck while I slip inside. I'll be in and out before anyone wakes."

"You're right. We'll definitely have the element of surprise. They think we're dead and with this weather, they'll never be expecting anyone to swim out to the boat."

"It sounds so easy," Jane said. "Maybe we'll get lucky and pull it off."

"We'll have to wait for dawn," Arthur said. "Otherwise we could swim past the boat and never know it."

They settled back in the sand and waited for daybreak.

CHAPTER SEVENTY-ONE

Sand swept across Jane, Walter, and Arthur. No one slept. The morning air turned from darkness to an eerie black-gray. They crawled out from their shelter and stuck their heads above the sand dune. Wind thrashed their faces as they looked at Bessy's yacht hobble-horsing across five-to-six-foot, white-capped waves.

"Look out there," Walter gasped.

"Come on," Arthur said. "It's only going to get worse."

"Wait," Jane said as she slipped off the red shoes. "We can't swim out there with that knife and boat hook." She reached up to the base of the bush in front of them and tied the shoes to it. The shoes flipped and turned. "Let's leave those weapons here. These shoes will flag the spot. If we're chased to shore, we'll have the upper hand."

Walter and Arthur slipped off their shoes and tied them. The knife and boat hook lay beneath their shoes.

Jane gave Walter a quick kiss. "That's for good luck." Walter lifted his shoulders, stood, and pulled Jane up. They leaned into the wind and moved across the small sand dune as large raindrops began to pound them. The yacht faded behind a curtain of rain.

It's going to be dangerous out there. Walter sucked in a deep breath and plunged into the breaking wave.

"Whoa," Jane sputtered as her head popped above a wave, "this water's cold." She kicked and pulled herself toward the next wave.

Arthur pointed his hands into the oncoming wave and

slipped through it, into another.

Walter lumbered across one wave after another. The roar of the wind and waves drowned out all the noise they created. They all focused on the dim silhouette of the yacht.

"Keep kicking," Jane yelled to Walter at the bottom of a troth. She wiggled and splashed up the approaching wave.

Up ahead, Arthur focused on the dive platform and kicked hard. The teak deck rose high into the air and then dropped into the water as the yacht pitched into the next wave.

Arthur lunged for and grasped the teak platform. He stretched behind for Jane. On the second effort, they locked hands. He pulled her in and then helped lift her onto the platform.

Walter splashed through the next oncoming wave, grabbed the teak wood, and hung on, half out of the water. As the platform dipped into the water, Arthur slipped up on it and then waited for the next dip and pulled Walter up. They were exhausted, but energized.

"Stay here. I'll be right back," Arthur said.

Walter and Jane huddled with rain pelting their bodies. Jane shivered. "We're coming with you just in case you meet up with Otman or Blair."

On the aft deck, Arthur tried the back door and to his amazement, it opened. He motioned for the others to follow him inside. The howl of the wind faded as the door closed.

Arthur teetered over to the table, then caught his balance, pulled out a chair, and handed it to Walter. "Use this to keep Otman and Blair away while everyone escapes. I'll be right back."

He crept downstairs, slipped inside the forward cabin, closed the door, and felt along the right-hand side, along the lower bunk until he found Bessy. A synchronized pounding echoed in the room as each wave slammed into the hull. He slipped a hand over her mouth and gently shook her. "Bessy."

She twitched and gasped.

"Shhh. It's me, Arthur."

Bessy threw up her hands and pulled Arthur into bed. "I love you so much. You've rescued me again."

"Not exactly. We have to get off *this* boat and find higher ground. A hurricane's heading straight for us."

She scooted off the bed and began to dress. "Didn't you find help?"

"No, and Otman didn't kill Walter and Jane. They're upstairs waiting."

"Really," Bessy said, in hushed squeal.

"Shhh. You're going to wake everyone."

Bessy pulled on a bright Bahamian tee shirt and navy shorts. She started putting on her tennis shoes.

"You'll have to tie those to your shorts," Arthur said, stopping her. "You won't be able to swim with them on. Come on." He eased open the door and they crept upstairs.

Bessy looked outside and saw large cresting waves. "Arthur, look out there at those waves."

"I know. We swam out here in them."

Bessy turned and saw Jane and Walter standing in the salon and tiptoed to them. She threw her arms around Jane. "I thought you were dead."

Jane grinned. "I'm a tough old woman. They can't get rid of me that easily."

Walter stepped beside them. "Let's get out of here before they wake up." They started for the back door.

"Wait," Bessy said, shaking her head. "We can't go ashore. I've always heard that a hurricane creates a tidal surge. If there *is* a surge, this low area would become covered with water and we'd be swept away. It's a proven fact that our chance for survival is greater by staying onboard. People that abandon their boats usually die. We have to move this boat to a protected anchorage where we can ride out the storm. It's our best option. We'll never outrun it. Not in those kind of seas."

"Wait a minute," Walter said. "I'm not going to wake up

Otman and Blair and explain that a hurricane's coming and expect a temporary truce. They'll end up killing Jane and me."

"I'd rather take my chances with that tidal surge," Jane said.

"Maybe we can stack the odds in our favor," Arthur said. "Walter and Jane can hide. We know we can't trust Blair or Otman, and after the hurricane passes, they'll lock Bessy and me back up." He looked at Walter and grinned. "That's when you can slip out of your hiding place and let us out. Then we'll all escape."

"That just might work," Jane said, smiling. "They think we're dead; they won't expect us."

"And with the devastation from the hurricane," Bessy added, "the Bahamian Government won't be spending the man-hours looking for us. They'll be restoring order to their country. Come on. Let's find the perfect hiding place."

"Anywhere but the forward cabin," Walter snickered.

They began searching the galley but none of the cabinets were large enough for Walter to climb into. The flybridge and the lower helm were ruled out as well as the salon.

"You know where a good place would be," Jane said, "one of the engine rooms. They'll never look there."

Bessy nodded. "That's perfect. There's plenty of room in there for both of you. We'll get everyone upstairs. It'll be noisy inside once the engines are cranked, so stuff tissue into your ears. Wait a few minutes until we're underway, then you can come out and wait downstairs. I'll keep them worried about the boat sinking in those big seas, so no one will venture down there."

Jane noticed Walter fidgeting. His face was sullen. She pulled him tight to her and whispered. "You'll be fine down there. We're not going to sink, and you won't get seasick. Trust me. I'll keep you from thinking about it."

Walter tried to smile. "If you can't, it's going to smell awful when that room heats up."

271

Jane forced a smile. *I've got my work cut out.*

"Once we're in a safe protected area and anchored," Bessy said to Jane, "you'll have to hide back inside the engine room."

"We can do it," Jane said, pulling Walter close into her. "Can't we?"

Walter nodded. "If you say so."

Bessy grabbed a small flashlight from inside one of the drawers in the galley and handed it to Walter. Then she led the way downstairs.

One at a time, Walter and Jane went into the forward cabin and changed into dry clothes.

Arthur collected the wet clothes and then took them upstairs and threw them out into the raging sea. *We don't want any evidence of them onboard.*

Bessy led them into the hallway and stopped between the two engine rooms, one on each side of the hallway. She opened the starboard door. "If you have to turn on the flashlight, put your hand over its beam. You don't want the light to be seen through this window." Both doors had a small, high window.

Walter turned on the flashlight and entered the engine room. Jane followed as they went to the back of the room and sat in the far corner against the outside wall. Walter put his arm around Jane and held her tight. He patted his shirt pocket full of tissue and turned off the light. Bessy closed the door.

"Now we've got to wake Blair and tell him." Bessy stepped back to the aft cabin and opened the door.

CHAPTER SEVENTY-TWO

Bessy steadied herself inside the dark cabin. Arthur stood behind her, bracing against the doorframe, one hand on each wall. The boat lurched as a wave swept under it and snatched the door from Bessy. It crashed into the wall.

Lightening flashed, exposing Blair, wide-eyed, lying on his back. "Who's there?"

Bessy flipped the wall-switch and the lights on the night-stands glowed. "Get up. We have to get out of here. There's a hurricane coming."

Blair leaped from the bed, wearing his pajama shorts. "Otman!" He grabbed Bessy. "How'd you get out of your room?"

Arthur raced inside. "She's telling the truth. There *is* a hurricane coming."

Blair tossed Bessy onto the bed and rushed Arthur. "I see you've become a meteorologist while you were gone, but I'm not buying it. You can't fool me."

Arthur grabbed Blair and slung him to the floor. "What part of the word hurricane doesn't scare you?"

Otman raced into the cabin and reached for Arthur, but the boat pitched and he stumbled into the wall. "What the heck?" he yelled, glaring at Arthur. After a quick push off the wall, he rushed back at him. The yacht lurched the other way and tossed all of them to the other side.

"We're in a hurricane," Bessy yelled, and lifted herself up.

Otman looked at them from the floor. "What?"

"Can't you tell?" Bessy yelled. "This isn't your typical

summer storm. A hurricane's coming, and if we don't get into a protected anchorage, we're all going to die."

The boat rocked, and Otman stumbled into the bed.

Arthur grabbed Bessy and pulled her from the room. "Come on. We've got to go before it's too late."

Blair leaned into Otman and whispered. "I hate to admit it, but if we *are* in a hurricane, we'll need their help, if we're going to survive. But once it's safely past . . . well . . . you know what to do."

"I've got the syringes with me," Otman said, and patted his short's pocket.

Blair and Otman teetered down the hallway as they chased after Arthur and Bessy. The boat's bow rose high, and the floor fell away from their feet. They plunged to the floor with a thud, as the next wave slammed into the bow. Neither said anything for a moment, nor moved. They just listened and held on.

Seconds passed. "We're in big trouble," Otman said. "Why don't we kill them and swim to shore?"

"Because, without this boat, we'll never get away and we'd be arrested by the Bahamian Government and handed over to the U.S. Now get upstairs."

They grabbed the handrail and pulled themselves up the stairs.

In the pilothouse, Bessy held tight to the steering wheel and turned the first ignition key.

Down in the starboard engine room, Walter and Jane stared into the darkness as they listened to the engine chattering to life. Walter feared they would be tossed into the moving parts. With faint rays of the flashlight penetrating between his fingers, the silhouette of the engine appeared. They scooted on their bottoms to the door. Walter grabbed the door, clicked off the light, and they eased out into the hallway.

Jane looked down the hall into the aft cabin. *There's less movement in that cabin. Walter is less likely to be seasick back there.* She tugged Walter; they slipped into Blair's cabin.

With both engines cranked, Bessy turned on the radar, GPS, and chart plotter. She opened a drawer, pulled out the *Explorer Charts,* and flipped through the pages until she found the chart of Andros; then studied the area. "We need to find a hurricane hole."

Arthur leaned over the chart and pointed. "Last night, the hurricane was down in this area." He pointed to an area that was beyond the range of the chart. "And it's heading west-northwest, at eighteen miles an hour. They predict it'll cross here." His finger slid across the page on the projected path and stopped. "The eye of the storm should hit us around noon-ish, but you never know. Hurricanes are unpredictable. It could turn, pick up speed, or slow down."

Bessy scanned the chart up the eastern edge of Andros. Her gaze neared Morgan's Bluff at the northern tip. She feared they'd never make it that far before the hurricane overtook them. Her eyes moved back down the edge. She studied the pass through the reef at Fresh Creek, but knew that with the waves from the south, they'd probably be blown into the reef. Sighing, her gaze moved south, focusing on the three Bights. Contemplating the north and the middle, she shook her head. *Very shallow, nowhere to anchor safely.*

"Where's Connie?" Arthur asked.

"Sleeping," Otman said. "Leave her. She'll just freak out."

Arthur wondered if Walter and Jane would run into her.

Blair fidgeted as he looked at the tempestuous clouds swirling above. He grabbed the dash as the boat pitched and rolled. "Look at the ocean." Frothy-white water was every-where. Six-foot waves curled toward them. Anxiety escalated into fear as the wind buffeted the boat. The doors rattled non-stop.

Bessy's finger pressed at the southern Bight. "There's something about this place." She pulled out the *Yachtsman's Guide to the Bahamas.* The pages ruffled as she thumbed through them and found South Bight. "This is it," she yelled.

"And it's not far from here. The entrance was dredged to twelve feet, years ago." Her eyes followed the Bight, past Driggs Hill, a tiny community. "I remember now, once we get out of the dredged channel, we'll have eight feet of water. In between these low islands we'll be protected from the heaviest of the winds and seas." She pointed on the chart to a bend in the Bight with a depth of eight feet. "We can ride out the storm here."

The boat jarred as a wave slammed into it. Otman clung to the ladder leading to the flybridge.

"We've got to go, now," Bessy said. She stared at another approaching wave, wide-eyed. The boat shuttered as they grabbed hold of anything they could find to remain upright. "We should all stay up here in case the boat sinks. You don't want to get trapped downstairs." She turned her head and smirked, when she saw Otman twitching.

"It's now or never," Arthur said.

Bessy's jaw tightened. *I've heard of sailboats riding out hurricanes, but never a motor-yacht like this. We've got a lot of windage.* Arthur rubbed Bessy's shoulders, as they stared into the storm.

CHAPTER SEVENTY-THREE

Inside the pilothouse, the GPS pinpointed their position on the internal chart, the island behind them, and the reef ahead. Bessy read the depth gauge—8.1 feet. "We've got to stay inside the reef until we get to this point." She pressed at the location they could pass safely through the reef and out into deep water. "We're going up here to South Bight." Her finger traced the path to the entrance. "We should be able to pass safely through. Once inside we won't have much wave action. Just a lot of wind."

"I'm steering," Blair yelled, and stepped up to the helm.

The boat rocked. Bessy staggered toward Arthur. "Get everyone to put on a life vest. If we sink, we'll be glad we're wearing them."

Otman grabbed Arthur. "*You* get the life vests. I'm staying here. But, remember, we have Bessy. Don't try anything." He shoved Arthur toward the stairs.

The yacht plunged off a wave. Arthur squatted to the floor and slid, one step at a time, down the stairs.

Bessy reached out for the windless controls. "Harry, are you ready?"

Blair grabbed the steering wheel with one hand and placed his right hand on the black transmission knobs. "I'm ready."

Otman stared through the front windshield. He clung to the dash and the ladder, as the yacht rolled across another wave.

Blair engaged the engines and Bessy pressed the windless button. Chain began to be pulled through the bow pulpit and down into the chain locker.

Arthur dashed into the forward cabin, grabbed both life vests, and hurried down the hallway to the starboard engine room. He opened the door and looked inside. Walter and Jane weren't there. Arthur smiled. He pulled the door closed and dashed up the stairs.

"Catch." Arthur tossed one life vest to Blair and the other to Bessy. Otman ripped it from Bessy's fingers and slipped it on.

Arthur disappeared back downstairs and entered Otman's room. He saw the black bag, opened it, and found it empty. *Otman has the syringes in his pockets.* He searched the room and bathroom, but didn't find Walter or Jane. He grabbed both life vests from the closet and hurried out into the hallway. There he dropped them on the floor to be grabbed on his last trip up the stairs.

The boat jostled and Arthur stumbled into the next cabin. "Connie, wake up; put on your life vest," he yelled as he flipped the switch for the light. He reached into the small closet and snatched both life vests from the top shelf, causing it to rattle.

"Otman! Help!" Connie yelled, as she sat up and clutched the pillow to her chest. "Get out of my room."

"You'd better get up," Arthur said, looking at her. "And put on something that's appropriate. There's a hurricane coming." He tossed her a life vest. "Put it on. Bessy says no one should be down here in case the boat sinks. You'll become trapped. Take this life vest upstairs to Bessy." He tossed it on the bed beside her.

The boat pitched and Connie toppled off the bed.

He ran out of Connie's cabin and to the aft cabin. Inside, he opened the closet door to see Jane leaning backward into Walter's chest, wrapped in his arms, already wearing vests. He grinned and closed the door. He hurried into the hallway, grabbed a life vest, and wrestled it on.

Inside the pilothouse, Bessy pointed to the map, at the cut

that ran through the reef. "That's where we have to exit." The boat rocked and their grips tightened. She looked out the front window. Dark clouds raced toward them. Waves crested as water droplets blew from their tops.

Otman stared across the agitated sea. "Maybe we shouldn't go out there. Maybe we should get to shore."

"Go ahead. No one's going to stop you," Bessy said.

The windless continued pulling in the chain.

Otman looked at Blair. "Maybe she should drive."

"I've driven in storms plenty of times. I'm driving."

Arthur picked up the other vest and climbed the stairs. "Put this on," he yelled, handing it to Bessy.

Bessy pulled the vest on and fastened the buckles. She reached under the bench seat and pulled out a large duffle bag. "Otman, take this emergency bag to the salon and put it at the back door. It contains our survival items, but hopefully we won't need it."

Otman looked past her to Blair, who was buckling his vest.

Connie stepped out of the stairway clutching one vest and wearing the other. "It's hot and muggy in here." She grabbed hold of the bench seat, and braced herself as a wave slammed into the boat, and spray geysered into the air, covering the deck and windshield.

"Connie," Bessy said, "take this duffle bag into the salon and put it by the back door."

Connie tightened her grip on the bench seat. "I'm not moving."

Otman grabbed the bag and pressed it into her stomach. "You're in the way in here; take the bag to the back, and stay there. Now!" Otman shoved her.

The boat lurched and Connie tumbled into the salon. She crawled to the door and placed the bag beside it, then scooted to the couch and rested against it.

Otman glanced forward and then behind, wondering what would happen once the anchor was up. Would they hit the shore or the reef first? His body quivered. He pulled at the buckles of his life vest, snugging them. Suddenly the sky around them lit up. The air shook with intensity.

Blair's knuckles were white. He took short, uneven breaths.

The bow of the boat rose free and the anchor settled into its cradle.

"Go," Bessy screamed. She scanned the waves crashing over the reef to the beach and back.

Blair's jitters intensified as he spun the steering wheel. The yacht moved sporadically.

"You've got to crab out of here," Bessy warned as the yacht moved toward shore. The depth gauge fluctuated between 5.9 in the troughs and 11.7 at the crest of each wave.

"Let her drive," Otman said as he dashed for Blair and knocked him from the steering wheel. "You don't know what you're doing."

Bessy grabbed the wheel and spun it. The boat began moving away from shore. She gave more power to both engines and the boat swung north and headed for the break in the reef.

The winds howled and rain pelted the windshield. The boat rocked one way and then the other. Their eyes strained to see through the sheets of rain.

CHAPTER SEVENTY-FOUR

A torrential downpour continued to pound the yacht, cascading down the front windshield, and obscuring Bessy's view. *Trust the instruments.* She brought her gaze back into the pilothouse, glancing from the depth gauge—7.2 feet, to the GPS that showed them getting closer to the cut in the reef.

"I hope we don't bump the bottom in one of the troths." The radar screen was solid black. She adjusted the gain on the rain control, and the radar began mapping out the shoreline. The boat moved closer and closer to the point of the cut.

I can do this. I can get us out of here safely. When the GPS indicated that the boat was at the cut, she spun the wheel, adjusting for the turbulence and gave more power to both engines. "Here we go." She gasped at the larger waves, outside the reef.

The bow rose high on a cresting wave and then plunged down. Plumes of water fanned outward. "Hold on," Bessy yelled as the larger wave, rolled toward them. They all stared, bracing for the impact. The boat shuddered, pitched, and groaned.

Bessy spun the steering wheel left and right, the yacht faltered, but moved ahead. Her legs trembled at the thought of crashing into either side of the reef. Eeriness hung in between large black waves and dark gray clouds that swept toward them.

Otman looked green as he stood by the side door with one hand on it, ready to flee if the boat were to break apart and sink. His eyes were closed tight, dreading to see any disaster unfolding.

Blair held his breath, as if readying himself for that moment he'd be in the water, fighting for survival. His body tensed, his eyes bulged, as the boat crested another wave. His teeth gritted, as the boat slammed back into the sea.

Connie pitched with each gyration the boat made.

Arthur hung to the bench seat and the dash beside Bessy.

The boat rose high again and the floor once again fell away from their feet. Their stomachs seemed to hang momentarily, then drop with a jolt.

"It's a good thing we left when we did," Bessy said. "If we had waited much longer, we wouldn't have gotten out of there."

Unable to see outside, Bessy breathed more easily as their marked position on the GPS indicated that they had cleared the reef. "We made it." A satisfied smile emerged. She pressed buttons on the GPS and located South Bight. She centered the cursor and entered their new destination. Finally, with the reef well behind them, she spun the steering wheel. The boat pitched and swayed as it came around and headed north, for South Bight.

Otman stared outside as a wall of water rose behind the yacht and they surfed down the wave. The bow plunged into another wave and rose up the back side.

No one said a word.

The radar screen plotted the shoreline, three miles to the west.

Bessy's legs ached. *Just a little farther,* she kept telling herself, *just a little farther.* An hour passed and then another, as hope flourished watching their plotted position grow closer. Finally, the radar screen painted a large break between two islands—South Bight. She gripped the steering wheel. "Hang on," she called, "we're turning in."

The boat oscillated as a large wave swept from the stern to the bow. Bessy spun the wheel to the right for a second and then spun it in the opposite direction. The yacht wobbled, but its bow raced forward.

Bessy increased power. The yacht surfed along with the following sea. When the band of rain eased, they could see the Bight between two low islands.

"Wow, this is better," Otman breathed as he released the death grip on the ladder and door molding, which hung loosely from the wall. He wiped his forehead.

Bessy watched the depth rise to twelve feet entering the dredged channel. She pulled back the throttles. The waves decreased and the ride smoothed out, but the wind continued to howl. The GPS's internal map ended, but the display continued to give digital longitude and latitude coordinates.

"Harry," Bessy said, as the yacht moved into what appeared to be a broad river, their depth now at eight feet. "You keep an eye out on the south side, and Otman, you keep an eye out on the north side. Let me know when we get too close."

Blair wiped the window with his palm. "Looks good on my side."

A shrill whistle sounded at the door.

Bessy pulled out the *Yachtsman's Guide* and opened it. She flipped to the dog-eared page in the Andros section and handed the book to Arthur. "Look for this spot in the bend. From here on, we're navigating by sight. There aren't any charts for these waters, only this hand-drawn one."

All eyes scanned outside. On the south side, a small harbour with concrete walls was visible. On the north side, sand, bushes, and small trees could be seen off in the distance.

Lightning zigzagged across the sky in front of the boat. They all jumped. "That one was too close," Connie said, rushing into the pilothouse. Her face was green. "How much longer will this last?"

Another band of rain pelted the boat. The visibility dwindled to zero. Bessy pulled back power to neutral.

"I can't see where we're going," Connie yelled. "Turn on

the headlights before we run into something."

Otman laughed. "You've got to be kidding. Boats don't have headlights."

Out of habit, Bessy reached down and verified the switch for the navigation lights was on. She knew the lights were useless for seeing other boats, but if another boat was anchored ahead and the captain saw them getting too close, he could blow his horn and warn of their location.

As the visibility returned, Bessy maneuvered the yacht up the Bight. Arthur studied the hand-drawn map and traced their position with his finger. Every now and again, he'd glance at the radar screen and verify that his finger was at the correct bend.

Another band of rain passed. Bessy glanced at the chart in Arthur's hands. She located a spot in eight feet of water. "That looks like a good spot to anchor," she said and pointed.

Blair's legs wobbled. "Any place sounds good to me."

The yacht moved across the eight-foot deep anchorage, as Bessy eased back the knobs, disengaging the props. "Let's drop the anchor."

Blair reached for the windlass button and pressed. They watched the anchor disappear under the bow pulpit. After approximately 150 feet of chain had been deployed, they waited, hoping the anchor would dig in and hold.

The boat swung around. The anchor was down. Bessy kept an eye on the GPS, and made a mental note of their position. She set the anchor alarm. Minutes passed. The alarm did not sound. "We'll be fine as long as the wind doesn't change directions. But we're a long ways from being safe. The winds are bound to increase." They stared into the approaching hurricane.

CHAPTER SEVENTY-FIVE

Every thirty minutes, for the next two hours, Bessy verified their position again. The numbers on the GPS remained constant. The alarm silent. The winds shrieked and vibrated the yacht. Downstairs in the aft cabin's closet, Jane and Walter nestled on top of blankets leaning up against the closet's end. Walter held Jane in a close embrace.

Jane eased the door open to allow the stale air out. She stared out the port-side window at the dark clouds. Sporadic lightening illuminated the room. The closet air now fresher, she closed the door. "I'm surprised this isn't worse, judging from all of those pictures we see on TV from hurricane-ravaged places."

"It probably would be if we were in winds over one-hundred miles per hour. I'm glad Bessy knew what she was doing and got us safely anchored. I can only imagine what the waves would be like out there now."

"So, tell me why you've never married," she said, changing the subject.

"It's a long story."

"We're not going anywhere any time soon. But, if you don't want to tell me, that's okay."

"I was right out of college and planned to marry my girlfriend of two years after she got back from a month's vacation in Europe with her parents. By the time she came back, I'd gotten a good paying job with a company in San Diego. She wanted me to move back home and work in her father's company. It's not what I wanted to do. I thought that after time, she would change her mind and join me. But she didn't. Anyway, we just recently got back in touch, and neither she nor I ever married. That's why I was so set on returning to Oregon. I . . . we were wondering if after all of these years we would still feel the same about each other."

Jane squirmed away, but Walter pulled her back. "It's all different now. I've gotten to know you, well, I . . . ah," he drew in a long breath, "I've fallen in love with you."

"Really," Jane said, a smile creeping onto her face.

"Yes. I'm glad you kept after me and didn't give up."

"Well, Bessy gave me a heads-up on you; otherwise I would have never known you were just doors down from me. If your best friend told you about me, you'd have done the same."

Walter snuggled next to Jane and kissed her. "If we get out of here alive, I don't want to make the worst mistake of my life. Jane Winchester, will you marry me?"

Jane whirled around on her knees and wrapped her arms around him. "Yes," she said, kissing him. "Oh, yes."

Creaks resonated through the yacht.

CHAPTER SEVENTY-SIX

The wind rattled the side door. The boat fishtailed at the end of the anchor line. Bessy stumbled back to the pilothouse. She glanced at the GPS again. The latitude and longitude position remained constant. *I can't believe that anchor is holding.*

A loud pop sounded behind her. Her head snapped forward. A branch had blown into the windshield, and then it was gone. Her eyes blinked as she focused on the horizon. *We've almost made it through the storm.* She beamed as she ran into the salon. "There's clear sky. The hurricane's about to pass."

Blair patted the flare gun, moved to the nav station, and looked out the windshield. The dark, swirling clouds sailed across. Far on the horizon, a distinct edge appeared. Blue sky emerged on the other side.

Otman rushed into the nav station and stared. His heart pounded with excitement. "We're going to make it."

Blair caught his attention, then looked at his pocket. "Get ready," he mouthed.

Otman dug his hands into his pocket and felt both syringes. He nodded to Blair, letting him know that he was ready.

Blair reached over to the ignition keys, pulled them out, and dropped them into his pocket.

Blue sky grew closer and closer and then was overhead. Suddenly, stillness filled the air. Their ears rang from the fading howl.

Otman watched as a bird swooped down and landed on the bow pulpit. He pushed the side door open. "We made it. We're safe." He stepped outside into the fresh, calm, cool air.

Connie rushed from the salon.

Blair stepped outside and approached Otman. "Keep an eye on them."

Otman ignored him for the moment and looked up at the shear edge. A canyon rose tens-of-thousands-of-feet up above. He gulped at the cloud bank and its appearance like that of a solid granite wall stretching into the heavens. "Judge, you might want to look at this."

Bessy and Arthur opened the back door, stepped out onto the aft deck, and looked up at the massive wall as it swept away. "It's so eerie, but peaceful," Bessy said. The air remained still. A perfect silence buzzed in their ears. The milky-white water lay calm.

"Where's the land?" Arthur asked as he scanned the horizon. "I thought you said the anchor held us. We've been blown into the middle of the ocean."

"No." Bessy moaned, as she scanned the circumference of the vertical wall. "We're in the eye of the hurricane, and a tidal surge has covered this portion of the island."

"It's kind of like the days of Noah," Arthur said, surveying the area.

"Yeah, and we'll be in big trouble when the water starts to recede. The water's going to rush back into the sea and pull everything with it." She stared south, but couldn't see the eyewall. "We've got to get at least one more anchor set before the eyewall passes over us. The one we have out now will pull out of the sand when the wind changes. With the combination of the water flowing off the land and the new wind direction, we could be pulled in two different directions. Come on, we've got to get a back anchor out."

"How are we going to do that?" Arthur asked as he followed Bessy back into the salon.

"I'll show you. It's going to take team work." She raced through the salon to the side door and out on the front deck.

"Stop right there," Blair said. "Where do you two think

you're going?"

Otman glared, his hand gripped both syringes.

"We've got to get another anchor out before the eye of the hurricane passes and the water sweeps back into the ocean."

"You mean there's more coming?" Connie asked, and looked south. "But, there's nothing out there but blue sky."

Otman now realized why he didn't see any sandy beaches. He had been in an eye once before and knew the backside would hit soon. "Connie, you need to get inside and stay out of the way."

Connie was glad she wasn't needed and obliged.

At the bow, Bessy bent down and untied the other anchor. She opened the cap covering the chain. "Arthur, grab the anchor, and walk it to the front windshield." She glanced at the water for a brief moment and was amazed at the silt that had been stirred up. The opaque water stretched to the horizon.

He grunted as he lifted the forty-five-pound Danforth anchor from its cradle. As he walked, Bessy pulled out more chain. The metal clattered across the fiberglass deck.

"Harry," she said, "you need to get up to the flybridge and grab the anchor from Arthur. Otman, go back to the aft deck and take the anchor from Harry. And Harry, keep the anchor on the outside of the antennas and the bimini poles."

Arthur grunted louder as he struggled to lift the anchor above his head. The chain clanked across the windshield.

Otman raced to the back door and stood out on the deck waiting for the anchor. "I've got it," Otman said as Blair lowered the anchor. "What do you want me to do with it? Throw it overboard?"

"No," Blair said. "Just hold it until I get there." Blair stood and stretched out the kinks in his back. *Dang that thing's heavy.*

Otman lowered it onto the deck and waited.

Blair scanned the sky and to the southeast and the south, He thought he could see a pencil line of gray on the horizon.

"We'd better hurry. The back side is coming."

Bessy turned and there on the horizon was a dark edge. Her heart beat wildly. "Have Otman heave the anchor as far off the back as possible," she yelled up to Blair. She pulled out more chain and lowered it into the water. Estimating 150 feet, she cleated it.

Otman stretched over the side holding the anchor and released it. A loud splash followed.

"Bessy, shouldn't we put out more anchors?" Arthur asked. "I thought you were supposed to put out four anchors during a hurricane."

"We should, but we don't have time. Hopefully one of the two anchors we have out will hold. One held us so far."

The boat drifted aimlessly between both anchors as the dark towering wall drifted closer and closer.

CHAPTER SEVENTY-SEVEN

Downstairs in the aft cabin, the closet door stood open. Jane and Walter peered out the port window at the blue sky. Calm filled the room.

"Walter, you're looking into the eye of the hurricane. I've lived in Palm Beach most of my life and never experienced this. I've always evacuated."

"I've never been in a hurricane." He stared out the window for a minute. "I guess we'd better get back in the closet before someone comes down here."

Walter eased the door closed. "Maybe we should rest while we're in a lull. You'll never know when we might need our strength."

Jane snuggled into Walter. "I'll go for that." She closed her eyes. "Maybe, I'll have a good dream about us."

"Hopefully, it'll come true." He rubbed her shoulders. "We've made it halfway."

"We've done better than that. The backside passes quicker. The worst is over."

"I wish that was true about Blair and Otman."

"With the element of surprise on our side, we might have seen the worst of them as well."

Walter chuckled. "I'll believe it when I see it."

CHAPTER SEVENTY-EIGHT

The canyon wall drifted overhead. The cabin darkened. Stillness and peace hung in the air. No one said a word. They waited in the salon, each in their staked-out area. Bessy and Arthur leaned up in the corner beside the back wall. Otman stretched out on the couch. Blair was in the recliner, and Connie lay sprawled on the carpet.

Suddenly, the boat shuddered as wind howled and buffeted it from the west. Horizontal rain pummeled the yacht. The back door popped open and slammed into the wall. Wind and rain surged inside.

Otman jumped up to close the door, but the tumultuous wind tumbled him backward into the table.

The boat rocked and swung around. Tight, white-capped waves curled eastward, with larger waves chasing.

Arthur put his head down and scooted toward the door. Wind and rain battered him. He lunged for the door and shoved it.

Otman crawled out from under the table and back on the couch, rubbing the back of his head.

"What force," Bessy said, as shivers swept her body.

Water swirled from the land, back to the sea. The current and the wind whipped and tugged at the yacht.

Bessy braced herself in the pilothouse, reading the GPS, watching to see if their position held. The second anchor line stretched tight. She cringed with every crack, pop, and thud from unseen objects bouncing off the windshield.

Arthur pulled himself along the wall and made his way up

to where Bessy was. "Is there anything I can do?" He shuddered at the sound of something crashing into the window.

"Not right now," Bessy replied, then her face broke out in a girlish smile. "I wonder what Walter and Jane are doing downstairs?"

"Shh." Arthur said. "Otman or Blair could be listening."

"Okay," she said, "but I've got a good mind to go down and check on them. I believe they might need a chaperone."

A flash of lightning and it's thunderous boom interrupted the frivolity. They saw bright lights for a second as they crouched on the floor beside each other.

"Bessy, we've been sitting beside that duffle bag. What's in it that's so important?"

"It's our survival supplies: a buck knife, bottles of water, sealed food, lights, and an EPIRB."

Arthur grinned, "An EPIRB." He knew that stood for Emergency Position Indicating Radio Beacon. "We should flip the switch. It'll send out a distress signal that passing satellites, aircrafts, and ships will pick up and relay our location to the U.S. Government."

"I'll try to distract them while you reach inside the bag and turn it on."

"How long will it take?"

"Depends on which EPIRB is in there and how fast the Coast Guard can send someone down here."

"Come on." Arthur scooted into the salon, up against the bag. Bessy stayed close to the front to keep an eye on their position.

"Hey," Otman yelled, causing Arthur to twitch. "What are you doing?"

A band of rain battered the boat. "Nothing," Arthur yelled.

Bessy slipped into the galley and filled a pitcher with water. She stacked five plastic glasses together, then carried the glasses in one hand and the pitcher in the other. She stopped at the coffee table. "I brought us something to drink."

Otman sat up and held out his hand.

Arthur eased the bag closer. He kept one eye on the bag's zipper and the other eye bounced from Otman to Blair. He eased the zipper open. As Bessy poured three glasses, he stuck his hand into the bag, rummaging for something he guessed would be an EPIRB. Pushing the bottles of water aside, he felt a rectangular object with one end larger than the other. A flexible object, he guessed was an antenna, protruded from the larger end.

Blair leaped from his seat.

Arthur snatched his hand from the bag.

"Don't drink that," Blair yelled as he pushed the cup from Otman's mouth. The cup tumbled to the floor. Water covered Otman and the couch. "The last time she so eagerly served us something, we fell asleep."

Connie looked at her half-drunk glass of water and held her throat.

"I didn't put anything in the water," Bessy said, and poured herself a glass. "See?" She tilted the glass up and gulped it down. With the empty cup in her hand, she looked from Blair to Otman to Connie. "I told you I didn't put anything in the water."

Connie breathed more easily.

Arthur's hand trembled as he thought about trying to stick his hand back into the bag.

A flash of lightning and an instant boom caused the cabin to reverberate. Eardrums rang as everyone cringed and Connie screamed. The room fell silent as they looked at each other.

"Did we just get hit by lightning?" Arthur asked, looking at Bessy and then at the bag.

CHAPTER SEVENTY-NINE

The aft cabin was filled with gray light, illuminated by less frequent lightning. Walter and Jane leaned against the back wall of the open closet, their legs protruding. Jane held a piece of cardboard and fanned Walter and herself.

Walter reached down to reposition himself. He felt moisture on his palms. "I've sweated so much that this blanket is damp."

Jane stretched her feet out on the carpet and noticed water oozing from around her heel. She reached out and felt it. "You've been sweating heavily," she said, chuckling in a whisper.

Walter glanced around the room. "Is water dripping from above?"

Jane slid out of the closet followed by Walter. "I don't see any," she said as she made her way to a window to look for leaks. She checked one side, while he checked the other side. They met in the center of the bed.

"All dry. Maybe the water's seeping in along the fiberglass and the paneling," Walter said.

"Maybe, but don't worry, the bilge pumps will keep it pumped out," Jane said, smiling while bouncing on the pillow. "This is comfortable. Why don't we sit here for now and stay off the damp floor?"

Walter fluffed his pillow. "Why not? It's more comfortable."

They reclined against the headboard. "I wonder what Bessy and Arthur are doing?" Jane asked.

The yacht rocked as another bolt of lightning flashed in the distance. Walter's eyes widened as he stared at the floor. "Uh, the floor is moving."

"What?" Jane swung her feet to the floor. Water squished between her toes. "This isn't good."

Walter jumped off the bed. "What do you mean? I thought you said the pumps would keep us dry."

"We've got to find the pumps. With all of this jarring, something probably fell into the bilge area and clogged them." Jane looked across the floor. "There's got to be a bilge under us." She dropped to the floor and pulled back the carpet, revealing a drop-in panel. She lifted it.

Water seeped out of the dark hole.

Walter turned on the flashlight from his pocket. Its weak beam didn't penetrate the hole.

"We need a stronger light," Jane said.

The room was searched, but no other flashlight was found. Walter flipped the light switch, but the lamps didn't come on.

"I think something's wrong with the boat's electrical system," Jane felt water on top of her toes. "You'd better sneak up the stairs and get Arthur or Bessy's attention. Someone needs to check the electrical switches. I think during all of that pounding, the breaker switch was bumped off."

Walter eased out of the cabin, down the dim hall, felt the first cabin door, and opened it. Additional light filled the hallway. To keep the door open, he propped one of Connie's suitcases against it. A little more light filtered into the hallway. He went to the next cabin, pushed open the door, and propped it open. The hallway glowed brighter. He hurried to the stairs, listened but heard no one, then climbed up. Peeking out, he saw Arthur in the salon, leaning against the back door. Walter waved and then motioned again.

After a minute or two, Arthur's eyes locked onto Walter. Arthur crawled up on his knees, then stood. "I've got to go to the bathroom." He looked at Otman.

"Go," Otman said from the couch, "but don't take long."

Arthur hurried to the stairs.

Walter backed down the stairs and waited as Arthur scooted downstairs. He grabbed Arthur's hand and pulled him into the hallway.

Arthur felt the water the minute his feet hit the carpet. "What's happening?"

"The pumps aren't working. Jane thinks a breaker switch might have tripped or was bumped in the rough seas. You've got to check it out."

Arthur nodded and crawled back up the stairs. "Hey, we're taking on water downstairs. Where's the breaker box?"

Blair dashed from his recliner to the pilothouse. "What do you mean we're taking on water?"

"There's water on the floor downstairs." Arthur located the breaker box. "That's strange, all switches are on. The pumps should be working."

Blair checked the battery's charge in the first house-bank. It was zero. He checked the next, and the cranking battery. It too showed zero. "How deep is it downstairs?"

Otman, Bessy, and Connie stared into the pilothouse, listening and watching.

"It was at my ankles."

Blair glanced at Otman and made eye contact, then turned his gaze to Otman's pocket.

Otman patted his pocket and nodded.

"That lightening strike must have blown out a thru-hole," Bessy said, glancing around at them. "All we have to do is plug it; that will stop the water from flowing inside. There aren't many to check; then we can bail the water out." She looked from Blair to Otman, then to Arthur. "Come on." She turned and stepped into the stairs.

Otman snatched out a syringe, minus the safety cap and grabbed Bessy. "You're not going anywhere."

Arthur moved toward Otman, but Blair held out his hand,

blocking Arthur's path. "I wouldn't do that. Otman, take them to their cabin and lock them inside. If either gives you any trouble, inject Bessy, then Arthur."

Otman pushed Bessy into the shadows.

Blair stepped backward so Arthur could follow.

Otman forced Bessy and Arthur into the forward cabin and slammed the door.

Connie stood frozen as she stared down into the dim light. *They'll drown down there.*

"Don't you want to put Connie in with them?" Otman asked, looking up. "She doesn't need to come with us."

Connie backed away from the stairs and into the salon. *I don't want to drown.*

"No," Blair said, "she's coming with me. Go down to my room and get my briefcase. We're leaving this boat before it sinks."

CHAPTER EIGHTY

Walter slipped down the hallway and into the aft cabin. He looked around the empty room and his heart stopped. *Where's Jane?* He heard sloshing in the hallway. *Otman's coming. Hide!* Once in the closet, he pulled the door almost closed.

Otman stepped into the cabin and stopped. Water sloshed around his lower shins. He saw the briefcase lying on the nightstand.

The yacht pitched; he tumbled onto the bed. A loud clunk sounded from the bathroom. Otman stared. He stood and crept to the door.

Walter watched from the slit in the closet door.

Otman leaped inside. "Jane!"

Jane lay in the bottom of the tub. Her eyes were glazed.

Otman stepped to the tub and snatched Jane from it. "Aw, you hit your head and have a concussion. That's too bad."

Jane's head rolled from one side to the other. She tried to focus. Her eyes blinked. "Otman?"

Otman dragged her out of the bathroom. "Where's Walter?" He glanced around the cabin.

"You killed him."

"I don't believe you. He's here somewhere, and I'm going to find him." He dropped her on the floor and stepped over to the closet. He yanked the door open, but the closet was empty. "Walter?"

Jane pulled herself up on the bed. "I told you he's dead. I sneaked back on board alone."

Otman surged through more than a foot of water. "You're

lying." He made a sweep of the cabin, but found no one. He moved to the door and looked into the dark hallway.

Out of the darkness, a board swung into Otman's head. The board cracked as Otman stumbled backward.

Walter jumped into the cabin sending a spray of water everywhere. He pulled back the board and swung again. The board snapped in half as an awful thud sounded and Otman fell limp into the bed.

Arthur rushed in with a board cocked behind his head. "These closet shelves are great. Step back and let me whack him. It's a shame these boards weren't in the forward cabin. We would have been able to escape sooner."

"I don't think you're going to need to hit him," Walter laughed. "He's out cold. Thanks for shutting those cabin doors and darkening the hallway so Otman couldn't see me coming."

"Yeah, anytime. Hey, I think you hit him in the same spot we got him when we rammed him with the bed at Southern Retirement Community," Arthur laughed.

"Come on," Bessy said from the doorway. "Let's get Harry."

Walter lifted Jane from the bed and steadied her down the hall to the stairs.

Bessy grabbed Jane's shoulder. "Leave her with me," she whispered to Walter. "You two, go get Harry."

Arthur climbed the stairs first, gripping his board. He looked into the salon and saw no one. He motioned for Walter to follow. Arthur crept into the pilothouse, then looked into the galley. As he stepped into the salon, he lowered the board. *Where are Blair and Connie?*

Walter stepped beside Arthur. "Look!" he said, pointing at the back window. "Blair and Connie are cutting the lines holding the dinghy."

Blair slashed the first rope and then the next. The wind snatched the dinghy and it flipped and flopped like a kite. Blair reached for the cut rope and pulled it down, handing it to

Connie who was standing on the dive platform.

"They're taking the dinghy," Arthur yelled. "They're getting away." He looked at the back wall where he'd left the emergency bag. "And they've got all of the emergency supplies."

Walter rushed back to the stairs and found Bessy helping Jane to the top step. He scooped Jane into his arms. "We've got to get on that dinghy before they get away."

Bessy sprinted for the door.

Walter lumbered through the salon.

Arthur pulled open the door. Wind howled as a light rain fell. The yacht vibrated as air whistled past. "Blair!" Arthur hollered.

Blair and Connie gasped as they looked up. The wind snatched the dinghy from their hands; it flipped and twirled in the wind, tethered on a single rope. "Grab the dinghy," Blair yelled to Connie.

Connie swatted at the dinghy keeping it from knocking her into the water.

Blair reached out and grabbed it, but the wet tube slipped from his grasp and fluttered again in the wind.

A crack like a rifle sounded, and the dinghy tumbled away.

"Look what you've done," Blair yelled up to Arthur. "Now no one's getting off this sinking boat." He snugged the straps on his life vest and clutched the emergency bag under his arm. "We're all going to drown."

CHAPTER EIGHTY-ONE

Inside the salon, Jane sat on the floor and Walter stood, holding onto the wall, looking from those on the aft deck to the stairs. *Otman's not going to sneak up on us.* The shrill wind eased. Outside, land was seen on both sides of the yacht.

Blair and Connie stood on the aft deck to one side. He held the bag in both hands, glad he upgraded last summer to the newest model EPIRB with an integrated GPS system. He looked up into the dark swirling clouds. He knew that once he activated it, it wouldn't be long before the signal would be intercepted.

Blair looked past them, but didn't see Otman. "Where's Otman?"

"Give us that bag," Arthur said, reaching for it.

"Stay back or I'll throw it overboard." He held it over the side.

Connie looked on with large eyes.

"Walter knocked Otman out and he's lying on your bed," Bessy said. "Now give us that bag."

Blair shook his head. *If I'm going to keep from going to jail, I'll need Otman's help.* "No. I'm keeping this safe with me." He unzipped the bag, pulled out the EPIRB, and stuck it out over the water. "I'll activate this as soon as Otman's up in the salon."

"We're not going to get him," Arthur said. "He'll kill us."

Bessy pulled Arthur close to her and whispered. "All we have to do is stuff rags into any thru-hulls that are blown out and the boat won't sink."

"It's too late for that. With the darkness and depth of the water downstairs, you'll never find where the water's coming in. We have to stay with that EPIRB if we're going to survive. If this boat breaks apart, we'll be swept out to sea and never found."

Connie pushed past Arthur and Bessy. "I'll get Otman." She rushed downstairs and into knee-deep water. She shivered and plunged into the dark hallway. *I have plenty of time to get him before we sink.* Inside the aft cabin, she saw Otman sprawled on the bed. "Otman," she yelled, but he didn't move. She cupped her hands, scooped up water, and tossed it into his face.

He sputtered and moaned, slowly opening his eyes. "What happened?" He cradled his forehead with both hands.

"Walter knocked you out," Connie said as she reached out and tried pulling him off the bed. "We're sinking, and Blair won't activate that thing until you're upstairs."

Otman looked blankly into the water swaying around Connie's knees and felt it as it swept across the bed. "We're sinking." His eyes focused and he pushed off the bed. "My head," he yelled as he stood and grasping it again.

Connie stared at the large welt on his forehead. "I'll get something for your headache." She dashed into the bathroom and opened the cabinet above the sink. She pulled out the bottle that read Ibuprofen and sloshed her way back to Otman. "Here, take what you need and come on." She tossed the bottle to him.

Otman twisted the lid off and dumped four pills out. He popped them into his mouth and swallowed them dry. After a few hacking coughs, he shoved the bottle into his pocket. "Where's Walter?"

"Come on. We've got to get upstairs so we can be rescued." Connie helped Otman from the cabin to the stairs. She glanced from him to the top opening in the stairs. *If I help him up, he could fall back on me and kill me.* "You're climbing up on your own." She scooted up the stairs.

Otman's knees buckled as he felt the first step. He got on his hands and knees and crawled to the top. He sprawled out on the floor beside the table, his head throbbing.

Walter glared at Otman.

Arthur stepped inside and handed the shelf to Walter. "I don't think Otman's in any mood to fight us, but if he does, hit him again."

Walter grabbed the board and eased toward Otman.

Arthur grabbed Walter. "Don't hit him yet. Blair has that EPIRB and we need its signal to pinpoint our position. Just keep Otman at bay."

Blair grinned as he flipped the switch on the EPIRB. He looked up at the swirling clouds and knew it would not be long before the signal would be intercepted and a rescue initiated. *Now, we wait.*

CHAPTER EIGHTY-TWO

The phone rang in the United States Coastguard headquarters, in Opa Locka, Florida, seven miles north of Miami. A young officer picked up the phone, "Air Station Miami." After jotting down the information, he slammed the receiver down and snatched up the intercom.

"Launch 65," resonated throughout the modern, three-story building and into the hanger attached to the main complex. Outside at Opa Locka Airport, blue lights marked the 8,002 foot east/west runway."

Lieutenant Hubert, the pilot, raced to sign out the short-range Dolphin helicopter. Attached to his uniform sleeve was an embroidered patch that read: The Busiest Air Sea Rescue Unit In The World. It is the same insignia that is painted on the building, above the center's front door. It acknowledged to all who entered the bravery and dedication of the men and women found inside.

Lieutenant Ricardo, co-pilot, raced upstairs for the briefing. "The distress signal is coming from a sixty-foot Hatteras documented to Bessy Tillman. The location is Andros, inside South Bight." The position of the signal was displayed on the chart. "You'll be flying into the back side of Hurricane Angelina. Winds are gusting to sixty from the West." Ricardo raced downstairs and out into the hangar. He ran past the Falcon Jet, sprinting to the second of three helicopters.

Hubert sat in the left seat, running through the preflight checklist.

The rescue swimmer, Pete, and the flight mechanic, Lee, buckled in and closed the side door.

Ricardo jumped into the co-pilot's seat as the large, blue metal doors of the hangar crept open. Twenty-mile-an-hour winds drove rain inside. A cart pulled the helicopter onto the tarmac, where the tow-bar was disconnected.

The twin turbine engines started to whine, then the massive overhead blades began to circle the craft. Navigation lights flashed red, white, and green.

Ricardo checked the instruments. "Let's do it."

"Rescue 6517," Hubert said into the radio, "requesting permission for take off."

"Rescue 6517, you're free to depart," the radio squawked.

The engines whined louder. Rain pelted the windshield as the blades slapped the air. The aircraft's tail lifted and then its nose. They flew straight into the easterly wind. The airport looked deserted; most aircraft had been flown to a safe location.

The thumping faded as the large metal doors closed. The helicopter's navigational lights disappeared behind a curtain of rain.

"I can't believe the flight brief," Ricardo said. "The embedded code came from the EPIRB registered to a sixty-foot Hatteras owned by Bessy Tillman. Good grief, we're going to rescue a bunch of old ladies in a hurricane."

"Why weren't they watching the weather report?" Hubert asked.

"They were probably playing bridge."

Ricardo turned his attention to the time and announced their fifteen-minute position back to Miami.

The helicopter buffeted in the sudden wind increase. Hubert tightened his grip on the yoke. "This rescue is going to be interesting."

"It could be worse," Ricardo said, glancing from the instruments to the rain. "We could be flying into the eastern side and snatching those women up in hurricane force winds. Can you imagine what their hairdos will look like?"

Hubert watched the radar screen. It showed strong rain to their right. He steered the craft directly east, remaining clear of it. "We should be over them within twenty minutes."

Now thirty minutes into their mission, like clockwork, Ricardo broadcasted the helicopter's position.

The helicopter shimmied as it entered another gust of wind and rain, then turned and flew due south toward the northern tip of Andros. Soon Morgan's Bluff appeared in front of them.

"Look at that Sundancer anchored and riding out the storm," Ricardo said. "Some boaters just don't pay attention to the weather."

"At least he's in a protected anchorage," Hubert responded.

"Pete," Ricardo announced over the headset minutes later, "we're nearing the drop zone. Be prepared to enter the water."

Pete zipped up his wet suit and pulled his mask on his forehead. He slipped his feet into the fins and rechecked his life vest. He gave a thumbs-up to Lee and waited.

Lee positioned his hand on the door handle.

"One minute until we begin our search," Hubert announced. "Winds are gusting at forty-six miles per hour, out of the west." He maneuvered the craft lower. Suddenly, white-capped waves disappeared as they flew across a beach and into South Bight.

Pete looked down at the land and water. Then he looked at Lee. "I'm glad I'm not going into those large seas."

"There they are," Hubert said, "straight ahead." He stared at the Hatteras. The waterline was at the portholes. "We got here just in time. Pete, get ready."

The helicopter began to hover. Lee hooked into his safety harness and slid open the door. Rain and wind blew inside. The blades thundered, kicking up backwash.

Pete looked down at the yacht. *I won't be needing my mask and fins.* He tossed each piece to the back of the helicopter.

Lee pushed the hoist cable out the door and handed the sling to Pete to hook into.

Inside the Hatteras, they heard the rotors beating. Blair raced to Otman and handed him the buck knife from the bag. "Keep them downstairs for now." He dashed for the ladder leading to the flybridge.

Otman popped the knife blade open.

Pete pulled off the headset and clipped in. "Ready." He swung out on the right side of the helicopter and Lee lowered him into sea spray, down to the flybridge.

Otman stood just inside brandishing a dining room chair in one hand and the buck knife in the other. "Stay back," he yelled to the others, as Blair took a step up the ladder.

"What about me?" Connie shouted.

Blair climbed out into the wind. He squinted as sea spray pierced his face.

Pete landed on flybridge.

He unhooked and the line was pulled away. Approaching Blair, he shouted, "Is anyone hurt?"

"Not too bad. I'm Judge Blair," he yelled above the wind and the pop of the rotor blades.

"I'm Pete."

Otman popped up out of the hatch, closed it, and stood on top of it.

Blair continued yelling, "That big man is my bounty hunter. The others downstairs jumped bail. We caught up with them and were bringing them back when this storm hit us. We were fine until we were hit by lightning. It knocked out our electrical system. We're taking on water."

"Are they dangerous?"

"Not now, they're scared to death we're going to sink. They'll do anything just to get off. I'd suggest you lift me first, then that man. We'll handcuff them as they're brought on-board. Otman will keep them under control."

Pete looked at Otman and smiled. "I bet he can control a

crowd."

Blair nodded.

Pete motioned for the sling. He grabbed it and wrapped it around Blair. Blair spun as he was lifted. Soon the sling was back in Pete's hands and he wrapped it around Otman. With a thumbs-up, Otman rose in the air.

Ricardo broadcasted Rescue 6517's latest fifteen-minute position.

The hatch on the flybridge popped open. Pete dashed to the opening. He held out both hands. "Stay down there."

"They're criminals," Arthur yelled.

"Get down," Pete yelled and blocked the opening. "Wait for my instructions."

Walter and Bessy stood on the aft deck. He helped her climb onto the flybridge. She rushed toward Pete.

Pete backed away from the hatch, pinned against the dash. He held one hand in front and kept the other by the sheaved knife strapped to his ankle.

Otman looked at Blair as he was pulled inside the helicopter. Blair stumbled forward, bumping Hubert. The helicopter dipped right, Otman bumped into Lee causing him to stumble out the door. Lee's safety harness snapped; he tumbled through the air screaming.

The helicopter banked hard left. Its red, white, and green nav lights disappeared in the heavy downpour.

CHAPTER EIGHTY-THREE

"Lee!" Pete gasped, watching him tumble thirty feet and belly flop into the water a foot off the anchor line. He thrashed wildly as the current swept him toward the yacht's bow.

Bessy raced to the side and reached for the safety ring, but it was missing. She yanked open the footlocker at her knees and snatched out a rope.

Walter watched Lee being swept alongside the Hatteras.

With one fluid motion, the knot loosened and Bessy tossed one end to the man who was bobbing past the dive platform. The rope tightened and Bessy's muscles strained. "Help me."

Arthur and Walter raced to her side, grabbed the rope, and pulled.

Pete slipped over the side of the flybridge, down to the aft deck and raced down the ladder to the dive platform. He grabbed the rope and pulled. "Hang on, Lee."

Bessy, Arthur, and Walter grunted and pulled.

Lee dangled behind the dive platform. Pete tried to lift Lee, but couldn't. Walter and Arthur hurried to Pete's side. They pulled Lee out and lifted him up to the aft deck, then carried him into the salon. Jane looked on from the couch, holding an ice pack to the back of her head.

Drizzle dotted the windows. Dark clouds sailed away as lighter silvery clouds appeared. The wind slowed to between fifteen and twenty miles per hour.

Connie clutched the EPIRB like a lifeline. She didn't move or say anything. *They left me.*

Bessy stepped up to Pete.

"Who are you?" Pete demanded.

"I'm Bessy Tillman."

"You're the owner of this boat?" Pete asked.

"Yes, I'm the owner."

"What happened here?" Pete asked, glancing around the salon.

"Those men held us hostage. After the storm struck, lightening hit us. We started taking on water."

"Who are those men?"

"Judge Harrison Blair, my ex-husband, and Mr. Otman, a loyal employee of his. They're dangerous. They jumped bail in the U.S."

Connie cowered, waiting to hear her name mentioned.

"And she's with them," Bessy added and pointed at Connie. "But now that they're gone, she won't be a threat."

Pete smirked. "I was told by Blair, that he was a judge and Mr. Otman was a bounty hunter. He said I shouldn't trust you."

Arthur now understood why Pete held the hatch closed.

"Well, the first man *is* a judge," Walter said, "but a crooked one. And the other is a killer. He killed seniors at a nursing home, just to make his job easier."

"What do we do now?" Jane asked.

"Exactly what we're doing," Pete said. "Stay calm and don't panic. That helicopter probably radioed for help and another rescue helicopter is on its way. With that EPIRB still sending out a distress signal, they'll know right where to look."

"But we're sinking," Walter said, envisioning Jane's yacht sinking. "How long will it take them to get here?"

"It depends on which aircraft they send," Pete said.

"I don't believe this boat will sink much further," Bessy said. "With the boat's draft and the amount of water downstairs, I'd say we're already sitting on the bottom."

"Now we wait." Pete scanned the sky. "With two missions underway, there's no telling when we'll be rescued."

CHAPTER EIGHTY-FOUR

In Opa Locka, Florida, torrential rain pounded the Coastguard complex. Water pooled around the buildings and covered the parking lots. Inside the command center, quiet eeriness filled the room as the young officer glanced away from the radio he had been staring at for the last fifteen minutes, and looked at the commanding officer. "Sir, Rescue 6517 missed its regular fifteen minute position announcement. It's been thirty minutes since we've last heard from them."

"Start a search and rescue. Get that Falcon jet airborne first and then another helicopter in route. Start the search at the Hatteras. Now!"

"Yes sir." The young officer grabbed the intercom. "Launch, 25."

The Falcon jet pilot raced into the hanger.

Back inside central command center, the young officer looked back at the commander. "Sir, the HH 60 Jayhawk helicopter from Clearwater is available."

"Send them. They'll love getting an opportunity to fly to the Bahamas."

"Launch 6022," the intercom blared.

Two blue hanger doors opened and the Falcon jet was pulled outside. Rescue 2511, with its flashing strobe lights, raced down the east-west runway and into the dreary sky.

Out in the hanger, Lieutenant Davis sat in the pilot's seat checking off the preflight requirements when Lieutenant Nickels, the copilot, sprinted up to the helicopter. She opened the door and climbed in. "Rescue 6517 hasn't been heard from in over thirty minutes. Their last known position was over a sinking Hatteras at South Bight, on Andros. The yacht's EPIRB is still emitting a signal. We're to fly down there and see if anyone is still on board."

Jason, the rescue swimmer and Hoya, the flight mechanic, climbed into the back and pulled the door closed. The cart pulled the helicopter to the departure pad as a steady rain fell. The twin engines whined. The blades began to rotate. Soon the rotors were spinning at full revolutions.

"We're clear for takeoff," Nickels said.

The helicopter ascended into the storm and flew eastward. Davis glanced with a rhythmic sequence at each instrument. Outside, gray light shrouded everything.

Nickels broadcasted their first fifteen-minute position.

Davis applied right pressure on the yoke and the helicopter began a slow turn. Their new heading led them toward the middle of Andros. The wind and rain slackened the further east they flew.

"Rescue 6022, this is Rescue 2511. We have visual on that Hatteras. It is taking on water, but at this time, there is no sign of activity." The Falcon slowed and banked, dropping to 500 feet.

"This is Rescue 6022," Nickels said. "Our estimated time of arrival is approximately twenty minutes."

Once the Falcon circled around and leveled out at 500 feet, it headed straight for the Hatteras for another fly-by. "Rescue 6022, people are emerging from inside. Repeat, there are people onboard."

"Copy that. We're standing by."

Minutes passed while Jason and Hoya developed and rehearsed their rescue procedures. Now they were ready and waited.

Davis announced their next fifteen-minute position.

With the hurricane moving away from Andros and approaching Florida Keys, the visibility increased to ten miles.

Davis pushed the yoke forward and the helicopter dropped in altitude. He and Nickels watched as the large trees disappeared under them and sand at North Bight emerged. "Look, down there," Davis said, pointing. "What used to be beautiful water is all white. It's hard to distinguish water and the beach."

Nickels stared at what appeared to be a stream of sand flowing across the beach. "I've never seen anything like that."

Jason and Hoya looked from the side windows in amazement.

Soon they passed the Middle Bight and were flying down the eastern edge of Andros. Out across the deep water, large waves bobbed, in a state of frenzied agitation. White water lined the barrier reef.

"There's South Bight," Davis announced over their headsets. "What a mess."

Nickels followed what appeared to be a slithering white snake from the beach inland. "There's the Hatteras." She picked up the mic. "Rescue 2511, this is Rescue 6022. We have a visual on the Hatteras."

"Roger. We're leaving the area in search of Rescue 6517." The Falcon banked and flew north.

Davis hovered the helicopter thirty feet above the Hatteras, kicking up rotor-wash.

Hoya clipped into his safety harness, pushed the side door open, and forced the hoist outside.

Jason hooked into the sling, was lowered to the flybridge, and detached. The helicopter pulled back and waited while Jason gave instructions.

The hoist was attached to Lee's bare hook—a hook attached to the center of all flight personnel vests for easy retrieval. He hadn't sustained any lasting injuries from his fall. Hoya brought him aboard. Soon all were extracted off the yacht and the helicopter banked right. A few patches of blue sky were visible out the windows. The helicopter flew northwest, across Andros. "Coastguard Miami, this is Rescue 6022.

We've rescued all from the Hatteras and are in route home."

Bessy watched her partially submerged yacht fade into the distance as Arthur held her hand.

Walter wrapped his arm around Jane and drew her close. "Arthur, Bessy, I didn't want to tell you while we were still held captive, but Justin has been killed and Shelly has been charged with his murder."

"What! Why didn't you tell me?" Arthur shouted.

"Hold on Arthur. I knew it wouldn't do any good, and besides, Jane's attorney recommended one of the best criminal lawyers in Palm Beach. We didn't want you to worry until after you were safe from Blair and Otman. It has been a little chaotic since then."

Arthur turned to Jane. "Thanks for helping Shelly."

"You're welcome."

Connie sat huddled in the back. Her thoughts drifted to herself. *What's going to happen to me?*

CHAPTER EIGHTY-FIVE

The Falcon Jet, screamed through the sky at 1000 feet. The pilots searched by nautical miles inside a 'box pattern' grid. Dipping its left wing, it departed the imaginary box and lined up on a new grid.

"Rescue 2511, this is U.S. Coastguard Miami."

"This is Rescue 2511, go ahead, Miami."

"We haven't intercepted any distress signals, and don't believe Rescue 6517 has crashed. Lieutenant Hubert probably set the helicopter down on a beach on Andros. Search the coastline."

"Roger, Coastguard Miami." The jet circled around, lined up on the beach, and flew north.

The beaches were strewn with seaweed, boards, plastic bottles, and limbs. Islanders were out walking around, inspecting the damage, and picking up items of interest.

The jet roared across the northern tip of Andros and banked hard left. "Down there," the copilot said.

The white and orange striped helicopter materialized under the tree line, with no apparent damage.

"Coastguard Miami. This is Rescue 2511. We have a visual on Rescue 6517. Repeat, Rescue 6517 is sitting on the northern tip of Andros at Morgan's Bluff."

The jet circled north of Andros out across the shallow waters, descending to 500 feet. With the northern beaches in sight and flaps down, it headed back to the downed helicopter, in slow flight.

"Coastguard Miami, this is Rescue 2511. There are no

signs of the passengers or crew at this time."

"Rescue 2511, please continue visual. We're sending a helicopter."

After receiving instructions, The Jayhawk helicopter, with the rescued passengers of the Hatteras onboard, diverted, and increased speed. After a short period of time, they approached the island's northern tip with the downed helicopter in sight.

"Set us down over there," Nickels said, pointing off to the side of the Dolphin helicopter.

"What do you think happened?" Bessy asked Arthur.

"With all of that bad weather, there's no telling."

The Jayhawk settled into the wet sand. The back door slid open, Hoya, Pete and Jason leaped out into the swirling wind. Pete outran them all and vaulted through the open side door. The back of the helicopter was empty. As he stepped between the two pilots, Hoya and Jason simultaneously opened both front doors. The pilots sat strapped in their seats, slumped over their yokes.

Hoya and Jason said, one second behind the other, "I've got a pulse."

Pete reached between the pilots and picked up the mic. "Coastguard Miami. Both men are alive, but we're unable to arouse them."

"Where are Blair and Otman?" Arthur asked, stepping up and looking inside. Walter and Bessy looked over his shoulders. Jane remained in the Jayhawk.

"Look over here." Walter pointed to footprints, leading down to the water's edge.

Bessy, Arthur, and Walter followed three sets of footprints.

"Look at the size of this set," Walter said, kneeling beside them. "They're enormous."

"I'd say they're a size fifteen," Arthur said.

"They could only belong to Otman." Walter looked across the water and then back to the bluff. "Arthur, this is Morgan's Bluff. Pirates used to hide out here and bury their treasures.

Jane and I stopped right out there and asked a fellow if he'd seen Bessy's boat." He glanced out to where the Sea Ray Sundancer and two others were previously anchored. "At least he got out of here before that hurricane hit."

Arthur looked back at the downed helicopter. "How ironic pirates landed here long ago and today, two modern-day pirates, Blair and Otman, landed here."

"So, one set belongs to Blair," Bessy said. "Whose are the third set and why would they come down to the beach and disappear into the water? There's no sign that a boat's been ashore."

Walter stepped too within a foot of the water. "Maybe they ran through the water to cover their tracks." He searched in both directions. "They could have gone anywhere from here."

Arthur turned and looked back at the helicopter.

"How would Harry have had time to call someone to pick them up?" Bessy asked.

"He couldn't have." Walter studied the footprints again and discovered one set of prints headed from the water to the helicopter. "But whoever it was came out of the water here and headed to the helicopter."

Arthur stood beside Bessy, staring back at the downed helicopter. *I wonder . . .* Arthur sprinted up the beach toward the downed helicopter.

"Come on," Bessy yelled, giving chase. "Arthur's found something."

Walter joined Arthur, who was staring through the front windshield. "What is it?"

"Walter, look at them. Don't they look like they're sleeping?"

Walter's eyes enlarged. "They look like they've been drugged. The last I remember, Otman had two syringes in his pocket."

"Do you think he used them?" Bessy asked.

"Sure." Arthur breathed. "And that's how they got away."

Pete and Lee moved around to the helicopter's side door. Pete grabbed the hanging harness and pulled the strap in all directions, looking for anything that might have cut it, causing Lee to fall during the mission. He looked closer at the harness. "This wasn't caused by abrasion; it was deliberately cut. It's not jagged at all. Look how smooth the cut is."

"That big guy cut my line." Lee reached for the safety harness. "He could have killed me."

Arthur turned to Bessy and Walter. "Finally, others are starting to see what we've been saying. Who knows how many he's killed."

Bessy and Walter nodded.

The two pilots were prepped and laid in the back of the helicopter. With limited space in Rescue 6022, Jason and Hoya remained behind, under the trees, and watched the Jayhawk lift off. They also were ordered to guard the downed helicopter.

The two pilots were dropped off at a hospital in Miami. Rescue 6022 was given orders to fly back to their home base in Clearwater and on their way, they made a slight deviation to Palm Beach Airport.

As the helicopter flew on final approach, Connie saw the flashing lights of the police cars and an ambulance. She let out a long sigh. *Where do I begin explaining what happened?*

The helicopter settled on the puddled tarmac. As the door opened, a light breeze blew inside. Silvery clouds drifted overhead. While the blades slowed, two police officers appeared, removed Connie, and led her to the back of a police car. It sped off with sirens blaring.

An ambulance rolled to a stop beside the now-quiet helicopter. As paramedics loaded Jane in the ambulance, she grabbed Walter's hand. "Are you coming with me?"

"I don't think the paramedics will let me. I'll catch a taxi." He bent to kiss her.

The two paramedics looked at each other. They both nodded. "Don't tell anyone that you rode with her. Come on."

Walter smiled and climbed in. He sat beside the paramedic and held Jane's hand. The back doors closed. The ambulance pulled out into the deserted street and sped away without lights flashing and sirens blaring.

Arthur and Bessy followed an officer into a private room where they were debriefed. Soon they were ushered to the front door where a taxi was waiting at the curb. As they started to get in, a police car pulled up.

"Mr. and Mrs. McCullen," Newberry said, leaping from the car. "Would you please accompany me to the police station? I'd like for you to sit in on Connie's questioning. You can watch from behind the mirrored window. She'll never know you're there."

"I don't know," Arthur said. "I just found out my daughter's being held for murder. I'd like to go see her."

"I understand," Newberry said, "but the jail is closed to visitors because of the hurricane. If you'll accompany me to the police station, I'll take you to see your daughter after I get finished with Connie's questioning."

"You'd do that?" Arthur asked.

Newberry nodded, and Arthur and Bessy slipped into his back seat.

CHAPTER EIGHTY-SIX

Floodlights cast an orangish glow around the West Palm Beach Police Station. Wind swirled and heavy raindrops pounded the facility. Streams of water gushed from the rooftop and pooled in the parking lot.

Inside the building, two people walked down a bright, but deserted, hallway.

Connie shifted in the wooden seat inside the interview room. She rested her elbows on the table as her eyes darted around the room. A light buzz hummed from the overhead fluorescent bulbs. The white walls intensified the brightness. She raked her fingers through her knotted hair.

What would Justin's advice be? She glanced up at the mirrored window.

Don't say anything without a lawyer present. She glanced back down at the table, sensing someone watching her. *If I ask for a lawyer, that could imply that I'm guilty.* She clawed her fingers across her scalp.

The door creaked as it swung open. "Hello, Connie. I'm Detective Mike Newberry and this is Detective Yvette Wheeler."

Yvette was five-eleven, short black hair, and muscular. Her badge hung on the front of her belt.

Connie watched Newberry step into the room, around the table, and sit with his back to the mirrored window.

Yvette walked around the other side of Connie and sat at the end of the table. She nodded and smiled. "We have four individuals that have filed disturbing reports against you."

"I didn't do anything," Connie said, looking down at the table.

"Kidnapping is a serious charge," Newberry said, flipping to a blank page in the legal pad.

"What?" Connie asked. "Kidnapping. I didn't kidnap anyone. I was forced to go with them."

"Nobody forced you," Newberry said, his face tightening. "I've read the complaints against you, and there's never a mention of a gun being held to your head."

Connie slumped forward. "No, I wasn't held at gunpoint," she said in a whisper, "but . . ." *Think, what would Justin say? What about all of those legal documents that I've typed over the years. I should be able to recall something I read to defend myself.*

"If no gun was used against you, then why didn't you help those four escape?"

Arthur and Bessy sat of the edge of their chairs, listening. A plain-clothes detective sat in the room with them.

"I tried, but that night I went into their cabin to let them out, they were all asleep and I couldn't wake them. I tried to escape myself, but it was dark and when I was standing on the dive platform readying to leave, I couldn't tell which way was shore. I was afraid I'd end up lost at sea; I went back to my bed and went to sleep. I never had another opportunity to help them escape or myself. If I'd been caught, Otman would have killed me."

"Otman had nothing to do with it. You enjoyed being waited on hand and foot. It was a lifestyle that fit you. You had your own servants."

Connie took short breaths. Her eyes brightened. *But that was in the Bahamas.* She sat up straight and stared at Newberry. *He can't charge me with kidnapping.* She leaned back in her seat and crossed her arms. "They were kidnapped in the Bahamas. That falls under Bahamian laws."

"So you admit you kidnapped them."

"I'm not answering any more of your questions. I'm innocent." She smiled as she tried to remember more of the documents that she had typed. *But what if they send me back to the Bahamas to stand trial?* Her smile faded.

Newberry opened another file. "What about you and Justin trying to overdose Shelly."

Connie stiffened. *Deny. Deny. Deny.* She heard Justin's voice coming from deep inside. "I don't know what you're talking about."

"Stop playing games, Connie," he said, while pointing to the paragraph he read. "You wanted Shelly dead, so you could have Justin for yourself."

Connie shook her head. "People get divorces every day."

"So," Yvette said as she scribbled a note on the legal pad, "you're saying that you and Justin weren't seeing each other?"

"Yes. No," Connie said, and lowered her head. "He loved me and I loved him. He was getting a divorce."

"And when was this divorce to take place?" Yvette asked.

Connie drew in a deep breath. A slight smile etched her cheeks. "The day we went to the airport."

"The airport!" Newberry said. His voice echoed off the walls. "So you were with Justin at the airport?"

"Yes," she answered, nodding.

Newberry leaned across the table, deep in thought. "So you were the last person to see Justin alive."

Connie froze. A lump lodged in her throat. *I think I should ask for an attorney.*

Yvette stared at Connie. *We've got her.*

"Connie!" Newberry proceeded, "Did you kill Justin?" He sat back in the seat, crossed his arms, and watched.

Bessy grabbed Arthur's hand.

"I-I want a lawyer," Connie stammered.

Newberry smirked. "Innocent people don't need attorneys."

"She killed Justin," Arthur mumbled, staring through the window at Connie. "I knew Shelly was innocent."

"I didn't kill Justin," Connie swore, her cheeks flushed.

"Then who did?" Yvette asked.

Connie stared past her lap to the floor, flicking at her fingernail.

"You're the last person known to be with Justin," Newberry shouted. He watched as Connie cradled her head in her hands. He glanced over at Yvette. They smiled at each other and then looked back at Connie. "The evidence all points to you. We'll hold you on murder charges."

"He did it," Connie said, under her breath, trembling.

"Who did it?" Newberry asked, leaning toward Connie.

"Blair killed Justin." Her head dropped to the table and landed on her crossed arms. A small sniffle emitted.

Puh-lease. Newberry's eyes rolled up. *What an act.*

"Blair," Connie mumbled, with short sniffling breaths, "hated . . . Justin." She rubbed her nose across her sleeve, "And blamed Justin for screwing up his life by having Arthur placed at Southern Retirement Community."

"Connie," Yvette said, "we want to make sure all of this is recorded." She pushed the recorder closer to Connie. "Sit up; speak clearly, and tell us what happened."

Connie rubbed her eyes as she sat up. "It was horrible."

"You're doing the right thing. Take your time and explain," Newberry said, while trying to read Connie's eyes. *Keep her talking, and sooner or later, she'll trip up.*

Connie glanced from Newberry to Yvette and back. "Justin and I went to Bali. Blair lured Justin back by claiming there was something wrong with Justin and Shelly's divorce papers and that the documents needed to be corrected. Blair's such a good persuader that Justin believed him even though Justin already had all of the money."

"Whose money?" Newberry asked.

Connie looked down at the floor for a long moment before continuing. "I don't know. He didn't tell me everything. Blair met us at the airport and was to drive Justin to the courthouse, sign the documents, and then we'd fly off to the Bahamas. Instead, when we got into Blair's Towncar, he drove us to the back side of the airport. There he exploded into a rage, screaming that Justin screwed up his life when Arthur arrived at Southern Retirement Community. Blair claimed Arthur was the reason he lost Bessy's money and her house. That's when Blair took out a pistol and shot Justin in the back of the head." She drew in a long breath. Her head sagged forward. She glanced out of the corner of her eye at the detectives.

Newberry scribbled illegibly: The Bahamas. *That's strange. Shelly was headed there when we arrested her. Hmm?* He stood. "Connie, how do we know you're telling the truth?" He stepped over to the mirrored window and turned around. "With what we know about you from Arthur, Bessy, Jane, and Walter, we're going to need some proof to verify your statements."

Connie cleared her throat. "Like what?"

"What did Blair do with the gun?" Newberry asked, with crossed arms.

"I don't know," Connie answered, shaking her head.

"Do you have any information about the crime scene that only someone who was there would know?"

"Yes, Justin was shot at the end of the runway at Palm Beach International Airport."

"That's common knowledge," Yvette said. "We need facts that only someone present could possibly know."

"He was shot with a hand gun."

Newberry controlled his smile.

"The paper said he was shot with a nine-millimeter," Yvette added.

Connie sighed. "Look, I'm telling the truth." She paused as she again searched her memory. "His body was rolled under a bush."

Newberry stepped away from the wall toward the table and sat. "All right. Who rolled his body under the bush?"

"Blair did." Tense lines furrowed in Connie's face.

"And what did you do?" Yvette asked.

Connie fidgeted. "I-I cried," her voice faded.

Newberry smirked. *She's getting an A for her performance, but I don't trust her.* "And then what?" He propped his elbows on the table.

"I demanded that Blair drop me off at the airport."

"The airport? Where did you fly to?"

"The Bahamas."

"When?" Newberry asked, narrowing his focus.

"That afternoon."

Newberry sat up. "On what airline?"

"Continental."

Continental? Shelly was boarding a Continental flight to the Bahamas when she was arrested. How many flights from West Palm would Continental have in the afternoon? Probably one. Newberry stood as he glanced into the mirror and nodded toward the door. "Just one minute," he said, and stepped out.

Yvette looked at the recorder and allowed it to continue.

Newberry closed the door and met the plain-clothes detective. "I need you to find out the tag number for Harrison T. Blair's Towncar. Then get over to the airport's parking garage and find that car. Impound it and have forensics go over it, now. That car might have been involved in the Roble murder. "Hurry!"

"You don't trust her, do you?" the detective asked.

"No, but we've got to start somewhere. Who knows, she might be telling the truth. Get out there and find that Towncar."

Newberry pulled out his cell phone and dialed, while the other detective hurried down the hallway and disappeared.

"This is Detective Newberry. I need the airport surveillance tape from Shelly Roble's file. Have it set up for me to view." *I bet Shelly and Connie were booked on the same flight. Connie is the one I should have arrested.*

Newberry froze. *Shelly's not the killer. She's innocent.*

CHAPTER EIGHTY-SEVEN

On the third floor of Palm Beach General Hospital, in a private room, Jane sat up on the side of the bed. The antiseptic smell permeated the room. "I'm not staying tonight," she said to the nurse. "I feel fine."

"That's just the medicine talking," the nurse said. "You need to follow the doctor's advice. He's admitted you over-night for observation."

"Observation, huh. He won't be here to observe me. He's going home and so am I. Walter, call a limo. I'm sleeping in my own bed tonight." She scratched out the phone number and handed it to him.

Walter smiled. "Yes, ma'am." He turned and looked at the nurse. "You might as well give up. I've known her for a short period of time, and I know for a fact she's going to do what-ever she says." He lifted the phone and dialed.

The nurse groaned. "The doctor's not going to be happy." She turned and stomped off.

"Thank you," Jane said, taking the phone from Walter. "This is Jane Winchester. I'd like for you to pick me up at Palm Beach General Hospital. Take me to my house and charge it to my account." She smiled and hung up. "The owner lives a few blocks from me."

Earlier while Jane had an MRI, Walter went shopping for clothes. Now that they were alone, he pulled the bags from the closet and sat at the foot of the bed. "I bought you something." He pulled out the first box.

"Oh, you shouldn't have," Jane said,

"I couldn't let you go home in that hospital gown."

Jane smiled as she lifted the lid. A bright flowered-print, button-up shirt shimmered. The box fell to the floor. "I love the colors. Thank you."

Walter pulled out the next box and laid it in her lap. "Hopefully the colors match."

Jane draped the shirt on the edge of the bed and picked up the box. She lifted the lid off. "Oh," she gasped. "They're beautiful." She lifted the khaki colored capri pants.

Before she could say anything, Walter pulled out the last box and held it out for her.

Jane leaned into Walter, watching.

Walter lifted the box top revealing a pair of red tennis shoes. "I think they're your size."

"Oh, Walter," she cooed. She scooted up on her knees and fell into his warm arms. She pulled him tight and kissed him.

"Do you like them?"

Jane kissed him again. With a short breath, she asked. "Can't you tell?"

"I'm glad. Garraway, the cop in Nassau, said I'd never lose you as long as you wore your red shoes."

Walter hurried from the room so she could change and they could leave. As he waited, he saw the nurse coming back triumphant with a young intern.

She stepped around him and entered the room. The doctor was one-step behind; Walter followed.

Jane brushed at the shirt; the wrinkles fell out.

"Tell her, Doctor," the nurse said.

"Ma'am, you really should stay the night for observation. It's for your own good."

"Thank you for your concern," she said, while adjusting the pants, "but I'll recover better at home." She straightened up and turned to Walter. "I'm ready to go."

"All right." Walter stepped around the nurse and held Jane's hand. "Thank you for everything," he said to the doctor, and they headed for the door.

"Sign here," the nurse snapped.

"What is it?" Walter asked as they stopped, and he took the clipboard.

"Jane needs to sign this AMA form."

"What?"

"It says she's checking out against medical advice."

"I'll be glad to sign," Jane said and picked up the pen and signed while Walter held the clipboard. He handed it back to the nurse, and they walked off, holding hands.

They waited a few minutes downstairs in the lobby until a white stretch limo pulled up.

"This is ours," Jane said.

By the time they reached the limo, the driver hurried around the back of the vehicle and held open the back door. "Hello, Ms. Winchester."

"Hello, Joseph. Thanks for coming."

"I'm glad you're okay."

Jane climbed into the cool air and slid across the back seat. Walter followed. Jane rested her head on his shoulder as the limo pulled away from the curb. She looked down at her new clothes. *And again, Walter doesn't have any clothes.* She looked up into his eyes. "Walter, I know these last few days have been adventurous, but I'm not ready for it to end. Are you?"

"A week ago, I would never have dreamed I'd be saying this, but I had a blast. I discovered many things. And you were the best discovery. My only regret was that you weren't able to show me that special island down in the Exumas."

"I have a lot of places I'd like to show you." She grinned. "But first we need to buy you some clothes." She looked into the front seat. "Joseph, don't take me home. We're going shopping."

"Yes ma'am," Joseph said. "Where to?"

"PBI."

Joseph stared into the rearview mirror.

Jane smiled. "That's right, PBI."

Walter looked puzzled from Jane to Joseph. *They're hiding something from me.*

Joseph's eyes shifted to Walter for a split second. Then the limo slowed, hung a u-turn, and accelerated.

CHAPTER EIGHTY-EIGHT

The receding breeze from the hurricane drifted across the barbed wire fence surrounding Palm Beach Jail. A dark, unmarked car pulled around back and stopped. Sprinkles dotted the windshield. The driver's door and the two back doors opened. Newberry handed an umbrella to Arthur and Bessy. They hurried up to the ramp to the second floor.

Shelly pushed open the door and stepped outside.

Arthur ran up and threw his arms around Shelly. They both pulled each other tight, unable to speak.

Bessy stepped up and encircled them.

Newberry stood and looked away for a few minutes. Then he joined them.

"Shelly, thanks for agreeing to come down and listen in on Connie's questioning and testimony. I want to make sure she's locked up for a long time. Thanks for telling us where the spare key to your house was. A forensics team is there now, collecting evidence. They've lifted prints from the guest bedroom where you were drugged. The preliminary reports show that Connie's fingerprints are all over that room."

"I knew it," Shelly said. "Even though I was drugged, I sensed Connie was standing over me."

"Shelly, I'm sorry I was so hard on you over Justin's murder. The evidence was overwhelming against you."

Shelly sighed with a half smile. "I'll forgive you this time, but don't ever do that to me again."

"Thanks. Let's go watch Connie squirm. You'll be a great help if we have a question that needs to be cleared up."

At the police station, Shelly, Arthur, and Bessy sat in the darkened viewing room. Shelly sipped coffee and stared at Connie through the large one-way window.

Connie glanced around the room, but averted her eyes from the window.

Shelly leaned forward. *How does it feel to be locked in a room by yourself?* She smiled and took another sip. *Just wait until you hear that metal door slam in your cell.*

The door swung open. Newberry and Yvette stepped inside. Newberry laid the folder down on the table and sat with his back to the mirror. Yvette sat at the end of the table.

Newberry opened the folder and pulled out the top sheet.

"It's late," Connie said. "How much longer? I'd like to go home. It's been a long day."

Newberry glanced up and then looked at Yvette. "I don't believe it'll take us long." He smiled. "Do you?"

"No," Yvette answered, and looked at Connie. "Not at all."

Connie smiled and leaned back.

"Connie," Newberry began, "we've found Blair's Towncar. Inside, we've found four sets of fingerprints that belong to Blair, Otman, Justin, and you."

Connie's smile faded as she stiffened. "So?"

"So," Newberry said, "you helped plan Justin's murder. Those prints put you at the murder scene. You set the whole thing up, didn't you?" He pulled out the toxicology report and laid it in front of her.

Don't answer until you've seen all of the evidence, Justin's voice warned.

Connie stared blankly at the document.

"This is Justin's blood analysis; it indicates he was heavily drugged." He stared hard into her eyes. "You slipped him sleeping pills. He never knew it was you, did he? Why'd you do it?"

Connie squirmed. "No, no I didn't." *Good. Deny everything. Don't give them anything.*

He turned and looked at the door. "Please bring in the TV."
A technician entered and set up the equipment.

"Connie, you're not telling the truth." He turned on the TV
and pressed the play button. The airport terminal appeared.

Connie watched pictures of herself dressed in Caribbean
clothing walking down the corridor. The motion picture froze
with her in mid-stride.

Newberry pointed to the motionless image. "Connie, is that
you?"

"Yes," Connie said, nodding slightly.

Newberry pressed the play button.

Connie hurried down the terminal, a pocketbook swung at
her side.

He stared at the pocketbook. *That's the pocketbook Shelly
was carrying when she was arrested.* He paused the tape; this
time he pointed to the pocketbook. "Is that your pocketbook?"

"Yes."

How did Connie switch pocketbooks with Shelly? He
pressed the play button and watched Connie sit and place the
pocketbook under her chair. While she sat there, she kicked the
pocketbook further under her seat. Soon, Shelly entered and sat
behind Connie. She placed *her* pocketbook on the floor beneath
her. The sitting area was in constant motion as passengers
waited for the flight and then began to board.

"We're boarding all other passengers at this time," the announcement blared. Shelly reached down and picked up a
pocketbook. *Shelly picked up the wrong pocketbook! That's
how it was switched.*

Newberry stopped the tape and slid Connie the first photo
of the pocketbook. "Is this yours?"

"Yes."

He slid the second photo in front of her. "This is the same
pocketbook, sprayed with Luminal." Dark splotches covered
the pocketbook. "Do you know what those dark areas are?"

Shelly leaned closer to the picture window. *Blood.*

Connie shook her head. "Dirt?"

"It's Justin's blood," Newberry said. "It's your pocketbook, and it's covered with Justin's blood. It places you at the scene, standing beside Justin when he was killed."

Connie froze, staring wide-eyed.

Yvette smiled with a slight nod. *You're guilty.*

Newberry's heart pounded with excitement as he lifted the next sheet of paper from the folder and laid it before Connie. "Do you know whose prints these are?"

Connie looked at the small fingerprints clustered together. "No," she murmured.

"They're yours. And do you know where we found them?"

Shelly let out a long sigh.

Connie trembled, then stared at the prints. "No."

"They were found in the guest bedroom at Shelly Roble's house." He leaned back and crossed his arms, confident.

Connie sat petrified and felt the room grow cold.

"It's proof that you and Justin were drugging Shelly."

Connie trembled, shaking her head.

"You pushed those pills into Shelly's mouth," Yvette said, leaning over the table.

"Why'd you do it?" Newberry pressed.

Connie's face brightened. "No! No, it doesn't prove anything. I'm not guilty. Justin was afraid to fly. He always took sleeping pills before he flew. When we were at the end of the runway, I begged Justin to give Blair the money, but Justin refused. I pleaded with Blair not to kill Justin. He snatched my pocketbook and held it between him and Justin before he pulled the trigger. I didn't do it."

"What?" Shelly moaned, glaring through the window.

Arthur and Bessy sat breathless.

Connie leaned over the table. "And those prints that you got from the guest bedroom. They're mine. That's the bedroom Justin and I always used when Shelly wasn't home. But that doesn't mean I tried to kill anyone."

"Liar," Shelly yelled. The scream remained inside the soundproof room.

"I'm telling you, I'm innocent."

"I don't believe you," Yvette said. "Once Blair dropped you off at the airport and you were safe away from him, you would have called the police and told us everything."

"I couldn't call anyone. He pressed the gun into my hands and said if I called anyone, the gun would mysteriously show up with my fingerprints on it."

Newberry stared at Connie. *We have nothing to hold her on.*

CHAPTER EIGHTY-NINE

The limousine changed lanes again. Overhead a sign indicated the right lane for the Palm Beach International Airport. Walter looked out the side window and saw airplanes parked on the tarmac. "Jane," he said, and chuckled, "where are you taking me?"

"I told you, shopping." Jane smiled.

The limo swerved off the interstate and merged into slow-moving traffic heading into the terminal.

"Why do you want to shop at the airport? That doesn't make sense. We passed a whole bunch of stores to get here."

Jane's smile widened. Her eyes sparkled.

"We're not shopping here are we?" Walter smirked. "I should have known."

Joseph looked into his rearview mirror. His eyes focused on Jane.

"Nope," she giggled and shook her head, "not at all."

Walter looked in the rear-view mirror at Joseph, who was looking at him. "Do you know where I'm going?"

The eyes in the mirror moved from side to side. Joseph looked anxious to know also.

"Watch out," Jane shouted.

Joseph looked ahead and stomped the brakes. They all swayed forward as they came to an abrupt stop. *That was close.*

Jane laughed as she looked into their eyes. "I can't spoil the surprise."

"I'll drop you a postcard and let you know where I end up," Walter said to Joseph and laughed.

The private Lear Jet raced down the runway into twenty-knot winds. The sky turned into night as they flew closer to their destination.

Out the window, Walter watched the lights of a distant island grow larger as the private jet descended. He yawned, popping his ears. He felt the warmth of Jane's hand in his. "What island is that?" he asked, turning to her.

She smiled, "St. Thomas."

"The Virgin Islands?"

"It is," she said as her hand squeezed his. "Isn't this exciting?"

A grin spread on Walter's face. Butterflies filled his stomach. The air in the cabin seemed warm. *Is it me, or the temperature?* His body tingled.

The jet's tires barked, as they touched down. The engines roared in reverse and the plane decelerated.

Outside the window, Walter watched the small terminal zip past.

The jet pulled up to the tarmac. Its engines whined to a stop, as the door popped open. "Welcome to St. Thomas," the female pilot announced.

Walter and Jane stepped down the few steps and out on the pavement. A faint breeze blew into their faces. Stars glimmered in the night sky.

"This is a lot different than this morning, isn't it?" Walter asked.

"Thank goodness," Jane said, grabbing his hand. "Come on." She led him straight for customs.

"I assume you've been here before." Walter heard the jet's engines roaring and turned to see its navigational lights flashing. *They're leaving?*

"Many times." She grinned. "But I've never been shopping where we're going."

Walter's face wrinkled. *Where hasn't she shopped?*

Walter watched as a faded yellow taxi zoomed up and

screeched to a stop. The driver's door swung open, and a skinny man jumped out and raced around the back end. "Where to?" he asked as he pulled open the door.

Jane nudged Walter in and followed. The driver slammed the door and then climbed in behind the steering wheel, which was on the same side. The engine revved. He looked in the rearview mirror for instructions.

"We're in a hurry," Jane said.

The man grabbed the steering wheel and pressed the gas. The car lunged forward and fishtailed as they merged into traffic. Again, he glanced into the rearview mirror for instruction. "Do you just want me to drive you around the island?"

Walter looked at the man with a puzzled expression.

Jane grinned. "Walter proposed to me this morning, and we're here to get married." She tossed a twenty-dollar bill to the cabby. "Go."

Walter chuckled. "Married?"

The cabby's wide eyes peered into the rearview mirror. *Poor guy. He's been shanghaied.* He eased his foot off the gas.

"I did propose, didn't I." Walter glanced out the window. "Why aren't you driving faster? We don't want to be late for our wedding." He pulled out another twenty and tossed it over the seat. "Drive!"

Jane kissed Walter.

The car lunged forward as the horn blared. "I'll take you to the judge." The car swerved left and rounded a turn. It accelerated around a smog-choking bus. "Get out of the way," he yelled through the open window. He looked into the rearview mirror. "It just so happens the judge is my brother-in-law. I'm taking you to his house."

The car skidded to a stop in front of a nicely manicured courtyard. Floodlights illuminated the bright two-story white house. "This is Judge Pablo's house."

The cabby leaped from his seat, ran around to the back door, and opened it. "Hurry, there's a wedding about to take place. You two don't want to be late." He grinned and dashed for the front door and knocked.

As Jane and Walter stepped up on the porch, the front door swung opened.

"Hello," the sixty-ish, gray-haired man said.

The cabby stepped aside and Walter took a step forward. "We'd like to get married."

"Wonderful evening for a wedding. I'm Judge Pablo. Who's got the marriage certificate?"

"Don't you have them?" Jane asked, as she looked at the judge.

"Not here. They're at my office."

Walter took a small step backward. "Can we meet you down there?"

The judge's jaw quivered with laughter as he shook his head. "You didn't call me in advance. It takes eight days to get a marriage license in St. Thomas."

Walter and Jane simultaneously sighed and their shoulders sagged.

The cabby grabbed their hands and pulled them toward the car. "Don't worry. I know where you can get married. There's a cruise ship down at the docks. They do weddings."

They all jumped into the cab and it sped off.

Their pulses quickened when they saw the terminal building for the cruise ships.

Each could feel the others pulse in their clasped hands.

The brakes screeched as the cab pulled alongside the terminal. Jane tossed the man a fifty-dollar bill. "Keep the change," she said as she opened her own door and jumped out.

Walter jumped out his door, ran around, and grabbed Jane's hand. Together they raced into the terminal and followed the signs that pointed the way to the ships. The cabby chased after them. "Hurry! Hurry! Hurry!" he kept repeating.

As they sprinted from the building, their momentum slowed. They saw the cruise ship moving away from the dock.

"We're too late," Walter said.

"And I was really looking forward to our honeymoon," Jane said as her voice broke. She looked deep into Walter's eyes as they came together and embraced. "I'm sorry. I guess it's not to be."

"Hey," the cabby shouted as he ran up to them. "Don't give up. You still can get married tonight."

They looked over at the man. "We can?" they said together. "How?"

"You can," he said. "I've a friend who has a friend that has a plane and can fly you to Isle De Flamenco." He smiled. "Otherwise known as the Island of Pink Birds."

"I've never been there," Jane said.

"How long will it take?" Walter asked.

"You'll be there before you know it."

"Just you wait." She squeezed Walter's hand. "It'll all be worth it."

The cabby placed a call from the terminal and made the arrangements.

Soon they were back at the airport, climbing into a rustic twin engine, and flying off to Isle De Flamenco in an Areo Commander, nothing more than an old two engine puddle-jumper.

The plane rose off the runway and out over the water. It barely reached 1000 feet before it began its descent. They looked at the grassy field below. "Where's the runway?"

"No problem, Mon," the pilot said as a grin spread across his face. The tires bounced on the lush grass.

The plane rolled to a stop beside an old metal hangar. At the front door, three people stood watching.

Walter and Jane dashed to the small group. Her little red shoes peddled across the grassy field.

The immigration officer completed their paperwork. The Justice of the Peace, who obviously started the celebration early, performed the ceremony, and the third man, the witness, chauffeured them away to their secluded bungalow. The full moon radiated the white sandy beach, outlining the small private bay.

Jane laughed. "Just hours ago we were tangled in the middle of a hurricane. Now we're tangled on our private island."

A fish splashed into the moon's reflection, sending a small ripple racing to shore.

CHAPTER NINETY

After lunch the following day, the unmarked car drove out the gate at Bessy's. Newberry reached out and caught the file folder before it slid off the seat. Shelly buckled up.

"I'm glad you had a good night's sleep. Thanks for agreeing to accompany me to the morgue. With a positive ID, the morgue will release Justin's body for burial."

"It'll help me bring closure to that part of my life."

"By the way, I spoke with the Coast Guard this morning. Both pilots from the Jayhawk claim they were forced to land at Morgan's Bluff. Once they shut down the helicopter, they both claim they felt a sting in the arm and then everything went dark."

"That's what Otman did to those elderly people at Southern Retirement Community."

"The pilots were asked if anyone else was onboard with Blair and Otman." Newberry slowed the vehicle and turned onto a side street.

"Why?" Shelly asked.

"Because of the third set of footprints found heading to the water's edge. Both pilots agreed that there were only four people on board when the helicopter set down."

"So, no one knows who the third person was?"

"After further questioning, the Coast Guard discovered a boat was anchored off the beach when the helicopter landed, but it was gone by the time the Falcon Jet found them."

Newberry pulled into the morgue lot and parked.

"Does the Coast Guard have any idea who it was? Sounds like someone was waiting for them. Or, maybe some Good Samaritan gave a helping hand and became another victim."

"We've checked to see if a missing person's report has been issued for any boaters." He shook his head. "No one's been reported missing."

Soon, they stood at the front desk. Newberry presented his badge. "We're here to ID Justin Roble's body."

The receptionist typed his name into the computer and then looked up at Newberry. "Mr. Roble's body was picked up this morning by Palm Beach Funeral Home."

"Come on Shelly," Newberry said, pulling her toward the front door. "We've got to get over there."

Fifteen minutes later, they were inside sitting in the funeral director's office. "Officer Newberry, I'm sorry, but that body was cremated right after lunch. His sister just left with the ashes."

"His sister?" Shelly shrieked. "It can't be. She died when Justin was in high school."

Newberry leaped from his seat, raced outside, and stared into the parking lot. *They're gone.*

Shelly walked up to Newberry. "Why would someone claim Justin's body?"

"I'm not sure. Sometimes a body is cremated to conceal evidence. Come on. We have one more stop to make."

"Where?"

"His dentist."

"His dentist?" She sprinted after Newberry

They slowed in the heavier afternoon traffic. Newberry kept reviewing the facts and drove in silence. Shelly fidgeted, wondering what they would discover at the dentist's office.

Finally arriving, Newberry and Shelly hurried inside. With Justin's file in hand, he stepped up to the receptionist's window. "I'm Detective Newberry, and I'm investigating one of your patients, Justin Roble." He flipped open the file folder and pulled out the x-rays. "I'd like to ask his hygienist a question about his teeth."

Shelly and Newberry followed the receptionist into the small conference room.

"I'm Lisa, Justin's hygienist," the petite brunette said.

"I'm Detective Newberry," he said, standing. "Can you identify his x-rays?"

"Sure."

"How can you remember all of your patient's teeth?" He handed Lisa the films.

She laughed. "I can't remember most of them, but Justin was in here a couple of weeks ago." She held the film up to the light. "These aren't Justin's x-rays."

"They're not?" Shelly gasped.

"How can you be so sure?" Newberry asked. "I picked these x-rays up from this office several days ago. They were in Justin's file."

"They're not Justin's. His teeth were perfect, and the teeth in these X-Rays are rotten."

"She's right," Shelly exclaimed. "He had perfect teeth. Someone must have mixed up the films."

"Is it routine for x-rays to get mixed up?" Newberry asked.

"Absolutely not," Lisa exclaimed. "This is the first time I have ever heard of that happening."

"So do you have Justin's x-rays here?"

"Give me a couple of minutes and I'll look for them." Lisa hurried from the room.

Shelly turned to Newberry. "How could the x-rays have been mixed up?"

"Well, I'm sure there could be many different possibilities of how it would have happened." He scratched the back of his neck. "From what you've have told me about Justin, I'd say he could have switched them."

"Why?"

"Maybe for a cover-up. . . . Shelly, when the hygienist works on your teeth, doesn't she have your file folder on hand?"

"Sure."

Lisa stopped flipping through the files as she overheard Newberry and Shelly's conversation. She moved to the doorway and listened.

"What would happen if the hygienist stepped out for a second or two to get some supplies? The patient could reach out and take whatever was in their folder."

"I suppose he could do that."

"If they had time to take something out, they'd have enough time to put something right back in before the hygienist returned."

"Like x-rays."

Newberry smiled. "Exactly."

Lisa cleared her throat from where she stood, dumbfounded, in the doorway. "Now that you mention it, I remember something from the morning I was cleaning Justin's teeth. I just finished and we were talking when I was paged for a telephone call. I stepped out to answer it. When I picked up the phone, no one was there. I came back and found Justin looking in his folder. Most patients don't do that. I questioned him, but he was short with me and left. I didn't give it much thought afterward."

"If those aren't Justin's x-ray's, then that wasn't Justin's body. Where is he?" Shelly mumbled.

"I don't know, but I have a good hunch who knows."

"Connie!" Shelly raced after Newberry to the car.

"Your perfect plan didn't work." Connie gritted her teeth and balled her hand into a fist.

"Take a deep breath. . . . Now exhale. You've done and said everything perfectly."

"It's easy for you to be calm. You're out of the country and don't have to face the cops. I can't do it anymore."

"Yes, you can."

"But, what if the cops find out. They'll come looking for me. They'll . . ."

". . . They'll never know you got the ashes. We've been through all of this before. I couldn't come back to the States and risk someone seeing me. That's why you came back alone to set up the perfect crime."

"It didn't work."

"So what if Blair's part of the plan didn't work. He screwed up. Not me. If he'd gotten rid of Bessy like planned, no one would have ever known she was missing. No one would have come looking for her. He would have her money and would never have to look back."

"Your plan didn't work either."

"You forgot to buy your airline ticket and had to settle at the last moment for the only international flight. If you had followed the plan, you would be here with me and we wouldn't be having this conversation."

"Well, what about Shelly?"

"So she's not locked up for life. She thinks I'm dead and will never come looking for me. You did a great job, telling those cops everything we rehearsed. Now we're free and don't have to worry about any of them. They believe Justin Roble is dead. Hurry, flush the ashes. Now."

Connie ran into the bathroom and dumped the ashes into the toilet and flushed. "Okay, they're gone. Now what?"

"Get out of there and don't go back to your apartment."

"Where should I go?"

"I don't care. For now, you're on your own. Go into hiding."

"You've got to come get me."

"Forget it. I'm dead. Remember?"

"I'll go to the cops and tell them everything."

Justin chuckled. "And incriminate yourself. I don't think

so. You'd never get out of prison. If I were you, I'd stay hidden. If the cops find you and question you, demand to have your lawyer present. Goodbye Connie." The phone went dead.

Newberry stood at the front door of apartment E-12, knocked, and waited. Shelly sat in the front seat of the unmarked police car, begrudgingly waiting for his return. Cold air blew in her face.

Shelly watched as Newberry turned and headed back to the vehicle.

He opened the door and climbed behind the wheel. "We'll find her sooner or later."

The curtain swayed an inch, back into its natural position. Connie grabbed a small carry-on suitcase and her cell phone and slipped out the back door.

The West Palm Beach air was muggy. Soft glows shown from the bottom floor windows at Bessy's house. Shelly stretched out on the sofa while Arthur and Bessy sat on the love seat. Three glasses of iced tea sat on the coffee table. A platter of fruit sat in the center of the table.

"That was some honeymoon," Arthur sighed. "I bet we could sell our story to TV."

"I'm not sure I'd like to see it," Bessy said.

"I don't know," Shelly teased. "I'd like to see the scene of Walter hitting Otman with that shelving, twice."

They all laughed.

"I still can't believe Otman and Blair hijacked a helicopter and disappeared," Shelly said.

"Well," Bessy added, "with the U.S. Government and Bahamian Government looking for them, they'll be caught quickly."

"And speaking of being caught," Shelly giggled. "I can't believe Jane caught Walter and they got married."

"You would have thought they'd have invited us to the

347

wedding," Arthur said. "We invited them to ours."

"Oh, leave them alone." Bessy smiled. "You didn't even think they belonged together."

"So, I was wrong."

"I knew they were perfect for each other, the first time I met Jane." Shelly sighed. "I'm glad they got married. Now, Walter will live close by."

Bessy snuggled into Arthur. "I'm glad we're all home, safe and sound."

HOWARD JONES lives in Florida with his wife and three daughters. Year after year, upon returning from their travels, he is asked to tell of their story-filled vacations. He finally realized that through him, people can see places they would never visit. Now he enjoys creating stories about intriguing people and fascinating places.

Howard appreciates hearing from his readers through letters and e-mails. Writing requires solitude, but the words from those letters keep him motivated. They are constant source of encouragement. You can write him at P. O. Box 277, St. Marks, Florida 32355, or e-mail sales@elliotfiction.com Visit his Web page at http://elliotfiction.com.

FIRST IN THE SERIES
BY
E. HOWARD JONES

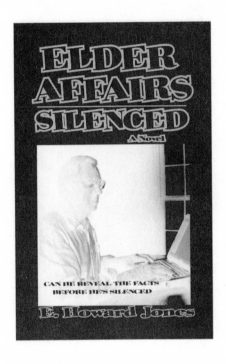

Arthur McCullen is enjoying his retirement years until a family member uses the legal system to manipulate him into a retirement home and take his money. The drama escalates as he encounters Mr. Otman, a male Nurse Rachet, who is determined to carry out the court order and keep Arthur "safe" inside. Arthur only gets deeper in trouble as he tries to prove he has been wronged. He meets some unusual characters, who join him in his quest to expose the truth and regain independent living. Can he reveal the facts before he is silenced?